Sasha

Congr

Your

♡

CW01464791

GUN MOLL

BOOK 1

BETHANY-KRIS
ERIN ASHLEY TANNER

Bethany-Kris

Published by Bethany-Kris and Erin Ashley Tanner

eISBN 13: 978-1-988197-11-1
Print ISBN 13: 978-1-988197-12-8

Cover Art © Jay Aheer
Editor: Nina S. Gooden

DEDICATION

For our fans, thank you.

CONTENTS

CHAPTER ONE 7
CHAPTER TWO 12
CHAPTER THREE 18
CHAPTER FOUR 26
CHAPTER FIVE 39
CHAPTER SIX 46
CHAPTER SEVEN 55
CHAPTER EIGHT 63
CHAPTER NINE 73
CHAPTER TEN 84
CHAPTER ELEVEN 97
CHAPTER TWELVE 106
CHAPTER THIRTEEN 127
CHAPTER FOURTEEN 135
CHAPTER FIFTEEN 152
CHAPTER SIXTEEN 166
CHAPTER SEVENTEEN 179
CHAPTER EIGHTEEN 193
CHAPTER NINETEEN 213
CHAPTER TWENTY 225
CHAPTER TWENTY-ONE 241
CHAPTER TWENTY-TWO 254
CHAPTER TWENTY-THREE 268
CHAPTER TWENTY-FOUR 283

CHAPTER TWENTY-FIVE 298
CHAPTER TWENTY-SIX 310
CHAPTER TWENTY-SEVEN 330
CHAPTER TWENTY-EIGHT 340

CHAPTER ONE

Deep down into the depth of her core, Melina Morgan could feel a blaze burning hotter and hotter. Her soul was on fire. Soon, she knew it would consume her, but there was nothing she could do. Life had already decided her fate and fate was a real bitch.

A droplet of water splattered her face as she readjusted the black umbrella she was holding. The sky was open, pouring water down all around her, but it didn't matter. Not much did anymore.

She watched with gritted teeth as the simple maple-oak-finished casket was lowered into the waiting plot in the ground. Melina stood alone as the first and only witness to the final resting place of a great man. A great man who'd been all but shunned and forgotten by everyone except her. Hot tears slipped down her cheeks, and as the thunder clapped overhead, she couldn't hold them in any longer. The despair and anger she'd been holding inside burst from her lungs like a train running at full speed.

Bitterness filled her mouth as she sobbed. Her knuckles cracked as she clutched the umbrella as if it were the only lifeline to hold her up. It wasn't fair. Those fucks had betrayed him, stripping him of everything he'd worked so hard for; everything he'd honored and held in high esteem, they'd taken it away. Melina shouldn't have been the only person at this funeral. It should have been filled with friends and colleagues of Daniel Morgan Jr. There should have been a line of men saluting him and placing the symbol of everything Daniel had ever stood for in Melina's hands.

But Melina held nothing except a worn, black umbrella that did little to keep the rain from chilling her bones. It was just too bad; the rain couldn't cool the fire in her soul. As the casket came to its final resting place, the gravedigger started to throw the first shovel of dirt in.

"Wait."

He threw dirt on the top of the casket.

"Damn it, I said wait!" Melina yelled at him.

"It's raining cats and dogs out here. I'm soaked."

"Well, so am I. Do you know who you're burying? Do you know who it is that you're giving less than a damn about?"

"Look, I'm just doing my job."

"So did he, and he got no respect for it. No appreciation. But today, you're going to give me a chance to show him the respect he didn't get when he was alive. Got it?"

The man glared at her, his muddy brown eyes were hard, but Melina didn't care. He was going to allow her this moment. Reaching inside her black trench coat, she withdrew a small souvenir. She'd had it since she was a small girl and now she was returning it to the one who'd given it to her. Staring at it with a measure of love and anger, Melina threw the small replica of the American flag down on top of the casket.

"You finished?" the insolent gravedigger asked.

"No, I'm not. You might want to get out of the way for what I'm about to do next."

"Can you hurry the hell up?"

Melina's russet brown eyes closed briefly before she opened them again. Reaching once more into her coat, she pulled out a black handgun with a worn grip and aimed it at the gravedigger.

"I suggest you shut the fuck up before you find yourself in a hole out here, too."

The man raised his hands. "I don't want any trouble. Please."

"Then be quiet and let me do what I came here for. You are welcome to continue your miserable excuse for a job, after."

"Yes, ma'am."

Melina raised her Smith & Wesson 386 towards the sky and fired one round.

"Lance Corporal Daniel Morgan Jr., thank you for your service. Thank you for believing that no man deserves to be left behind. Thank you for taking a stand and sticking by it, no matter what it cost you in the end."

Melina blasted another round off into the sky. The gravedigger jumped, but she ignored him. She wasn't finished yet. Her voice wavered as she continued talking.

"When others would've simply turned a blind eye, you stuck to your values and you always did the right thing. When life fucked you any way but right, your spirit let you hold on and keep fighting. Few knew your pain, but I saw it, no matter how much you tried to hide it from me. Few will ever know the real cost you paid for serving your country as an honorable man, but I know and I remember."

With tears streaming down her cheeks, Melina raised the gun and fired one last time.

"This isn't goodbye. It's just an 'I'll see you later' and when we meet again, you'll be the man you once were. The man who looked at life through shining eyes with the hope and belief that no matter what, doing the right thing would always save you in the end. Rest now and know that the pain of this life is over, and you're in a far better place. See you later."

As the rain slowed to a light downpour, Melina

put her gun away and nodded towards the gravedigger. "He's all yours now."

She turned to walk away.

"Ma'am, I don't mean to pry, but if he was a vet, why didn't he have a military funeral?"

Wiping her eyes, Melina swallowed the lump in her throat and faced the gravedigger with the familiar coldness already settling in her heart.

"While in Afghanistan, a small group of men under him were trapped behind enemy lines and ordered to be left behind. He disobeyed orders and went back for them; two of those men died. My father lost his right forearm. Instead of giving him a medal for risking his life for his fellow man and for losing a limb, they discharged him dishonorably. He was an example for other men, and nothing more."

"That was mighty shitty of them to do that."

"Yes, it was."

"What about the men he saved? Why aren't they here?"

"I was unable to get the contact information for the ones who survived."

Melina turned away and started to walk.

"He was your father, wasn't he?" the gravedigger called from behind her.

"Yes, he was."

Taking a deep, cleansing breath, she started to walk through the graveyard and to her car. It was over and she would never return here. Contrary to what many thought, there was no sentimental value to visiting a grave. The person you loved was gone. There was no lingering spirit, waiting around for you to come visit. Only a body remained. A body that had already begun to deteriorate and would soon return to the earth from which it came.

No, Melina was done here. There was no reason to visit a headstone, especially one that did not even begin to convey the true measure of the man buried beneath it.

GUN MOLL

The rain continued to slacken as Melina walked back to her vehicle. A loud beep made her stop. Opening her purse, she reached inside. Her fingers closed around a black beeper that was outdated and behind the times, but necessary, according to her boss. The number "711" flashed across it. Putting it back inside her purse, Melina kept walking. She'd just received another lesson from life: *It doesn't matter what the fuck is going on, the world keeps moving. Deal with it.*

Sad, but true. Anyone else would have the time to grieve properly, to get affairs in order. Hell, just a little time to sift through their father's belongings and reminisce. But not her.

It was time to dry her tears and close the vault to her heart permanently. She was in this world alone, and she had to make it the best she could. Even if she cringed every time the numbers 711 came across her beeper. Even if her stomach turned, imaging what kind of desperate fool she'd have to entertain tonight. It didn't matter. She was an escort and tonight, she belonged to the highest bidder, whoever he might be.

CHAPTER TWO

"James, come taste this for me."

Mac beat back his immediate urge to correct his mother when she used his given name. She was the only person he let get away with that shit. "I'm busy, Ma."

"James."

"Ma, I'm busy."

"*James*, come taste. Don't make me tell you again."

He was twenty-six-years-old, and all his mother had to do was use the fucking *tone*. Every good Italian child knew what the tone was. Age, size, or gender didn't make a goddamn difference. When an Italian's mother used that tone, they knew to listen, or get out of the way.

Sighing, Mac jumped down from the ladder he'd been balancing on for the last ten minutes. His mother needed her living room fan fixed and he still wasn't any closer to figuring out what was wrong with it.

Needs a new one, he thought.

Mac knew that's what it was. But Cynthia Bella Maccari wasn't the kind of woman to ask for money or complain. He took care of his mother, as far as that went, but he did it without asking or telling her he was doing it. Sometimes that meant showing up with his Challenger's trunk full with groceries, or sneaking her stack of bills off the table and taking them to the bank.

Cynthia never said a word.

Neither did Mac.

It was just too damn bad James Sr. didn't get the memo.

Mac's father was useless in all things—women, family, and money. Expecting him to handle his estranged wife's business was like asking the doorknob to turn without touching it. It wasn't going to happen.

James Sr. liked to think that because his wife had kicked him and his cocaine-abusing, women-running, asshole-self out all those years ago, that he didn't have a responsibility to Cynthia or the two children they shared.

Mac took care of it all. Whatever his mother or sister, Victoria, needed, Mac did it.

"All right, Ma, give it to me," Mac said, leaning in the kitchen entryway.

Cynthia turned from the stove with a wooden spoon in hand. A thick, red sauce covered the tip as his mother blew on it to cool it down. She held it out for him to taste once she was close enough.

Mac hummed as the rich flavors soaked his taste buds in familiarity.

Home.

It tasted like home.

"Damn," he groaned.

"James!"

There was that tone again.

Crass language had never been acceptable in his home growing up. They'd been dirt poor and lived in a pretty shoddy neighborhood, but his mother always held some kind of standard for her children.

Mac never really learned to follow those rules.

"That mouth of yours, my God," Cynthia muttered.

Mac winced. "Sorry."

Cynthia's brow puckered in her disapproval as she shook her head and dropped the spoon. "I know you run around on the streets going on like that, but in this home, James—"

"I'm sorry, Ma," he interrupted before she could really get started.

Apparently, that wasn't going to soothe Cynthia's temper.

"No, listen. What have I always told you, huh?"

"Bad language and acting like a fool isn't going to get me a real job."

Cynthia smiled. "And what are you doing for work lately, hmm?"

Shit.

Mac wanted to get his mother off that topic and quickly. If his bad language had tripped her anger up, his choices on the job front really would. His mother wasn't stupid, she knew he ran the streets like her estranged husband did. He made up schemes, worked with a crew, and brought in money however he could. Even if it was fucking pennies. It was work. The only kind of work he cared to know.

It was the one thing Mac had in common with his fuck-up of a father.

La famiglia.

The family.

Mafia.

Mac's introduction to the Pivetti crime family had happened when he was just six-years-old. A lot of his younger years were spent in the passenger seat of an old Cadillac while his father collected money and watched the streets for his brother. Mac's now-deceased uncle had once run the streets of Hell's Kitchen as the top Capo in the family. Marco had been terrifying, and cold as hell. But then Marco Maccari met the wrong end of a bullet when a war broke out between rival New York families, and what could have been the Maccari reign in the Pivetti family ended.

James Sr. found his shame in white lines of cocaine,

effectively ruining any chance he had of getting made in the family. It was embarrassing and undignified.

Mac wouldn't be his father. He'd worked far too hard to separate James Sr. from Mac Maccari in *la famiglia* to let it be screwed up by something so stupid. Mac even went so far as integrating himself as a soldier for the Vasari crew in the Pivetti Cosa Nostra, while his father worked under the Audino side.

There was no need to stain himself with his father's mess, after all. Appearance was everything to Cosa Nostra. A man's worth was determined by his actions, honor, and loyalty. James Sr. had none of that.

But Mac couldn't please his mother by being a wise-guy, either.

Double-edged swords.

Cynthia had never hidden her disapproval of Mac's choices, regarding Cosa Nostra. If she chomped down on that bone, they would be glaring at one another all night. Mac had shit to do in the Kitchen in the morning, and he needed to be gone from Amityville before dawn broke.

"Ma, let's not start in on that again," Mac warned, hoping it was enough.

Cynthia sighed. "I want you to be a good man, Mac."

When she used his nickname, Mac knew his mother was serious. Cynthia only did that when she wanted something from him, or she needed him to listen.

"I am a good man," he replied quietly.

In all the ways that count, he held back from adding.

"Being a wise-guy—"

"I'm not James, Ma."

Cynthia pursed her lips. "I know."

Guessing by the way his mother dropped his

stare, he figured the conversation was over. Sometimes, it was all about picking the right battles with Cynthia. Maybe she just wasn't up for the argument that night.

God knew it would come on another.

"Sunday," she said.

"What about it?" he asked.

"Church."

Ah.

Yeah ...

"Ma, I've got some stuff to do this weekend and all that. Next Sunday, okay?"

Cynthia's hands met her hips.

The tone was coming again. Mac knew it.

"Fine, Sunday," he said quickly.

Mac would have to make an excuse to his Capo to get out of collecting dues from the bookies, but whatever. Family came first. Sometimes that didn't always mean the family that was supposed to be first.

"And make sure you check up on your sister this week," Cynthia ordered. "She doesn't call me enough."

Probably because Victoria was smarter than Mac, and knew not to poke the bear that was Cynthia Maccari.

"Yes, Ma."

Before Cynthia could say another thing, a loud clap of thunder rang out. It practically shook the roof and walls of the small, one-level home. A sheet of rain followed the noise, banging the roof hard.

"Oh, darn," Cynthia mumbled, glancing upwards.

Mac followed her gaze and noticed a water stain on the ceiling. When had that gotten there? Chances were, that stain was from a roof leak. With another storm passing through, it was only going to get worse.

It needed to be fixed and soon.

Mac, frustrated with another thing being added to his list, tried to figure out how in the hell he was going to come up with the kind of money to fix the roof. A patch wouldn't do. Maybe for a short while, but not long-term.

The house was old and a roof was just one of the many improvements it could use.

"Ma?" he asked, knowing he didn't need to say another thing.

Cynthia made a dismissive noise under her breath. "It's nothing, James."

"Ma, that water stain is a foot long and three inches wide. How long has it been leaking?"

"A few months."

A few months?

"Ma!"

Cynthia wouldn't meet his gaze. "The house is old."

"I'm aware."

The rain kept pounding at the roof. Mac gritted his teeth and pushed his frustrations back. It wasn't his mother's fault that her useless husband couldn't even take care of her or their family.

But sometimes he wished all of this hadn't been left to him.

"I'll have someone here next week to fix it, Ma," Mac said.

"But—"

"No arguing. It needs done."

"Fine," Cynthia said heavily. "That's going to be a couple of thousand dollars."

"I'll figure it out."

And he sure as hell wouldn't tell her how, either.

CHAPTER THREE

Melina stared at herself in the mirror. Her hair hung down her back in tousled waves. A nude lipstick moisturized her full lips. The fitted, black bodycon dress she wore accentuated the round curve of her ass and the gentle swell of her hips. Tugging up the bodice of the dress, she cursed under her breath. It seemed the ten pounds she'd packed on had gone straight to her breasts. It was getting a little harder to squeeze into her clothes—her top half anyway. But it wasn't all bad. If anything, it would keep tonight's customer firmly focused on her assets instead of forcing her to suffer through small talk and boring attempts to excite her.

Satisfied with her appearance, Melina walked down the short hallway to the living room area of her hotel suite. *Nothing to do now but wait.*

Moving over to the wet bar, she poured herself a gin and tonic. Glass in hand, she sat down in the soft, black lounge chair and pulled out her smart phone. Opening the email from her account, she scrolled through the information Dulcea had sent over.

Sweet. Yeah, her boss was sweet all right. Like a poisoned apple. Dulcea Massellini was a self-made woman. Nothing and no one was going to get in the way of her business.

Melina had seen her fair share of women cut off without warning. She didn't even want to think what happened to those women. When you dealt with a woman like Dulcea, it wasn't a bed of roses. Yes, the money was good. Great, in fact, but screw up and there would be consequences. Melina never wanted to be in that predicament. Besides, she needed the money now more than ever. The rest of her father's funeral arrangements had to be paid for. Taking a drink, Melina pushed the thought away and focused on the information in the palm of her hand instead. *Tonight's date.*

Garrett Jameson. CEO of Jameson Investments. Millionaire. Forty-five years old. The last piece of information made Melina grit her teeth.

Married, father of three.

Bastard.

Mr. Jameson should be taking his wife out tonight instead of her. Melina had no respect for a man who didn't honor his commitment to a woman, especially when that man was also a father. Scrolling down, she scrutinized the picture Dulcea had sent along. The man wasn't bad to look at, in a young Mel Gibson sort of way, and she was sure that he was well aware of it.

Just great. Another night of putting up with groping hands. Melina took another drink and kept looking. Dulcea was anything if not thorough. A list of her client's likes and dislikes always accompanied the dossier she sent to each of her girls.

Caviar.

Champagne.

Moonlight walks.

Same shit. Different face. Nothing ever changed, and Melina was rapidly losing faith in the male species.

Get the fuck over it, girl. You've got money to make and bills to pay. Melina drained the last of the one drink she allowed herself before each of her dates. The last thing she needed was to be off her game when she had a job to do. A knock at the door drew in her attention. *Showtime.*

Setting her glass down on the coffee table, Melina walked leisurely to the door. Looking through the peephole, she carefully readjusted her dress before opening the door.

Six feet of white-collar asshole greeted her. Or rather, greeted her breasts. His icy-blue eyes couldn't stop staring at them.

"My face is up here."

Garrett Jameson blinked quickly and then met her gaze. A low whistle came from his throat. "Man, are you a looker."

A looker? Really? That was the only line he could come up with? Pathetic. Absolutely pathetic.

"I'm well aware of that," Melina said curtly.

"A lady usually thanks a man for complimenting her."

"I'll do that when you compliment me. Now, are you ready?"

He gave her a sardonic smile. "I get it. The aloof attitude is all part of the game." Garrett leaned in closer to her. His fingers twirled a lock of her hair. "Well played. This should be an entertaining evening."

"That all depends on you."

Melina turned and pulled the door shut behind her, forcing her date for the evening to take a few steps back. His hand slid around her waist, bringing her into close proximity to him. The scent of pine needles assaulted her senses. The man had obviously bathed in cologne before coming to pick her up. He smelled like he belonged in a damn forest, with the other dying logs.

"Shall we?"

"I'm all yours," Melina said. With cold detachment, she gave him a practiced smile and started walking towards the elevator. She could sense the man's desire before she felt the gentle nudge of an erection along her backside. As the elevator doors opened, she glanced at him. He raised a brow, as if daring her to say something.

"Did I miss something?" she asked.

His gaze darkened, and Melina laughed softly as she stepped inside. Garrett followed, staring at her with narrowed eyes.

"For the kind of money I'm shelling out tonight, this isn't what I expected."

Folding her arms, Melina appraised him. Charcoal gray suit. Probably Italian. Easily over two-thousand dollars. Silver cuff links. Her gaze roved lower. She was pretty sure those weren't Stacey Adams on his feet, either. The man screamed money, but she didn't care. She was getting paid, regardless if this date lasted thirty minutes or three hours.

"And pray tell, what did you expect?" she asked.

"An exciting evening with a woman beautiful enough to make Jesus sin."

"You're in for an exciting evening, but there are a few things we need to address."

The elevator doors opened and Garrett offered his arm. Melina took it and allowed him to lead her through the lobby. People milled around them, seemingly lost in their own worlds. That is, until they saw Melina. She couldn't resist the small snicker that escaped when a poor sap was slapped by his wife for ogling her. It was part of the territory and by now, Melina was used to it.

"I'm a lucky man. No one can take their eyes off you."

"Indeed."

Melina rolled her eyes as he led her outside to the limousine parked on the curb. You'd think a man could be original every now and then. She'd seen and ridden in more limousines than she could count anymore.

"Only the best, my lady."

Stepping forward, Mr. White Collar opened the door for her. Melina slid in without another word. A moment later, he was beside her, arm draped casually over the seat behind her. As the limo started to move, Melina carefully crossed her legs and shifted to look at her date for the evening. He was watching her like a young man ready for his first piece of pussy. She was not impressed. Reaching for his white tie, she curled it around her fingers.

"Mr. Jameson, just so that there's no misunderstanding about just what kind of service I provide for you, I'm an escort. I'm not a whore or a prostitute. If and when I decide to fuck a man, it's on my terms and because I want to. So, while in your company this evening, I will play the part of the beautiful, young woman who hangs on your every word—but don't be mistaken. It will go no further unless I say so. Is that clear?"

He wet his lips, a gleam in his eye. His hand rested on her thigh, fingers easing under the tight fabric of her dress.

"Do you mean to say that being in the back of this limousine with a multi-millionaire doesn't turn you on just a little bit? Most women would be creaming their panties by now."

"I'm not most women."

"So I see." Jameson's fingers continued easing up the hem of her dress, exposing the soft smoothness of her thigh. "You're like a dominatrix and a schoolgirl, all wrapped in one. A man never knows what he's going to get with you. I understand why you came so highly recommended."

"Then you also know that the further your hand goes up my thigh, the more you owe at the end of the night."

"Money is no object."

"I wasn't talking about money."

Before he could react, Melina had a knife at his throat.

"What the hell?"

"Obviously, you weren't paying attention to what I

said, so let me say it again. Keep your hands to your damn self until I've given you the go ahead to touch me. Otherwise I'm going to make your wife a wealthy widow. Got it?"

He swallowed, nodding his head. Melina eased the knife down and shook her head. The bastard had an erection at full mast. *I've picked up a closet freak.*

Sliding the small knife back into the holster strapped to the inside of her thigh, Melina leaned close, intentionally rubbing her breasts along his arm. "What's the matter? Cat got your tongue?"

"Hardly. I'm just trying really hard not to embarrass myself right now," he muttered.

Melina smiled knowingly as her palm lightly grazed his fly. "And why is that?"

"Because I'm so turned on right now."

"Are you now?" Melina ran a finger along his jaw line.

"Yes. Twenty thousand for a hand job. Right now."

"I wouldn't even let you smell it for twenty thousand, but you know what? If you're a good boy, for fifty thousand, I'll spank you later." She squeezed his crotch.

"Oh, God."

He shuddered and Melina knew exactly what was happening. Leaning back, she watched him as he was caught up in the throes of what had to be the most shameful orgasm he'd ever felt. This was exactly why men kept coming back to her. While other girls had to resort to sucking and fucking to make their money, Melina brought satisfaction without ever taking off her clothes. She had a talent. A natural sensuality that drove men crazy and guaranteed that she would always have a steady stream of customers. Jameson's hand palmed her breast and she let it.

"That'll cost you an extra twenty grand."

He nodded, eyes closed. Beside her, his body still trembled. Melina smirked as he finally stilled beside her. His eyes opened and he quickly removed his hand from her breast. She tapped her manicured fingers on her thigh.

"I'm waiting," she said.

"Of course."

Reaching into his pocket, Garrett Jameson pulled out his checkbook and quickly wrote. Tearing the check out, he handed it to her with trembling fingers.

"Thank you." Melina folded the check in half and tucked it into her cleavage. Twenty grand, just like that. Her nipples hardened and she patted her date's leg. Power over a man. That's what turned her on. Not a man with money or class. Garrett Jameson was nothing. A means to an end and before this night was over with, Melina was sure that his checkbook would be making yet another appearance.

An underground fight. Melina would've never pictured this as a place Garrett Jameson would choose. It was true that anyone could surprise a person. After sitting through a boring business meeting with Garrett and some potential new clients, Melina had more than earned her pay. After smiling and fawning over Jameson as if he were the end all to end all when it came to men and being unfailingly polite to the male clients eyeing her like a slab of prime ribs, all she'd wanted to do was go back to her hotel room. A little wine, some Netflix, and a King-sized bed seemed the perfect way to end the evening.

If only things were that easy. Hoping to seal the deal, Jameson had insisted that she accompany him and the men to the latest in entertainment for the rich, bored and ungrateful. As an amateur kickboxer herself, Melina could appreciate the physicality and training any athlete had to endure when preparing for a sport. But underground fighting was a different breed altogether. In Melina's mind, it was barbaric. Grown men bashing in each other's faces while a bunch of snotty, rich people bet on them like they were a bunch of fucking animals.

Doing her damnedest not to curl her lips in disgust, Melina allowed Garrett to place his hand on the small of her back and lead her to a ringside seat. In front of her was a square boxing ring, surrounded by a chain-link fence. An extraordinarily thin woman stood inside the ring, wearing a red string bikini. *Male chauvinism at its best.* Melina rolled her eyes.

"I'd give my right nut to see you wearing that," Garrett whispered in her ear.

Melina laughed. "Your right nut is exactly what it would cost you, too."

"Just one nut? I think a lady like you is definitely worth two," a new voice said near her.

Melina shuddered. Like an invisible force drawing her, she turned and found a pair of hazel eyes that stared straight into her soul.

CHAPTER FOUR

She was gorgeous.

Not in the usual hot body and pretty face kind of way, either.

No.

Gorgeous.

In a tight dress that showcased an amazing set of curves—made to fit a man's hands—and full lips set into a natural pout as she stared at Mac, she caught him. Sexy. Confident. Womanly. The brief glimpses of her profile that he had managed to get over the last hour hadn't been nearly enough to do her justice.

Beautiful women didn't trip Mac up. He'd seen more than enough of those pretty faces over the years, and taken his taste of a few along the way, but this woman was something else entirely. Dark-caramel skin, russet eyes, and wavy, black hair that was long enough to wrap his fists in and pull.

Shit.

He wondered if she would like that.

She had a take-no-bullshit demeanor that he'd heard her grace her companion with more than once throughout the night. Mac was willing to bet she was the kind of woman who enjoyed fucking men over, but had yet to meet the one she didn't, or better yet, couldn't.

The man who could trip her up.

Like she was finally coming to her senses, the woman

blinked and smiled slightly. "I beg your pardon?"

The man at her side wrapped his arm around her waist and pulled her in close. Mac didn't miss the disgusted shudder the woman tried to suppress.

Right then, he knew.

This woman was an escort. High-priced, guessing by the man's appearance and attitude mixed in with hers, not to mention where they were. These underground fights didn't let the fucking dregs in, after all. It was common for the very wealthy men and women who attended the events to bring along someone other than their spouse.

Like a hired date.

The woman looked Mac over again. For the most part, he would have called her glance dismissive, except she lingered far too long on the way his suit hugged his frame and the collar of his dress shirt that was opened at the top two buttons.

"Two nuts, huh?" the woman asked.

"Oh, you're certainly worth two," Mac replied. "But I think you'd have a lot more fun with a man who wasn't willing to give them up just to get a taste. You know, the kind of man that makes it worth your while to show it off."

The man at her side sneered. "Hey—"

Mac held up a hand, silencing the guy instantly. "I'm not talking to you."

He knew better than to piss off patrons at the Ferro fights. Frankly, Mac knew better than to be at the underground fights, which were organized and run by a rival New York Cosa Nostra family. *La famiglia* was all about loyalty, after all, and playing fun with another family's business was a dangerous game.

Mac needed the money, so he signed up for a fight.

"Melina," the guy murmured in the woman's ear, "let's go find a better view of the cage, yes?"

Melina.

He tried her name in his mouth silently, liking the way it felt. Escort or not, Mac wanted to know this woman. Especially when she flicked him with a look that screamed disinterest on the surface but burned with curiosity all the same.

Mac loved a good challenge. He made a mental note to find this Melina again after the fight, if he was able, and her *date* didn't sneak her off early.

The guy openly glared at Mac.

Sorry to ruin your evening, cafone.

"Mac, my boy, you're up next! You've got five minutes to get ready. *Capisce?*"

Melina's gaze caught Mac's and he winked at her.

"Get used to hearing that name," Mac murmured, still smirking like a motherfucker. "It'll be said a lot tonight."

She didn't respond; the fool pulled her away.

"All right, Macky boy, lemme tape up those hands of yours good and tight."

Mac sighed, willing away his irritation with the fight manager. Pissing off the guy who could get Mac into the cage or throw him out of it didn't seem like a good idea. Why did people just assume they could take his name and twist it however they saw fit?

"Just Mac, Cordial."

"Yeah, well, I like Macky. Shut your mouth. You're better with your fists anyway."

Perfetto.

Mac dropped it. "What's the payout?"

"If you lose, nothing."

"I'm not going to lose."

Cordial chuffed under his breath as he wrapped another line of tape across Mac's knuckles and under his palm. "You're too cocky for your own good, boy."

"Have I lost a fight in here before?" Mac asked.

"No, but there's always a first time for everything. And an arrogant attitude is the fastest way to get there."

"Payout?" he asked again.

"I won't know until you're in the ring. They changed up the betting. Frankie didn't want to have a list of fights for the night. He wanted the betting to be spur-of-the-moment and straight out of the stupid, excited pockets."

Mac laughed under his breath. "It's no wonder there's free liquor in here now. I was curious about that earlier, but I think I get it now."

Cordial smiled. "Bang on, my boy. The drunker they are, the more excited they get, and the bigger they bet. You always seem to draw a good number."

"Is Tank still meeting me in the cage?"

His companion's smile faded fast.

"What?" Mac demanded.

"Tank had to bow out last minute," Cordial said quietly, focusing all of his attention on taping up Mac's other hand. "Don't worry about it. Just get in there, fight, and don't pay attention to the last name of your opponent."

Shit.

That did not sound good.

"What's his last name, Cordial?"

"Ferro."

Fuck.

"Frankie's boy?" Mac asked.

Cordial nodded.

Mac figured. Junior was the only Ferro that Mac knew who occasionally liked to step into a cage and fight. The guy was good, as far as that went. He could take care of himself and he wasn't liable to get beat to death or something during a match.

But he was still a fucking Ferro.

In Cosa Nostra, men didn't fight one another. Part of the oath men took when entering into the life explicitly forbade made men from physically hurting another made man. It was against every rule Mac had ever learned in *la famiglia*. It also didn't help that the two men came from rival families and word might get out that Mac had taken a Ferro son on in the cage. Despite having his Capo's okay for the fights on occasion, Mac didn't have the main boss's okay.

Then again, he'd never gotten close enough to the Pivetti Don to ask anything.

But with this fight tonight, going hand to hand with a made man in another family, Mac might be asking for trouble he didn't want or need. Junior was made, as far as Mac knew. Mac wasn't, but beating the hell out of the guy wasn't a quick way to get his button. Especially if someone caused any trouble about it.

Sore losers, and all that jazz.

"You want to fight or not?" Cordial asked, slapping Mac's fists hard.

Money.

Mac needed some.

That goddamn roof at his mother's wasn't going to fix itself. He had his car payment and rent due, plus his sister had mentioned she was looking at a starter home. Mac wanted to help Victoria out with that, even if she hadn't asked for money.

Cash, cash, cash.

It was a fucking mantra Mac couldn't escape. He'd wanted to be a wise-guy because he thought that was how money was made. That, getting in with a family, and earning his button properly, would keep his family from suffering in poverty.

They were still drowning in poverty at times, just like they always had. When Mac had money, things were good. When he didn't, his family was barely able to keep their heads above water.

"Yeah," Mac grunted, pushing off the table. "I'm going to fight."

"Good." Cordial held out the mouth guard that Mac brought along for the evening and he shoved it in his mouth, biting down hard on the rubbery piece. Everything had to be checked before it went into the ring. Even something simple, like a mouth guard. "Keep your chin tucked in and your eyes on his right side. He favors harder hits, rather than several smaller ones. Watch for when that hit comes, Macky. He puts a lot of power behind it and he won't have much left to spare. You're a good old southpaw, so keep that locked up tight until you get the chance to take the best shot. Make that one count. He's quick on his feet, so you might wanna get him on the mat. Got it?"

Mac nodded. "Yes."

"Let's go."

***

Mac ignored the cheers, jeers, and pounding feet as he stepped into the cage. Their faces were nameless and unimportant to him. It wasn't the excitement of the crowd that got him revving for a fight. It wasn't the flushed, turned on faces of women or the bloodthirsty men.

Mac didn't fight for any of that.

Nor for approval, validation, or release.

No, he fought to win.

He fought for money and nothing more.

All those late nights at shoddy gyms when he was a teenager had paid off over the years. Between running on the streets for dealers and delivering messages for his uncle to his father before Marco died, Mac found time to kill, in gyms and a punching bag. He learned a few skills in boxing and Kung Fu, which worked well inside a cage when matched with his quickness and sharp eye.

"Open up," the girl wearing the smallest bikini ever and a fake smile said.

She was rake-thin, with bleach-blonde hair and not Mac's type. Unfortunately, the crowd loved a good show when the fighters got into the cage together, so he had a part to play. Making a point to wag his eyebrow and smirk at the girl, he opened his mouth and pushed his mouth guard out with the tip of his tongue. She took her time inspecting his mouth before he felt her hands slide under the boxing shorts he wore.

Mac beat back the cringe threatening to form as the girl's hand roved over his junk once, twice, and then a third time.

"Searching for something particular?" he asked when she didn't remove her hand.

"Just checking," she replied sweetly.

Too sweetly.

"Well, if you're looking to find something for you, you're not going to find it in there, babe," Mac muttered. "Takes a bit more than a touch to get me hard, girl."

Slipping his mouth guard back in place and taking a step away from the girl, he winked. It forced her hands out of his pants, anyway. And it still gave the crowd some idea that maybe he liked what she had done with her hand down his shorts, if their loud cheers were any indication.

"You're wearing jewelry," the girl pointed out. "It's not allowed."

His leather wristband with the M embossed in gold had been his grandfather's. The cross around his neck had been a gift from his grandmother. Both had passed when he was a teen. The two items didn't come off his person unless someone ripped them off.

And if that happened, the fool better make damn sure they were good and gone before Mac got ahold of them.

Mac cocked a brow. "The leather wristband has been vetted by the organizer and the necklace is a personal choice. They're not coming off or they already would have, before I stepped into the cage."

With a scowl, the girl turned on her heel and stalked to the other side of the cage.

Mac bounced on his heels as Junior Ferro stepped into his side of the cage. Neither of the men spent too much time looking one another over, as Ferro was checked in the same fashion Mac had been. Guessing by the leer on Junior's face, he liked the chick's hand on his dick a lot more than Mac had.

Sloppy, sweaty palm seconds.

Maybe that was Ferro's thing.

Mac didn't give a damn.

"Eleven K," came a shout from outside Mac's side of the cage.

He turned to see Cordial mouthing the words again.

"Eleven?" Mac asked, just to be sure.

No way.

That was the highest payout he'd ever seen from the Ferro fights.

Cordial nodded. "Eleven K to the winner of the fight. That's not including the payouts to everyone else. A record, apparently. Seems someone's bound and determined for you to lose, Macky. The largest bet came in on Ferro for you to lose against him."

Shit.

Mac's gaze swept the crowd quickly, trying to find the stupid fucker in a sea of people that was bound and determined to see him lose. Almost instantly, he found a pair of russet eyes meeting his stare closer to the cage than he was expecting.

Melina.

The gorgeously cold face was still mocking him in the back of his mind.

Her companion looked smug as fuck with an arm around Melina's waist as the fool nodded in Ferro's direction.

Shined shoes. Perfectly managed hair. Expensive tux. Silk tie.

Money.

Mac had guessed it about the guy earlier, but his cocky attitude and arrogant posture practically screamed it. Growing up like he had, in the thick of the streets with men who made their living off scheming from fools like Melina's companion and whoever else they could fuck over, gave Mac the ability to sniff out easy money.

That fool was easy money.

Chances were, that was the idiot who betted against him. Apparently, the guy's ego was still a little bit hurt after their encounter from earlier.

Mac caught Melina's gaze again as the cage was cleared. She looked surprised to see him in there. Given that he had been wearing a suit earlier and not the cage look he sported now, it wasn't such a surprise.

"Middle!" the ref shouted.

Why the Ferros even bothered with having refs in the cage, Mac wasn't sure. It wasn't like the idiots did anything except call the winner. On more than one occasion, Mac had witnessed the refs ignore just about every dirty move that could be used, even if it resulted in someone being carried out and shoved in a trunk.

Mac met Junior Ferro in the middle of the cage. Ferro put his taped fists out and Mac met them with a bump of his own.

"Clean fight, boys," the ref said.

Mac scoffed behind his mouth guard.

Even Junior sneered.

The moment the ref stepped back from the two men, a familiar bell dinged. Junior charged Mac fast and furious, like a goddamn bull in heat. Quickly, Mac stepped to the right just before Junior reached him and with a fast step on his heel, Mac swung to the side with all his body weight, lifted his left foot from the floor and let his heel connect with the middle of Junior's chest.

Easy hit.

Junior stumbled forward like he'd been surprised at the move, sucking in a hard breath of air. Yeah, a kick to the chest hurt. Placed right, it could break a rib and take a man's breath away. Mac wasn't looking to do serious damage to Junior. There was no reason to embarrass the guy any more than he already would once he won the match.

Why hadn't Cordial told Mac that Junior liked to charge a guy in the cage?

This fight could have been over instantly.

Turning fast to regain his balance from the kick, Mac met the rapid-fire fists of Junior, one after the other. Using his taped hands and arms as a shield, Mac blocked the light punches easily.

He favors the harder hits, rather than several smaller ones.

Well, Cordial fucked that one up big time.

Seemed like Junior had either taken up a different style or he was trying to trip Mac up. Just as Junior dropped back like he wanted more room for a swing, Mac prepped to block a hit and toss out one of his own.

Instead, his back met the fucking mat hard.

It took him an entire second to realize he was on the floor and Ferro was on top of him, raining quick, unrelenting punches over his head and chest.

Goddamn.

Mac needed to get out of this, and fast.

Ferro sneered behind his mouth guard, making damn sure Mac saw it. It was the opening Mac needed—just that one second of distraction. Mac's elbow flew up and cracked Ferro hard under his jaw, sending the man's head flying backwards. Blood dripped from a slice in the fool's bottom lip.

With one swift kick, Ferro was tossed off Mac.

Being upright had never felt so good to Mac.

Bouncing on his heels again, Mac ignored the screaming roar of the crowd and the volcanic noise around him. If he focused in on that shit, that's all he would hear.

Those people weren't important.

Winning was.

Ferro stood, pissed and ready to charge again.

Mac let him.

Unlike the first time, when Mac moved out of the way, he didn't move this time. Ferro pulled back for the swing Cordial had warned him about, Mac ducked the hit, and the southpaw came out to connect with Ferro, right under the right rib with enough force to crack the bone.

Instantly, Ferro shouted from the shock of the hit, crumpling in on himself. Mac tossed out two more hits, each landing to the half-assed protected face of his opponent.

The second Ferro lifted his head, Mac let his body move with a familiar roundhouse.

It connected to the side of Ferro's head with a solid thud.

Junior hit the mat, out cold.

Mac didn't wait for the ref to step in and call it. He knew what it was. A win by knockout. Stepping back, Mac finally let the overwhelming noise of the crowd seep into his focused senses. A cage door was opened to let him out.

Cordial was there to meet Mac with an icepack and a stick of super glue.

"Shit, lemme see that cut, boy," Cordial demanded.

Mac blinked, unsure of what Cordial meant. Then, he felt the drip of something warm and sticky slide down his cheek. Touching his eyebrow with his taped fist, Mac winced. Pain ricocheted over his forehead.

"Ouch," Cordial muttered.

"Just get it closed," Mac mumbled behind his mouth guard.

Cordial tipped Mac's head back, wiped the cut with a wet cloth, and then applied the glue. After ten seconds of holding the cut closed, Cordial let it go.

"Blink for me."

Mac did as he was told.

"Looks good," Cordial added.

Mac spat his mouth guard into the plastic tub Cordial offered.

"He's out, yeah?" Mac asked, not wanting to turn around and look back inside the cage.

"Out cold," Cordial confirmed. "They're waking him up now. You've got a minute or two before you need to go back in and let the people fawn over you."

Great.

Mac sucked in a breath, letting the lingering adrenaline from the fight fade away. His gaze caught a pair of brown eyes off to the side, watching him with interest.

Unable to stop himself, Mac offered Melina a grin.

Her companion didn't miss it.

"Is that what you call a fucking match?" the guy shouted. "Fancy feet and quick fists don't make a good fighter!"

Mac laughed as the guy's face turned red. "How much money did you lose betting against me? You didn't have to shell out more cash for the night than you already have, man."

Embarrassment was a horrible thing to feel,

especially when cash was involved.

Melina's gaze caught Mac's again as he was shoved backwards into the cage for the winner to be declared. Earlier in the night, her interest in the fights and people had seemed nonexistent. Now, there was a flush to her caramel skin and her cold stare held a familiar heat as she looked him over.

Sex and sin.

He bet a night with her would be worth all the trouble she caused.

Smirking, Mac mouthed, "I'll see you again, doll."

CHAPTER FIVE

*M*en. It didn't matter what they looked like or who they were. At the end of the day, they all shared one basic characteristic—the desire to prove themselves as an alpha male to a woman. Case in point, the two men last night who'd acted as if Melina were some female they were rutting over: Garrett and Mac.

Different men, at opposite ends of the male spectrum.

One with an arrogance brought on by wealth.

The other with an arrogance brought on by an unassuming confidence in himself.

And for some odd reason Melina was strangely attracted to one of those men.

Though she'd been annoyed from the moment she'd laid eyes on Garrett Jameson, the hazel-eyed Mac was a different story altogether. Built with the body of a Greek god and tough enough to take a man down before he knew what was happening to him, Melina couldn't deny that there was something about Mac that interested her.

Maybe it was the way he'd looked at her. As if he could see through the tough exterior that had become a constant part of her life.

But then again, maybe it was the total disregard he'd shown for her date. Where there were sure to be men who would've allowed the privileged Jameson to emerge as the alpha male, Mac had risen to the challenge of showing which man really was the leader of the pack.

Doll.

One word. She couldn't get it out of her mind and she didn't like it one bit.

Feminine endearments had always bothered her for some reason. Perhaps it went back to her catching her first "boyfriend," whispering those endearments on the phone … to another girl. Yep. That was probably it. She was no one's "sweetheart", "honey", or whatever other stupid pet name men liked to use. Her name was Melina and Melina only. Mac calling her a "doll" had only reminded her of something she'd rather forget. No doubt, he thought he was being cute. In reality, "doll" was a throwback slang word used to describe a pretty but unintelligent or expressionless woman. Melina was none of the latter.

But she'd spent enough time thinking about the fighter. He was just a man, a rather attractive man, but still a man like all the rest of them.

Parking her black Nissan Altima in front of a nondescript, gray brick building, Melina killed the ignition and exited, locking the car behind her. Walking unhurriedly, she opened the door in front of her and entered. The front foyer of the building was empty, but that didn't matter. She knew better than to be deceived by appearances. Melina found the wooden stairs that lead upstairs and took them two at a time. When she reached the last stair, the strains of jazz filled the air.

Pushing open the red painted door in front of her, Melina came face to face with a red-haired woman wearing a silk dressing gown.

"Melina, dear, I thought I heard someone come in."

"Expecting someone else?"

Dulcea rolled her green eyes. "You remember the first cardinal rule, never kiss and tell."

"Well, since your lipstick is still intact, I'll assume you haven't kissed anyone yet, so, it wouldn't technically be considered kissing and telling."

"One of these days, somebody is going to come along and tame that tongue of yours."

"You mean when Jesus returns? I assure you, he's the only man capable of that feat."

Dulcea gazed at her with shrewd eyes. "We'll see. Do you have something for me?"

"As always." Melina opened her purse and pulled out two folded checks, handing them to Dulcea.

The redhead unfolded the checks and looked at Melina, her eyes stretched wide.

"Damn girl. What did you do?"

"Not what you're thinking."

"Come on, now. This old girl has been around the block a time or two. No judgment here if you did."

Crossing her arms, Melina stared at her boss. "You know I have no problems with owning up to my shit, but Garrett Jameson was in no way appealing to me. I hate men who think their shit doesn't stink because they have money."

"And yet, you entertain these men and are quite good at it. What a conundrum you are."

Dulcea turned and walked back into the room, beckoning for Melina to follow her.

"The moment you figure a person out, the mystique is gone. You taught me that, remember?"

"Indeed, I did."

Laughing, Dulcea turned the dial to open the large wall safe. Placing the checks inside, she pulled out two stacks of wrapped bills and handed them to Melina.

"Wow, this looks like more than the usual take."

Dulcea shut the safe and faced Melina. "Of course it is. You brought in an extra thirty grand, in addition to the fee I've already collected from your gentleman. Just make sure you don't spend it all in one place."

Placing the stacks of money in her purse, Melina gave Dulcea a terse smile. "When have you ever known me to be a frivolous girl?"

"Never, but it is all right for you to live a little. You're a young, beautiful woman. The world is whatever you want it to be."

"The only thing I want from this world, it can't give me."

Dulcea patted her arm, her eyes shined bright. "I know. Just take it one day at a time, okay?"

Melina nodded. "I am. Until next time."

With a wave, Melina was off and going up the stairs. She'd just banked eighteen grand. This was the most money she'd ever made on a date. *You're really coming up in the world.* Sure she was. This would be the first money she'd earned that wouldn't be going to pay medical bills. A tear slipped down her cheek. For so long, she'd worked with the hope of crawling out from under the debt that had become a part of her life and now that part of her life was finally over. She should be elated for what that meant, but Melina would go out with jerks for the rest of life if it meant having her father back. There really were some things money couldn't buy.

"All right, let me see those hands in the air. Run in place."

Melina smiled at the kids spread out in front of her. Ranging in age from six to fifteen, they were regulars at the Boys and Girls Club, and she loved them all.

"Let's do ten jumping jacks. Let's get that blood flowing."

42

"I'm going to be tired before we even get started," fifteen-year-old Ursula said.

Melina laughed as she joined them in their exercises. This was exactly what she needed. Time with people still young and impressionable, not yet tainted by the bitterness of the world. After all the ugliness she'd seen, these young boys and girls were a ray of sunshine.

"I'm tired, Miss Melina," six-year-old Ellie said.

"That was the last one, Ellie."

"Yay," a few of the kids yelled.

Waving her arms to signal them all to stop, Melina quickly paired the kids up in twos and helped them to put on the protective mitts and face masks they used whenever she taught them kickboxing.

"I'm ready to kick some butt," nine-year-old David said, hitting his gloves together.

"I'm not teaching you guys so you can kick some butt. I want you to know how to defend yourself if something ever happens, remember?"

"Yeah, but do you know how badass the girls think it is when you tell them you're a kickboxer?" fourteen-year-old Mykel asked.

"They must not be too bright if they believe you," Ursula said before she started snickering.

Mykel glared at Ursula, but before he could say anything, Melina swiftly redirected his attention by telling the kids to all start practicing the punches and kicks she'd worked with them on last week. For the next half hour, Melina taught the kids. A smile never seemed to leave her face, but all too soon it was over. Glancing down at her watch, she brought the practice to a halt.

"That's enough for today, guys. Put up the equipment and go get yourselves cleaned up. Pizza should be here in about fifteen minutes."

"Thank you," some of the kids said in unison.

"You're welcome. Good work today."

She watched as one by one, the kids removed their equipment, wiped it down with alcohol wipes, and put it away until the next class.

Renee, the main operator of the Boys and Girls Club, joined Melina. "You wear these kids out every time you come here."

"I try my best, Renee," Melina said.

The older, salt-and-pepper-haired woman smiled at her. "You do a darn good job of it. So many start off here but they never stay. You're the exception."

"I love the kids. Coming here is the highlight of my week."

"I'm glad to hear that. They love you, too."

"I know. Listen, I've ordered pizza and a few other things for them. Here's the money to cover it."

Melina handed Renee a wad of bills. The older woman cocked an eyebrow at her.

"This is way more than pizza costs."

Melina shrugged. "I know, but things come up. Sometimes they need things. Just hold on to the rest of it for when they need something."

"Melina, this is over three thousand dollars!"

"My dad always used to say "Be a blessing to someone else, and the Lord will bless you with even more"."

"He was a smart man."

"Indeed, he was. I'll see you guys later."

Before Renee could say anything else, Melina slung her purse over her shoulder and exited the building. Her heart felt lighter than it had in days. Walking down the sidewalk towards the epicenter of the shopping complex, she decided a treat was in order. She could almost taste the Caramel Macchiato she was going to order. The wind blew around her, whipping her hair around her face. Running a hand through it, Melina tugged the silky strands away from her face.

"You promised," a female's high voice said.

Melina turned her head in the direction of the voice. A blonde-haired girl had her arms wrapped around a man whose face Melina couldn't see, as too many people were flooding the crosswalk. With hands stuffed in his pockets, he allowed her to drag him across the street. Melina kept walking until she was at the stairs to the entrance of the epicenter.

"I know I promised, but this isn't my scene."

"Well, it's mine and today is all about me. That's what you said. Get used to it."

Melina shook her head. Apparently, guys were into the needy type these days. Speed walking in hopes of avoiding the couple, Melina missed a step and went tumbling. A pair of tan, muscled arms caught her before she fell.

"Hey, doll."

Melina knew that voice.

Mac.

CHAPTER SIX

With a grin, Mac righted Melina to her feet, taking in the fact she had lost the tight dress, sky-high heels, and makeup from the night before. Today, she looked like a regular young woman dressed in Converses, skinny jeans, and a Henley.

Mac had to admit, the steel-tongued woman wore both looks well.

Goddamn well, actually.

"Mac?" his sister asked behind him.

Mac gave Victoria a wave without looking back, hoping she'd take the hint and be quiet for a second. He doubted it would work. Victoria Maccari didn't know the meaning of "quiet" and she was nosy as hell. He loved his sister, to be sure, but she was one of a kind.

Kind of like the woman he was still holding.

Mac offered Melina a slow, easy smile as she turned to face him. "Well, well. Funny meeting you here. I didn't expect to meet up with you again so soon."

Melina took a step back and Mac let her, dropping his hold. "Uh, thanks. I'm not usually so ..."

"Clumsy?"

"I'm not clumsy."

"What would you call it?" he asked.

"I was trying to get inside quicker and missed a step; that's all."

"There's lots of daylight hours left, doll. What's the

rush?"

"You ask a lot of questions," Melina said coolly.

Mac let her attitude bounce right off him. He had a feeling that under her sharp-as-glass exterior was a woman who probably had a few things to hide. People who tended to keep others away usually had those kinds of secrets to tell.

Besides, he didn't mind a challenge.

"You didn't answer them," Mac replied with a grin.

"I'm not required to," Melina said, tossing him a smile. "I don't know you and you don't know me. I didn't realize it was commonplace for strangers to have chitchats about their personal lives."

"Actually, we know quite a bit about one another. I frequent fights and you entertain at fights. Apparently, we come to the same shopping center." Mac waved at the building, ignoring the people who passed them by. "And lucky for you, I was here to stop you from bruising up those beautiful legs of yours."

Melina's mouth popped open.

Speechless.

Mac chuckled. "Was that all it took to quiet that attitude of yours?"

Melina's eyes narrowed into slits. "Hey—"

Shit.

"Hey, doll, I was just kidding around. No harm meant. It's a joke, you know."

"It'd help if you'd cut out the 'doll' nonsense," she muttered.

Melina's anger came in the form of fire-blazing eyes and pink cheeks. Mac didn't think the woman realized how good she looked when she was pissed off. Angry women were fun women. They had passion and a hunger that most women lacked.

Maybe he liked that a little.

"What's the problem with doll?" Mac asked.

He'd grown up hearing every sweetheart of every man he knew being called that on one occasion or another. It'd never been used in a derogatory way, and in fact, was held in regard for those who were special to a man.

"You mean the unintelligent, emotionless doll of a woman who looks pretty on a man's arm and does very little else?" Melina asked sweetly.

Sugary sweet.

Like cyanide.

Damn, this girl was tough.

"Is that what you think it means?" Mac asked back. "What, do you have a slang dictionary on hand or something? Does every endearment a man might offer make you think it's intended to lower you or dumb down your status to him?"

Melina blinked, her cheeks reddening. "Well ..."

"Well, what?"

"Sometimes, yeah. And then sometimes endearments are just another way to disarm a woman and make her vulnerable."

Mac appreciated her honesty, but she was ten shades of wrong. "Doll actually started as reference to a man's mistress and a shortened version of the name Dorothy. Then, it was used to describe a woman who was of the pretty but silly type."

Melina huffed. "Exactly."

Mac laughed deeply. "But considering how silly you act over an endearment meant to show how much a man cherishes a certain woman in his life, and the fact you're mighty damn pretty, I think doll fits you awfully well."

Maybe that was the wrong thing to say.

Melina didn't seem like the type to like a man who would challenge her, but it was hard to tell. Mac wasn't the kind of guy who would roll over and play dead, just because a woman liked to sharpen her stilettos.

When Melina stayed quiet, Mac cocked a brow.

"What, did you think I was all looks, with some fast fists, and no brains, doll? I've got a dozen more surprises where that one came from. Maybe you'll let me show you sometime."

Melina openly glared. "You are one cocky—"

"Careful," Mac interrupted with a smirk. "A lady never swears in public."

"Who said I was a lady?"

"Certainly not me."

A hint of a smile graced the corner of Melina's lips as she tucked a strand of hair behind her ear.

Mac thought she had a beautiful smile.

She did like this. Mac could see it in the glimmer still burning in her brown eyes and the way she looked him up and down. She was agitated, sure, but she damn well liked it. If he had to guess, Melina didn't find a man willing to challenge her very often.

"Are you here for something particular?" Mac asked.

Melina pursed her lips. "Coffee, actually. I was going to get one before I headed home."

"Let me buy you one."

Melina lifted a single brow in response, but said nothing.

"Mac," Victoria said again, more insistent the second time.

She was probably tapping her little black pumps on the pavement behind him.

Impatient little ...

"I think your girlfriend is getting annoyed," Melina said, a bitter twist lighting up her words.

Jealous.

It flared to life in her pretty features and in the way her lips tightened as she glanced over Mac's shoulder at Victoria. Melina practically dismissed Mac's younger sister with a flick of her fiery brown eyes and the coldness of a scowl.

"My sister," Mac corrected quietly. "Victoria Maccari is my *sister*, not my girlfriend. Seems my mother thinks I've not been watching over Vic enough, so today was her day to do whatever she wanted, since I won the fight last night and could treat her to anything."

Melina's stance softened, but barely. "A spoiled woman is one who can't care for herself. No woman should depend on a man for anything, much less spoiling her."

Jesus.

This woman was something else.

"Or maybe the kind of men you've been dating haven't been spoiling you right, doll."

Just like that, Melina's invisible wall slammed back up again. Her gaze hardened and all amusement on her features left, leaving a cold mask in its wake. It took Mac all of three seconds to realize his mistake. He knew she was an escort just from her date the night before, but his words hadn't actually been directed towards that.

"I'm—"

Melina held up a single, manicured hand, silencing Mac's apology before he could even get it out. "Don't bother. There's really nothing left to say."

With that, Melina pushed past Mac on the epicenter's steps and walked down without even looking back once.

Pride was an awful thing. It was the kind of thing that could make or break a man. Especially a man like Mac, in a profession where pride made the man. A man had to have some kind of pride in being who he was, or he was fucking nobody.

So, when Mac felt his pride take a hit from Melina's rejection, he couldn't let it go like that.

"Hey, doll?"

Melina's back tensed and she stopped up short in her walk. Flicking him with a stinging glance over her shoulder, she asked, "What?"

"I'll be around when you get tired of playing with

pups."

"So ..."

"Shut up, Vic," Mac warned.

Victoria smiled slyly. "You know I'm not going to."

"Shut up and get your nails done like you wanted."

"But—"

"Victoria, I swear to *Dio*, I will leave you here to pay for this spa day all by your little pretty lonesome."

Victoria frowned. "You would not, Mac."

All right, so he wouldn't.

Still ...

"It's none of your business. Leave it alone," Mac said.

She wouldn't. Mac knew it. Nosy Victoria was at it again. She'd sniffed something in his personal life and like a shark, she would bite down and wouldn't let go until she'd ripped out a nice bloody chunk to chew on.

When she had wanted to come to the epicenter—to visit her favorite spa and be pampered for the day—Mac had been more than happy to drop his sister off with a thousand dollars and let her go batshit crazy. He figured he didn't have to be right there for her sessions, or the clothing shopping she wanted to do after.

He was wrong.

She wanted to spend time with him. Mac didn't know how to say no.

Family was everything.

"So, who is she?" Victoria asked.

"Someone I met last night and met again today," Mac answered honestly.

"Is that seriously all you're going to give me?"

The nail technician clicked her tongue chidingly and grabbed Victoria's finger, which she had waved at Mac.

"That's all I have to give, honestly," Mac replied. "I just don't know the woman, all right?"

"But you want to," his sister pressed.

Maybe.

"Leave it alone, Vic."

"Where did you meet her last night?"

Sighing, Mac wished the wall would swallow him whole. "Out somewhere."

"Where?"

"Do you have some kind of tape to shut them up when they don't quit talking?" Mac asked the technician.

His sister glared. "Asshole."

"Vic, where I go and what I do when I'm there is none of your business. It's better you don't know, anyway. That's how it works. You know this."

"How *la famiglia* works, you mean," his sister muttered.

Mac forced his mouth to stay shut and not bark off the retort he wanted. Like his mother, his sister always had something or the other to say about his choice in being involved with Cosa Nostra.

"I chose this, Vic," Mac settled on saying.

"Have you gotten what you wanted from it yet?"

"It's not about getting something you want from it. It's about becoming a part of something that's bigger than just you. I'm damn good at this."

Victoria blew out a quiet breath and thankfully, dropped the topic. "That girl seems like a nasty one, Mac. I never knew you to go for the ball-breaking type."

"I don't usually."

"Then what's up with her?"

Mac shrugged. "I don't know, Vic."

"You don't know?"

"Nope."

"Boo, you suck," Victoria crowed.

Mac chuckled. "What do you want from me?"

"You seem to like talking to her."

"Because just talking to the woman is like foreplay. And you can't find many women like that."

Melina also made his dick harder than steel with just a look, made his blood hot just by being close, and got his darker urges thrumming deep with the sound of her voice. Mix that all up with her sharp tongue, and he'd bet she was crazy in the sack.

The crazy ones were fun.

Mac liked fun.

Victoria's face crumpled. "I don't want to hear that."

"Then stop asking."

Before Victoria could say another thing, Mac's phone rang in his pocket. He recognized the tune instantly and pulled the device out of his jacket pocket.

"Skip," Mac answered as he picked up the call. He turned his back to his sister and took a few steps away from the station, hoping she couldn't overhear his call with the Capo. "What's up?"

"That shit with the trucks you worked out is happening tonight, Mac," Guido Vasari said. "You need to be in on it to make sure it gets done. You've got the contacts with the trucks, so make sure the drivers are well paid for the hell they're about to receive in the Kitchen. Make it look good. Stop by my restaurant later and I'll give you some cash to cover feeding their mouths so they can cover up their bruises. The stuff better be hidden in the warehouses by morning. I also hear you've got some dues to be collecting down in the Trifecta with Carlos. Dallying around like a fool isn't going to earn you any money, kid."

Mac winced, taking in the orders and what all of them meant. "I was heading down to the Trifecta tonight, actually. The rackets are good. They pay. Carlos has them on a schedule."

"Fuck his schedule. You pick up the checks when I want you to, not him."

Forcing back his irritation, Mac said, "Yeah, on it."

"And the trucks."

"And the trucks, Skip."

Even if that meant he wouldn't sleep for the next eighteen hours.

"Call me in the morning and I'll let you know if you're needed for something else," Guido said.

"Will do."

"*Ciao*, Mac. Don't fuck this up."

The phone call hung up before Mac could say goodbye. This was how most of his conversations went with his Capo. Frankly, Mac was lucky that he had gained enough attention and respect from the Vasari Capo that he was on the man's phone contacts. Most soldiers simply answered to someone else who answered to Guido.

But it still pissed Mac off like nothing else.

He worked his ass off for Guido, who took all the credit when it came to the family boss for the schemes and work Mac did, and was given very little for thanks.

Except a phone call with more demands.

Mac was getting tired of it.

"Mac?" his sister asked.

Turning on his heel, Mac shoved his phone in his pocket. "Sorry, *sorella*, but I need to cut this short. Work and all."

Victoria frowned, but didn't argue. "Okay."

"Apologize to Ma for me, too."

"Why?"

"I won't make it to church, after all."

CHAPTER
SEVEN

All of it was gone now, except for a few precious things. Melina could hardly believe that one small box was all that remained to remember her father by. Blowing out a breath, she raked a hand through her hair. It had been an emotional week for her. She'd kept putting it off and making excuses, but she'd finally forced herself to clean up the three-bedroom apartment she'd shared with her father. Without him, the place no longer felt like home. It was just a set of rooms that were haunted by the ghost of a man too good for this world. Melina wiped away a bitter tear.

With every box she'd packed, the sorrow in her heart had grown just a little bit heavier. Clothes. Shoes. The hats her dad had been so fond of wearing. It hurt to hold onto them. It was better to give them to someone in need. There was one special piece of clothing she'd kept, but even that had been a long debate within herself.

The uniform.

A mark of Daniel Morgan's rank and selfless service.

A reminder of the country that had spit on his service and let him down in the end.

Part of her wanted to set it on fire and watch it burn to nothing; but regardless of how badly she hurt, Melina knew her father wouldn't have wanted that.

No. He would've wanted her to honor his

commitment to his country. It didn't matter that he'd lost everything. It didn't matter that he'd been scarred for life after the horrors he'd seen, because regardless of everything, he'd been proud to serve his country. And it was because of that selfless love that Melina had his uniform and all the insignias of his rank framed in a large memory box. Each day that she looked at it would be a subtle reminder that no one could be trusted, least of all the US government.

Trust no one and they'll never have the chance to disappoint you. It was the creed she'd adopted long ago. Melina would live by it until she took her last breath. Taking one last look around the empty apartment, she nodded. The place was spotless and the apartment manager would have no choice but to give her back her full deposit.

The men from the Salvation Army had been more than happy to pick up all the items she'd donated. Furniture, clothes, and a few knickknacks here and there. Yes, everything had gone except for her clothes and a box of her father's keepsakes. There were so many photographs. Melina hadn't realized that there were so many pictures of them. Hell, she didn't even know that so many photos of her mother remained, either.

Sarita Ann Morgan. Kindergarten teacher. Loving mother. Amazing baker.

Dead at twenty-seven from ovarian cancer.

Life was a bitch that kept fucking you over.

Melina had been eight when her mother passed. Old enough to remember the way her mother had always smelled like vanilla. The way she'd always had a smile on her face for anyone that came in her path.

***

"Look at you. You're growing into such a beautiful young

lady."

"*Just like you, Mommy?*"

Melina stood beside her mother. The two of them stared into the mirror, looking at their reflections.

"*No. You're going to be even more beautiful than I am. Don't forget you've got your Daddy's looks, too, and we both know he's no slouch in that department.*"

"*No, he isn't.*"

They both burst into laughter and Melina turned, hugging her mother's waist. Sarita ran her fingers through her daughter's long, black hair.

"*What are you two in here, giggling about?*"

Melina's eyes followed the voice and she let go of her mother.

"*Daddy!*"

Going down on one knee, he opened his arms and enveloped her in a warm hug. "How's my princess today?"

"*Wonderful.*"

"*Wonderful, huh? That's good to hear. And how about my queen?*"

Daniel rose, holding Melina, and stepped towards his wife. He kissed her on the lips and Melina made noises in the back of her throat.

"*Better, now that you're here,*" *Sarita said.*

"*You two are so lovey dovey.*"

Daniel tickled his daughter. "Well, why shouldn't we be? We love each other and we love you, the most adorable little girl in the world."

Melina laughed and squirmed until her father put her down. Then she took her place standing between her mother and father. One big happy family.

If only she hadn't been fool enough to believe

that was the way things would always be. At twenty-five, she was alone in the world. Her mother's parents had stopped bothering to even keep in contact after Sarita had died. Daniel's parents were long gone, and with no aunts and uncles from either side, Melina was truly alone. Some moments it hurt, but other times she didn't care. Either way, she would be okay. If Eve could survive getting kicked out of the Garden of Eden and incurring God's wrath, then there was no doubt Melina could. Besides, Melina had one thing Eve didn't ... street smarts.

Laughing, Melina walked to the front door and opened it. Stepping halfway out, she gave the apartment one last glance and shut the door behind her. All she had to do now was return the keys and this would be another piece of her past she could put to rest ... forever. Sometimes a body wasn't the only thing that needed burying.

***

This is a bad idea and you know it.

Melina parked her car and silently swatted away her pesky inner voice. This might be a bad idea but right now, she just didn't give a damn. After squaring away things at her old apartment, Melina had spent the rest of the day waiting around for the movers to deliver the new items she'd purchased for her two-bedroom apartment. She had a lot of work ahead of her, with decorating her new place and unpacking the mountains of clothes she had, but she'd get to that all in good time. Tonight, she was taking Dulcea's advice and throwing her cares to the wind. She was young, beautiful and single. Why not live a little? Especially when you never knew when the opportunity would be taken away from you.

Checking out her reflection in the rearview mirror,

she wiped away a stray smudge of copper-colored lipstick. Her hair hung in loose curls down to her shoulders. Her eyes were rimmed with dark kohl and her lashes fanned out. The soft, black leather dress clung to her curves like a second skin. The dress was strapless and studded with gold beading around the bodice and ended at mid-thigh. Paired with ankle high black boots, her ensemble was the perfect mix of bad girl sass. Melina had no doubt that tonight she would have her hands full keeping the men at bay. But it wasn't anything she couldn't handle.

Stepping out of her car, she locked it and quickly walked towards the packed club. It was a good thing she'd learned how to walk in heels a long time ago. The club was a block away and with the line of people that she was sure would be waiting outside, there was no doubt she'd be on her feet for a while. She held her clutch and enjoyed the bite of the wind across her back, and in a few minutes, the club was in her view and the line was already crazy long.

Taking her place at the end of the line, Melina watched the people around her. Throb was supposed to be one of the hottest new clubs in the area. Local gossip also claimed the place was backed by mob money, but Melina didn't buy it. The mob was dead, as far as she knew, and if it wasn't, she didn't care. Tonight was about her and she didn't give a damn about anyone or anything else.

Ahead of her, a group of teenage girls screamed and flashed their breasts, begging for attention. Pathetic.

There was nothing wrong with being sexy. Melina thrived on the power she had as a woman, but she also knew when to draw the line. Mystique was everything. Today's females needed to learn that if they shared everything, they'd have nothing left for themselves, including respect.

The line inched ahead and Melina went with it. Suddenly, broad shoulders were pushing into her, making her lose her balance.

"What the fuck?" she asked.

A pair of hands gripped her shoulders and Melina looked up. A tall, dark-haired man with olive skin and chocolate brown eyes smiled at her.

"Please, forgive me. I didn't mean to bump into you."

Melina nodded and took a step back. The man released her.

"Let me make it up to you," the man said.

"That's not necessary."

"Please? A gentlemen does right by a lady, when he can."

Melina laughed. "What did you have in mind?"

"Well, I happen to be close associates with one of the owners of this place. I can get us in past the line and into the VIP area, all free of charge."

Melina raised a brow. "Really? I'd like to see that."

"Your wish is my command, lady."

He held out his arm and against her better judgment, she took it. With a smooth pace, the man eased them to the front of the line. The bouncers took one look at him and opened the doors, letting them inside. She smiled.

"Okay, I'm impressed. Let's see if you can keep it up."

"Just you wait and see."

As they entered through the entrance leading to the main floor, music filled the air. The dance floor was a connecting sequence of clear squares. Each square was illuminated by colored lights. Overhead strobe lights spun all around. It was pretty impressive, but what really drew Melina's attention were the two silver-barred cages elevated from the dance floor. Inside danced two women. Their movements were fast and frenzied as they moved to the beat of the music.

"Well, what do you think?"

"No matter where you go, there are half-naked women," Melina said.

Her companion laughed, his eyes settling on her.

"Trust me, with a real woman like you here tonight, nobody's paying them the least bit of attention. Let's get a drink."

Melina allowed him to lead her towards the large bar, located at the back of the club. There were wall-to-wall bottles of liquor. Taking the empty seat in front of her, Melina waited to see what her handsome benefactor would do next.

"Hey." He snapped his fingers at one of the bartenders. "Whatever this lady wants, she gets. It's on the house."

"Yes, sir."

The bald, muscled bartender turned his attention to Melina. "What can I get you?"

"Long Island Ice Tea."

"Coming right up."

As the man turned away to prepare her drink, Melina felt a hand on her shoulder. Lips brushed her ear.

"I hate to rush off, but I need to speak with one of the guys who run the place. I'll be right back."

"I'm a big girl. I'll be fine."

"You sure are."

The man winked at her and then he disappeared through the crowd.

Not a minute later, the bartender was back. "Your drink, ma'am."

"Thank you."

Melina picked up the glass and took a long drink. The liquor hit the back of her throat. Cold and refreshing with tones of lemon, this was exactly what she needed. Three more swallows and the drink was gone. Moving from her seat, Melina disappeared into the crowd on the dance floor. The sounds of Jazmine

Sullivan's *Let It Burn* filled the air. She loved the soulful melody and the old-school music it was based on.

Moving her body to the music, Melina danced to the song while silently mouthing the words. She wondered if she would ever find someone who made her fire burn like an inferno that would never go out.

Mac.

Mac.

The voice inside her head whispered the name. No. He was arrogant and too cocksure.

He had a smart mouth.

But he was also sexy as hell.

Hazel eyes and a brooding face.

She liked the look of him and part of her couldn't help but wonder if there was more to him than smooth words and a handsome smile. From the way he moved in the ring, she surely hoped he had that same finesse in the bedroom. Arms slid around her waist, pulling her against a warm male body.

"I'm back. Let's party."

"Let's see if you can."

A hit of liquor in her system and a handsome man on the dance floor with her. Maybe Dulcea had the right idea, for once.

CHAPTER EIGHT

"Could you get those girls any more naked than they already are?" Mac asked, watching two women dance above his head in cages.

Guido chuckled. "Skin is in, as the saying goes."

Mac beat back his scowl. Guido was a good thirty years older than the women he was leering at, not that his age made a difference to the guy. The Capo still worked with the kind of mentality that came with every old-school wise-guy Mac had ever come across. Females were toys to be used well, used hard, and thrown away when the men finished with them. Move on to the next before the last turned clingy.

Guido was also married—happily, or so he claimed to Mac—to a good, old Italian woman who knew her place and turned her cheek.

Yeah, a wise-guy.

Mac was no saint. He liked women and he had more than a few over the years, but he never liked to fuck with a woman's head like some of the mob guys did. He knew men who had upwards of five or six different women they were running alongside the wife and kids they kept at home to keep face. Others had entirely separate homes from the one the world got to see, including *goomahs*, illegitimate children, and all that shady business.

Mac just couldn't do it.

He thought of his mother and her struggle to manage her house while her husband ran around with any woman who would take him. He considered his father, and how the man only ever stumbled home when he needed to save face for the mob. To show he was keeping up the family side of things.

That was not the life Mac wanted to live.

"Come," Guido demanded.

Mac followed his Capo through the throng of moving, sweaty bodies on the dance floor. With the bass of the music pumping through the space and the lights overhead flickering fast enough to make a person dizzy, it was a lot to take in. Mac enjoyed a club every once in a while. It was a good way to meet someone who was looking for the same kind of thing he was that night and to blow off some quick steam.

Unfortunately, that wasn't why he'd come to Throb tonight. Mac hadn't actually been inside the place since Guido opened the doors to the club a month ago, but he'd heard enough to know it was a hotspot and making more money than a lot of people knew. It wasn't just the liquor and door fees making the cash, either.

Guido had hands on the floor selling anything and everything from acid to ecstasy. He also had girls who didn't look like hookers but worked the backrooms like they were.

Or so Mac heard.

Sometimes, with Guido Vasari, it was better not to ask.

Chances were, the rumors were true. Guido was the sole owner of Throb, as well as five other hotspots in the city. The Capo's other clubs were full of mob money and mafia business. Modern mafioso had to be a little more careful about how and with whom they did dealings, after all. With changes in the world, came changes in the mob.

Men like Guido had to step their games up.

Mac might have had a hand or two in that, but his Capo never cared to give him the credit for it.

"Ah, here we go," Guido said, pulling out a key.

Mac turned to glance over the crowd one last time as Guido unlocked a door to expose a staircase leading up to a dark hallway. As his Capo stepped inside and called his name, ordering him to follow, Mac swore he saw someone he recognized.

Chocolate eyes.

Dark hair.

Caramel skin.

Mac froze, his gaze zoning in on the crowd again.

Could it …?

"Mac," Guido barked.

Mac shook the odd feeling off.

The Capo glowered at him. "We have shit to discuss. Get out of your head, *capisce?*"

"Yeah, I got it."

"Good. I'd hate to smack you out of it."

Mac held back his scoff and that was only for the sake of respect.

Respect.

That's what the mafia was all about.

Mac gave Guido what the man wanted—again. "Let's talk about the issue we're having with the Corelli crew and how to get it settled, Skip."

Guido smiled. "*Grazie.* Good to know my best *soldato* has his head on straight tonight."

Solider.

Because that's all Mac was to Guido.

"Are you ever going to get me the button?" Mac asked.

Mac wanted into *la famiglia.* For now, Guido was Mac's only way to the Pivetti Cosa Nostra and the button.

Guido laughed. "Not if you keep asking

questions like that, Mac."

With a wave, Guido directed Mac up the enclosed staircase. The passage was so small, it felt like the walls were closing in. At the top, Guido flipped the keys in his hand until he found the one he wanted and unlocked the second door. Guido knocked once before he pushed the door open.

Mac tried not to act surprised at the sight of a bleached-blonde hanging off the arm of Guido's enforcer, Tip. Well, everybody called the guy Tip, but his real name was Sammy. Mac still hadn't figured out how Tip got his nickname and chances were, he didn't want to.

Tip held the female's hair back as she bent over on his lap with a rolled up bill in her hand, stuck up one nostril. The distinct sound of snorting followed and white lines of powder disappeared off the glass coffee table.

"What'd I fucking tell you, huh?" Guido asked as Mac closed the door.

Tip shrugged as he yanked the girl by her hair and pulled her into a straight position again. She was blitzed out of it, if her pupils were any indication. Tip looked to be in the same shape, if not worse.

This was the kind of enforcer Guido had watching this joint when business was going down?

Fucking useless.

"Having fun, Boss," Tip said, a slow smile curving his lips.

God, the man was stoned out of his mind.

Mac took note of Guido's frown, but the Capo just seemed defeated at the scene. What in the hell was going on, anyway? Any other Capo would have kicked the enforcer in the teeth and gotten him the hell out of the joint to save some face. Maybe even got the guy whacked, to end the nonsense altogether.

Hard drug use had never been acceptable in Cosa Nostra, as far as Mac knew. People turned their cheeks to a little bit of substance use here and there, but full-on addicts were something entirely different. It just wasn't allowed.

"Get her out of here," Guido growled.

Tip laughed. "Yeah, all right."

"And clean yourself up before you come back," the Capo added.

"Sure, sure."

Mac waited while the giggling blonde and the enforcer made their way out of the large office. Guido said nothing as he hit a few switches on the wall panel and lit up the room with more lights. Hardwood floors, buffed and polished, gleamed. High ceilings with bronze fixtures rested above their heads. Guido's large, cherry-oak desk rested in the middle of the room, commanding attention.

The Capo took the leather seat behind the desk, pushing the papers on the top out of the way. "Goddamn."

Mac figured it'd be rude not to ask about Guido's troubles, even if he was annoyed with the Capo for overlooking him constantly. "Something wrong, Skip?"

Guido glanced up, his dark eyes flashing with tiredness. "I'm getting too old for this game, Mac."

"I don't know, you do all right."

He was still one of the highest earning Capos in the Pivetti family, after all. That was something to take note of. Even if all of Guido's earnings were made by his crew and their hard work, who really cared?

Apparently, no one.

"I didn't know you were having issues with Tip," Mac said.

Guido waved the statement off. "I'm not. He's just going through some shit, that's all. His wife is due to have their kid right off soon and Tip's just doing what he does to manage the stress."

Wait, what? The guy had a wife and a baby on the way, but he was spending his nights in a club getting high with whatever female was handy? And Guido was turning cheek to that kind of behavior?

Mac did a double take of his Capo. "Skip—"

"I'm not in the mood to discuss my enforcer's business, Mac. We have other things to handle tonight."

Mac nodded. "Fine."

"Your boys fucked up."

"No, your boys did," Mac corrected. "I was there and told them to wait, Skip. I said the truck wouldn't be beyond the Corelli lines. They were cocksure and went in without my approval. By the time I got in on them, they had already picked the truck clean and clipped the driver."

Guido scowled. "The driver was supposed to be paid off, not killed."

"Like I said, they went in cocksure and stupid. That's what arrogance does."

"The fact remains," Guido barked, "you have a problem."

No, Guido had a problem.

Mac chose not to correct the man on his mistake again.

"The job was a screw-up," Guido said, sighing harshly. "A major one, Mac. Now, I've got Anthony Corelli and his crew sharing words and fists with any Vasari crew they can find. It's bad enough that it has made its way to the boss. And now I've got the threat of Luca settling the feud, if Anthony and I can't get it corrected ourselves."

"So give Anthony his share of the truck," Mac said.

Simple fix right there.

Anthony Corelli was a Capo of another Pivetti crew. His territory lines hugged Guido's in the Kitchen in several different spots. Parts of Little Italy were still considered no-man's zone because no one really knew who the fuck it belonged to.

Nonetheless, Anthony was due his take on the truck. The men Guido had sent to Mac for the truck job had been useless, ignorant idiots. A bunch of street thugs in need of a good ass kicking. Usually, Mac got a few good guys mixed in with the bad— guys who would keep an eye out for the fuck-ups and keep them in line.

This time, he got nothing.

Nada.

A mess, that's what.

And Guido wanted him to take the blame for it.

"Give Anthony his take," Mac repeated. "He's owed it, Guido. They skipped onto the truck in his territory, there's no questioning that."

"Still my crew," Guido said, unfazed. "And that *cafone* just likes to cause me trouble."

Mac had to wonder about that, considering the stance Guido was taking now. The rules about territory and cash were clear. If it was someone else's streets, you paid them their dues. Guido knew this even better than Mac did.

"If Pivetti steps in …" Guido trailed off, scowling again.

Luca Pivetti was almost like a damned myth to Mac. He'd heard the man's name whispered and seen the guy's picture splashed across news broadcasts, but that was about it. Luca was the face of the Pivetti crime family—he ran the organization and he ran it hard, fast, and cruel. Mac, being as small of a fish as he was, had yet to have the pleasure of actually meeting the Cosa Nostra Don.

But he sure as hell wanted to.

Luca had three daughters and an illegitimate son, with the oldest being the boy who was thoroughly mixed up in Cosa Nostra. The daughters were held in esteem to the family, the perfect *principessas* in waiting. What they were waiting for was a mystery to outsiders, but to anyone inside the organization, they knew the truth. Marriages. Arranged ones.

"What do you want me to do, huh?" Mac asked. "They didn't follow my directions."

"And in turn," Guido said, pointing a finger at Mac, "you didn't follow mine, *soldato*."

"*Sì*," Mac admitted, though it nearly killed him to do it. "I'll figure out a way to fix it—maybe kill the problem by paying Anthony out with my money."

What little he had left, that was. After the bills for his mother's home and the bit of savings he'd given to his sister—not to mention his own—Mac's money well was running dry again. Another fight was an option, but that was like playing with fire when another family's organization was involved. Too much integration with another family and Mac would find himself in a makeshift grave before he even knew what happened.

Then again, Mac didn't even know if he could make up that kind of money in a quick time frame. It would probably top twenty grand or more, knowing the kind of electronics that had been inside the truck. A loan shark was an option, but the interests were a killer. Literally.

"I'll figure something out," Mac repeated.

"Do that, or we'll end up having to take out a rival."

"What can I get you?" the tattooed bartender asked.

"A beer," Mac replied.

Something he could chug fast and get a hit from. Nothing too strong, just something good enough to take the edge off. After his discussion with Guido, he'd earned the drink.

The cell phone in his pocket buzzed with a call, but Mac ignored it. The electric feel of the music and the cold beer the bartender passed him was enough to lull him into a calmer state. He wasn't about to ruin that with nonsense like a phone call.

Besides, it was probably his mother wanting him to show at church in the morning.

Mac was in no mood to travel all the way to Amityville for Mass.

Tipping the bottle up to his lips, Mac chugged half the beer in a single go. As he brought the bottle down, a flash of russet eyes and caramel skin caught his eye. Just like earlier, he took notice. He knew that face and that feisty smile.

Shit.

Melina.

Bad timing, Mac thought as he glanced around the club. It wasn't a good place to be getting mixed up with a woman, not with it being mob-owned. *But what were the odds*, he wondered. It seemed like the more he turned around, the more he kept running into the dark-skinned, sexy-as-fuck woman. Her sharp tongue and sassy demeanor never failed to surprise him, either.

Mac had a lot going on.

Too much to be messing with a woman who clearly had some kind of attitude problem.

He wished he would have listened to his inner voice, but when he noticed one of Guido's guys—a made man who made his money by crossing off names when asked—dancing with Melina like he wanted to take a bite out of her, Mac was already pushing off the bar. A hot ball twisted in his gut, sending him across the club's floor quicker than he thought was possible. Not a single person got in his way, but that might have been because they noticed the pissed off look he wore.

No claim.

Mac had no claim on Melina, but he didn't like

the sight of a man touching her. Certainly not a man like Vincent Carracci.

Jealousy was a goddamn monster.

Mac wore that monster well.

CHAPTER NINE

Melina swayed to the beat of the music. The drink she'd had was giving her a slow buzz and the pair of strong arms around her weren't too bad, either.

"You're so damned beautiful. You know that," her mysterious dance partner said.

She smiled. "I've been told that a time or two."

"Good. Nice to know there are still some honest people left in the world."

"And would you be one of them?"

"Hardly."

That voice.

Melina's eyes narrowed as she calmly took a step away from her companion.

"You know, I think this might qualify as stalking," Melina said.

She stared into a pair of mocking hazel eyes. Arms folded across his chest, head tilted to the side with a small smirk, Mac Maccari was a sight for sore eyes.

"Mac, what are you doing here?"

"You know, Vin, the usual. Business."

Melina stared between the two men on either side of her. The air was suddenly thick around her.

"You two know each other," she surmised.

"Yeah, we do, doll."

Melina momentarily gritted her teeth. "I thought

we'd established that I don't like that word."

"And I thought you understood what I meant by that, Melina."

His gaze bored into hers with the intensity of a thousand suns. She swallowed hard and was forced to look away.

"Look, Mac, I don't know what kind of game you're playing but this lovely lady and I were enjoying ourselves before you so rudely interrupted, so beat it and spare yourself some embarrassment."

Vin's hand slid around Melina's waist and she took notice of him. His eyes were hard and a muscle worked in his jaw. Clearly, whatever relationship Vin and Mac had, was not an amicable one to say the least.

"Vinny, I think you'd do good to remove your hand, before you lose it."

Melina put a hand to her waist. "Mac."

Mac's eyes flicked to her briefly, before they turned back to the man with his hand still resting on her waist.

"Who the hell do you think you are? I eat guys like you for breakfast. No one's buying the tough guy act you're putting on," Vin said.

"That's too bad. Don't say I didn't warn you."

Before Melina could blink, she was spinning away from Vin and he was hitting the floor. Mac stood with the heel of his shoe pressed against the man's throat. The smirk never left his face.

"The next time I ask nicely, you'd do well to listen."

People were starting to pay attention to them now. Melina's eyes were open for security to show up at any minute.

"You can stop worrying so much, doll. Nobody's coming to kick us out," Mac said.

"You're a piece of shit, Mac," Vin said in a choked growl on the floor, "just like your old man."

For the first time, Mac's smirk slipped. Veins started to bulge in his neck and his hands formed tight fists. The heel of his shoe pressed down harder into Vin's windpipe. The man's face turned red and his hands grabbed at Mac's ankle.

"Don't you ever compare me to him. You're lucky I don't crush your fucking throat."

Melina's heart felt as if it were on a rollercoaster, rising high up in her throat and then plunging back down to her gut. Even more strangely, she didn't know whether she should be scared or turned on. She gasped as Mac's fingers circled her wrist and pulled her towards him.

"Melina and I will be leaving now."

Without a backwards glance at the man he'd just sent sprawling to the floor, Mac started walking, dragging Melina with him.

"Let me go. What the hell do you think you're doing?"

Mac ignored her and continued moving her towards the outskirts of the dance floor. His grip was firm and strong. The club goers around them had already lost interest. Melina would get no help from them. It was up to her, like always. Digging in her heels, Melina stopped walking and jerked away from Mac with all her strength. He stopped walking briefly, glared at her, and then picked her up and put her across his shoulder.

Melina slapped Mac in the back. "I swear to God if you don't put me down, you are going to regret it."

"I'd love to see what kind of regret you have in mind, doll."

"Stop calling me that."

Melina tried to squirm from her position, but Mac wasn't budging. He continued walking, until he led her into what looked to be a small storage room and kicked the door shut behind them. He eased her down so that she was sitting on the side of a small black and gold table. The second she was free, Melina swung at Mac but he easily dodged her fists. Grabbing her wrists, he easily bent them down to the table. At the same time, he maneuvered himself to step between her legs.

"Now, that's better," Mac said.

She could feel the hard ridge of his cock pressing into the junction between her thighs. Melina wanted to ignore it, but she couldn't.

"You're a real asshole, you know that?"

Mac shrugged. "I've been called worse, but considering I just saved you from making a colossal mistake, I think you could call me something other than an asshole."

"What the hell are you talking about? I was just dancing."

"Yeah, with a known enforcer. Vincent Carracci is not a guy you want to mess with."

Melina rolled her eyes. "Please spare me. He was the first decent-acting guy I've come across in ages."

"Then you need to get out more, doll, but not to a place like this. You're just asking for trouble coming here."

Melina shifted on the table, but Mac didn't let go of her wrists. The fool had the nerve to smirk as her moving brought them into even closer proximity with each other. His gaze dipped down lower to her breasts and consciously, Melina tried to address the rising and falling of her chest. What was it about this guy that left her tied up in knots? One minute she wanted to knock the smirk off his face. The next she wanted to fuck his … no, she wouldn't go there.

"Throb is the latest hot spot. I'm just here for an enjoyable evening. What could possibly be so bad about me being here?"

Mac leaned closer to her, until their lips were only a breadth apart.

"Because this place is mob-owned, sweetheart. They chew up and spit out beautiful women like you. They hook a girl on decent drinks and good-looking men, slip them whatever will make them fly, and then keep reeling them in until they've got no choice but to come back for what they need, what they're provided with here. You have no idea how men like Vincent work or what they do for this club."

Melina cocked a brow. "Come on. Everyone knows the mob is dead. You're going to have to do better than that."

"Sometimes ignorance is bliss, but not in this case. Why do you think I was acting like that?"

Melina shrugged. "I thought you were just being your usual arrogant self."

Mac laughed. "Cute, but no. I wanted Vincent to think you were my girl so he'd back the hell off. There are rules in the world of mafioso and messing with a man's woman is a big one to break. You don't need to be mixed up with a guy like him."

"So I should be with a guy like you?"

"Maybe. Maybe not, but whatever you do, please don't come back here, Melina. I wouldn't want to see anything happen to you."

She licked her lips. "And why is that?"

"Because I don't want to be held responsible for killing the next man dumb enough to put his hands on you."

Melina swallowed hard. "Kill?"

Mac rubbed his nose against hers. "Mmhmm."

She knew she was poking a bear. Melina could feel the change in the atmosphere. Suddenly, she felt achy and hungry at the same time.

The moment his mouth descended on hers, Melina knew fire. Mac's kiss burned a path from her breasts to her sex. Her pelvis tilted towards his. She couldn't help herself as her mouth opened to him. His tongue slipped between her parted lips, exploring and teasing her own. He tasted of beer and mint.

Bitter and sweet, all at the same time. Mac moaned against her mouth and she could feel the vibration all the way down to her pussy.

Melina didn't fight it when he released her wrists and slid his hands around her waist. One of her legs curved around him, holding him to her aching core. Her breasts tingled, begging to be touched. As if sensing her unspoken desire, one of Mac's hands ghosted up to fondle her. His hand rubbed her nipple through the material of her dress slowly between his thumb and forefinger. Melina whimpered and he squeezed tight, causing her nipple to turn into a sharp, hard point as a bite of pain chased close behind the bliss racing through her blood. She was wet for this man. She wanted him to fuck her right there on that table.

Things had gone far enough.

Gathering her wits, Melina pushed Mac away, breaking the kiss. His breathing was ragged as he stared at her with his jaw tight and lust burning brightly in his hazel eyes. Melina wouldn't be the least surprised if her own face was flushed. There was something between her and Mac and it was dangerous. She didn't let men have control over her. She wouldn't start breaking that by giving her control over to this man.

Mac's tongue peeked out to sweep his bottom lip. "I knew a mouth that inviting had to be sweet."

"That has to be the lamest line I've ever heard."

"There's no need to go for a line when telling the truth is so much easier."

Melina eased off the table. "The truth is, that you saw me with another man and got jealous, so you made up this story about the mob to get me alone. Isn't that the truth?"

"I wish it were, doll, but there really are things out there that go bump in the night."

Melina smiled. "Are you one of them?"

"Depends on who you ask."

"Dodging the question. Typical man."

"There's nothing typical about me, sweetheart. I'd be more than happy to show you whenever you're ready."

Melina traced a finger over Mac's collarbone. "I'm not sure you're ready for me."

With a small laugh, she moved around him and headed towards the door.

"I'll always be ready for you, doll."

Melina tossed a smile over her shoulder. "We'll see about that."

Opening the door, she stepped out into the hallway and left Mac behind. A deep breath escaped her as she headed back towards the front entrance of the club. She'd kissed him.

What the hell is wrong with you? You don't even like him. Okay, maybe that was a stretch. Was he cocksure and confident? Absolutely. Did his smart mouth get on her nerves? Without question. But the moment their lips had touched, she'd started to burn. Mac had unleashed something inside of her that she thought she'd never feel.

Want.

Lust.

Need.

It scared the absolute hell out of her.

She didn't know a thing about Mac.

Does that really matter, when he kisses you like that?

Pushing open the doors to exit the club, Melina shook her head at the long line of people still waiting to get inside. Good luck to them. Throb had looked like it was at maximum capacity already. These poor fools were going to be waiting in vain.

Yes, they were fools, but Melina was not.

There was an old saying, "If you stick your hand in the fire, you're going to get burned."

She'd been burned and there was no way she would allow herself to be consumed. Men and emotions made a woman vulnerable. Melina wasn't going to allow that to happen to her. Shivering at the remembrance of their kiss, she headed down the block towards where she had parked her car. If a simple kiss was causing her so much turmoil, it would be better if she didn't see Mac again. There was no telling what would happen if she did.

The sound of crunching gravel made Melina stop and turn around. Her breath dried in her throat when she saw two men behind her with guns pointed straight at her. Raising her arms, Melina's purse dropped to the ground.

"Please don't shoot me."

One of the men opened his jacket and removed something. He held it up for Melina to see, all the while keeping the gun steadily trained on her. It was a shiny silver badge.

Fuck.

"Melina Morgan, you have the right to remain silent. Anything you say can and will be used against you—"

"I haven't done anything."

The dark-haired man holding his badge continued to read her the Miranda Rights while his orange-haired partner put his gun away and proceeded to cuff her.

"You have to at least tell me what the charges are," Melina said.

"Solicitation. Let's go."

Melina nearly stumbled as she was unceremoniously jerked and dragged behind the undercover officers.

This couldn't be happening.

This was supposed to be a night out. A night to throw her cares to the wind and have some much-needed fun. Instead, she was heading to the slammer.

As Melina was shouldered roughly into the backseat of an unmarked SUV, she caught sight of a familiar man coming down the street. Mac. Melina opened her mouth to say something, maybe to warn Mac off, even though she had no reason to, but something made her stay quiet.

Maybe it was the way Mac's gaze caught the glint of the cuffs Melina wore before his fist slammed into the concrete support beam. Then, he turned fast on his heel and disappeared.

Great.

Even Mac wasn't going to help her.

She was on her own.

Again.

Not that Melina was surprised.

Life was a bitch and once again, Melina had been fucked over.

Melina sat in the dark room, handcuffed to the table in front of her. She could see people moving through the large glass window to the right of her. Her mind had still failed to process that she'd been arrested.

Solicitation.

A prostitute was the last thing she was. Besides, she wasn't buying any of this. It was too random. There was more at play here than she was being told, there had to be. Her gaze narrowed when the door opened and the two men who'd arrested her waltzed in. The ginger-haired one took a seat on the opposite side of her, while the dark-haired man took a spot leaning in the corner watching her.

"Ms. Morgan, I'm Detective Parks. My partner is Detective Keaton," the ginger-haired man said.

Melina said nothing. She simply stared.

"You're a very beautiful woman. It's easy to see why men can't help themselves around you," Detective Keaton said.

"It's not a crime to be beautiful."

"Indeed, it isn't." Detective Parks leaned back in his chair and regarded her with a smirk.

Melina itched to put her stiletto through his throat.

"No. It's not a crime to be beautiful, but it is a crime to solicit," the other detective said.

"I went to a club," Melina replied, unaffected. "Last time I checked, going to a club was in no way related to soliciting."

Detective Keaton came towards the table and sat on the edge next to his partner.

"It is when your patrons include two members of the Pivetti crime family."

"What the hell are you talking about?"

"Don't play stupid. We watched you in action tonight. You're good. I'll give you that," Parks said.

"You guys really need to get out more."

Keaton tapped his partner's shoulder. "We've got a smart aleck on our hands."

"Seems that way, but I bet a night in the slammer will make her talk."

Were these fools for real?

Melina crossed her legs. "Threats aren't going to work on me. I've done nothing wrong and the last thing I'm going to do is let two dimwitted cops intimidate me."

"We've got you, Ms. Morgan, if not for soliciting, then you are definitely working for them in some other capacity. Maybe you're a mule or a messenger. We've been watching that club for long enough to know what beautiful women like you are used for inside that business."

"This is not *The Godfather*. Are things really that slow that you have to result to harassing innocent citizens?"

"If you're so innocent, make it easy on yourself and be a good citizen. Tell us what we want to know."

Melina would not have been surprised if flames started shooting from her eyes.

Be a good citizen.

They could go fuck themselves.

"Why don't you two stick this illegal interrogation up your asses? And while you attempt to pull it back out, let me have my phone call. I'm done talking."

Melina turned her head and refused to look at either of them. She gritted her teeth and closed her eyes. Yes, she'd just told them a few words, but if they acquiesced and let her have her phone call, who would she call? Dulcea was out of the question. No way would her boss want to be within a mile of the cops, especially with them saying Melina was soliciting at the time of her arrest.

She had no one to call.

Melina was alone in the world and the hard reality of that was staring her right in the face.

CHAPTER TEN

"Ah, Mr. Maccari, I wondered which one of Miss Morgan's patrons would come to her rescue this evening."

Mac turned at the sound of the weasel-like voice, only to come face to face with a plain-clothes police detective. Smiling slowly, Mac looked the cop over. Seemingly tired and worn, the man's clothes were wrinkled, his shirt sleeves were rolled up to his elbows, and the top two buttons had been undone to loosen the collar around his neck.

Apparently, illegally interrogating people could make a man exhausted.

"Patron?" Mac asked. "I can't say I know what you're talking about."

"Melina Morgan—escort extraordinaire. I found it interesting that the Pivetti family is shelling out the dough for a hooker of Melina's caliber. That's quite a cost, James."

Mac lifted a brow, refusing to show his annoyance and confusion. "First off, it's Mac."

"Ah," the detective said, smiling, "your father is the James of the family, yes?"

What in the hell was this guy playing at?

Mac didn't give him an answer.

"How about I just call you Maccari?"

"How about you get these fucking tools you call desk workers to enter in the bail money I just paid them, approve the bond, and release Melina like the law demands?" Mac asked, tired of the games.

"They will," the man assured, "once we have a little chat. As I said, I find it interesting the Pivettis have such a high-priced escort working one of their clubs, when we both know they can have more than enough women to take care of that business. Is the boss stepping up his game, Maccari?"

Fuck this.

"I have nothing to say to you," Mac said simply.

And he never would.

Frankly, Mac had no idea what the detective was going on about anyway. Melina had no ties to the mob and whatever work she did as an escort had nothing to do with the Pivetti family. This guy was pulling at straws and would come up with nothing. Mac didn't plan on helping him along in that game.

"Funny, Melina said the same thing. Nothing to say, no calls to make, no info to give. But rest assured, Maccari, my department has been watching Guido's club for a while, as well as his crew and the rest of Luca Pivetti's business. We caught a lucky break with Melina being at the club. I'm sure the task force working the escort scene won't mind opening their case files to us so we can have a little look at what they know, too."

Good to know.

Mac didn't give a damn, nor did he know, what they could or would find.

They could have fun trying.

His plan was simple—get Melina the hell out of jail. As it were, she'd been in there all weekend. Mac had waited until Melina was arraigned on false solicitation charges the day before, and then that morning, he skipped down to the jail with money in hand to bail her out.

Nothing was ever simple and Mac had a mess to

clean now.

The police was just one of them.

Mac smirked. "Then I suppose my girl gave you everything you need to know."

"Well—"

"The bail has been paid," Mac interrupted coolly. "I'd appreciate it if you released my girlfriend."

Mac seriously hoped Melina didn't have a fit when she heard that little title. It wasn't like Mac had much of a choice. He could have brushed off the scuffle he had with Vin the night at the club, but then Melina got arrested. Guido got wind of a woman being arrested outside of his club for solicitation, and when he added in the fact that the same woman had been the source of discontent between two of the Capo's guys … well, Mac had to make up something worthy to explain that shit away to his Capo.

So, Mac's girl she was.

Melina would have to suck it up until Mac came up with a better plan.

"Do you often allow your woman to dance with another man like she's single and ready for the taking?" the detective asked.

Mac bristled at the comment, but hid it well. "Watched that, did you?"

The man grinned, but said nothing.

"Good to know you pigs are inside the club. I'll be sure to let Guido know, so he can make sure you don't get inside again."

The detective's haughtiness faded fast.

"As far as who my girl was dancing with in Guido's club and what she was doing," Mac continued calmly, "I don't think there's very much to be concerned about. I invited her to the club and while she was waiting for me to finish up some business, she danced with another man."

"A man you clearly took issue with."

"I handled it. Vincent won't make the mistake of pushing up on my girl again."

"Him, not her," the detective said, shaking his head.

"Because he knows better."

All made men did.

Claimed women were untouchable.

Melina just got branded, whether she wanted to be or not. Mac figured it would keep her ass out of trouble until both the police and Guido's interest in the woman had faded. Then she could do whatever in the hell she wanted.

"High bail," the detective noted, looking over the paperwork Mac had signed on the receptionist's desk.

"Three grand isn't bad."

Mac had paid higher for himself on a weapons charge, actually.

"I'll have Melina released within the hour."

"I'm sure she'd appreciate that," Mac replied.

"Yes, well, we'll have a few more discussions with her, I'm sure."

Mac scowled. "When you do, there'll be a lawyer there."

"Like the public attorney assigned to her case at arraignment?"

Don't give him what he wants, Mac told himself. "My suggestion is that you drop these bullshit charges on her before you start climbing down a rabbit hole you can't get out of."

"The woman is an escort, Maccari."

"I didn't say she wasn't."

"And she was in Guido Vasari's club, a joint known for the backroom hookers."

Mac's jaw ticked, his agitation beginning to boil over again. "Maybe so, but my girl isn't one of them. She wasn't working that night."

"She sure looked like she was."

Mac resisted the urge to punch the guy in the

throat.

"The bail is paid," he repeated for what felt like the hundredth time. "Release Melina Morgan."

The detective waved at the woman waiting behind the desk and then turned on his heel without another word.

Mac took that as a battle won.

Melina snatched the heels and purse that were pushed out to her in a plastic tub through the hole in a Plexiglas window. She had yet to notice Mac just fifteen feet away, waiting for the right time to step in. It was likely that she still didn't know who had gotten her out of jail.

She had her dress from the club on but her face had been washed free of makeup and her hair was piled high on her head in a messy bun.

Jail was not a good look on a lot of women.

It kind of looked good on Melina.

Mac chuckled to himself as the woman behind the glass rambled on about the things that Melina had given up when being taken into the jail. Melina looked like she was two seconds away from ripping the poor girl's throat out.

Touchy, touchy.

"Thanks," Melina said, clipped and angry, snatching a pen to sign the document that had been handed over to her.

Turning on her heel, Melina's gaze met Mac's from across the room and she froze.

"Doll," Mac drawled. "You look like you're ready for a fight. Good thing I've got fast feet, hmm?"

Briefly, Melina's shoulders loosened. The detective who had been bothering Mac earlier waltzed in behind the Plexiglas window. Another ginger-haired man followed behind. As the two looked over the paperwork and chatted with the woman who had signed Melina's things out, they also kept an eye on the meeting between Mac and Melina.

"You didn't think I'd leave you in here to rot, did you?" he asked when she stayed quiet.

"I—"

Mac couldn't let Melina ruin the cover story he'd created for her with the detectives. It was better for him to cull the possibility of that nonsense as quick as possible. His goal was only to keep her out of further trouble, whether she liked it or not.

"I take care of my girl," Mac said, flashing Melina a smile. "Isn't that right, doll?"

The stiffness in Melina's posture and the fire in her gaze returned in an instant. Mac could practically see the retort forming on her tongue.

"How many times do I have to ask you not to call me that, Mac?"

Pushing off the wall with a slow confidence that drew Melina's gaze downward, Mac crossed the fifteen or so feet separating them. If much more came out of her mouth, she might blow his cover story with the detectives still in hearing range. Melina didn't want the kind of trouble that might follow her if those bastards believed she was involved with Cosa Nostra or Guido's business, beyond her personal involvement with Mac.

Melina stiffened as Mac caught the heels she held with two of his fingers. Without her heels, Melina was a couple of inches shorter and had to stare up at him.

"Let me help with these," Mac said quietly.

"I—"

Mac leaned forward and silenced whatever Melina was about to say with a hard kiss. Instantly, the tension in her body released and Mac used that opening to move closer, close enough that her chest was pushed against his and her hands fisted into the bottom of his T-shirt. Her kiss was no different than the first time. Her mouth was still as hot as sin with a sweetness lingering right behind. It still made him harder than steel, too. Then, Mac felt her hand open and her palm press against his midsection as if to push him away.

He let her pull away, but he grabbed her waist to keep her close.

"We have guests," Mac said under his breath, shooting a look over Melina's shoulder.

Melina's gaze flicked up to meet his, wary and tired. "Oh?"

"As of now, they're under the impression we're very close. I'd like for them to believe that for a while longer, and it would be in your best interest if you did, too."

"I had no one to call," Melina whispered.

Mac softened at that admission. Guessing by the defeated expression Melina wore, she had been let down one too many times in her life by people who should have given a damn. Sometimes, life was an awful bitch like that.

"I came, doll."

"Thank you."

Two words spoken so softly that if he wasn't so close to her, he might not have heard them.

Mac ticked two fingers under her chin, forcing Melina to look up again. "You're welcome. You might be tough as shit with enough stubbornness and fire to rival Satan himself, but you've got a lot to learn yet, woman. Right now, I want you to smile, let me put these shoes on you, and then you can take my hand, and let me escort you out of the jail like the good boyfriend I am. I want those detectives to believe we're together so they'll stop digging for things that don't exist. It needs to be believable. Can you do that?"

"Yes."

"Don't sound too excited now."

Melina smirked. "I'm not used to a man saving me."

"I'm not used to being a hero."

"Put the damn shoes on me, Mac."

"Your wish, my command, doll."

Melina didn't say a word that time.

***

"The mob isn't dead."

The words had been spoken so quietly beside him that Mac almost missed Melina's statement. Without responding, Mac found the closest turnoff point he could that was safe to do so on the busy street and turned his car off.

"No," Mac admitted, "It's very much alive and as active as it always was in New York."

Melina frowned. "They have ... oh, my God, they have rooms dedicated to you guys."

"Rooms?"

"With boards and pictures ... everything. Under each one is bullet points of info." Melina rubbed at her temples with the pads of her fingers. "They paraded me through the rooms, past the info and pictures, like they were trying to get me to say something. It's like they thought I was in with it all or something. They thought I knew what I was looking at—they believed that crap."

"When was this?" Mac asked.

"Before they took me to the jail and charged me."

Mac blew out a slow breath. "Do you remember anything specific about—"

"Jesus, if it's not them, it's you," Melina cut in angrily. "What, do you want to know the info I got from the cops, too? Not very much, Mac, considering they figured I knew everything there was to know anyway."

"All right, chill, woman."

"Sorry. It just … that was a lot to take in. I didn't expect to get out of there anytime soon. I had no access to money and no one to call."

Yeah, she'd mentioned that at the jail, too.

"What about family?" he asked.

"Dead."

Ouch.

Melina's tone offered no room for discussion. Mac dropped that topic. "Your boss, doll?"

Melina scoffed, avoiding his stare by glancing out the window. "You have a pretty good idea of what I do for a living, don't you?"

"You're an escort."

"Exactly. I'm sure my boss would love to find out I ended up in jail on solicitation charges. That would go over just perfectly fine. She probably would have paid my bail the very first second she could."

"Nice use of sarcasm," Mac noted.

Melina shrugged like it didn't make a difference. "It is what it is."

This girl was so bitter, it practically radiated off her. Someone or something had done her terribly wrong and she likely believed everyone else was out to mess her up in some way, too.

"I think you've been stuck getting fucked over by a lot of different things and instead of going out and getting something better for yourself, you've just been demanding the wrongs of the world should start doing you right for once. That's not how it works, *bella*."

Melina cocked a brow as she regarded him again. "Italian, right?"

Mac grinned. "Yes."

"Beautiful."

"*Bellissima.*"

Melina wet her lips. "The *most* beautiful."

"Bang on, doll."

"I don't expect the world to hand me anything," Melina said quietly, "but I haven't been in the right place to do anything about what I've been given, either. Not lately."

"You'll get there. Give it time."

If there was anything Mac knew about life, it was that the damn thing kept moving forward.

"Maybe."

"About your boss," Mac said as he turned the car on and pulled back onto the road.

"What about her?"

"You should know you won't be able to go back to that job."

Melina's lips thinned. "Excuse me?"

"Right now, the cops believe you're somehow involved with whatever schemes my Capo—"

"Guido Vasari."

Mac shot her a sly smile. "So, you do remember some of what you saw on those boards, huh?"

Melina shrugged. "A bit."

"Good to know."

"They're not really sure what you are or where you stand, I think."

Mac chuckled. "Fuck, girl, me either."

"Kind of crappy work, if you don't even have a title, isn't it?"

"I'm looking for a button, not just a title. Any man can have a title—*soldato, Capo, stolto.*"

Melina's nose crinkled in her confusion. "*Stolto?*"

"Fool."

"Ah."

"Every man in the mafia is some other man's fool. It's knowing which one you're willing to be a fool for and who thinks you're his. Trust me when I say, knowing the two makes all the difference."

"I'll take your word for it."

Mac smiled as he took a corner smoothly, his Challenger's wheels not even skipping once on the wet pavement. "Like I was saying, the cops believe you're somehow involved with the Pivetti Cosa Nostra and that your profession as an escort ties into it. By the way they talked, I think we can safely assume there's a taskforce that already had your name pinned down under whoever you're working for."

Melina swallowed hard. "Yeah?"

"Seemed like it."

"Damn."

"Don't worry about it," Mac said, seeing the concern flicker in Melina's hard gaze.

"That's hard to do when my one job just became a choice between income and risking jail."

"I think that's an easy choice."

"It is," she muttered, "but it still leaves me screwed."

"Not really. The police think you're with me, anyway, so you'll be sticking close to me for a while until their mess blows over. Just to be safe," Mac added quickly when Melina opened her mouth with an obvious rebuttal right on the tip of her tongue. Before she could get in a word edgewise, he continued with, "And they are not the only ones you have to worry about. The cops should be the very least of your fucking worries right now, Melina."

"I beg your pardon?"

"You caught more attention the other night than just mine," Mac admitted.

Melina stiffened in the seat. "What?"

"My Capo took note of the fact that the woman who caused a ruckus between two of his guys also happened to draw the attention of cops outside his club. That doesn't look good on Guido and he's quick to cull any person who draws any sort of attention to his business, you see. Especially the official side of things. No person in the mob wants that mess around."

"But I was just—"

"An innocent patron enjoying a night out, I know." Mac sighed, taking another corner sharply as he said, "I'd already got Vin off your back by making a statement about who you belonged to. That was for your own good, but the idiot took the info back to Guido. I kept it going so Guido would leave you alone on the basis that the cops were just trying to mess around with his guys in a new way. It wouldn't be a stretch."

Melina finally seemed to take note of where they were as Mac pulled into an underground parking garage. Throb's parking garage was empty but for a few vehicles and a couple of soldiers, who Guido liked to make watch his car when he wasn't inside it.

"What are we doing here?" she asked.

Mac turned the car off and faced her. "You have to trust me."

"To do what?"

"Honestly?"

"Yes."

"Doll, I'm not even sure yet."

"Great," Melina mumbled.

Mac drummed his fingers to the steering wheel. "My boss let me know I should bring my girl around to properly meet him once I got her out of jail."

"But I'm not your girl."

"But he believes you are."

Melina rubbed at her forehead again. "So what now?"

"Now, you make a good show for him and make him believe the cops didn't infect you with a desire to turn rat. You've got no place here, Melina, and trust me when I say you want Guido to let you go on your merry little way."

"Will you let me go on my way after, too?"

"For the most part," Mac said. "Once everything is clear with the cops."

"Is it really that serious?" she asked quietly.

Because Mac opened his mouth to make a claim on her just to keep a fool away and Guido decided to get involved, yeah, it kind of was serious.

"This isn't a life for games," Mac murmured.

"Playing pretend is a pretty serious game."

"Good thing you're the kind of woman who doesn't seem to like to lose, doll."

CHAPTER ELEVEN

Melina couldn't believe the difference in Throb. Where it had been a wild and crazy scene when she'd left a couple of nights before, now it was a ghost town. For a moment, her steps started to falter. Mac stopped walking and looked at her.

"What's wrong?"

"What if I screw up?" she asked.

His eyes, usually so expressive, held not a hint of warmth. "You can't afford to. Not with a guy like Guido. Not when it comes to the mob. There are no second chances."

Melina exhaled slowly. "That doesn't make me feel any better."

"It's not meant to. You should know by now that I'm not one for bullshit. I'm not going to sugarcoat this shit."

Melina looked down.

Mac placed his finger under her chin, forcing her to stare up at him. "Whatever happens, I'm right here with you. You're not in this alone."

"I'm always alone, Mac. This time isn't any different."

Straightening her spine, Melina marched away, leaving Mac to catch up with her. It didn't matter what he said. If she wanted to make it out of this situation without a bullet in her head, then she had no one to depend on but herself. Mac's loyalty was to his boss, not her. As she opened the door and stepped inside the quiet establishment, Mac grabbed her arm and whirled her around to face him.

"Listen to me. Now is not the time for you to go off half-cocked. I know you don't trust anyone, but today I'm asking you to trust me. Please, Melina? At least until I get us out of this."

She stared at him hard. His eyes shifted back and forth, watching her intently. Melina felt unnerved under the force of his gaze. *Get it together, girl.*

She nodded. "Okay."

He offered her a lazy smile. "Good. Now go in there, and be the ball-breaking doll I know and like."

Melina arched a brow. "And here I thought soft and sweet was your type."

"Hardly. I like a woman who can give it as good as she gets it. Keep that in mind."

Winking at Melina, he grabbed her hand and walked her through the empty floor and to the right wall of the club. When he stopped, she waited to see what he would do next. She could barely believe it when Mac swung the panel open, exposing a staircase that led up to a hallway shrouded in darkness.

"What in the hell?"

Mac laughed. "You aren't scared, are you?"

"Yes, but I can't let that stop me."

Without a second thought, Melina took the stairs two at a time up to the hallway. Behind her, she could barely hear Mac's footsteps. When his hand slid around her waist, she tried not to be startled.

"Told you. I'm right here with you."

His lips were pressed to the shell of her ear. She could smell his cologne, and for a minute, she forgot that she was about to be interrogated by a Cosa Nostra Capo. All she could think about was their close proximity, and the way it made her body feel.

"Doll, if you don't get moving, I'm not going to be responsible for what people might see if they decide to come out into this hallway."

Melina shook her head, offering him a half smile. "You don't know when to quit, do you?"

"It's part of my charm."

"Charm? Yeah, right. How much further?"

"Just up and around the corner. Let me make the introductions and just go with the flow. Remember, we're together."

The hand holding her waist suddenly felt too warm. Too intimate. Especially with his lips still brushing her ear.

"I got it."

His hand slid from her waist to grip her hand again. Melina allowed him to lead her down the dark hallway until they reached another door with light filtering out underneath it. She could hear men's voices raised in boisterous laughter. She didn't say a word as Mac opened the door and ushered her into the room. For a moment, she was blindsided by the light as they stepped out from the darkness.

When her eyes finally focused, she surveyed the men in the room. Sitting behind a desk was a heavyset man with dark eyes. His black hair was thinning on the top. He wore a bright gold chain that nestled into the wiry hair that was bared beneath the two buttons left open at the top of his shirt. The dark suit he wore definitely hadn't come off the rack. She could spot the expert tailoring a mile away.

Yes, this man was important. She'd bet her life that he was Mac's boss.

"Skip, this is Melina Morgan, my girlfriend."

"Ah. Mac, you've done well for yourself. She's a real looker."

A looker? Who in the hell still talked like that? Melina bit the inside of her cheek to keep from saying anything. Now was not the time for her to let her mouth write a check she had no way of cashing.

"Thank you, Guido. Sometimes you luck up and land a good one."

Mac turned his eyes on Melina and she saw the softness in them before it was quickly replaced.

"If landing a prostitute is good, that is."

Melina's eyes focused on the hulking man that stood next to Guido. Visibly corded veins stood out on his gigantic neck and forearms. *So, Mr. Steroid King wants to talk shit.* Melina smiled and ignored Mac visibly tensing beside her. When he made a step to move forward, she placed her hand lightly on his arm, meeting his gaze briefly, before turning back to the asshole standing in front of her.

"Trust me, a guy like Mac doesn't have to pay for it. You, on the other hand … I'm not sure there's enough money that makes taking you to bed worth it."

Guido laughed, slapping his hand on the desk in front of him. "Damn, Tip. I think this girl just cut your balls off with that one."

Tip glowered at Melina, but she lifted her chin in defiance.

"She has her own particular charm. It's one of many reasons being with her is never dull," Mac said.

He lifted her hand to his lips and pressed a kiss to her knuckles. As he winked at her, Melina couldn't help but smile back. She could do this. There was nothing to worry about.

Just a bunch of men, trying to measure who had the biggest cock.

Nothing new.

"I'm not buying it."

Mac's arm slid around Melina's waist, and he held her close as he turned his attention to the man that had been sitting quietly on a chair in the corner. Melina swallowed as recognition dawned on her face.

Her other dance partner.

Vincent Carracci.

Enforcer.

"And why is that, Vin? Because you tried to push up on my girl and got shut down?"

Mac smirked. His hand drifted casually up and down Melina's waist in a firm mark of possession. Deciding to play along, she leaned her head on Mac's shoulder as they waited for Vin to respond.

"Hardly. Pretty girls are a dime a dozen. I just find it suspect that *your girl* tries to hook up with me and then is taken away by the cops. I don't believe in coincidences."

"Vincent does have a point. The last thing I need is cops snooping around my business."

Melina shifted so that she was facing Guido again.

"Then let me put your mind at ease. I'm no fan of the cops, and with the business I work in, I don't need them focusing on me either."

Guido lifted his hands. "But how do I know this? How do I know they didn't let you go with the intention to use you as an informant?"

"She's on the level, Skip," Mac said.

"I know you want to believe that, my boy—especially from the way she looks—but it might be better for all of us if she wasn't a part of the picture. If you get my drift."

Cold fear stabbed through Melina like a sharp sword. She wasn't dense. She understood perfectly what they were saying.

She needed to die.

"Wow. I didn't realize the mob was frightened of women. Interesting."

"We're not scared of anything. Least of all a piece of pussy," Tip said as his face twisted into a snarl.

"Who said anything about the mob?" Vin asked,

sneering.

Melina's gaze flitted to Mac instantly, searching for a direction to go.

"I've had about all the disrespect I'm going to take from you two. I brought Melina here out of respect to Guido. Now, if either of you would like to keep running your mouth about my woman, perhaps we need to leave this office and handle it in a different fashion."

Mac's eyes were hard, like stones. A muscle moved in his neck. She could feel the tension radiating from his body.

"Is that right, little man?"

Tip moved from his spot next to Guido behind the desk, and came around to face Mac. Though Mac was not a short man by any means, Tip still had a good few inches on him. Melina opened her mouth to say something when Mac eased her behind him. Against her better judgement, she kept quiet. Things looked like they were primed to explode at any minute, and she had no desire to add fuel to the fire.

Mac laughed. "That's right, asshole. I protect what's mine."

Melina watched the exchange between the two men, all the while, keeping an eye on Vincent in his chair. An amused smirk tilted the corners of his mouth. She itched to wipe the smirk off his face.

"Who's going to protect you?" Tip asked.

Everything happened in a blur. Melina was propelled away from Mac, and had to catch herself to keep from falling. Mac and Tip locked up and Vincent moved from his seat. Guido sat, silent and amused, watching the events with nary a word coming from his lips. Melina's breath froze painfully in her lungs. She knew that Mac could handle himself. She'd seen him fight, but that was a different story when two men were coming for him at the same time.

The sound of punches landing was sickening. It

looked as if Mac might be gaining the upper hand against Tip, when a blow to his kidneys from Vincent nearly sent him to his knees. Tip took the chance to envelope Mac in his massive arms in an attempt to crush his windpipe. Melina's eyes widened as she noted Mac's face turning red. Standing in front of Tip, who was holding him, Vincent kicked Mac in the stomach.

"Stop!" Melina yelled.

"Shut up, bitch. You'll get yours next," Tip said.

Pushing herself up from the floor, Melina's eyes darted left and right. She had to do something. They were likely going to kill Mac and then come for her. She wasn't ready to die today.

Then she found salvation.

Grabbing the black nine-millimeter casually tucked into Vincent's gun holster, she aimed and fired.

Tip released Mac and fell to the floor. A bullet hole poured blood from between his eyes. He was dead before he even hit the floor.

"What the fuck?" Vin asked, stumbling slightly back from Mac.

He wasn't far enough away yet. Melina turned the gun on him. He stared at her, eyes open wide with shock.

"Back up." Her voice shook and she could feel moisture forming on her palms.

Raising his hands up in the air in surrender, Vincent moved further away from Mac. He took his position sitting in the chair he'd earlier vacated.

"See. We're all good here. Give me the gun, girlie."

"So you can shoot me? No. I don't think so."

Vin glowered at her as he sat, but Melina didn't give a fuck. Keeping one eye on Vincent, she almost accidently squeezed off another round when the sound of clapping startled her. Mac stared at her as he rolled his neck and flexed his shoulders. Behind him, Guido clapped.

"Well, well. Mac, you've really got yourself something with her. I'm fucking impressed."

"So am I. Every time I look at her." Mac's voice was soft as he breached the distance between them.

Inside, Melina could feel herself shaking, but she held the gun firm and refused to lower it. Mac's hand wrapped around hers and he eased the weapon from her grasp. He nodded as if saying that everything was all right. She wanted to melt into his arms, but she couldn't. No matter what Mac was signaling, Melina wouldn't be at ease until she was out of this office.

"So, maybe she's not a rat," Vin finally muttered.

"At this point, I'm thinking not ... Besides she did just kill a man," Guido said. "As worthless as that man was to me."

"He was going to kill Mac. I did what I had to," Melina said, her throat thick and tight.

"Mac was never in any real danger, sweetheart. I've seen him get out of worse situations than this little tussle you witnessed."

Melina raised an eyebrow. "So what are you saying? You set me up?"

Her eyes shifted briefly to Mac before they went back to his boss.

"Not intentionally. I planned on testing you to see if you were a rat, but I had no idea Tip would fly off the handle like he did, providing me an even better chance. Thank you for getting rid of him, by the way. You saved me the trouble."

For the first time, it dawned on Melina that she'd just killed someone. She'd taken a life without a second thought. The weight of that reality hit her like a freight train. She sagged against Mac, who held her tight. His lips pressed against her temple in a soft kiss.

"If there's nothing else, Melina and I are going to go."

"I don't blame you, Mac. I'd be eager to get your little gunslinger home and underneath me as soon as possible, too, if I were you."

Melina's teeth gritted as Mac held her. Guido was a chauvinistic pig and she hoped she never had to see him again.

"We'll see you later, Guido," Mac said.

Gently, Mac turned Melina towards the door. He placed the gun she'd taken from Vin into the waistband of his pants. Opening the door, he allowed her to step out first, but he paused at the threshold.

"Vin, I'm sure you'll understand me not giving this back to you. I think by all rights it belongs to Melina now. Later."

He closed the door securely behind them. Melina's knees shook as she descended the stairs. Mac's hand remained at the small of her back. "Melina?"

"Yes?"

Behind her Mac blew a loud breath. "Have you ever heard of a gun moll?"

CHAPTER TWELVE

"Are you hungry?"

Melina continued to stare at her clenched hands in her lap, like she hadn't heard Mac's question. She had been like that ever since they departed from the club. Mac didn't need to ask why, he knew.

Killing somebody was a killer.

It was even harder to deal with when those around you didn't act like you had done anything wrong. Or worse, when they gave you the impression you had done something good and right.

Killing was killing, to Mac. It was just another part of the Cosa Nostra life he'd chose. Melina, however, hadn't chosen it.

It bothered him that she was struggling. Mac wasn't a fucking machine, despite what his Capo liked to think about his *soldato*. He had feelings and right then, they were thoroughly tangled up in the beautiful woman in his passenger seat with nothing to say. She didn't have to say anything. Her emotions might as well have been bleeding out on her sleeve.

"Melina," Mac said, willing away the thickness in his voice.

Finally, she glanced up at him. "Yeah?"

"Are you hungry, doll?"

Mac expected a retort from Melina for the pet name, but she surprised him.

"Not really," Melina said.

"That's too bad."

"Why?"

"Because I know jail food is garbage, and you probably haven't eaten all day. It's almost six, so you have got to be starving inside. Just because you don't feel like eating doesn't mean you're not hungry, Melina." Mac waved at the building he'd parked in front of and added, "We're already at one of the best places in the Kitchen. Let me buy you a meal, get you warm again, and see if your bark comes back."

Melina passed the restaurant a look that said she was just realizing Mac had parked the car. "If the bark comes back, so does the bite."

"I look forward to it, doll."

With that, Mac got out of the car. He was around the front and at the passenger side before Melina had even gathered her purse. Opening her door, he offered his hand to her.

She stared at it warily.

"What are you?" she asked.

Mac laughed. "Pardon?"

"You, what are you? You're giving me whiplash. You're cocky as shit, you fight like a pro, you've got affiliations to the mob, and a dirty mouth. Yet, I've seen you take your sister out, you came to get me out of jail when someone else wouldn't have done it, and you open a woman's door. What are *you*?"

"The man my mother raised," Mac said quietly.

Melina blinked at that answer. "Oh."

"You forgot a few other things, doll."

"Like what?"

"I also like good food, a hard fuck, and a Sunday morning prayer."

Melina's lips popped open, but nothing came out.

"Hungry?" he asked.

"Yes."

"You don't sound so sure."

Melina took his hand he was still holding out. "I'm not sure of anything."

Mac chuckled. "Because of me?"

"Don't flatter yourself."

"Too late."

⁂

"Why do you keep staring at me like that?" Melina asked.

Mac twisted his fork around in the spaghetti pasta and kept one eye on Melina all the while. "You've got me curious, doll."

"You're never going to drop that, are you?"

"No. I like it."

Melina pursed her lips. "Fantastic."

"About you, though, you've made me wonder."

"Wonder, what?"

"If all your tough act is just a show," Mac murmured. "Deep down, you're bothered about what you did in that office. You're playing with your food and distracted by the people. You keep looking over your shoulder and sometimes, you just stare at the wall. All that bravado you had is … gone."

Melina cocked a brow and squared her shoulders. "It wasn't bravado. Fear makes you do strange things sometimes."

"Yes it does. Will talking help?"

Mac would let her chat it out if she needed.

"No," Melina said simply, "it won't."

"Okay." Mac tossed her another look, noting the fire returning in her eyes. "Are you pissed at me for something?"

"Maybe. I haven't decided yet."

"It helps if a man knows what he's done, doll." Mac chuckled, saying, "And the doll thing doesn't count, because you always turn stiff in the collar over that."

"No, not that nonsense. You led me on in that office, Mac."

Mac straightened in his chair. "I did not."

"You did. You could have gotten out of their hold, and I never would have ..." Melina's gaze swept the neighboring tables before her voice lowered. "I never would have done what I did. It was unnecessary and you know it."

"I don't know anything of the sort. What I do know, however, is that two men were on me, I couldn't breathe, and you were scared. You were frightened enough that you felt you had no other choice than to turn a gun on someone. You made that choice and it was the right one for you at the time."

"And you?" she asked softly. "Was it the right choice for you?"

"As long as I make it out alive, it is always the right choice."

Melina sunk into her chair. "None of that makes me feel better."

"The mafia will do that to you. Nothing about it feels particularly good, but once you step into it, there's no getting out and you're in it for life. Then, it's all about making it work and doing so carefully."

"I don't understand."

Mac shrugged. "I know."

"What is it you do exactly?"

"Whatever Guido needs me to do," Mac replied before shoving a bite of pasta into his mouth.

"So, there's no normal nine-to-five."

Mac swallowed his food before saying, "No. I

do anything from managing a few men, running a scheme on something, keeping care of his rackets with the construction companies, or even being a middle man between Guido and his guys for … other things."

"Like what?"

"You ask a lot of questions."

Melina smiled coldly. "You could answer some."

"I've already said enough. Do with it what you will," Mac said quietly.

"Basically, you make money."

"Try to, yes."

"For Guido."

"For the family," Mac corrected. "Guido is just the Capo I work under. He, like everyone else in this business, still has someone he has to answer to."

"And who is that?"

Mac sighed heavily. "Too many questions."

"Is it Luca Pivetti?" Melina asked.

"Could be."

"He's the boss for the family you work with, right?" Melina tapped her nails on the table. "Inside the room where the detectives took me, his picture was there with his title under it. Luca is the boss, that's what it said."

Mac leaned back in his chair, smiling at his companion. "You know, there are rules for this sort of thing, doll."

"Oh?"

"Yes."

"Do tell," Melina said.

"The most important one is that we never talk about business in public."

Melina's mouth snapped shut.

Mac winked. "I appreciate it."

He went back to eating without another word. Melina pushed around the food on her plate in silence, too. After a few minutes passed, she glanced up at him with a bright curiosity burning.

"What now?" Mac asked.

"Will you ever tell me more about it?"

Melina had earned her stripes, as far as Mac was concerned. She had killed a man for him. The woman was golden. She wasn't out to hurt him or get him messed up with the officials. But that didn't mean she was ready for what his life entailed.

He didn't know that much about her.

Not enough for that, anyway.

"Maybe," Mac finally said.

Melina laughed under her breath. "Well, I guess we won't have to worry about it."

"Why is that?"

"After today, we part ways. Right? We just had to convince—"

"Doll," Mac said, interrupting her before she could say anymore, "... things might change after everything that happened. It might not be as easy as saying goodbye and going on our merry little ways."

Melina dropped her gaze. "Why not?"

Mac passed a look over her shoulder. "For one thing, because you took out a Pivetti enforcer and others might not take it as well as Guido did."

"And for two?"

"For two, there are a couple of Guido's guys sitting three tables behind us. They came in about ten minutes after we did. They ordered coffee, sandwiches, and nothing else. They followed us from the club. Chances are, they're going to keep following us."

Melina shot an inconspicuous look behind her and asked, "Should we be worried?"

"No," Mac said, scoffing. "Guido likely wants a report from them to confirm what he believes and to make sure I'm on the up and up with it all."

"But what does he believe, Mac?"

"That you're my girl, Melina."

"I knew that. I just wanted to be sure."

"Mmm," Mac hummed. "How do you feel about dancing?"

Melina's eyes widened. "You're joking, right?"

"No. It seems we're expected to give our new babysitters a show. As it is, you've barely touched your food and I'm finished. Dinner typically follows a date. You like to dance, if the other night is any indication. I would like for you to go dancing with me."

"With you."

"Yes," Mac said, flashing his signature smile.

"A date."

"You've already let me take you out to dinner, doll."

Melina's shoulders stiffened. "On one condition."

"What is that?" Mac asked as he pulled out a few bills to leave on the table and pay for their food.

"You drop that word."

"Not a chance."

Melina gaped at him like she couldn't believe him. Mac simply grinned back at her as he stood from the table, moved around the side, and held out his hand. Melina stared at it, hesitance weighing her pretty features down.

"I know you're going to go with me," Mac said.

Melina's gaze snapped up to his. "You don't know anything."

"Yes, I do. You see, you might like to be the queen bitch in the room, but I get the feeling that somewhere inside you, there's a woman who would die to have an assertive man take control."

She swallowed hard.

"Am I right?" Mac asked.

"I haven't found one yet that does anything like that for me," Melina replied.

"Then maybe you should close your mouth and give me your hand, doll. While you're at it, take a breath and get some of that heat out of your cheeks. The turned-on look is a good one to wear, especially on you, but if you're trying to hide it, work a little harder."

Melina's tongue peeked out to wet her bottom lip. "I—"

"Take my hand and let's go dancing," Mac demanded.

Her palm slid into his without a word.

With his arm tight around Melina's waist, and his lips to her ear so she could hear him above the pounding bass of the music, Mac said, "Our guests are still around. I noticed them at the bar."

Melina *tsked* under her breath. "Drinking on the job."

"Not a normal job." Then, Mac brushed the stray waves of Melina's hair away from her neck, letting his knuckles graze over her skin. She was soft and hot under his touch. He kept finding himself wondering what other parts of her felt like. "Dance with me."

"The last time I danced with a good-looking man, it got me into trouble."

Mac kissed the shell of her ear and felt her shudder under his hold. "Because you didn't dance with me. Instead, you danced with a fool."

Melina tried to hold back her smile, but she failed. Mac took that as a victory.

"Is that so?"

"Yes," Mac said.

"Can you even dance?"

"Don't be offensive."

"Should I add that to your list of things?" she asked.

"That, and this, too," Mac said, letting his

knuckles ghost over her neck again.

Melina's smile grew into a sexy little grin as her brown eyes found his. "What?"

"Touching you. I'm discovering I like doing that a lot, too."

"Okay."

"Is that all you've got to say?"

Melina shrugged. "No. I might like it, too. Dance with me, Mac."

Mac was already pulling her out onto the floor and into the smothering crowd before she could even finish her sentence. Melina gasped the sweetest sound when Mac snagged her wrist in his palm and turned her fast to face him. Swallowed by the people, they were just another couple under the flashing lights and loud music.

"Closer," Mac said, tugging Melina into his body. "You need to be closer for this, doll."

Mac drove a hand down the small of her back until his fingertips danced just above the swell of her ass. His fingers wove with hers as he pushed against her back until she was tucked firmly into his chest.

"Closer," he demanded.

Melina's bottom lip caught between her teeth when Mac pushed her even closer, until their noses touched and his groin was pressing to her pelvis. The music vibrated the floor with its heavy bass. Mac was too focused on the way Melina's hips moved with his and her hands fisting into the sides of his T-shirt.

Her movements were sensual and left behind the feeling of sex. She stayed close to him the entire time and never once did her gaze waver from his. Mac wasn't sure he could remember a time when he'd had a woman like this one in his hands. He was pretty damned sure Melina was in a league of her own.

Mac let his barriers drop as the music turned up in pace. His hands roamed over Melina's curves, imprinting them to memory for a moment. What would she look like in nothing but caramel skin and waves of her hair?

"What is a gun moll, anyway?" she asked.

Mac slowed their dancing, surprised at her question. When he'd asked her about it at Guido's club, she had given him a blank stare and no answer. Mac decided to let it go. She clearly hadn't been in the mood for it then.

"Mac?"

He let go of her waist to skim his thumb over her chin.

"She's one hell of a woman," Mac finally settled on saying.

"Is that it?"

Not even close.

"She's the one that no one ever expects. She's the pretty face in the corner that everyone overlooks. She smiles and bats her lashes, but when you turn your back, she'll cut your fucking heart out from behind. She's dangerous. She's amazing. She's a mobster's girl, the unsuspecting lady with a gun hidden under her coat, and the only thing a man can trust to follow through. That, doll, is a gun moll."

Melina's fingers wrapped around Mac's belt. "Why would you ask me about one?"

Because Mac figured she'd make a damn good one.

"Spend the night with me," he said instead.

Melina opened her mouth to speak, but nothing came out.

"I know you want to say no. It's just your goddamn nature. Don't say no, Melina. Give up a little bit of that control and ice queen persona. Just for a night. What will it hurt?"

"A lot, maybe," she whispered.

"Spend the night with me, doll." Mac drove Melina into his body again, letting her feel the hard ridge of his erection under his jeans. She should know what her tight curves, brash attitude, and sexy smile did for him. "It would be damned good and you know it."

Melina sucked in a harsh breath. "Oh, that's one thing I don't doubt."

"I want to take you somewhere. I want under this dress, Melina. I want you on a bed, bent over, or on your knees. I want to taste you when I bury my face between your thighs. I want you to shake and scream. I don't care where or how, but I want it. Tonight."

"Men always ask."

Mac smirked. "And I bet you always say no, don't you?"

"Because they ask."

Assertive men, he knew. Melina liked to think she was in control. Men who thought they were in control with her always lost because the girl was a fucking shark. Mac was positive she could smell a man's weakness and she got off on it.

"I bet you've had weak men all over you, right?" Mac laughed and shook his head. "Pussy-weak men who don't have the first clue how to handle a woman like you and they don't know what to do with you. I think what you need the most is a man who will put you on your knees because he knows you'll fucking like it and ask for more. You want a man that'll be rough with you, one that will take you and own you, because he knows you want it like that, not because it's the one and only time he gets control over you. How close am I?"

A heat pinked Melina's cheeks and her breaths came out harder than before. "You're getting there."

"There's no question here, doll," Mac said, taking a step back from her. "You either go with me or you don't, but I won't ask for it. You won't see me beg for it. I'm not that kind of man."

Melina nodded. "I know."

"And you like it."

"I do."

116

GUN MOLL

Mac unlocked the door to his apartment and pushed it open. Standing back with a hand to the door, he let Melina walk in ahead of him.

He let the door close and then shrugged off his jacket. Out of the corner of his eye, he watched Melina take in his small, two-bedroom apartment. The open concept of the place hid nothing except the closed bedrooms and the bathroom at the far end. The earthy tones, modern furniture, and pieces of art on the walls were mostly compliments of Mac's sister, Victoria. She liked to decorate. Mac didn't give a damn what his place looked like, as long as it was decent.

"Nice place," she said, hanging her coat and purse on a hook.

"Thanks. It's livable."

"It's comfortable, cozy."

Melina smoothed her dress down by running her hands over her sides. The action had her hips and ass swaying a little. Mac's gaze and body instantly tuned in to that and nothing else. Melina was sexy as fuck and the woman didn't even have to try. While he admired the view of Melina in his apartment, Mac kicked off his shoes.

"Did you notice if your boss's guys followed us from the club?" Melina asked.

Mac was done worrying about Guido's nonsense for the moment. "Hey."

Melina tossed him a look over her shoulder. "What?"

"I don't know if they followed us or not. I've been too focused on you to care."

"That's not very smart."

"I have priorities, doll," Mac drawled with a sly grin.

"Like getting me into your bed."

"I'm not trying on that end at all. You're already here."

Melina laughed. "So, why are we still talking?"

Why, indeed?

"The heels stay on," Mac said.

Melina's brow furrowed. "My heels?"

"The heels stay on, doll, until I take them off."

Mac didn't give her a chance to respond. Before she could blink, Mac was on her. His hand tangled into Melina's hair and he tugged her head back. Wide, brown eyes gazed up at him with a heat burning brightly. Mac grabbed her waist tightly and gave a little yank on her hair. Those pink lips of hers parted with a quiet moan.

"I'm sure you know, but you're beautiful."

Melina released a shaky breath. "Thank you."

"Never thank me for the truth, doll."

The sharpness was back in Melina's eyes in a flash. Mac felt her fingernails score into his midsection through his T-shirt. Pleasure danced up his spine at the sting her touch left behind.

Melina yanked on his shirt. "Kiss me, Mac."

"You don't make the calls here, Melina."

She pouted.

She fucking pouted.

And it was goddamn *beautiful.*

"But—"

Mac didn't let her get whatever she was going to say out. He kissed her instead, bruisingly hard. Melina's gasp allowed Mac the chance to dive into the heat of her soft mouth all over again. He hadn't forgotten what she tasted like, but he still felt starved for it all the same. Pulling her hair again, Mac tipped her head back until she was bent in his hold and under his power. Without his hands holding her up, she would surely fall.

Melina trembled under the kiss. Her tongue danced with his, fighting for control. Mac refused to let her have it. He kissed her deeper, feeling her teeth scrape over his lips until the soft pants of her breaths turned ragged.

Pulling away, Mac flashed his teeth in a wicked smile. "But I'll kiss you for doing that, doll."

Melina's tongue peeked out to swipe her lips. "What did I do?"

"You'll figure it out. You're a quick woman."

"Can we stop talking now?" she asked.

Fuck, yes.

Mac released his grip in Melina's hair and spun her around. He found the tiny little zipper at the top of her dress and yanked it down. Once the dress was opened and split down her back, he ran his palms from the bottom of her spine all the way to the top. A shudder worked its way over her body as Mac pulled the dress down over her shoulders and let it drop. Under her dress was nothing but navy blue lace and caramel-toned skin. Mac took a couple of steps backwards just to admire the view.

"Step out of it," Mac said.

Melina turned in the little puddle of clothes and stepped forward. Her heels clicked on the wood floor. From the swell of her breasts to the curves of her hips, she was all woman. The flat, smooth contour of her stomach led straight down to the lace boy-shorts she wore. Her skin was unmarked, beautiful, and begging for his hands to be all over it.

Every inch.

He wanted to feel, taste, and explore every inch of this woman.

"Tell me one thing you want," Mac said, his tone gruff and thick.

Melina glanced away. "Why, won't you just say no?"

"I told you to tell me, doll. Stop wasting time, or I'll just give and you'll take. No doubt, you'll enjoy it all the same, but I'd still like to know what you want right now."

"I want you on your knees."

Mac took her admission in. "Does that make you feel powerful when a man is on the floor for you?"

Melina laughed, but it came out breathy and deep. "How do you know this shit?"

"So, it does."

"I like it," she said simply.

Mac hooked a finger and then pointed in front of himself. Melina crossed a few steps between them.

"Take it off," Mac said, waving a hand at her brasserie.

Melina unhooked the clasp holding the cups of her bra together at the front. Her thumbs skimmed under the straps and she tugged it down over her arms. The moment her breasts were free, Mac took the chance to cup them in his hands. He grazed his thumbs over the hardening peaks of her nipples until Melina's eyes were closing and her head tipped back.

"I'm feeling sorely underdressed at the moment," Melina said softly.

"Hush, doll."

"But—"

"The quicker I take my clothes off, the faster this will end."

Melina snapped her mouth shut. Mac chuckled.

Then, he dropped down to the floor. He kept his gaze on her face all the while.

Melina's eyes popped open when Mac's right hand fisted her boy-shorts and began to pull them down her shapely legs. Using his left hand, he snapped the inside of her thigh to make her widen her stance. Melina did without argument. Between her thighs, the sliver of her sex peeked out at him. Bare and smooth, he could already see the lips of her sex were wet with her arousal.

"It's terribly sad, you know," Mac said when Melina stepped out of the underwear.

"What is?"

"That not one single man has ever gotten down on his knees for you, while still being capable of making you lose control."

Melina's hands balled into fists at her sides. "Never."

"Well, this should be fun for you. Be sure to let me hear every sound you make, doll. I like a loud woman."

"You are—"

"Fucking wonderful," Mac interrupted with a cock of his brow. "It's something people learn to accept over time."

That was the only thing Mac gave Melina before he grabbed her thighs, pulled her forward, and then buried his face between her thighs. His mouth encased her hot sex and his tongue slid from her wet slit all the way up to her throbbing little clit. The nub pulsed under his tongue when he teased it with gentle, short flicks. One of Melina's hands found its way into his hair and grabbed tight enough to hurt.

Mac didn't mind.

"Oh, my God," she breathed.

Mac grinned, watching her shake above him. Fast, sharp jabs of his tongue moved from her hard clit back down to her slit. Mac's fingers bit into her thighs, spreading her wider for him. He wanted more of her, all of her. The tartly-sweet flavor of her come flooded his taste buds as he fucked her pussy with his tongue and teased her with nips of his teeth.

"Christ ... *Mac!*"

The harder her body shook for him, the faster he worked her sex. Melina held him firm to her body, her hips rolling into his face with every swipe of his tongue and lips on her pussy. Mac pulled back, just enough to let the climbing wave of her oncoming orgasm fade away. He held strong to her thighs, refusing to let her come any closer to his mouth as he bit a path along the inside of her thigh. His lips came close enough to her sex that he could taste the smear of her come on her skin.

"Ask me for it, doll," Mac murmured before kissing the hood of her sex.

Melina sucked in a sharp breath. "*No.*"

Melina swayed above him, her heavy breasts heaving and her fingers tightening in his hair. Her resolve was breaking and Mac knew it.

"If you want that, you have to ask me for it," Mac said.

Letting go of her right side, Mac slid two of his fingers between her thighs and ghosted the digits over her sex. Her body rocked with slight tremors. The quieter she turned—with her blazing brown eyes boring into him down below—the more Mac stroked her sex. He let the tips of his fingers glide against her slippery entrance and stretch her open just enough for her to feel his digits inside her pussy.

Mac was dying to bend this woman over and fill her full of his cock, and see if she could really let it all go.

"You're soaked, Melina. All over my mouth, my fingers, and this beautiful pussy of yours. You are fucking soaked. Just ask me for it like I know you can and I'll give it to you. I'll fuck you with my fingers while my tongue fucks your clit until you can't breathe, you can't think, and you're begging me for more. Ask me, doll. That's it. Open that pretty mouth of yours and ask me for it."

Melina whined. The sound came off broken and aching.

"So good," Mac whispered against her skin. "You sound so damned good."

"I want to come," Melina said breathlessly.

"Not what I asked for."

"*Please* make me come."

A slow, easy smile spread over Mac's lips. "*Perfetto, bella.*"

"Please," Melina said in a breath. "I want it. I want to come, *please.*"

"Nice and loud, doll. Remember?"

Melina nodded.

Mac gave her what she wanted. His fingers slid into her tight core the very second his mouth encased her trembling sex again. Drawing her clit into his mouth, he teased the swollen nub with his tongue and teeth while his fingers worked a hard and deep beat in Melina's pussy. He could feel her inner walls hugging him and flexing around his intrusion.

Melina choked out a broken cry. "Jesus Christ."

Mac curled his digits hard into the fleshy spot inside Melina's sex as he sucked hard on her clit. Her juices flooded his fingers as she shouted his name loud enough for it to echo in the dark, quiet apartment. Keeping his gaze locked on hers, Mac watched the sliver of a tear fall from the corner of Melina's eye. Shaking and riding out the final waves of her orgasm, Melina damn near crumpled when her knees buckled.

Mac was up off the floor and holding her up before she could fall. Taking her face between his palms, Mac kissed her trembling lips. Melina didn't shy away from the taste of her come on his mouth or the roughness of his fingers digging into her jaw and cheek.

"More," she demanded.

Mac felt her hands at his pants, working the belt to get it off. Mac grabbed the foil packet he knew was in his back pocket before she could get his pants off completely. He let her fumble with the belt until it was yanked off and his jeans were being shoved down. The heavy, thick length of his erection strained against his boxer-briefs as he kicked his pants aside.

Melina, gasping for breath when Mac attacked her neck with his mouth, drove her hands up under his shirt to pull it off, too. He only let go of her long enough to get the offending fucking clothes off.

Skin on skin.

That's what he wanted.

All over this woman.

Mac *needed* it.

Grabbing the backs of her thighs, Mac lifted Melina off the floor. He turned her around until he could steady her against the wall. Melina's hands grappled for something steady, but she only yanked the coats off their hooks in the process.

"Fuck," Mac groaned when she rolled her bare sex into his erection.

Christ, it felt so good.

But it hurt, too.

"Fuck me," Melina begged. "*God*, please."

There was no order to her words, not a demand in her tone. She was weak under his hands and Mac took that in like a drug.

"It'll be my pleasure, doll."

Kissing her until he couldn't breathe and his cock was harder than steel, Mac ground his pelvis into her wet center. He could feel her arousal dampening the fabric of his boxer-briefs and leaving her mark behind. The heels of Melina's shoes bit into the backs of his thighs while her fingernails scored lines over his shoulders.

Mac let Melina drop to the floor on shaky legs. "Arm of the couch, now."

Melina's hooded gaze fell down to where Mac's cock was straining inside the underwear he wore. "*Jesus.*"

"Now," he repeated darkly.

She didn't need to be told again. Mac watched Melina's ass sway back and forth as she crossed the space from the entrance to the couch. At the arm, she placed her hands to the supple butternut-colored leather and bent over. All over again, her wet, pink flesh of her sex peeked out at him.

Promising.

Begging.

Needing.

Mac shoved his boxer-briefs down and grabbed ahold of his cock. Melina watched him over her shoulder and sucked on her bottom lip as he stroked his member. Then he tore open the foil pack and sheathed his length in latex. He quickly closed the space between them until he was behind Melina and running his palms over the sexy swell of her ass. Mac let his erection rest on her backside. It gave him just enough friction to keep his body awake but not nearly the amount that he craved.

A single snap of his hand cracked against her ass. The sound bounced off the walls. Melina backed into his palm, moaning.

"Like that, do you?" he asked huskily.

Melina's head dipped down, her hair hiding her face. "I just want to fuck."

"You want me to fuck you."

"*Yes.*"

Grabbing the base of his cock, Mac dragged the tip down the crack of her ass and through her fleshy lips. At the entrance of her sex, he pushed in just enough to stretch her open like he had before with his fingers. With his hand pressing down on the small of her back, forcing her to stay bent over the arm of the couch, she couldn't move or back into him.

"We'll do this again," Mac promised.

Melina sighed shakily. "Will we?"

"Oh, yes. Because tonight is going to be fast, hard, and dirty. Next time, we'll take a little more time. You don't mind that, do you?"

"No."

"Good."

Mac let go of his cock and slid home with one hard thrust. The grip Melina had on the arm of the couch let go from the force of Mac entering her. Keeping his one hand on her back, he used his other to fist her hair and pull it aside. He wanted to see her face when he fucked her. He wanted to know what she looked like when a man was owning her like this.

She didn't disappoint.

With her teeth biting hard into her bottom lip, and her eyes wide open, Melina was the sexiest sight Mac had ever seen. She struggled for a grip on the couch as he pounded into her from behind. Her rolling cries seared into his mind, promising to stay there long after the night was over. She backed into his cock, meeting every crack of his hips. Mac could see how wet she was when he looked down, and he was lost watching the view of his cock disappearing into her supple, pink pussy.

Skin on skin.

Perspiration dotted down her spine. Pleasure licked up his.

He could still fucking taste her in his mouth.

Her scent was all over him.

Mac's fingers ached from holding her so tight.

"Harder," Melina pleaded.

Mac tugged on her hair, forcing her head back until her teeth bared for him and the muscles in her neck strained. His pace was punishingly hard and so fucking brutal. The sounds of slapping skin mixed in with Melina's sweet music beautifully.

"Come," he growled.

Melina whined.

"Come on, doll, I want you to milk me fucking dry."

She broke under him all over again. He pushed her deeper into the couch and fucked her harder.

This was going to be a long night.

Mac was just getting started.

CHAPTER THIRTEEN

Melina stretched and rolled right into a hard body. Her eyes opened wide.

"Morning, doll."

Melina groaned as the events of last night came rushing back to her. She'd had sex with Mac, and not just a hot meeting of fumbling bodies. No, it had been a great deal more than just sex. Mac had taken her body to heights of pleasure she'd never experienced before, and no doubt, heights she would never find again.

"Melina?"

His hand captured her chin and forced her to face him. They lay side by side, gazes meeting.

"Yes?" she asked.

"What are you thinking about?"

In usual Melina fashion, her defenses climbed higher to keep from allowing her thoughts and feelings from being known. "Look, just because we had sex does not mean I'm going to be sharing my deepest, darkest secrets with you."

"Why not? You already shared something else pretty significant with me."

Melina punched Mac in his arm. "You did not just say that!"

He caught her fist and held it before pulling her closer to him. A half-grin tilted the corners of his mouth up, making his usual strong, sexy features even more boyishly handsome in the morning light. His eyes were soft and unguarded in a way she'd never seen him before.

"I most certainly did. I think after a man spends half the damn night with his face between a woman's thighs, that qualifies him to say whatever the fuck he wants to."

Melina frowned at him. "A gentleman doesn't kiss and tell."

"I never said I was a gentleman, doll."

"Indeed, you didn't."

Mac's fingertips ghosted over Melina's skin, barely touching her as he traced the curves of her body. She pressed her thighs together, but it didn't help. It only intensified the ache that was starting to build all over again.

"I can see your wheels spinning," Mac murmured.

"So, you're a mind reader now?"

"It doesn't take a mind reader to know what's going on in that beautiful head of yours."

"Well, since you have all the answers, pray tell what thoughts are rolling around my mind."

Melina bit her lip as one of Mac's fingers traced lazy circles on the top of her pubic bone. Her nipples turned to tight pebbles, and Melina didn't have to wonder what was coming next. Mac's eyes said it all.

"You're thinking that you shouldn't have let me fuck you. You're afraid that because you opened yourself up to me, and showed me the raw and uninhibited side of you, it means you've lost your edge. When it comes to sex, you like to have the power because you figure if you're in control, then you're safe. It's supposed to be just sex, feeding a desire, Melina, and nothing else. Last night was much more than just sex and you're scared, but I'm not going to let you run away from me."

Momentarily rendered speechless, Melina gasped when Mac's hand found its way between her legs and began to stroke her. The pad of his thumb rubbed her clit slowly and methodically, while another finger dipped inside her. Mentally, Melina cursed herself. Her body was betraying her once again, and Mac was right, no matter how much she hated to admit it. Last night had been something entirely different from just a tumble in bed.

Mac had taken his time to please her in every way. To dominate her and take control. To show her his vulnerable side and put her needs above his own.

She hadn't been expecting that. What she'd hoped for was a quick fuck that would prove Mac had more bark than bite, and that his less than stellar performance would do away with whatever feelings she might be harboring for him.

It hadn't.

And now, as her body hummed to life beneath the expert skill of his hand, she realized that she was about to be screwed again in more ways than one.

"Say something, doll. It's not like you to be so tight-lipped. Looks like I need to give you some help."

Before she realized his intentions, Mac forced her to her back and covered her body with his own. His fingers never stopped their slow torture between her thighs. Stroke after firm stroke of his fingers inside her wet sex; circle after slow circle of the pad of his thumb to her throbbing clit. Sparks of pleasure cascaded over her skin, promising release.

"You're not playing fair," she whispered.

Mac flashed a sinful smile. "I never do when it comes to something I want."

He leaned down and kissed her hard. Her mouth opened and allowed his tongue inside. She savored the flavor of Mac's mouth while his lips owned hers. Melina whimpered against his mouth as her body hovered on the precipice of another orgasm.

And then the phone rang.

"You'd better get that." She somehow managed to groan out the words.

"Whoever it is, they can wait," Mac growled.

His tongue warred with hers as the phone kept ringing. Mac's fingers worked her clit in time to the phone's rings and Melina came.

Hard and hot all over Mac's hand.

"*God.*" She moaned, giving into Mac's wants and her own wants.

"No, it's Mac, sweetheart. Remember?"

A retort rolled off her tongue, but it was silenced by Mac's phone ringing again. She wished she could catch her damn breath.

"You'd better get that this time," she finally said.

He kissed her hard. "There's something else I'd rather get."

Melina bit her lip and smiled as Mac rolled off her and reached for his phone.

"Mac here."

He sat up straight in the bed like someone had lit a fire under his back. Melina rolled onto her side to watch him, leaning up on her elbow. A furrow formed between his brows before his eyes opened wide.

"You're fucking kidding me. Why?"

With one arm folded across his torso, Melina's eyes were drawn to his defined muscles and his washboard abs. As much as she hated to admit it, the man had a beautiful body. A real work of art. Not to mention, a particular part that was standing proudly beneath the bed covers. Still watching him, Melina slid her hand under the covers and grabbed his cock with a firm grip. He was hard, hot and heavy in her hand. Mac's eyes hooded with lust as she stroked him from base to tip. It was the only reaction he gave to her teasing.

"I see. I'll make it happen."

Mac ended the call and placed his phone on the bedside table. His eyes narrowed on Melina.

"What? Why are you looking at me like that?" Melina asked.

"Because as much as I'd like to let you continue, we need to talk and I need to be focused in order to do that."

Melina's hand stilled. "Okay. Shoot. What was that call all about?"

"You've made waves, really big waves."

"Meaning ... what?"

"The boss wants to see us," Mac explained.

"I've already made Guido's acquaintance. I'm in no hurry for a repeat performance."

Mac shook his head. "I'm not talking about Guido."

Melina sat straight up clutching the sheet to her chest. "You can't mean ..."

"Yeah, I do. Luca Pivetti."

Melina swallowed hard as Mac's words sank in. The boss of the Pivetti family wanted to meet her. She didn't know why, but she was pretty sure that whatever the reason was, it couldn't be good.

"He wants me dead, doesn't he?" she asked.

"No. If the boss wanted you dead, you would be already."

"So what does he want then?"

Mac shrugged. "That, I don't know."

Mac opened his arms and she moved into them, leaning against his chest.

Melina's eyes closed as his lips pressed to her forehead. She was tired and deep down she was scared. It was one thing to deal with cops. It was something else entirely to be on the radar of a mob boss the police were trying to take down.

"What happened?"

Melina tensed. "I don't know what you mean."

"Yes, you do."

"What happened to you?" she asked turning in

his arms to face him.

"We're not talking about me. We're talking about you. I know opening up is not easy, but sometimes it helps to get it out."

Melina was silent. He was right. The burden of everything she was dealing with weighed on her like an elephant sitting on her chest, crushing her vital organs. In a perfect world, there would be somebody she could tell her secrets to; someone that she could trust, no matter what. Mac seemed to want to be that person, but people seemed to be a lot of things until the going got tough.

"Not today, Mac."

Before he could stop her, Melina was out of bed and hurriedly dressing.

"You're running away now?"

"I'm not running. I just need time."

"Time for what, Melina?"

"To know just how much I can trust you." She faced Mac. A muscle moved in his jaw and his eyes grew dark. "Okay?"

"I see."

"Nothing personal. I just …"

"You have to protect yourself. I get it."

Melina nodded. "Good. I'm going home."

"I'll be in touch. Until we find out what's going on, we need to keep up appearances."

"That won't be a problem. No one is better at keeping up appearances than me."

With a smile, Melina turned on her heel and was gone. Mac was getting too close, too fast. There were too many changes in her life now. She couldn't afford another.

Especially when her heart was involved.

For so long, the vault to her feelings had been closed. Anger had become her way of life, the way in which she coped with one disappointment after another. She wasn't ready to give Mac a chance to become yet another disappointment, no matter how much her heart might want otherwise.

***

This shit had to stop.

It had been two weeks since Melina had killed Tip, and she was being followed.

Again.

Fresh anger burned like lava in her throat. Hadn't she been harassed enough during lock up? Now they were upping their game by following her everywhere she went. They thought they were so smart in their unmarked cars, but Melina was smarter. She could spot a cop a mile away. The air stunk with their stench.

She'd tried to get back to her life. The only problem was that she didn't know what that was anymore. Escorting as a way to make her money was out of the question. Even if the cops weren't watching her, Dulcea had told her she was done working with Melina. The attention from the official side of things made her boss run scared.

Once again, Melina was on her own. No job and no one to lean on. She'd thought going down and hanging out with the kids at the center would make her feel better, and it had … for a little while.

Now she just felt empty inside.

"Yo, Morgan. No tricks today?"

Melina kept walking, ignoring the voice that mocked her.

They were pigs. Every last single one of them.

"Hey, Morgan, how much for something quick? I'm looking for a good time."

She stopped walking, and turned to face the unmarked car that had pulled up beside her. Melina recognized the two detectives that had interrogated her, Parks and Keaton.

"A whore doesn't have options. A lady does. Learn the difference, assholes."

Melina started to walk away.

"A whore with a smart mouth. That's a new one."

She'd had enough. The constant surveillance she could deal with. After all, a man watching her was something she'd long ago gotten used to. But the comments, they were too much. Melina blinked back tears that were threatening to fall. Turning back to face her tormentors, a red haze was the only thing she saw.

"They're not worth it, doll."

Mac.

Even though she wished she didn't feel so goddamned relieved at his voice, she was.

It seemed once again that he'd come to her rescue.

Right on time.

CHAPTER FOURTEEN

Tossing a glare at the plain-clothed cops in the unmarked car, Mac slipped his hand into Melina's before he leaned close and planted a searing kiss on her lips.

"Hey!" Mac heard one of the detectives bark.

Mac ignored the asshole. "Seriously, doll, don't ruin your day by letting fools that have nothing better to do than harass an innocent woman get you upset."

Her posture softened and a tiny smile edged the corners of her lips upwards.

"I hadn't thought of it that way," Melina said quietly.

Mac couldn't resist letting the very tips of his fingers ghost over her jaw. The flicker of lust darkening Melina's gaze said that his touch had affected her deeply.

"Hey, James," one of the detectives said. "Don't you have your hired fuck on speed dial like the rest of her clients?"

Mac didn't grace that insult with a response. He also let the fact that they used his given name slide. Instead, he took note of the way Melina's smile dropped slightly. She hid her hurt well enough, but he could tell the man's words affected her.

"Don't let them do that to you, Melina," Mac said too low for the pigs to hear.

Melina's gaze cut to Mac's in an instant. "That's

easy for you to say. It's not you who is being called a whore every time you turn around. It's not you being followed by these idiots, Mac."

"Maybe not, but you're still giving them the power to hurt you when you react. It doesn't matter if your reaction is in anger or pain—you're still giving them what they want. Don't do that. They're not worth the fucking spit from your beautiful mouth."

Melina stood straighter at those words. "Yeah, you're right. Not worth it."

"Good." Mac held out a hand. "Care to spend the afternoon with me?"

"Doing what, exactly?"

"Whatever you want, doll. We'll say the day is my treat to clear your mind of stress."

Melina pursed her lips. "What, like pampering?"

Mac smirked. "I do love to spoil a woman."

"Spoiled women are useless women, Mac."

"Or maybe the right man hasn't been spoiling you, Melina. Stop being difficult, even though I know it's terribly hard for you to even imagine being something akin to delightful and appreciative, and take my hand so we can get away from the detectives."

Melina took his hand. "Now what?"

"Did she give you a cost for the day yet, Maccari?" the other detective taunted. "We're trying to find out if her price range is out of our budgets."

That time, Melina barely showed any emotion to the cops' rudeness. Mac was proud as hell. He tugged her in close and moved them down the sidewalk, further away from the detectives and their prying eyes and ears.

Mac looked over Melina's fingernails, letting the pad of his thumb run over her fingers. "When was the last time you had your nails done, doll?"

"A couple of weeks."

"That's a shame. A woman's outer beauty and confidence should reflect what is inside her. Any man who gives a damn about his girl should make sure he not only tells her how gorgeous she looks, but takes special care to provide her with whatever she needs to physically feel beautiful, as well. You've been biting the hell out of your nails, doll. Stress, right?"

"Possibly."

Mac winked. "How in the hell do you plan on leaving another set of your marks down my back with a mess like this?"

Melina's jaw dropped. "Mac!"

"Well, it's an honest concern. My treat, let's go."

Mac swept Melina's heeled feet into his hands and rested her shoes in his lap. She tossed him a curious glance, but kept quiet when he pulled her shoes off and pressed his thumbs into her ankles.

No matter what a woman liked to say about the topic, heels were hell when they were walked in all day.

The Asian woman buffing Melina's fingernails down gave a sweet smile in Mac's direction as she continued her work.

"Good man," the woman said, her accent thick. "Good man please woman."

Melina sighed, averting her eyes from Mac's grin. "So they say."

"Your poor hands," the Asian woman muttered to herself. "You treat them horrible."

"Lay off," Mac told the woman. "She's had a rough couple of weeks."

"You not good man then."

Mac cracked up, chuckling loudly. "I am."

"These hands say no, mister."

"That's why I brought her to you."

The Asian woman smiled, her eyes crinkling at the edges. "Ah, good man."

Melina shook her head at the exchange. "You seem comfortable here."

Mac shrugged. "My sister spends a few hours a month between here and another salon she likes."

"Oh?"

"Yes. I usually pick up the tab, depending on how much time I've spent with her that month. It's like my way of giving her one-on-one attention. Now that we're older and she's off into her own life, we're not as close as we were when we were younger."

Melina's gaze softened briefly. "Huh."

"Is that a surprise or something?"

"No, I just ..."

"Spit it out, doll."

Melina rolled her eyes. "It's nothing. It just surprises me that family seems to be such a huge thing for you. Most people don't see it the same way. Once they're adults and out of their childhood home, they forget about where they came from and the siblings they grew up with."

Mac's hands stilled in their massage of Melina's ankles. "Family is absolutely everything, Melina. In my family, it's even more important that my sister knows she has someone to go to other than my mother if she needs a person to talk to."

He had always been a cornerstone for his sister. Mac couldn't imagine letting Victoria stumble through life on her own. Given she had no one else but their mother who still struggled to maintain her own house and home, Mac didn't think that would be a very honorable thing to do to his sister.

"What about your father? Aren't most a daddy's girl of some sort?"

Mac had to force himself not to react to Melina's innocent question. She didn't know a thing about his history with his drunk father, or the way he and his sister grew up. He couldn't expect her to, either, so he didn't fault her for the curiosity.

"Not for Victoria," Mac settled on saying.

His words came out lame and disinterested, but the heat of resentment trailed close behind in his tone. Melina cocked a brow at him. Clearly, she had heard it, too, but thankfully, she didn't call him out on the slip.

"So," Melina drawled.

"Hmm?"

Mac had gone back to rubbing her ankles and calves, which took up a great deal of his attention. The silky feel of her smooth skin under his palms was a surefire way to get his cock hard and his mind in a less than innocent place.

Kind of like where it was right now.

"Mac," Melina said.

His head popped up fast. "Have I told you how much I like your legs?"

"Yes. I think you called them beautiful once."

"You need to be told again. Especially when you're wearing a dress. Sexy as sin."

The lady on the other side of the table giggled, but kept her head down on her work. Mac didn't miss the way Melina's fingers twitched, or how her thighs momentarily tightened.

"Not the place or time, Mac," Melina said, heat coloring her words.

"The place is relative, doll. And any time is a damn good time for that."

Melina pressed her lips together like she was holding something back. Mac simply smiled at her non-response and went back to rubbing the kinks from her legs.

"It was kind of lucky that we ran into each other today, wasn't it?" Melina asked after a moment.

"If you want to say that."

Mac wasn't a liar, after all.

"How would you say it?" Melina asked.

Sighing, Mac took his time to put Melina's heels back on and drop her feet on the floor. He leaned back in the chair and said, "I told you that I would be around and keeping an eye on things. What did you think that would involve, Melina?"

It took a couple of seconds, but Mac watched the realization come to Melina's pretty features. Anger skipped over her furrowing brow as she regarded him through thick lashes.

"You've been following me?" she asked sharply.

The Asian woman made an "oh" sound under her breath, but never once looked up from her work. Mac, despite being amused at the woman's enjoyment over her customers, paid her little mind. Melina was more important at the moment.

"Chill out, doll."

"I told you that—"

"You wanted time and space. Everything that happened—it was a lot," Mac said, choosing his words carefully. "I was letting you take what you needed, but there's a lot of shit at play between the pigs that have been trailing you and the other side that's watching you, too."

Melina's shoulders stiffened. "The mo—"

"Careful," he warned.

Mac thoroughly believed Melina was born to be a mobster's girl, even if she didn't know it. The woman could handle a gun, kept a calm head in bad situations, and wasn't afraid to get a little dirty.

That had "gun moll" written all over it.

But she had a lot of learning to do in the world of mafia.

A lot.

"*They're* following me, too?"

"They are," Mac confirmed. "Guido has had Vin

checking up on your place, but there's been some other activity I noticed by people I don't recognize as well."

"How do they even know where I live?"

"As long as a person has money, nothing is unreachable," Mac answered simply.

"Jesus."

"I was giving you what you asked for, Melina, but we have an image to maintain, too. We told them one thing, and we can't appear as another thing. Okay? So, yeah, I've been around. I made sure it would be noticed that I was coming and going from your new apartment building. I made a trip to the center one day when you were working with the kids, but you never noticed me. I stayed out of your way."

Melina sucked in a hard breath. "The kids? My new place?"

"Yes."

"How do you know about those things?"

Mac cringed at the edge in Melina's voice. It was sharper than a goddamn razor and it would probably cut deeper than one, too. "That morning you left my place ..."

"What about it?"

"I trailed you."

Melina's expression fell dark before she blanked completely. Slowly, she turned in her seat to face the Asian woman instead of Mac while her nails were being buffed and readied.

"Miss?" the woman asked.

"Yes?"

"He's idiot."

Melina didn't even smile. "Yes, he is an idiot."

"But he's idiot with good taste because he pick you."

Mac grinned when Melina passed him a burning glare.

"That's just about the one thing he's got going for him right now," Melina muttered.

Hey, Mac would take it.

Mac sipped from a to-go cup of hot coffee and leaned against the window of the salon. Across the street, the unmarked police car sat running with the two fools from earlier inside. The detectives chatted back and forth while watching the business and Mac.

He understood Melina's annoyance at the fuckers. They were like blood-sucking mosquitos that a person wanted to swat with their hand and kill, but could never quite catch in time before the pain of the bite.

Bastards.

In his pocket, Mac's phone rang. He answered the call on the second ring.

"Mac here."

"*Soldato,*" Guido greeted.

Mac frowned. "Skip. What's up?"

"Just checking in to make sure you're ready for tonight."

"Of course."

"Good. You know, Anthony will be at the dinner as well."

Mac's irritation level climbed higher. "Is that so?"

"*Sì.* Tonight is the perfect time for you to try to acquaint yourself with the Capo and perhaps some of his men. Use the old Maccari charm. Your father knows how to use it well enough when he isn't drunk off his ass. I'm sure you'll be even better at it."

Mac's jaw clenched so hard his molars ached. Obviously, his Capo was still on the kick of ridding his rival in the Pivetti Cosa Nostra. Mac had very little interest in being involved in Guido's plans for Anthony, but it didn't seem like he was going to be given a choice in the matter.

"I'll see what I can do," Mac finally said.

"Good, good. And your girl? How is she?"

"Well."

Mac could practically see the leer that Guido was wearing when the Capo replied, "I look forward to seeing her again. Any woman who can aim and shoot like that one has got to be a wild thing in the sack. Broads like those are hard to find nowadays."

Respect.

Mac chanted the word over and over to keep from barking at his Capo to shut his disgusting fucking mouth. Jealousy was an awful, terrible monster. He was finding that the more people looked at Melina like she was a piece of meat, and the more words people said about her, the worse his jealousy got.

He didn't want other people looking at his girl like that.

Except she wasn't his at all.

"Melina will be her usual self at the dinner, Skip," Mac forced out.

"Perfect. Tonight, then. Pivetti mansion at seven. Do not be late, Mac, or you won't like what happens."

"Seven it is."

Guido hung up the call without another word.

More frustrated than ever, Mac shoved the phone back into his pocket. He couldn't help but check on Melina, just to be sure she was still enjoying herself inside the salon. After she finished getting her nails done, he had made sure to add that she was to have whatever else she wanted added to the tab, including her hair and makeup.

Mac knew that Melina was going to be pissed off

to the heavens when she found out that she had unwillingly been invited to a dinner at the Pivetti boss's home later that night. He sincerely hoped a day of pampering would soften her up just enough to get her to agree.

Well, it wasn't even a matter of Melina agreeing or not. She had to go. Mac simply preferred to have the nicer side of Melina come along, rather than her angry side.

Not that an angry Melina wasn't a fun one.

Mac liked that, too.

Dammit.

Pushing those thoughts away, Mac caught the unmarked police car in his sights again. One detective nodded to the other one before getting out of the car. The fool started a trek down the street towards the coffee shop. It was noon and that place was packed, so it wasn't likely that the detective would be back anytime soon. The other detective rested back in the passenger seat and closed his eyes.

Lazy asshole.

Mac grinned, an idea setting in and refusing to let go. As much as he believed in turning the other cheek and being the bigger person, he figured the two detectives needed a lesson in humility.

For five minutes, Mac watched the detective in the car until the guy's mouth popped open in what looked to be a snore. Sleeping on the job. Lazy, indeed. These fools could use a lesson or two from a Cosa Nostra Capo on what happens when a man falls asleep during a scheme.

Keeping one eye on the sleeping detective in the car, Mac strolled across the street. He casually tossed his hands into his slack's pockets as he rounded the back of the vehicle. Checking to be sure the other cop wasn't coming back down the sidewalk, and the other idiot was still sleeping, Mac pulled a pocketknife from his pants.

When a gun couldn't be carried, a knife was just as good.

The street was quiet, even with the few people strolling on past. No one ever paid anyone else any attention on the streets of New York. It was almost like an unspoken rule that people needed to mind their own damn business.

Bending down, Mac left a two-foot long scratch across the back of the trunk with the tip of his knife. Then, as he strolled past the car to cross the street again, he stuck the blade into the tire and jerked the hilt a bit to let the air out. When he pulled the knife from the tire, the air hissed as the tire began to deflate slowly.

Smirking at the sight of the sleeping fool in the passenger seat, Mac quickly crossed the road again. In this part of town, businesses didn't have cameras on the outside. Most of them didn't even have them on the inside.

Mac took his place leaning against the window again. It took a whole fifteen minutes before the other cop returned. Instantly, the fool must have known something was wrong, given the way the car was leaning hard to the left.

The detective found the scratched trunk and the slashed tire. Mac watched, entirely amused, as the two detectives shouted at one another. Then, the cop that had gone to the coffee shop looked across the street. His eyes found Mac's instantly, narrowing with angry understanding.

Suspecting and proving were two different things.

Mac smirked, lifted his cup of coffee as an acknowledgment, and then disappeared back into the salon.

How's that for an option, boys?

"Beautiful," Mac appraised.

Melina smiled coyly as Mac ran his fingers through her blown out waves. Three hours later, and she now sported cherry red and deep violet highlights throughout her dark chocolate hair. It wasn't a combination he would have thought of, but it looked damn good on her.

"Thank you for not arguing too much about the pampering," Mac said.

Melina shrugged. "It's not usually my style to let a man spend money on me like this, but I have a feeling you would have tied to me to a chair."

"Maybe."

"Thank you. It was nice."

"You're welcome. Like I said, men who care about their women should show them."

"*Their* women, huh?"

Mac chuckled. "I know. Don't bite my fucking head off. I'm just saying. Besides, what man spends half of an afternoon in a salon with a woman if he's not interested in her, right? It was a good show for the detectives, if nothing else. And if anyone else happened to be following you today, then they probably got the message, too."

"Is that the only reason why you did this?"

"No," Mac admitted.

Melina huffed. "You're trying to get me into bed again."

"No on that front, too, doll." Mac ticked two fingers under her chin. "And not that I have to point it out, but we both know if I wanted to get you in bed, you would already be there."

Goddamn, she tried to hide her shiver, but she couldn't. Mac took that as a battle won and left it alone.

"Why do this, then?" Melina asked quietly.

"I told you that I wanted to know you, Melina. I've given you two weeks to get your thoughts in order. Sometimes women like you need a good shove to get you out of your crazy head. Maybe that had a little bit to do with it."

"But not all."

"No, not all," Mac confessed, blowing out a heavy breath. "We have one more thing to do this afternoon."

"Oh?"

"Yes, you need a new dress."

Melina's brow furrowed. "Why?"

"To go with your new hair and your beautiful face, doll. Something sexy as sin to show off your legs and curves when I take you to dinner tonight at Luca Pivetti's mansion."

The rebuttal and denial was on the tip of Melina's tongue. Mac could see her argument and refusal forming right before his eyes.

"Before you start," Mac said, lifting a single brow to keep Melina quiet, "… this is not an option, Melina. This is a formal invitation. Remember those rules I told you about?"

With a tight jaw and a heated glare, Melina nodded. "Yes."

"This is one of them. You never shun a Don, babe. Let's go pick you out a dress."

Melina scowled. "It better be a nice one."

"Anything you put on will be perfect."

***

"I didn't think to mention it before, but you have a nice ride," Melina said.

Mac flashed her with a grin. "Oh?"

Just to make a point to her statement about his Challenger, Mac revved the engine when he shifted gears. The engine roared in response and Melina laughed.

"Yeah, it's not bad," she said.

"It's not a Mercedes or a Porsche, but it's a damned good car."

Melina arched a brow. "How much money do you have under the hood? Because I would be willing to bet that regardless of what a car looks like on the outside, it's what is inside that counts. Am I right?"

Mac shrugged. "You might be, doll."

In fact, she was bang on. He had as much money under the hood of his Challenger as he did in the purchase of the entire car. It was better people weren't aware of that fact until they needed to know.

"So," Melina drawled, turning her head to watch the highway fly by out of the passenger window. "Is there anything I should know about tonight? Rules, or whatever?"

"Yeah, there's a bit."

"I'm listening, Mac."

"Respect, doll. That's it. That's everything. Nothing else matters, nothing else is acceptable. Only respect."

Melina pursed her lips. "To who?"

"Anyone in that mansion. They're there for a reason. They got there either because of their last name, what they've done for *la famiglia*, or how close they are to the boss. It's that simple. No matter how much you might dislike someone, you're not to outwardly show it unless they disrespect you in a very obvious way. And even then …"

"What?"

"Even then, you let me handle it."

Melina scoffed. "Is it some kind of woman thing? Because I have a uterus, I can't stick up for myself?"

"No, it's a Cosa Nostra thing," Mac replied quietly. "It's a respect thing between men and their women. That's all, Melina."

"Oh."

"Mmhmm."

"Anything else I should know?" Melina asked.

Mac eyed her from the side, taking in the slinky silver dress she wore. It draped over her shoulders, half on and half off, and hugged her curves perfectly. It showcased the delicate line of her throat and collarbones, decorated with a silver, low-hanging necklace.

Melina was all woman. Every inch of Mac knew it.

"Smile, Melina," Mac said.

"Smile?"

"Beautiful things tend to stand out in a room, and as much as you might want to blend in, you never will. You deserve to be admired and envied. I'm incredibly lucky to be the man showing you off tonight."

Melina sucked in a quiet breath. "Thank you."

"Clearly, you're not told how beautiful you are nearly enough."

"Not like that, Mac."

She'd said those words to him once before.

"I still think that's a shame, doll."

"All your charm is a dangerous thing, Mac."

"It can be." Mac took an exit ramp when the GPS directed him to turn. "Another few minutes and we'll arrive. There is something else I should mention, Melina."

"What is that?"

"Earlier, when we were talking about my sister, I avoided something. I might not be able to avoid it tonight. You see, way back when I was a kid, my uncle, Marco, was a family Capo. The Maccari family had a longer leg in the mob when he was alive."

"Why do I hear a 'but' in there?"

"But," Mac added, chuckling dryly, "my uncle was killed in a street war. He was the one thing that kept the Maccari family present and noticed. He was influential enough in his position that he was capable of wiping away the mistakes of his younger brother."

Melina frowned. "Your father?"

"If that's what you want to call him, then sure. Mostly, I just refer to him as 'James' or I don't refer to him at all. He's a drunk, and he's got a taste for street women and coke. When I was younger—maybe five or six—he wasn't so bad. He had his shit under control while my uncle was alive, for the most part. Then, Marco died and nobody gave a shit. James went downhill fast. He only came around enough to make it look good for *la famiglia*."

"Why would that even matter?" Melina asked.

"Because family is everything."

"You told me that earlier."

Mac smiled, but it felt forced. "I did. I meant it, too. My father, however, only used his family when he needed to, so that his Capo would think he was on the up and up with it all. No matter what James tried to make it look like, he was still a fucking fool on the streets. Drunk, high, and screwing up every other day. I don't know how he's even still alive. My mother worked her ass off doing two jobs, feeding and clothing two kids, and trying to keep her house afloat. The moment I could start helping out, I did. But the only thing I knew was where I came from—mafia."

"What does this have anything to do with tonight, Mac?"

"Sons follow their fathers, Melina. That's what is believed in this world. You are only as good and as honorable as the man you came from."

"And yours is shameful."

"Very shameful," Mac murmured. "I often take shit for my father."

Melina glanced down at her hands resting in her lap.

"Is that why you go by Mac? I mean, the cop called you James earlier, and the other one called you Maccari. You go by Mac."

"Yes. That's exactly why."

"You don't know that anyone will say anything about your father tonight. You didn't have to tell me this, you know."

Mac disagreed entirely. "Maybe you're right, but I wanted to. You want to trust me, doll. That's what you said."

"It was."

"I'm simply helping that along by sharing. My father is just one of the reasons that being invited to this dinner has me nervous."

Melina laughed lightly. "You don't seem nervous."

"Don't mistake poise for boldness, Melina. They're two entirely different things. I've been waiting for a night like tonight for a very long time. I've been kept at arm's length from the boss and anyone even remotely close to him because of my father's history. This is the closest I have ever been to Luca, and I would prefer not to fuck it up somehow."

"This is it for you, isn't it?" she asked softly.

"Hmm, what?"

"The mob—Cosa Nostra. This is all you want to be."

Mac didn't even have to think about it. "Yeah, it is."

CHAPTER FIFTEEN

Melina had seen plenty of wealth in her former career as an escort. Some of her clients had been multi-millionaires, while the rest toted bank accounts that certainly weren't anything to scoff at. Fancy cars, massive homes, private jets, and more. Melina had seen it all.

She had never seen anything like the Pivetti home.

Actually, that was kind of a joke. It wasn't a home. It wasn't some large, two or three-level structure with a big garage, a large yard, and a couple of nice cars in the driveway.

No, not at all.

The four-level structure sported what looked like three massive wings, a garage that was big enough to be a small warehouse, stonework from the bottom of the walls to the roof, and windows that were as large as an eighteen-wheeler. Specialty lighting put the decorative walkways on display. The long, winding driveway was lined with birch trees. The doors to the garage were wide open and the lights were on. It showcased the highest luxury of cars on the market in a rainbow of colors. All-terrain vehicles had been lined up in one of several sections.

The place rested on a private section of land that, guessing by the length of the driveway, had to be a few acres. Situated on the outskirts of the city in an expensive, private suburb, the Pivetti home was not at all what Melina had expected.

It dripped in money.

She had thought that maybe it would be a large home—something worthy of a crime boss—but certainly not this.

"Oh, my God," Melina mumbled, staring up at the structure before her.

Her gaze caught the dozen or so security cameras that were visible in eaves and over doors. No doubt, someone was probably watching their vehicle. She was thankful for the dark-tinted windows keeping them from view as she gaped like a fool. It was only then that she noticed the black-clothed men standing in inconspicuous locations. Guards, likely.

Melina didn't know what to think.

"Close your mouth, doll."

Her jaw snapped shut. "This place is huge."

Mac put the car in park, eyeing the home. "I've never seen it up close before, but I'd heard stories about it. I'd seen a couple of pictures, but nothing more. My imagination didn't do it justice, I can tell you that."

"It's ... what is it?"

"Excessive."

Melina wholeheartedly agreed. "It's a little ostentatious for a crime boss, isn't it? Isn't the whole point of your business to stay under the radar? Nobody is saying he has to live in the slums, but this is ..."

"Excessive," Mac repeated with a chuckle. "Luca Pivetti comes from old money. Keep that in mind. His grandfather's father had a large share in one of the biggest banks in the USA. He also has a huge ownership in the casino market in Vegas, and a few overseas real-estate endeavors in Europe. So yeah, the man might be a crime boss, but he's also a major business man with some very legal ventures."

"I can smell the money from here."

"Oh?"

Melina crinkled her nose for show. "Smells like entitlement and arrogance."

Mac laughed hard. "Keep those thoughts to yourself when we're inside, doll."

Jesus Christ.

She hadn't even thought about the inside of the home.

"Please tell me the floors aren't paved in gold and the wallpaper isn't made of diamonds or some nonsense," she said.

Mac shrugged. "I have no idea."

"Great."

"But let's go find out."

Even better ...

<hr />

Melina's coat and clutch were taken from her by the waiting staff the moment she stepped into the home. The quiet woman who bent down to wipe the soles of Melina's heels wore a gray uniform, trimmed with white and comfortable looking black shoes. Confused, Melina allowed the woman to clean her heels as she watched a man do the same to Mac.

"Thank you, Miss," the woman said, her voice barely above a whisper. "Mr. Pivetti welcomes you to his home to celebrate his youngest daughter's eighteenth birthday with a dinner and party. Enjoy the evening, and please find one of the help if you need anything. We're happy to serve you, ma'am. Follow the hallway to the entrance where the staircase is located. Another staff member will be waiting to direct you up the right staircase to the second level where the rest of the guests are in the ballroom."

Ballroom?

There was a ballroom in the fucking place?

The man who had cleaned Mac's shoes stood and recited the very same thing to him. Melina raised an eyebrow in Mac's direction as the woman scurried away into a connected room with the man right on her heels.

"What was that?"

Mac looked as confused as she did. "What wealth can buy?"

Melina didn't think so. Those people didn't feel like normal house staff. Usually, maids and so forth were not as robotic and stiff. Sometimes, they even smiled. Those people had done neither.

It felt all wrong.

Glancing down at her dress, Melina asked, "Am I underdressed for a ballroom?"

"No," Mac answered. "According to Guido, it's where Luca entertains for dinners and parties. It's big enough and it keeps everyone in one place instead of wandering his house. I guess the boss gets pissed as hell when people snoop."

Taking in the large foyer that had expensive art and tapestries on the wall, and the marble floor beneath their feet, she wasn't surprised that Luca didn't allow people to wander. In the middle of the room, a silver statue of horses rearing back that was nearly as tall as the ceiling rested below a glittering chandelier full of crystals.

Probably one-hundred percent real crystals.

Overwhelmed, Melina took it all in in silence.

"Come on, doll," Mac said.

Melina allowed him to guide her down the hallway. Painted photographs lined the dark-wood walls. Gold plaques under each named the individual or individuals in the paintings. At the very end of the hall, Mac stopped and nodded at the final two paintings.

One was a man who Melina recognized, sitting alone in what looked to be a library. Short, dark hair combed neatly to the left and the large ring on his right finger caught Melina's eye first. With brandy glass in one hand, a cigar in his other, and steel gray eyes staring out at them, the man in the painting seemed cold and distant. His posture was straight and stiff in the large leather chair he rested on. His wealth surrounding him made him seem almost unobtainable—untouchable.

Luca Pivetti.

Melina knew his face from the photographs the detectives had shoved at her.

"Whoever painted that has a knack for putting reality into art," Mac muttered.

"I thought you never met the man?"

"I haven't, but I've heard enough." Mac nodded at the second painting. "His daughters."

Melina took in the second painting, noting the three women standing around their father with an ornate, massive fireplace behind them. All of the girls were beautiful and young. The oldest probably couldn't be much older than twenty-five, at the most. What stunned her most about the girls were the color of their skin.

Dark caramel, like hers.

"I didn't know his wife was …"

"African, yes," Mac said.

"African only?"

"South African with an Italian-African father, actually. Diamonds are a huge trade, you know. Luca's father got mixed up in that mess and in the process, met a man that might have been a little more dangerous than even he was."

"Luca's wife's father?"

Mac smirked. "Good guess. Her father had dual citizenship between Africa and Italy. He spent the majority of his adult life in Africa running diamonds."

Melina's gaze narrowed. "Blood diamonds?"

"I think so. Anyway, when a deal went south between Luca's father and the diamond king, a deal was struck, a marriage happened, and it's been quiet going ever since."

"An arranged marriage?"

Mac eyed her before saying, "It's actually not uncommon in this lifestyle."

"Wow."

"Yeah. She came over here to the States and they married. They had three girls. Cosa Nostra overlooked the fact she was only half-Italian, seeing as how the Italian came from her father's side."

"No sons?" Melina asked.

"Rumors say there's a son or two in *la famiglia* that belong to Luca. Mistresses for mothers, or so the story goes."

"You seem to know a lot of the story."

Mac's hand slipped into Melina's before he pulled her alongside him to walk again. "I wanted to know the man I was meeting. So let's do that, doll."

The second Mac and Melina were directed into the ballroom, Melina found the person who the talking, laughing, and dancing people probably considered the most important man in the area. In the middle of the very spacious room, a marble fountain of naked women had water spouting from the ladies' outstretched hands. Sitting on the edge of the fountain with his ankle crossed over his knee and a glass of red wine in hand was a laughing Luca Pivetti.

The man was surrounded by men and women alike. They looked on at his laughter with their own as drinks were poured and servers moved from person to person with plates of finger foods in hand. The moment Luca stopped laughing, the people around him quickly followed suit. With a wave of his hand, the people scattered away from him. Luca stood as a young girl dressed in a pink chiffon dress came up beside him. Standing on her tiptoes, she kissed his cheek and Luca patted hers in return. Melina recognized the girl instantly as one of Luca's daughters in the painting.

He was clearly commanding. He owned the space. He was important.

Melina learned all of that in just a few quick seconds.

"I thought this was supposed to be a birthday party-slash-dinner?" Melina asked Mac.

"It is," he murmured in her ear. "But with these people, it is just as much about the boss celebrating his youngest child's eighteenth birthday, as it is about the girl herself."

"Why?"

"She's of age, I guess."

"To what, Mac?"

"Marry," he said simply.

Melina sighed. "She's a girl."

Mac's face was stone-cold and impassive as he replied, "Yes, but she's also a Don's daughter. It is what it is, doll."

"Mac, my boy."

Melina inwardly flinched at the voice of Guido, Mac's Capo. Mac's arm tightened around Melina's waist as they turned to face the older man. He was classed up in a tailored suit, a sharp tie, and a sly smile. Gone were the undone buttons on his shirt showing chest hair and the gold chain around his neck. Guido appeared to be a cultured, well-dressed man ready for a classy party.

Appearances were deceiving.

Melina knew that fact better than most.

"And, Melina, it's wonderful to see you again, too,"

Guido said.

"Skip," Mac greeted with what sounded like forced politeness.

Guido looked straight past Mac to Melina. The leer on his chubby face was enough to make Melina cringe.

"You're looking mighty fine tonight, sweetheart," Guido said.

Mac's fingers pressed roughly into Melina's hip before he pushed her closer into his warm side. His lips pressed to her temple with a brief kiss. A heat spread in her stomach at Mac's touch and kiss, shooting straight down between her thighs. She would recognize a sign of possession anywhere, and that one was written as clear as day.

For the sake of show, Melina let Mac do what he wanted.

The *show*, right.

Melina would keep telling herself that and ignore the way she felt. It would work ... eventually.

"She is looking beautiful, isn't she?" Mac said, flashing a grin at Melina. "She spent the day being spoiled, so she's ready for a bit of fun with me tonight."

Melina smiled back. "Mac always does know how to show me a good time."

Guido chuckled. "Broads like you deserve to be spoiled every once in a while. I'm glad to see this man of yours is treating you properly."

Mac scoffed. "I know how to treat a woman."

"Treating and handling are two different things, Mac." Guido's leer deepened as he eyed Melina's chest openly. She beat back the desire to bark at him to look at her eyes. "But I'm sure you have both under control, hmm?"

Mac turned Melina a bit in his hold to put her slightly behind him as he grabbed a piece of blue cheese from a serving tray as one of the wait staff walked by. It was a subtle way to take Guido's eyes off her. Melina appreciated the move.

"You know it, Skip," Mac said.

"Come. It's time to say hello to the boss." Guido waved a hand and spun on his heel.

Melina's throat constricted with anxiety over the simple statement. Mac shot her an inquisitive glance when she didn't move forward with him to follow behind Guido.

"You okay?" Mac asked.

Pushing the nervousness away, Melina nodded. Lying seemed the way to go for tonight. This was all about the show. "Yeah."

Mac intertwined his fingers with Melina's and pulled her close again. She felt better at his side, strangely, and chose to stay there as they strolled across the ballroom floor. Melina ignored the curious gazes of the people she didn't know. Their whispers traveled, but not loud enough that she could hear them clearly.

The closer they came to Luca Pivetti and the two men standing beside him, the quieter people became. At just a few feet away, Luca held up one hand and passed Mac and Melina a dismissive glance.

"A moment," the man said sharply.

Melina blinked, stunned.

She listened as the Don of the Pivetti crime family discussed the weather for the next week, the latest game he'd watched, and what he'd purchased for his daughter for her birthday. He held an entire ten-minute conversation with the men while Guido, Mac, and Melina stood off to the side, waiting to be introduced into a conversation that didn't seem all that important.

They were the lesser to these people, she realized.

Outsiders.

Newcomers.

Quietly, Mac said to Melina, "On the left of the boss is his underboss, Enzo. On his right, his consigliere and lawyer, Matthew. Remember their faces and names, doll. They're important men. They're the closest any man will ever get to the boss without being him. You understand?"

"Yes," Melina whispered.

Taking another look at the two older gentlemen talking with the Pivetti Don, Melina realized she did recognize them. Their pictures had also been shoved in her face with demands for information. The cops hadn't focused on them nearly as much as they'd focused on what she might know about the boss, however.

"Okay, good."

"Yes, let's do that," Luca said, chuckling loudly. "Put five down on them for me. They're going to win the series, I'm telling you."

"Just five?" Matthew asked.

"No, let's make it ten thousand on the game. Might as well go all in."

"I'll let Mickey know."

Then, Luca turned to face Guido with a tight smile. "Guido, how are you, my old friend?"

"Well, Boss," Guido replied. "Happy birthday to your daughter, of course."

Guido's tone held no hint of his earlier rudeness or arrogance. He suddenly seemed like a whole new man with his hands limp at his sides and his head bowed slightly. Stepping forward, Guido took the hand that Luca outstretched and kissed the ring on the man's index finger without hesitating. Then, Guido stepped back just as fast.

"Yes, thank you. Lora is vibrant tonight, isn't she?" Luca glanced over Guido's shoulder at Mac and Melina. "And who do we have here?"

Guido tipped his head to the side. "James Jr. Maccari and his—"

"Female," Luca interrupted coolly.

The man's gaze traveled over Melina with a disinterested stare that burned. She wasn't so much offended by his rejection as the coldness in his eyes. Somehow, instantly, she knew this man disliked her. He practically radiated it.

Mac stiffened beside Melina, and his hand held hers tighter. "Boss."

"You prefer Mac, yes?" Luca asked.

"Yes."

"Good. James reminds me of your father, and that makes me want to blow your brains out. If it weren't for his ability to clean up, when need be, I would have done that exact thing to him years ago."

Mac cleared his throat and said, "I'm not my father."

"Damn good thing," Luca muttered around the rim of his brandy glass.

"Could we—" Guido started to say.

His words were interrupted by the hand that Luca raised.

"Quiet, Guido." Luca flicked Melina with another cool stare before turning it on Mac. "You and I should have a chat, Mac. We're due one. After all I've heard about you, it seems a shame that I've yet to meet one of the best *soldatos* that my *famiglia* has to offer."

Guido's cheek ticked at that statement. "We can do that, Boss."

"You've been keeping this boy a secret, Guido," the man on Luca's left—Enzo—said.

"Not a secret, just—"

"It's not important," Luca interrupted. "Come, we can go to my office and have a proper drink without everyone watching."

Melina could practically feel Mac's tension release.

"Sure," Mac said, stepped forward to follow the Pivetti Don as the man turned.

Melina moved to go, too.

Luca said over his shoulder, "Not her."

Mac stopped his walk, his grip on Melina's hand turning almost painful. "Pardon, Boss?"

"Not her," Luca repeated without even turning around. "I'm sure she'll be fine to mingle with the crowd, Mac. This shouldn't be such an unusual event for a woman of her ... business. Their typical dates tend to be wealthy. She knows how to act, how to talk, and whatever else. Besides, I happen to know that Melina also attended a few events in a ballroom while growing up, although I believe the military usually throws them for charities, awards and things."

Melina straightened like someone had poured ice water over her head.

Military?

How did he know that?

Mac swallowed hard, passing Melina a look that asked a million questions.

"I'll be okay," she told him. "Go ahead."

But she wasn't. Not at all.

More than ever, Melina wanted to high tail it as fast as she could away from these people and the Pivetti boss.

The man didn't like her and he knew too much about her.

That screamed bad news.

Mac released Melina's hand. "Smile, doll. You look too beautiful not to smile."

Melina forced a smile on her face for Mac's benefit and nothing more. She could tell by the frown he tried to hide that he knew it was false.

"Go," she told him.

"If I have to repeat myself," Luca said, "then I will simply go to my office without having a meeting with you, Mac, while my men escort you from my property."

Melina turned on her heel and walked away, not giving Mac a choice in the matter at all. Over her shoulder, she caught his gaze as he checked on her while he followed behind the boss, his Capo, and the other men.

Avoiding the people in the ballroom, Melina stole a glass of champagne from the servers as tables of meal platters were brought out. More tables followed with chairs as the ballroom was transformed from an open space to a large dining room for the guests.

Unsure of what she should do, Melina stayed to the far wall and amused herself with the whispers of people around her. Mostly, they were talking about her. It only really became annoying when the color of her skin was mentioned more than once by a group of bitchy, statuesque women with plastic-looking faces that was huddled in a group only a few feet away from her.

They had to know Melina could hear them.

She refused to give them a reaction.

"Ladies," a heavily accented voice said.

Melina found who the voice belonged to almost instantly. She recognized the accent as South African as a beautiful, dark-skinned woman stepped between Melina and the other women. Her dress was a long flowing, black number that showed off her tightly braided hair and her delicate neckline.

No doubt, Melina had a feeling she knew who the woman was. She just didn't know her name. Mac hadn't mentioned what it was earlier when he talked about the wife of Luca Pivetti.

"Since when has the color of a woman's skin been an issue in this home?" the woman asked.

The other ladies gaped like fishes before scampering off when the woman flicked her wrist at them. She'd done it with such a flair that almost made it seem like she was shooing away garbage.

Once the group was gone, the woman spun around to face Melina. Her face was pixie-like in nature, though her lips were full and her eyes were a deep, dark brown.

"Thank you," Melina said quietly.

"Oh, darling, don't thank me for that. My God, they work every last nerve I have. What is your name?"

"Melina Morgan."

"Hello, Melina." The woman held out a hand, and Melina took it. "It's nice to meet you. I rarely forget a face that enters my home, so I assumed you must be a new guest. I apologize for not coming over sooner. I'm Neeya Pivetti."

Melina smiled. "It's nice to meet you, too."

"I noticed you talking with my husband earlier. I hope he didn't make you too uncomfortable. Luca doesn't do well with newcomers."

"It wasn't that bad."

"Liar. Luca is a tyrant and I know it."

Melina laughed along with Neeya.

The woman's husband might not have acted like he liked Melina very much, but his wife did. Melina would take it.

Women tended to hold the power, after all.

Men simply thought they did.

CHAPTER SIXTEEN

Silently, Mac followed behind the Pivetti boss and his men. As Luca sipped from his brandy glass, he barely acknowledged the people and staff he passed. The man was stiff like a board, and a certain air radiated from him in waves.

Melina had been right.

Money did smell like arrogance and entitlement.

Reminding himself that respect was the most important word of the evening, Mac stuffed his opinion of Luca down where it wouldn't bother him. It certainly hadn't helped that the Don seemed less than friendly to Melina, and his words to her came out even colder.

Behind the boss, Matthew and Enzo trailed close. They still kept a far enough distance from Luca that spoke to Mac of placement in the family. Luca held the highest spot, and so he walked ahead first. Matthew and Enzo backed their boss up as a consigliere and underboss, and so they walked second, behind the man in charge.

Mac and Guido walked side by side.

Strangely, Mac didn't feel like the lesser. He knew he was to these men—a *soldato* for the family, working towards his button with a drunk for a father and little else. It was a known opinion, as far as that went.

Mac refused to let it affect him.

What he couldn't ignore, however, was the nagging voice in the back of his mind reminding him over and over that he had been forced to leave Melina behind. That was not a part of Mac's plans in anyway. He didn't like the thought of her being left to fend for herself against people she didn't know.

Not that someone might cause her issues, but Mac couldn't be sure. Either way, it left a bad taste in his mouth and a sinking feeling in his stomach. No doubt, Melina could handle herself if need be. It still made Mac feel like a giant piece of shit.

"You good?" Guido asked.

"Sure, Skip."

"Put your little woman out of your mind while we get this meeting over and done with, Mac," Guido said too quietly for the men a few feet ahead of them to hear. "Luca's got a hard-on for making sure no newcomers around his men and family are out to get him in some way. Once this night is over, you won't have to worry about Luca again."

Mac frowned, but hid it by glancing down at the floor. Guido made it sound like this would be Mac's one and only meeting with the Pivetti crime boss. Mac fully intended to work his way into the Pivetti Cosa Nostra, and in doing so, would need to be front row and center for the boss to see Mac at his best, and unfortunately, some of his worst moments. He would need to be available for the boss, should Luca need something or call on him. It was how a solider went from the streets, to an associate, to eventually a made man in *la famiglia*.

It was a process. It sometimes took years, and for others, decades. It could be relentless, brutal, and demanding. Cosa Nostra was a bastard in that way to the men who were determined to join. Nothing about the mafioso life was easy or simple. Men gave everything to get their button, and more often than not, the button was the only fucking thing they were left with when it was said and done.

A man didn't get his *in* to the family simply by knowing someone who knew someone else. Guido was very aware of all that shit.

The man also knew how badly Mac wanted his button.

Something was off with Guido. Maybe it was being close to the boss. Men tended to act differently when important people were around. It could have been that Guido was concerned about Mac's first time having a conversation with Luca, too. Or, maybe it was something entirely different.

Mac decided to go along with whatever Guido wanted, or rather, make the man think that's what was happening until the Capo's intentions became clearer.

"You good?" Guido asked.

"Perfect," Mac assured, grinning confidently.

Guido must have been satisfied with the response, because he rolled his eyes and patted Mac on the shoulder like he usually did when he was pleased with his *soldato*. "Good, good. Just keep quiet unless the boss asks something important from you directly. Otherwise, I'll handle the talking."

"I'm not an idiot, Guido. I can handle a single conversation. I do just fine when I go out into public by myself, you know."

Guido's hand landed hard to Mac's back with enough force to sting. Mac didn't even wince, but he got his Capo's unspoken statement.

Shut up, do what I say, and follow the fucking rules, Mac.

"This isn't the public," Guido said low, eyeing the men walking ahead of them. "This is Cosa Nostra, my boy. Let a man with the button show you how it's done."

Mac's jaw ticked in his agitation. Once again, Guido was shoving him behind to take center stage. Usually, he did nonsense like this whenever he wanted to take credit for something. Tonight, there was nothing to take credit or get praised for.

"Whatever you say, Skip," Mac forced himself to say.

"Remember that, Mac."

"Mac," Luca called.

Mac's gaze drifted to the boss. Luca shot a look over his shoulder and smiled. The sight took Mac by surprise, considering the fact that since he met Luca, the boss's expression had barely changed from an emotionless disinterest.

"Yeah, Boss?" Mac asked.

"What do you prefer to drink?"

Nothing.

Mac didn't drink at all.

He also couldn't refuse a boss. Refusing was as bad as shunning. It screamed foul and rude for a man to reject a boss when he was being gracious with his time and space. Men earned themselves bullets for ungrateful behavior.

"Whiskey, neat," Mac lied.

"I'll have that ready for you, *soldato*."

"Here you are, sir," a mousey-looking girl said.

Mac took the glass of whiskey she offered with a smile. The girl didn't return it. The only reason Mac thought of her as a girl and not a woman was because she seemed far too young to be working in someone's home as a maid ... or whatever she was. Her tiny frame did little to fill out the uniform she wore, her small hands were fit for a child, and her quiet voice barely broke a whisper. A child was more like it. The top of the girl's head barely reached Mac's chest.

She was dressed like the people who had cleaned his shoes earlier in the night had been clothed, with a drab gray uniform, black shoes, and her hair pulled back tight. She didn't look him in the eye, kept her head down, and scurried from the room like someone might snap her with a stick the moment Luca cleared his throat.

"Amusing, isn't it?" Luca asked.

Mac stared in the direction the girl had gone. What about that was amusing?

"How old is she?" Mac asked, curious.

Luca tilted his head to the side like he was considering the question. "About how old would you say, Enzo?"

Enzo glanced up from the book he was looking over on Luca's large, cherry-colored oak desk. "Marcus said fifteen when he sent her. If he was being truthful, then she's about sixteen now."

Mac recognized the name Marcus as belonging to Luca's father-in-law. What he didn't understand was the rest of Luca's words. *Sent her?*

Luca must have noticed the confusion cracking Mac's stony mask. "My wife's father has a hand in a few different … trades."

"Like diamonds," Mac said.

"Ah, you've been doing your homework," Luca said, a teasing praise coloring his tone.

It didn't sound entirely innocent.

Matthew chuckled. "Nothing wrong with that, Mac. It's good to know who you're meeting. Don't believe everything you're told out there on the streets. More often than not, by the time a story has made it to the people outside of this house, it's been changed and exaggerated so much that more of it is lies than it is truth."

"Or," Enzo drawled, smirking wickedly, "… it's entirely true and whatever it was that happened is so shocking, people don't trust that anyone will believe them, regardless if they are being honest or not."

Luca laughed darkly, tilting his glass towards his men. "Always on point, boys."

The camaraderie between the men was just about the only thing that felt normal to Mac. He honestly believed that Luca was close, if not best friends, with his underboss and consigliere. There had to be a certain level of trust between the three for them to work together, after all.

A quiet Guido sipped a glass of spiced rum as he sat in a corner chair, watching the exchange with a guarded gaze and nothing more.

"As I was saying," Luca said, turning back to give his attention to Mac. "My father-in-law has a hand in a few trades. He fancies himself a hero of sorts. One of his trades often crosses paths with an auction of sorts."

"And that girl comes into any of this how?" Mac asked, carefully choosing his words.

"They're gifts, of course. Marcus believes he's saving them when he can, taking them from something horrible, and putting them somewhere better. It's the best they can have with no names, no history, and no real life. If you understand what I mean, Mac."

He couldn't be talking about …

Was he?

"Trafficked humans," Mac said quietly.

Both Enzo and Matthew watched Mac as if they were assessing his tone and reaction to the news. Mac refused to let them see how disgusted the idea of trafficked souls actually made him. There was nothing he could do about the girl, or the other people he'd met earlier. And if he believed what Luca told him, then they were treated far better here than they would be elsewhere.

"Well, the term used at auction is 'slaves'," Luca explained, sounding entirely bored. "At least, that's how Marcus described it. He's known to trade certain things for the ones he believes can be saved, for whatever reason. Occasionally, he sends them here. My wife is good with them—she's had her own experience in all that nonsense, but I won't get into that."

Mac took some sense of comfort in knowing the … *slaves* … were treated well, and that Luca's wife took care of them in some way. It still didn't settle quite right, but Mac didn't have a choice but to drop it.

"As I said," Luca added, shrugging, "I find them amusing."

Mac swallowed hard, lifted his glass to hide the bobbing of his Adam's apple, and pretended to take a sip of whiskey. When Luca spun on his heel to chat with his two men for a moment, and Guido's attention was diverted to the boss, Mac tipped his glass into the bamboo tree in the corner, and dumped out a quarter of the contents.

Drinking was not an option for Mac. He would fake it for someone else's benefit—or to trick a man, if a situation called for it—but he wouldn't willingly drink. Not after watching his drunk of a father use alcohol like a crutch for most of his life.

By the time the boss's attention was back on Mac, nothing looked amiss. The glass of whiskey was back up to Mac's mouth as if he was taking another drink.

"So, let's chat," Luca said.

"I'd be happy to," Mac replied. "I just don't know about what exactly, Boss."

"Your female, for one."

"Melina."

Luca's nose crinkled like he'd smelled something bad. "I'm aware of Miss Morgan's name. How did you come about dating an escort, anyway?"

"We met at an event we both attended and hit it off. Luck, I guess."

It wasn't a total lie.

"And how long have you been dating?" Luca asked.

That was a difficult question.

Thankfully, Mac had an answer prepared. "Time kind of bleeds with Melina. You don't really notice it passing by."

"Your Capo wasn't aware that you had a girl."

"Mac's always been quiet about that sort of thing," Guido said from the corner.

Luca ignored the older gentleman, keeping his attention on only Mac. "And do you often allow your females to behave abhorrently in both their career choices and personal life?"

"What's wrong with Melina's job?"

"She's a whore," Enzo said, scoffing.

Matthew nodded his agreement. "A little checking is all it takes to find out who she's been … working, so to speak."

Luca waved at his men. "There you go. Doesn't it bother you at all?"

"That she needed to support herself and did so how she could?" Mac asked quietly. "No, that doesn't bother me at all."

"Call a whore a whore, Mac," Luca said.

It took all Mac had inside him to keep from barking at the Pivetti Don that Melina was no man's whore, and she didn't deserve the title. What in the fuck was his problem with Melina, anyway? "As far as I know, she wasn't fucking men for money, Boss."

"But it's possible."

Mac chuckled. "You should spend some time with my girl. She's not the kind of woman who has a price, Boss."

Guido snorted, and then shrugged when all eyes turned on him. "Sorry, but Mac has a point. Melina is quite … headstrong and independent. She doesn't scream 'hooker' to me. Sure, the job is a little questionable, but maybe she's one of those girls who doesn't need to fuck to earn her buck, Boss. That's all I'm saying."

Again, Luca ignored Guido.

"Well, her father was quite sick, and essentially tossed aside by the government after he'd done his duty for this godforsaken country," Luca murmured. "I can see how she would need something to support him with his medical issues, as well as her own home. I'll let the job pass, Mac, but you'll do well to keep her from going back to something similar."

Mac took that info in. He hadn't known that. Somehow, Luca did. That told Mac the boss had been looking into Melina. What was it that he'd mentioned earlier before they came up here to chat?

Military?

Yes, that was it.

"After the mess with the cops," Mac said quickly, "my girl knows that the escorting really isn't an option anymore. As far as the behavior you mentioned on the personal side of things, I'm just guessing here, but you must be talking about Vin. I handled that, Boss. Both on his side of things, and hers."

Luca smiled like that pleased him. "Good. The cops have me concerned."

"Me, too."

"Probably not in the same way. This girl of yours … she practically comes out of nowhere. I asked about the length of your relationship because I want to make sure she hasn't been planted or—"

"Absolutely not," Mac interrupted.

Luca cocked a brow. "I beg your pardon?"

The coldness in the man's tone might as well have slapped Mac in the face. "Sorry, Boss, no offense meant … I just get a little touchy when people start climbing my girl's back about that nonsense. She's no rat, and she's not a fucking cop wearing a pretty dress. She's just a girl— mine. Hell, she put a bullet in a man for me."

Luca sucked in a heavy breath, watching Mac closely as he said, "Yes, Tip. I'd heard about that unfortunate event."

"He had it coming."

The faintest hint of a smile tugged at the corner of Luca's mouth. "You do realize that had it been you who put a bullet into a made man, I would have returned the favor."

Silence covered the room in a heavy, awkward blanket.

Mac nodded once. "I wouldn't expect anything different."

"I'm glad we got that cleared up, then," Luca replied. "But on the topic of your *girl* ..."

All over again, Mac got the distinct impression that Luca wasn't fond of Melina and had no intention of ever liking her. Mac had heard stories of how difficult the boss could be when it came to accepting newcomers into his folds. To Luca, Mac probably wasn't considered an outsider, what with his old family ties to Cosa Nostra, his father's involvement, Mac's own work, and whatever Guido had been saying about him.

But Melina?

She was nobody to Luca.

"What about her, Boss?"

"I'm sure you know some of the details concerning her family history, yes?" Luca questioned quietly.

"Yes," Mac lied.

Praying to God up above that Luca wouldn't question specific details, Mac almost missed Luca's reply.

"Then you know to be careful with her," Luca said. "We all must be careful with whom we associate and have around, Mac. You, more than anyone, should be aware of that little fact, what with the effort you've put into keeping a distance between your father and yourself."

Guido coughed in the corner, dropping his gaze down.

Luca passed the man a cool stare. "Although, I must say, I was surprised to learn that one of Guido's best *soldatos* happened to come from filth like James Maccari."

Mac let the comment roll off his shoulders.

Guido shrugged. "I told you, Boss, I didn't think the kid was ready."

What?

Mac almost shouted the question out loud, but somehow managed to keep it inside his head. His Capo, the man who taught Mac practically everything about the streets and how to run them, didn't think he was ready?

When had hell frozen over?

What was Guido trying to prove?

"Yes, well," Luca muttered, setting his glass to the table, "… you've not given him much of a choice but to be noticed now, Guido. First the truck incident with Anthony's territory, then the girl, and now the Tip nonsense. Frankly, you couldn't have done a better job of bringing him to my attention, had you asked him to jump my fence and try to get past the guard dogs."

Mac's brow flew high at that statement. "You have dogs?"

"Yes. Another gift from my father-in-law. Beautiful creatures."

"Vicious creatures, you mean," Guido mumbled around the rim of his glass. "Little bastards."

Luca smiled a cruel sight. "Ah, watch it, Guido, or I'll have you be their babysitter the next time I have to leave the city for some time."

Guido's mouth snapped shut instantly.

Mac chuckled under his breath, but it quickly faded when Luca turned on him again.

"My first inclination is not to trust your woman," the Don said honestly. "Given what I know about her and also what I don't know about her, I can't see my opinion changing. There is an unfortunate amount of attention on her right now from the official side of things, so I will be keeping watch."

"Like you already have been?" Mac asked.

"Noticed, did you?"

"I'd be dead if I didn't notice things."

"Good point," Luca said, flashing a grin. "Be that as it may, I am still watching, Mac. And if I happen to find even one thing on that woman that could bring harm to my children, my wife, or my Cosa Nostra, I will put her down like a dog."

"There's nothing to find," Mac said, willing away the sudden thickness in his throat.

"There had better not be, or you'll find yourself in a grave next to hers." Luca flicked his hand in Mac's direction as if to dismiss him. His next words sealed the deal. "Go, enjoy the evening. Find your woman and make sure she behaved while you were away from her side. I'm sure this won't be our last encounter, Mac."

Mac smirked. "I hope not. Just maybe for a different reason next time."

"Keep working at it," Luca replied. "Good men get noticed, Mac, but the honorable ones get the button. While you're downstairs, I suggest you begin working on the honor side of things by finding Anthony and working some kind of arrangement out that pleases him to make up for the truck and money incident."

"Yes, do that," Guido echoed, smiling a little too slyly.

Mac shot his Capo a hard look he hoped voiced his anger. Guido went back to drinking like nothing was amiss.

"Mac?" Luca asked.

"Yeah, Boss?"

"I said you were to leave. It wasn't a request."

Mac got the point. He disappeared from the room before he needed to be told again, and dumped the remainder of his whiskey into another plant as he passed it by in the hallway.

Now, he had to find Melina.

His little doll wasn't going to like what he'd just learned. His concern over her safety was now at a critical level. Luca had eyes on Melina, and the man seemed almost intent on finding something awful on her. Something worthy of killing her.

Mac couldn't—wouldn't—let that happen. Melina hadn't asked for this. She was innocent. A bystander that got caught up in something that had little to nothing to do with her life. The chance of Mac being able to cut his ties with Melina and let her go scot-free was unlikely, too. Luca might take that as a sign of Mac's dwindling care for the woman and decide to take her out if he felt she was still a liability.

Goddammit.

Plus ... her family history.

What was that about?

Everything about this night felt ten shades of wrong to Mac.

But he still had shit to do.

CHAPTER SEVENTEEN

Neeya Pivetti was an interesting woman.

Regal.

Strong.

Melina liked her and she was fairly certain the Pivetti Don's wife was warming up to her as well. That still didn't take away the fact that she was a guest in a hostile environment.

An unwelcome guest.

Though Neeya had done her best to engage Melina in conversation and patron her presence, nothing could make Melina forget her brief encounter with Luca Pivetti. The man didn't like her. That much was obvious and normally she wouldn't have cared, but things were different when a man that didn't like you was a Cosa Nostra Don that knew things about a past you didn't advertise.

Yeah. That was when things got sticky.

Melina had enough problems in her life. The last thing she needed was Luca added to the mix. And what about Mac? He'd been gone for a lot longer than she'd expected him to be and that could only mean one of two things. His meeting was going very well or had gone very badly and her would-be "boyfriend," was on his way to a body bag.

Grabbing another glass of champagne from a passing waiter, Melina gulped it down in an effort to calm her nerves. Mac was a big boy. He could take care of himself. She'd seen that firsthand, but this wasn't just an everyday occurrence. From the moment they'd entered the Pivetti monstrosity of a mansion, the stakes had been upped. It had been a long time since Melina had prayed, but if sending up a few words to the Big Man Upstairs was what it took to get her and Mac out of here breathing, she was willing to do just that.

"Doll, you look a little tipsy."

Melina's eyes flew to Mac's face. His hand rested possessively just above the swell of her ass but he wasn't looking at her. Instead, his attention was focused across the room on a dark-haired man with a slight build. A burning cigar was held between his lips as he engaged in conversation with a waitress.

"How do you know how I look when your attention is across the room?"

The words came out more harshly than she intended for them to. Mac smirked before his eyes locked onto her in a bold stare. She swallowed hard.

"Just because I'm not always looking at you, doesn't mean I don't see."

"And exactly what does that mean? More cryptic mob talk?"

A furrow formed between Mac's brows and for the first time, she noticed the unease that hung between them.

"Mac, what's wrong?" she asked him.

He sighed. "A lot of things, doll, but we'll handle them however they come."

"What aren't you telling me?"

Mac glanced around before he took her hand and led her away. He was walking so fast she was having a hard time keeping up with him. He was holding her hand so tight she could feel the tension in his body. This wasn't the Mac she knew. The Mac she knew was confident to the tee and unafraid of anything. The man holding her hand now was strung up tighter than a steer at a rodeo. With purposeful steps, he led her down a short hallway, haphazardly opening up doors as they went and peeking inside. When they came to almost the end of the hallway, Mac opened a door and pulled her inside before shutting and locking the door behind them.

Melina jerked away from his grasp and he let her. She watched him as he stood silently leaning against the wall, arms folded. He watched her but said nothing.

"Mac?"

He pushed off the wall and came towards her in one fluid motion. As he pulled her towards him, Melina cocked a brow.

"I'll explain everything but first…" he trailed off.

"First what?" she whispered.

"I need you."

His lips met hers in an open-mouthed kiss that had a hint of whiskey and desperation.

Mac didn't drink. Ever. He had mentioned that to Melina during their evening together when she'd asked about having some wine brought up with food.

Something was very wrong. She pulled away.

"Mac, whiskey?"

Ignoring her question, he kissed her again with no hint of gentleness. His mouth sought to dominate hers and for once, Melina let down her guard. It didn't matter what had happened or what would happen. Right now, she was in the arms of a man who wanted her, who needed her. And deep in the back of her mind, Melina was slowly starting to think she might need him, too.

With his hard body pressed into hers, one of his hands slid down her waist to pull up the hem of her dress. She glanced at their surroundings and noticed they were in a small bedroom. A queen-sized bed on a dais dominated the room.

"We've got a bed," she whispered against his lips.

"Why do you think I picked this room, doll?"

Rolling her eyes, Melina allowed Mac to guide them over to the bed but just as the back of her legs hit the bed, she spun around and pushed Mac down. His hands grabbed her waist bringing her with him. Pushing against his chest, Melina straddled him.

"I don't know what's gotten into you, but I think it's time I reminded you exactly what kind of woman you're dealing with."

Mac smirked as Melina reached for his pants with deft hands. Undoing the top button, she lowered his zipper and reached inside, freeing him from the confines of his pants. He was hard and thick in her hand and growing larger as she slowly stroked him. Below her, Mac gritted his teeth. She loved the power he let her have over him and the way he willingly ceded his control to her. But Melina sensed he didn't need her to be an alpha female right now. What Mac needed was to reassert his dominance.

Releasing her grip on his cock, Melina rolled to lie beside him and pulled her dress up over her hips. Then she turned and kissed Mac. He pulled back to look at her.

"What are you doing?" he asked.

"Giving you what you need. I don't know what happened in your meeting, but instincts don't lie. My instincts are telling me that right now you don't need me to challenge you. All you need is for me to be your lover."

His stared at her long and hard before his hand came up to caress her cheek. Melina leaned into his touch.

"You never cease to surprise me, Melina."

"Keeps things interesting, doesn't it?"

"In more ways than one."

Mac's mouth crashed down on hers and Melina kissed him back, nipping at his lips. Her body relaxed as he pushed her back firmly against the bed. When she felt the brush of his fingertips at her hip bone, she moaned. Their kiss deepened as he eased the scrap of black lace down her hips. Melina lifted up off the bed to allow Mac to pull her panties all the way down her legs, before he tossed them onto the floor.

"Open for me, Melina."

She gasped as his warm fingers found her wet slit, exploring and stroking. Mac's tongue teased hers in the same way his fingers were. Thick and strong, his digits swept over her folds as his thumb worked her clit. Her body burned to have his cock inside of her. Melina whimpered when his mouth left hers. His lips trailed down her neck and she pulled him closer, silently urging him to take what she offered.

When his mouth replaced his fingers between her legs, she bit her lip to keep from crying out. With the tip of his tongue, he teased her soft lips before licking her slit greedily from front to back. Melina's thighs trembled as he leisurely tasted her. Pleasure hummed through her body, building in intensity with every hot lap of his tongue between her legs.

This was crazy.

Absolutely fucking crazy.

They were in the residence of a Cosa Nostra Don, locked in a room where Mac was eating her pussy like his life depended on it. He sucked her clit into his mouth hard and Melina came apart.

"*Mac.*"

Her body trembled as the force of the orgasm shook her to the core. Why was it that every time this man touched her, she lost her sanity? He kissed her and she tasted herself on him, tart and forbidden. When he shifted atop her and thrust inside of her with one smooth motion, she wrapped her legs around his waist. He pounded into her, and she met him thrust for thrust. Mac's eyes held hers as he took her, scorching her with the intensity of his gaze.

Her hands held onto his shoulders as he

pumped in and out of her welcoming heat. The hard, thick length of his cock touched every aching spot inside of her as the tempo of their fucking came faster and faster. Mac's breath came out in harsh pants and just as the force of another orgasm made her cry out, he grunted his own release above her. Collapsing atop her, she stroked his back as both of them struggled to breathe.

"Damn it, Melina. This wasn't …"

His words are cut off as the sound of a doorknob turning stopped them cold.

"Is someone in there?" a voice called from the other side.

She recognized it at once.

Neeya Pivetti.

"Get dressed," Melina ordered.

Pushing Mac off her, she got off the bed and searched for her underwear. She found the lacy panties lying next to the bed and quickly slipped them on before she smoothed down her dress. Melina spared a glance at Mac, who was up and straightening his own attire. She had no mirror to see how she looked, but she could imagine that she had a case of bedhead that nothing could explain away.

"Hello?" Neeya's voice came again. This time, there was a hint of anger.

Running her fingers through her hair in a half-hearted attempt to look presentable, Melina finally gave up and rushed over to unlock and open the door. Neeya Pivetti stood in the hall, arms crossed. When she saw Melina, the look of annoyance on her face disappeared briefly as she cocked a brow.

"Melina, is something wrong?"

Melina shook her head. "No. I just needed—"

"We just needed a few moments to talk privately. Please forgive us for encroaching on your hospitality, Mrs. Pivetti," Mac said smoothly.

Melina forced a smile as his arm slipped around her

waist in a firm but gentle grasp.

Neeya glanced from Melina to Mac and back again as an eyebrow lifted in silent understanding. The hint of a smile ghosted across her lips.

"Then I hope your talk went well," their host finally said.

Melina didn't miss the undercurrent to Neeya's words.

"It did, so we should return to the festivities now. I wouldn't want us to be missed," Mac said.

Neeya nodded. "I agree, but first Melina might want to fix her hair."

Patting Melina's arm, Neeya walked away. Melina closed her eyes, certain that her cheeks were burning bright red. Behind her Mac, laughed softly. She spun around to face him, hands on her hips.

"It's not funny. Neeya and I were getting along, and now I have no doubt you've got her thinking I'm some kind of slut that fucks around in other people's homes."

Mac's eyes crinkled at the corners as he gently ran his fingers through her thick hair.

"Did I tell you how much I love these highlights in your hair? They really bring out how beautiful your skin is."

"Mac!"

"I heard you, doll. Neeya doesn't think you're a slut. If anything, she's probably wondering if I made it worth your while. If she ever asks, you can tell her I left you well satisfied."

Melina swatted his hand away and he stopped smiling. His mask was back in place and she swallowed hard. She could feel the coldness emanating from him once again. The man who'd just taken her so fiercely was gone and in his place was a soldier navigating his way on a constantly changing battlefield. Mac wore the look of a man trying to survive against all odds. Melina knew that look all too well.

"We need to get going," he said.

She nodded, sensing that now was not the time to argue with him. "Okay."

Melina allowed Mac to lead her from the bedroom. She expected Mac to lead them back towards the hustle and bustle of the gathering. When he headed in the opposite direction, she slowed her pace.

"Keep walking, doll."

"I thought we were going back to the party."

"If you want to keep breath in that beautiful body of yours, then I suggest you stop questioning me and let's get the hell out of here."

Mac pulled on her arm, but Melina stood firm.

"I don't know what's going on but if you don't stop manhandling me, I'm going to ram these stilettos in your groin and make you a eunuch."

"Damn it, Melina. Luca Pivetti wants you dead. Now please, sweetheart, let me get you out of here."

Luca Pivetti wanted her dead.

Fear exploded, bitter and hot in Melina's mouth. Her eyes flew to Mac's face. His eyes were hard, but there in just the shadows beneath was a touch of something she'd never seen from him.

Fear.

Swallowing hard, Melina nodded her head. "Okay."

Mac's hand closed around her waist and he nudged her forward. It was all Melina could do not to stumble as he all but forced her down the hallway. She couldn't believe what was happening. Her life was in danger. As if it wasn't bad enough that the cops were dogging her every move, now a Cosa Nostra boss wanted her dead. Tears blurred in her eyes, but she refused to let them fall. She couldn't show weakness.

Not now.

Not ever.

But she was scared. More scared than she had ever

been in her life. There had to be a reason that Luca Pivetti had it out for her and one way or another, Mac was going to tell her what the hell was going on. The entrance they'd come in loomed ahead of them.

Freedom.

And then the man Mac had been watching earlier appeared. His steely green gaze swung from Mac to her. She didn't like the way his eyes roved over, measuring her worth like a prized mare he was considering breeding with. As they came closer, he offered her a thin smile.

"Mac."

"Corelli."

Melina could feel Mac stiffening behind her. His grip tightened on her waist and she was sure before she made it home tonight, she was going to have bruises that looked like Mac's fingers.

"I don't think I've had the pleasure of being introduced to your beautiful companion this evening," the man said.

Melina didn't like the look of him. He reminded her of a weasel, sneaky and unpredictable.

"Melina, this is Anthony Corelli. Skip, this is my girlfriend, Melina Morgan."

Anthony graced Melina with a predatory smile before offering his hand. The last thing she wanted to do was allow the slick bastard to touch her, but at this point there was no reason to piss off another connected man.

"Melina, no wonder Mac has been hiding you. If I had a woman as gorgeous as you, I wouldn't want to have other men looking at you, either."

He took her hand and brought it to his lips. Revulsion bubbled up in her stomach, but she forced a quick smile.

"Mac is not to blame for hiding me away. If anything, I've been keeping him busy."

Corelli's lips lingered on her skin for longer than she would have liked before he released her hand. His brow raised.

"Is that so?" he asked, directing his question towards Mac.

"You're looking at her. What man wouldn't be smitten with Melina? Beautiful, quick-witted, entertaining. I've stumbled upon a rare woman."

Melina smiled, quietly touched by Mac's vocal praise of her. She knew that they were still playing a game, trying to maintain their image as a couple but it was more than that. His lips pressed a quick kiss to her forehead and she leaned into his touch. Anthony Corelli watched the exchange between the two of them, missing nothing.

"Indeed, you have. A man can't help but be envious," Corelli said.

Mac laughed. "A man like you, Skip?"

The dark haired man lifted his shoulders in a small shrug. "Perhaps."

"We all have our crosses to bear, but I'm glad we were able to speak before Melina and I departed," Mac said.

"Is that so?"

"Yes. I owe you a debt and I intend to repay it."

"Ah, yes. The unfortunate incident that went awry. I'd wondered when you'd get around to that."

Melina glanced at Mac. His eyes went dark. No doubt there was some bad blood between him and Corelli.

Just great.

Another problem to add to their ever growing list.

"I'm a man of my word. Whatever debt I owe, I will repay."

"A Maccari that's a man of his word. That will be a nice change of pace."

The atmosphere changed and Melina was sure that if she didn't do something, Mac would do something he might not live to regret.

"Mac's the most honorable man I've met in a long time. If he gives you his word, he's good for it," she said.

Anthony smiled at her. "It's rare to find a woman who will step up and defend her man so passionately."

"Not many men are worth defending."

"Indeed they aren't," Anthony conceded.

"I will make arrangements for the drop as soon as I have it," Mac finally said.

"I'm sure, but perhaps you might be more amenable to a different arrangement. Some things are worth more than money, after all."

Anthony's pointed gaze fell on Melina, openly eyeing her breasts. His gaze was that of a man eager to sample some new fare. The unspoken question he was asking Mac hung heavy in the air between them.

A whore.

That's all she was to any of them.

It didn't matter that they thought she was beautiful. At the end of the day, she was nothing to them. A commodity to be used and then discarded and branded. The black and white truth of the matter stabbed Melina in the heart like an ice pick. Quickly, she turned away and buried her face in Mac's shoulder in an effort to get her warring emotions under control.

"With all due respect, Melina is mine and mine alone." Mac's hand stroked her back in a soothing manner.

"Understood."

"Good. Have a good evening, sir."

Melina straightened in Mac's arms and gave Antony a withering glare.

"To you as well. It was a pleasure meeting you, Melina. Perhaps our paths will cross again."

With a lingering smile, Corelli started walking

back down the hall towards the party. Melina breathed a deep sigh and wasted no time reaching for the front door that would let them out. Mac followed behind, neither of them speaking until they were in his car and away from the monstrous estate.

"Are you all right, doll?"

The word hung in her throat. "No."

"I didn't figure you were. I know that you can handle a lot, Melina, but even you must be near your breaking point right now," Mac said.

She sighed. "I need to understand what's going on. Why does Luca Pivetti want me dead?"

"It's complicated."

"Well fucking simplify it, Mac. This is my life we're talking about."

"It's like this, in the short time you and I have crossed paths, you stirred up a lot of shit. The cops arrested you outside of Guido's club and you killed a made man."

Melina folded her arms in the darkness. "What's your point?"

"Luca Pivetti hasn't gotten to where he is by being stupid. He's careful and runs a tight ship. No outsiders. And then here you are unleashing a firestorm, so he has to wonder exactly what your motives are," Mac explained.

"My motives."

"Yes. In his mind you're either just a whore I let get too close or you're undercover. Either way, to him, that puts your head on the chopping block."

Melina gritted her teeth. This was complete and utter bullshit. "I am the last person in the world who would work with those pigs on anything. I'd rather go to jail."

Mac's hand found hers and gripped it tight as they stopped at a red light. Leaning over the space between them, he kissed her cheek. "I know that because I know you, but no one else does. Luca is just being cautious, like he's always done."

"I don't care. I'm tired of people taking one look at me and assuming they know who the hell I am or what my story is. I'm no one's whore. I've never had sex unless it was what I wanted to do and even in those cases, there was never any money involved. I take care of my damn self."

"These days, it's easier to assume than for people to bother to take time, but it's their loss. I don't want you to take any of this to heart, doll. It's cutthroat, but in the end it's really just about business."

"Business? It's business to call a woman a whore, while at the same time, having a wife at home and women on the side you fuck? It's business to proposition a man to sleep with his girlfriend like she's some damned piece of meat to be passed around? Well, excuse me but I don't care for this particular business, Mac."

"Cosa Nostra is … something else."

"Mac, I've always had to fight and sometimes you just get tired."

"No one understands that better than me, but listen to me, Melina. Cosa Nostra is all about how things are perceived. It's ugly and unfair how you've been dragged so far into this, but I'm going to protect you. All eyes are going to be on us even more than they already are. I need to stay close to you, and I need you not to fight me on this."

"How close?"

"Closer than your own shadow." He squeezed her hand.

"I'm used to having my own space."

"I know that, and I've done my best to respect that, but that can't go on any longer, Melina. My presence will ensure that even though you're being watched, everything is on the up and up with you. Besides, I'd like to spend a little more time with you."

"You would?" she asked.

"Of course I would. There's so much about you I don't know."

She didn't like where this line of conversation was leading.

"There's not much to know."

"I think there is, starting with your father."

"He's dead."

"Stop hedging, doll. Luca brought him up for a reason, so how about you tell me why a Cosa Nostra Don is so interested in a dead veteran."

CHAPTER EIGHTEEN

"Your place or mine?" Mac asked.

Melina twisted her hands in her lap, watching the buildings pass by as the car flew down the road. "Mine, I guess. You might as well see the inside, seeing as how you've been hanging around the outside enough."

Mac chuckled. "You were listening, after all."

"I listen, Mac."

"Me, too," Mac murmured. "So, here's what I've heard coming from you, even if you aren't outright saying it."

Melina cleared her throat, seeming surprised. "Try me."

"You're frightened and worried because you don't know how to handle what's happening around you, or how to control it. You're out of your element, your safe place where you are top dog, and that's unsettled you. You're uncomfortable with how you were treated by the men at the Pivetti mansion, while the wives were respected like little queens. How close am I?"

"How do you do that?"

"You're not so hard to read, doll."

Melina scowled. "I like to think I am."

"You're like ice to me. Crystal-clear, strong, and cold all over."

"Ouch."

Mac flashed a smile. "I never said I didn't like it."

"I'm not always cold, thank you."

"No, you're certainly not. I had you pretty hot earlier, didn't I?"

Melina's cheeks tinted with a light pink. "Hey, now—"

"Keep your bark, Melina."

"Mac!"

"Save the bite for later," he finished with a wink.

Melina huffed, crossed her arms, and glared at him from the passenger seat. "Does this really seem like the right time for you to go on with your usual cockiness? Do I look like I'm in the mood for any of that?"

"You look like you need a break," Mac answered honestly.

And she did.

Melina's eyes were tired, her usual fight was dulled. She wasn't sitting as straight as she usually would in her seat, and a wariness emanated from her.

"So," he continued, drawling out his words, "... forgive me if I'm trying to make you relax a little bit, doll."

"Relax, huh?"

"Yes. It seems as though we're going to be spending a lot of time together in the near future, and not all of it will be fun. Relax. Get comfortable. Right now, we're safe. Chill the fuck out and don't sweat the rest."

"Easy for you to say," Melina muttered. "No one wants to kill you."

"You do realize that my public statements about being with you put me on the same platform as you, right?" Mac asked quietly. "Calling you mine, vouching for you, and bringing you into the fold like I did, makes me responsible for you, Melina. If Luca decides to pull the trigger on you, then I will quickly follow."

Melina quieted in her seat. "Oh."

"Yeah, 'oh'."

"I didn't know it was like that."

"The mob sees a man for what he is underneath his charming smile and nice clothes. A human—one with a word and blood. If his word can't be trusted, then his blood can be spilled. You have my word, Melina. Please let me keep the blood from spilling, too."

"Okay," she whispered.

"That all you got?"

Melina sighed. "No, but I'm too tired and confused to come up with something better. I think relaxing sounds pretty damn good right now."

"I agree. How big is your bathtub?"

"Excuse me?"

"Your bathtub. How big is it?"

"Big enough," she replied.

"For two?"

Melina glanced away, but Mac had seen the hint of her smile before she did. "I guess we'll find out."

"I guess we will, doll."

***

"This was not what I thought you had in mind when you asked if my tub could fit two people," Melina said softly.

Mac grinned, continuing his massaging of Melina's ankles and calves from the other side of the large bathtub. Her smooth, caramel skin, wet from the hot water and bubbles, felt like satin under his fingers and palms.

"Is that so?" he asked.

"I thought ... well, never mind."

"Sex. You thought I wanted sex."

Melina shrugged. "Don't most men?"

"Haven't you figured it out yet, doll?"

"You're not most men," she said, sinking lower under the water.

"Well, I try not to be." Mac laughed a husky chuckle. "I won't deny that I'm not thinking about sex with you in this tub right now, but that's not what you need."

Melina opened one eye, watching Mac over the mounds of bubbles and sloshing water. "How do you know what I need?"

"The same way that you knew what I needed earlier at the Pivetti mansion. It's no different. People pick up on things, doll. Now, shut that pretty mouth and let me work here."

She did, but not without a playful glare.

Mac went back to his exploration of Melina's legs. Her quiet little moans filled the bathroom as he massaged away the stress in her muscles and washed her mile-long legs.

"A good man always takes care of his girl," Mac said quietly.

Melina's eyes opened again at those words. "But I'm not really your girl, Mac."

"So? I should still take care of you."

"What if I was?"

"My girl?" Mac asked.

"Yes."

Mac cocked a brow, eyeing Melina as she grabbed a loofa off the ledge of the tub and began dropping dollops of milky-colored body wash onto the frilly cloth. "I don't understand what you're asking."

Melina drew the loofa over her arms, covering her slick skin in white suds. "If I was your girl, then what would you do, Mac?"

Ah.

Mac smiled, leaned forward, and snatched the loofa from Melina's hand. He ignored her quiet "hey" and started running the loofa up and down her legs with smooth, long strokes.

"Mac, I asked you a question," Melina said.

"I would spoil you rotten," Mac said, shooting her a look through his hair that had fallen down over his gaze. "Whatever you wanted, whether you needed it or not, I would make it happen. I'd make damn sure you felt as beautiful as you looked, regardless of what you needed to feel that way. I'd take you out every chance I could, just to show you off to the people who can't have you because you're all mine. But I'd have my fucking hands on you all night, so that they'd know to stay away. It'd probably feel like my fingerprints were burned into your skin because I'd be holding you that tight."

Melina's tongue peeked out to wet her bottom lip. "What else?"

"I'd always keep an eye on you, even if you didn't know I was doing it, just to make sure you were good and safe. I'd wake you up in the morning, every single morning, with my hands all over you and my mouth kissing all the spots I could find. I'd make sure that whenever you were stressed out, or something was on your mind—bothering you—that you could take some time away from life and the world to be just you again. Simple stuff, you know."

"Simple." Melina scoffed. "Right. That sounds more like worshipping, Mac."

Mac didn't see the difference. "If a man cares enough, worshipping his woman should be the simplest, easiest, and most obvious thing for him to do every day, doll. She should be the most important thing on his mind. The first and last thing he considers every day and night."

Melina's gaze flitted from Mac's face and then down to the bubbly water. "Oh."

Oddly, it bothered Mac like nothing else that he could tell Melina had never been given the pleasure of having a man treasure her like she should be treasured. No one had every loved her enough to worship the very ground she walked on, or had seen her for the beautiful gift she truly was.

It nagged in his chest.

Poked at him like a needle.

Over and over.

Like a damned tattoo was being penned permanently to his skin, reminding him that Melina deserved someone who would treasure and treat her the way she should be cared for. Didn't he have enough going on where this girl was concerned, without adding something like that to the pile as well?

Mac sighed, shaking off the strange feeling. "I suppose it doesn't matter, anyway."

Melina sucked in a quiet breath before asking, "Why not?"

"You're not mine, doll. Or at least, you don't want to be."

Melina didn't respond, but she wouldn't meet Mac's eyes again.

He continued washing her stress away.

Mac didn't need a response.

Mac lifted the cup of coffee to his lips and took a sip of the hot liquid. The coffee settled on his tongue, heady and bitter, as he took in Melina's apartment again. The place was in need of decorating, as it was just the basics for furniture and the walls were bare. With several wide, large windows overlooking a quiet part of the city, it had a great view. Mac bet the place looked spectacular in the morning, with sunlight flooding in through the glass and spiraling across the hardwood floors.

"Admiring my view, huh?"

Mac spun on his heel at Melina's uncharacteristically soft voice. She stood in a simple cotton shorts and tank ensemble. Her bare toes wiggled against the hardwood floors as she watched him with a smile.

"It's pretty nice," Mac admitted. "You're higher up than I realized."

"Do the heights bother you?"

"Not a bit. Besides, a bit of fear keeps a man awake. What doesn't kill you, and all that nonsense."

Melina laughed. "You have a funny way of looking at things."

"Yeah, I try. I was wondering about something else, though."

"Shoot."

"The cost of this place," Mac said, carefully choosing his words. Melina was not the kind of woman who would like a man pointing out that she had clearly picked an apartment that was far above her price range. Independence and all that garbage. "Can you afford it?"

Melina's lips drew thin. Instantly, Mac wondered if he had stepped over a line.

"I could have afforded it, before, when I first got it," Melina admitted.

Mac frowned. "And now you can't because you have to give up the escorting."

"Probably. Twelve-month lease says I'm still on the hook."

"Damn," Mac said, feeling a weight press down on his shoulders.

Responsibility was a bitch.

One Mac didn't know how to shake. In a roundabout way, his involvement in Melina's life forced her into a bad situation. She had to give up her job, she was left with a place she couldn't afford for long, and now she had a mark on her head that could put her into an early grave if Mac couldn't get the attention from Luca Pivetti to wane.

It was shitty all the way around the board.

Melina, seemingly seeing the guilt raging on Mac's features, said, "Don't worry about it. I'll figure something out. I am nothing, if not a survivor. I don't know how to fail."

"Easier said than done, doll," Mac settled on saying.

"I was thinking about something."

The strange softness in Melina's tone had Mac turning to look at her again. "What's that?"

"What you said earlier to me."

"In the bath."

"Yeah," Melina murmured.

Mac ignored the heat traveling through his body at warp speed. His little plan to let Melina relax and be cared for instead of worrying about the stress and craziness surrounding them had left him with a semi-erection that just wouldn't go down, no matter how hard he tried. Touching this woman, cleaning her, listening to her little sighs and her sweet voice while they were close in a bath of hot, soapy water had been perfect. It had also taken all the control Mac had inside of him not to reach out, pull Melina into his lap, and fuck her raw.

Once they were out of the bath, dressed again, and some time had passed, Mac was still semi-hard. But he was able to disregard it with some distance between them.

"What about it?" Mac asked.

"I thought about what you said," Melina replied quietly. "You know, about what you would do for someone who was your girl."

Mac lifted a single brow high. "I said you, doll. If *you* were my girl."

"Okay, me."

"Glad we got that cleared up."

Melina smiled slyly, and shook her head. "Anyway,

my point is that I realized something."

"Like what?"

"Like everything you said you would do, you have done. For me, I mean."

Mac held back his smirk, but barely. He wondered how long it would take Melina to put two and two together about his earlier statements. "Oh?"

"Yes. You're not as slick as you think you are, Mac."

"Actually, I'm even more so, but we'll leave that alone for another time."

Melina pursed her pretty pink lips like she was considering arguing with Mac. Thankfully, she didn't. "Nonetheless, I wanted to thank you for doing all of that for me. You don't have—"

"I do," Mac interrupted smoothly. "Because I want to. And as I told you earlier tonight, I want to know more about you, doll. If I didn't give a damn, I would leave you to fend for yourself. I have a feeling there is a lot more to you than just what I've seen so far. I'm still interested in learning the rest. Don't mistake my interest for simply kindness. I'm not kind to just anyone, doll. I don't care about just anyone."

Melina swallowed hard. "But you do care about me."

"Yes."

"Okay."

Mac laughed under his breath. "Again with this 'okay' nonsense. What happened to the Melina with her sharp responses and her quick wit?"

Melina lifted a single shoulder like it didn't matter. "She's still there. She's just ... processing this awful day."

"It'll pass," Mac promised.

"Good. But right now, I want to sleep. I'm tired. It's late."

"Go ahead. I'll take the couch."

Melina fiddled with her fingernails. "I was going to ask if you wanted to share the bed."

Mac's throat tightened as his cock thickened. "To sleep, or …?"

"Smooth, really."

"Hey, I'm not in the business of hiding my intentions, doll. If you want me to jump in bed with you and fuck you until you fall asleep, let me know. I'm up for that."

Melina grinned wickedly. "Rain check, Mac. Tonight I just want to sleep beside someone. A familiar, safe someone."

Mac let her words settle in.

He was familiar to her.

And safe.

Mac put his darker desires away in a locked box. "I can do that for you, doll. Whatever you need. All you have to do is ask."

Melina nodded, but her smile fell slightly. "Thanks."

"I buried my father the same day I met you," Melina said.

The words had been whispered into the dark. Mac was sure that Melina probably believed he was asleep already, or that he couldn't hear her. He decided to stay quiet and let her talk.

"Next to the priest who said a few words before leaving quickly, and the man who shoveled the dirt back into the hole, I was the only person there," she continued.

Mac swallowed back the lump forming in his throat. "What about your mother?"

"She died when I was eight. Ovarian cancer."

"I'm sorry," he said.

Melina sighed softly, and turned in the sheets. Mac

felt her hand skim closer to his side, but she didn't touch him. He stayed still with one arm under his head, and the other resting over his bare midsection.

"I have a few memories of her. All good ones. Even at the end when she was sick and knew she was dying. She never showed it. That's probably where some of my stubbornness comes from."

Mac managed a smile in the darkness. "At least you know where your roots come from, doll, and what makes you … you, so to speak. What about your father?"

"Dying to know, are you?"

"Only what you want to tell me." Mac rolled to his side and used his arm as a prop to hold himself up. He found Melina watching him with a mixture of wariness and curiosity. The way her dark eyes burned into him felt like fire spreading over his nervous system. It didn't really burn, but it felt damn good. "And guessing by the fact you brought him up while we're getting ready to sleep, I think you want to talk about him, too."

Melina's gaze dropped quickly. "Maybe I do. I haven't got anyone to talk to him about. No family. No friends."

"Loneliness looks terrible on a beautiful woman."

"Does it?"

"Come a little closer and you won't feel so alone."

The corner of Melina's lips lifted into a smile. "We're supposed to be talking."

Mac didn't give her another chance to refuse him. Reaching out, he snagged her wrists in his palms and dragged her to his side of the bed. Melina instantly softened in his arms when he wrapped them around her. Her head tucked under his chin, and her hands balled into fists against his chest.

Comfort.

Sweet-smelling skin.

Soft hair.

Silky lips pressed feather light to his pec.

Mac drew in a quick breath. "That's better."

"It is," Melina whispered.

"Talk to me."

"Daniel, my father, was a former Marine. Lance Corporal."

Mac stiffened. "A military brat."

Melina laughed. "Is that all you got from that?"

"It explains a lot, Melina. About you, for one. But for Luca and his opinions, too."

"Maybe I should have told you, but I didn't think it was important that my father had been in the military. It wasn't like it fucking mattered to anyone else, that's for sure."

The unhidden anger in Melina's tone managed to take Mac by surprise. "You don't sound like you're very proud of him and his service."

"Him?" Melina released a shaky breath. "Him, I adored. Him, I couldn't be more proud of."

"Then what is it?"

"The military. He was dishonorably discharged for disobeying orders to leave a small contingent of his men behind enemy lines in Afghanistan. He ended up losing his left arm up to the elbow in the attack. When he came back … when he came back, he—" Melina stopped abruptly, and her fists balled even tighter.

Mac ghosted his hand from the small of her back to the nape of her neck in gentle swipes until he could feel the tension start to release. "It's all right, doll. You don't have to tell me more if you don't want to."

"I do, though. My father suffered from PTSD. The night terrors were the worst. Sometimes he drank, which only exasperated his issues. He had severe anxiety and we just didn't have the money to get him the help he needed. I started escorting to pay for his medical bills. I wanted him to get better, because no one else gave a damn. The military forgot about him. The government overlooked him and his service. The men he saved were allowed to return to their posts, while he had been shamed and stripped of his position for what he'd done. My father was a good man—an honorable man who took care of his family and his men."

"And his country," Mac murmured.

"Well, his country turned on him. They didn't give a shit about what happened to him. He was the little guy—the forgettable one. He was left to handle what he'd seen and the things he'd been forced to do on his own, without so much as a fucking thank you or a proper funeral when he died."

Melina's bitterness practically wafted off her.

Mac let it roll off him. He figured it made a hell of a lot of sense. "I get it, now."

"Get what?" Melina asked sharply.

"Hey, none of that, doll." Mac pressed the tips of his fingers into Melina's back, just to let her know that he was still there, holding her. "Keep your attitude at bay for five minutes. Don't turn it on me because you're angry at the world. I'm not the world, Melina. I'm just one man looking out for you. That's all."

Melina glanced up at him with wetness coating her bottom lashes. Just as quickly as she'd looked up, she was hiding her face again. "You're right, I'm sorry."

"Thank you. As I was saying, I get it. Your attitude, your distance, and your lack of approachability. It makes sense. You hate anyone with any ounce of authority. The ice queen persona is a hell of a lot easier to maintain than the poor little me one, right?"

"Ouch, Mac."

"Sometimes the truth hurts, doll. Either way, you have a right to your feelings. You can protect your emotions however you want to. You might find it easier when you let some people in beyond your high walls. No one's saying you need to break them all down and let the world in or anything."

"Just the one man looking out for me, right?"

Mac grinned. "Why not?"

"Maybe I'm not used to having anyone look out for me, Mac."

"Hmm. I figured that."

Melina moved closer until all the curves of her body had molded to Mac's. It was dangerous and wonderful at the same time. There was no hiding the hard ridge of his erection pressing against the toned contour of her stomach. Mac simply didn't act on his wayward thoughts. Melina wasn't finished talking, after all.

"What happened to your father?" he asked.

"Killed by a drunk driver."

"Shit. That's rough."

Melina nodded once. "It was. I wanted him to get better. I was desperate enough to escort behind his back to make the kind of money we needed for his medical costs, right? He could be better, I knew it."

"PTSD is hard to manage."

"Yeah," she said, "it is."

"I'm sure he appreciated what you tried to do, doll. And he no doubt loved you."

Melina tipped her head lower, but Mac felt it all the same. Her tears. Wet and hot. They dropped from her cheeks and hit his bare chest. Melina tried to wipe the proof of her pain away, but it was already too late.

He'd felt it.

A tightness wrapped his chest, taking away his air and allowing a dull pain to settle in his middle. Mac couldn't make the ache go away, no matter how hard he tried.

No woman should cry in bed with a man.

Melina, for that matter, should never cry with him.

"Don't cry," Mac whispered into her hair. "Not with me, doll. It cuts me up inside. Please."

Melina's hands wiped at her face again. Mac found her chin with his palms, tilted her head back, and used his thumbs to sweep her jaw line.

"I'm sorry," Melina said quickly. "I'm not the kind of woman who cries. I didn't mean to cry. It's just that I've not talked about it and—"

"Don't apologize. Let me help, all right?"

Melina said nothing as Mac wiped away her tears until her face was dry and her lashes fanned her cheeks. The natural pout of her lips drew in Mac's gaze and he pressed a quick, soft kiss to her mouth.

Instantly, Melina's eyes opened wide again.

"No tears when you're in bed with me," Mac said firmly. "Or I'll be forced to make you stop by whatever means necessary."

Melina smiled. "Is that so?"

"Yes."

"I'll have to remember that."

"Do," Mac said.

"You were right, though," Melina said quietly. "I am angry. I'm pissed off at everyone that turned their back on my father and left him to survive alone after all he did. It makes me fucking cold inside. Then I'm just numb from the anger and it's all I ever seem to feel. It's easier."

"Cold enough to burn, doll."

"Sometimes."

"You do realize that you have to burn through yourself before you burn anyone else, right?"

Melina blinked up at him. "I hadn't thought of it that way."

"Most people don't realize it until it's too late."

"Should I thank you for letting me in on the

little secret, then?"

Mac chuckled deeply. "Babe, if you'd like, I'll make sure you have at least one thing to thank me for every single day, as long as you keep me around."

"I'll consider it."

"Good."

Then, Mac rolled to his back and pulled Melina with him under the sheets. She gasped out a breathy laugh when she realized she was on top of him, straddling his waist. Grabbing her face in his palms again, Mac pulled Melina down so that he could kiss her hard. The moment her soft lips opened, he deepened the kiss until her fingers wrapped into his hair and her tongue answered him back in a sweet, tantalizing dance.

"What game are you playing tonight, Maccari?" Melina whispered against his mouth.

Mac smirked, let his hands travel down to her rounded ass, and grabbed tight. He pulled her into his groin, letting the softness between her thighs grind against his hard cock. "You've had a rough night. Why don't you let me distract you for a little while?"

Melina sucked her lower lip in between her teeth. "Yeah?"

"Say the word."

"Which word is that?"

"Please. But if you add my name into it as well, I'll really make it worth your while, doll."

"Do tell," Melina teased, rolling her hips over his groin again.

Mac held back his groan. "If you're a good girl, I'll let you climb on top of my cock, and ride yourself straight to heaven, Melina. Just say the fuckin' words."

Melina's eyes fluttered closed and a little moan escaped when Mac squeezed her backside again. "I'm not a good girl, Mac."

"I might be a little biased where being good is concerned. And you know how I like your sass. Give me what I want, and then I'll let you take what you need until you can't feel anything else but my cock in your pussy and my name in your mouth."

"God, that's …"

"Wonderful. It is fucking wonderful. You know it will be, Melina. Give it to me, come on."

Melina's tongue swept her bottom lip before she breathed, "Please, Mac."

That was all he wanted to hear.

Without warning, Mac let go of Melina's backside, fisted her flimsy tank top, and pulled it from her body. He made quick work of yanking her shorts down over her thighs, and then pulling them from her smooth legs when she lifted off him enough to remove the clothes. She pushed the sheets away with shaking hands before she tugged his boxer-briefs down.

From that point, Mac let Melina take the lead.

She needed it. He could feel it in his bones.

To control. To take. To *fuck*.

 Sometimes simply feeling was needed. Not talking, wondering, or explaining. Simply feeling.

Melina leaned over Mac's form, dug into the bedside table, and pulled out a foil packet. He watched her through hooded eyes as she tore open the condom, and then quickly rolled it down his length with far steadier hands than before. Mac shuddered, groaning low at the sensation of her fingertips gliding down his length.

"Fuck," he muttered heavily. "Do you know how beautiful you are above me?"

Melina laughed—a sexy sound—moving back over his body with the grace of a woman who knew that yes, she looked damn good. "I only have to look at you watching me, Mac, and I know."

The wet heat of her pussy settled on his cock. Melina shifted her hips, letting her core rub against his length with every little movement of her body. Mac grabbed her hips and grinded his cock harder into Melina's pussy, feeling the tip of his cock glide through the fleshy lips with each flex.

"Do you like that?" Melina asked, breathy and grinning. "Feeling me rubbing against you like this? Could you come like this, Mac?"

"I could, but I don't want to. I'd rather be in you while you milked me dry, doll."

"I think I can do that."

Then, she was lifting just high enough to grab the base of his cock, and dropping back down before Mac could get another word out. The tight heat of her pussy engulfed his length and suddenly, Mac couldn't fucking breathe.

He could feel.

God, could he ever.

Her wet walls flexed around him, shuddering and taking him deeper. Her pussy hugged him tight enough to make his cock throb and ache, while the air rushed out of Mac's chest in a whoosh. Melina's hands found his chest, her nails scored into his skin, and then she was lifting from his length to begin a rhythm that was as fast as it was punishing.

"Lean up," Mac demanded, somehow managing to find his voice.

He sounded coarse and rough. Like he needed water and air.

Melina bit her lip and did as he demanded grabbing onto his thighs to brace herself. She kept her pace up, lifting and lowering her body onto his length. Mac had the perfect view of his cock disappearing into her pink, slippery sex. She took his cock in over and over, her juices coating his latex-covered length and her inner muscles fluttering around his cock harder with every thrust.

The sound of her sex taking him in, sucking him deeper, and their skin meeting in the darkness was music.

Perfect, dirty music. It was fucking filthy and he loved it.

Melina's quiet, rising cries were far better.

"Goddamn, look at you," Mac ground out through clenched teeth. He grabbed her hips harder, pulling her into his cock with every lowering of her hips. "You look good on me, Melina, riding me like that. Do you feel it, doll? Is it right there?"

"Yes," Melina whined.

"Get it for me, and then I want you to make me fucking come."

"*God.*"

"Come on, you know you want it. Give it to me. Milk me fucking dry, doll."

Melina's fingernails scored another set of lines across his chest. Mac didn't mind the sting. How could he, when all he could hear was his name in Melina's mouth? Why did it matter when all he could see was her pussy riding his cock like she fucking needed it, her breasts swaying with each lift of her body, and the small shaking rocking her shoulders like she was getting ready to lose control?

"Make me come," Melina demanded.

Mac didn't know how to deny Melina a thing when she wanted something. His hand slipped between her thighs and found her clit, hot and hard under the pad of his thumb. He circled the little nub with fast strokes.

"Oh, my God, Mac."

"Louder," Mac demanded, loving his name in her mouth.

Melina choked out a cry and his name came out far more broken than before. She was right there. Her legs quaked and a sheen of perspiration dotted down her chest. Her eyes squeezed shut a second before her stomach muscles clenched and her body tensed all over.

Right there ...

"Fuck."

Mac pulled Melina down as she shattered around him. He brought her trembling lips to his, and kissed her through the orgasm.

Hot.

Soft.

Needy.

When Melina had calmed enough to ask Mac for more, he put her on her knees, made her ask again, and then gave her everything she wanted.

A good man didn't deny his girl, after all.

Melina was his.

Mac decided.

Simple as that.

CHAPTER NINETEEN

She couldn't figure him out.

And that scared the ever-loving hell out of her.

Lying beside him in bed as the sun's rays peaked in through the blinds, Melina could only wonder what to expect next. Ever since the moment she'd laid eyes on Mac, her entire world had been shaken so much that it would never be normal.

At least, never be normal for her.

Melina had a lot to figure out, but she had a measure of comfort that for once she wouldn't have to figure it out alone.

Mac was there.

For her.

For whatever went down.

And she was strangely happy about that.

"How long are you going to lay here frowning?"

The deep timbre of his voice made her body tremble, startling her. She swallowed hard.

"Have you been watching me?" she asked.

"Yep."

"Why?"

"Because I like watching you. Because in those rare moments when you think no one is watching you, you let down your guard and I get to appreciate just how beautiful you really are. Inside and out."

His hand reached for her chin, tilting her head to

look up at him. His eyes were soft and clear. The faintest hint of stubble was visible along his jawline and he'd never looked more appealing to her.

"Somebody taught you how to do this romantic stuff well," she teased.

Mac frowned for a second, before it disappeared. "It sure as hell wasn't my father."

He shifted in the bed and pulled her closer. Picking up on the visible tension in her lover's face, she used the tip of her finger to draw lazy circles on his chest.

"I'm sorry," she finally said softly.

"For what?"

"For reminding you of things you'd rather forget."

"You didn't. Actually, you just reminded me of how happy I am to not be like him."

He brushed his thumb over her lips and she sighed as a dull ache started between her legs. What was supposed to be a night of cuddling and sleep had turned into a night of full-on fucking.

And she'd loved every second of it.

His eyes watched her, darkening as she opened her mouth, subtly giving him permission to ease his thumb into her mouth. Mac chuckled before pulling his hand away.

"What's so funny?" she asked.

"So you do wake up like a sweet kitten in the morning. At what time do you turn into a lioness again?"

Melina rolled her eyes. "Oh, you've got jokes now, huh? I see it didn't take you long to go from Mr. Romance back to Mr. Arrogant."

Mac shrugged. "It's how I am and I embrace it. Now, as much as I would love to stay in bed all day—fucking you properly all over again—business waits for no one."

Melina tensed. "What kind of business?"

"Why don't you come with me and find out?"

She sat up and pulled the top of the sheet around her breasts. "Do you think that's a good idea?"

Mac leaned against the headboard. "Why not? We're supposed to be a couple who can't stay away from one another. What better way to show that, than by having you by my side? Besides, it's time you got an inside view on how I make my money."

"So you want me to be your side kick?"

Mac shook his head. "My gun moll."

"How do you know I don't have something planned today?"

He cupped her chin in his hand, staring deep in her eyes. "If, after last night, I can't convince you to spend more time with me today, then I didn't do something right. Looks like I'll have to rectify that immediately."

His mouth covered hers with a slow, sensual kiss that nearly stole her breath away. Mac nibbled at her lips before slipping his tongue inside and kissing her deeply. Melina shuddered as his tongue rolled slowly across hers. She couldn't help moaning against his mouth as she grew wet for him. Melina pushed Mac away.

"I can't trust myself around you," she said.

Mac cocked a brow. "And that's a bad thing?"

"For a person used to being in control, it is."

"Sometimes we all need to let go, especially you, doll. Now get up and get dressed before I change my mind and keep you here all day."

He leered at her and Melina quickly took the opportunity to head towards the shower. She needed a chance to get her head together. There was no telling what kind of work she would be doing with Mac today.

She looked good.

Damn good.

Mac hadn't been able to keep his eyes off her or his hands, for that matter. As she watched him driving, barely holding the steering wheel, his right hand rested possessively on her leg. The black leather mini-skirt and thigh-high matching spiked-heel boots made her feel powerful.

And very aware of her own sensual femininity.

Christ.

What the fuck was wrong with her?

Lifting the long, thin silver chain that hung between her breasts, she twirled it between her fingers.

"Are you purposely trying to drive me to distraction, doll?"

Melina bit her lip, glancing at him. "I don't know what you're talking about."

He rubbed her thigh before he slowly slid his fingers underneath her skirt.

"Yeah, the fuck you don't. Leather looks good on you and those boots ... don't get me started on your red lipstick and the cleavage you're showing. If I didn't have men waiting, I'd pull this car over and give you the ride of your life."

Melina gasped when he rubbed her clit through the soft silkiness of her panties. "Mmm. You never play fair, Mac."

He flashed her a grin. "Where's the fun in that?"

"You're too much, Maccari. Too much."

"But that's exactly why I keep you interested ..." he trailed off.

The winsome smile he'd just given her was gone and replaced by the blank mask and cold-eyed expression she'd seen him adopt at the Pivetti mansion. When he stopped touching her and parked the car, she grew faintly alarmed.

"Is something wrong?"

He faced her and shook his head. "No. I just need to

make a few things clear. I brought you with me to observe. I don't want you participating in any of this shit. If something goes down you see nothing, you hear nothing, and you know nothing. Got it?"

"I'm not some wilting wallflower, you know? I can handle myself."

"You don't have to remind me of that. I just don't want you getting your hands any dirtier than you have to."

Melina smirked. "Okay. We'll do this your way."

Mac leaned across and kissed her softly on the lips before he exited the car. Before she could touch the door handle, he was opening the door and helping her out. When she stood beside him, he gave her a low whistle of appreciation.

"Watch yourself, Maccari."

"No time for that. I have to watch you."

Grinning at Melina, he took her hand in his. As she walked with Mac, she took in her surroundings. This was a part of town that she'd never been in before. Then again, there seemed to be a lot of firsts, when it came to Mac. A light sheen of snow and gravel crunched under her boots and even though there was still snow on the ground, Melina was grateful that no cold wind blew. The black leather coat she wore kept away most of the chill.

A rusted silver warehouse rose up in front of them. There were spider-web cracks in the windows and a sliding aluminum door that stood open. Shiny silver chains hung from the door handles.

"Is someone here already?" Melina asked.

"They'd better be or there's going to be hell to pay."

From the look on Mac's face, Melina didn't doubt it. He let go of her hand and opened the doors of the warehouse. He motioned her back as he took out his gun and stepped inside. She waited a minute, trying to keep her nerves calm in the process. When he stepped back outside, his gun was in his pants and he motioned for her to follow him.

When she entered the warehouse, Melina nearly gasped. The place was full. There were boxes from the floor to the ceiling. She didn't even want to ask what was inside of those boxes. Sitting in the middle of the warehouse were six vehicles, being taken apart piece by piece. Melina leaned close and whispered in Mac's ear.

"Chop shop?"

"Among other things. Give me a minute, okay?"

Melina nodded before Mac walked away and headed towards one of the men directing the dissembling of the vehicle. She watched the two men shake hands and start talking, but she couldn't hear what they were saying over the noise of the machines. When Mac nodded in her direction, the man he was speaking to gave her an appreciative glance. From the glare Mac gave the man, it seemed her lover was two seconds away from giving the man a hit to the face to remind the man that he was walking a subtle line between disrespect and appreciation. A few minutes later, Mac walked back to where she was standing.

"Follow me," he said in a terse tone.

She allowed him to lead her to a corner of the warehouse that housed a small room with a plate glass window. Inside was a small office with a desk and fold-up chair.

"Let me guess. You want me to stay here while you work."

"Yes. You'll be able to see everything and keep out of sight if anything starts to pop off with any unhappy customers."

"How long are we going to be here?"

Mac shrugged. "As long as it takes."

"You know, I could've stayed in bed if this was all you had in mind."

Melina flopped down into the folding chair. Mac kneeled down beside her.

"I told you I brought you with me for appearances sake, and while that part is true, it's not the whole truth."

Melina crossed her legs. "So, what is the truth?"

"The truth is that I like having you close, even when that means I'm being selfish in the process."

"So, he finally admits that he has flaws. Wow. This is a big day. I'm going to mark it down on my calendar."

"If wanting you is a flaw, it's one I'm damned-well happy to have."

He stood up and winked at her before he turned on his heel and headed back out into the main part of the warehouse.

So, he liked having her close.

She wished that she could ignore the butterflies fluttering in her stomach, but she couldn't.

There was something real developing between her and Mac that she'd never expected. Yes, circumstances had forced them together unexpectedly, but he could've walked away from her at any time, leaving her to fend for herself.

But he hadn't.

Instead, he'd been there with her every step of the way, helping her navigate her way through a life that she knew nothing about.

A new life that could very well be the cause of her death. Somehow, she knew Mac wouldn't let that happen. Whatever happened, they were in this together and as she watched him take down and open boxes, she couldn't help but be glad that there was someone who finally cared about her enough to watch her back.

Almost two weeks had passed and things were quiet, which was not at all what Melina had expected. After all, with her on the Pivetti boss's list of people to watch, she'd been waiting for something to happen. Perhaps someone tailing her, but that hadn't happened. Even the cops had backed off and for that, she couldn't be happier. Those ridiculous charges had mysteriously been dropped, as well.

She and Mac had settled into somewhat of a routine. He slept over a few nights out of the week. Those nights usually ended with them tearing up the sheets, enjoying their fill of one another. Having sex with Mac was slowly becoming her new addiction, and it was one she didn't mind having. But she was starting to enjoy more than just the sex. Mac had a way about him. She found herself laughing and smiling more than she had … since she was a child.

The realization had startled her earlier that morning, when she'd left her place with Mac. They'd been together pretty regularly, as she accompanied him some days while he worked. She'd seen Mac and his fellow crew members unload more hot goods than she could keep count of. Not to mention, the stolen car parts they'd sold. Her eyes had grown as big as saucers when she saw the stacks of money Mac made every day. Then she'd promptly let loose a stream of curses when Mac told her he only kept thirty percent of his take.

Bullshit.

She pushed the thought from her mind as she leaned against the wall of the store, watching Mac. Today they were doing the collection bit. That morning, Mac had allowed her to collect the money from the more upscale of those businesses, before giving her what was his cut without batting an eye.

"I told you I'd take care of you, didn't I?" he'd asked softly.

So far, Mac was proving to be a man of his word. Her landlord had called her two days ago and thanked her for paying her rent early for the next two months. When she'd asked Mac about it, he'd just shrugged and smiled, pretending he had no idea what she was talking about. She was learning that was his way. He liked to do things without receiving recognition. The man liked to move in silence and shadows, but sometimes you needed to step out into the light. Perhaps she could persuade Mac to do that, at least for tonight.

"We're out of here, doll."

He reached for her hand and led her outside.

"Are we done for the day?" she asked.

"Don't tell me you're tired? Not the invincible Melina," Mac teased.

"Hardly."

"Then what is it?"

He squeezed her hand.

"We haven't had much time to spend together, since you've been working so much."

Mac stopped walking and looked at her. "We've been together almost every day."

"But you've been working. There hasn't been that much time for …"

"For what, doll?"

He stared at her hard.

"For us."

His hand caressed her cheek. "So there's an 'us' now?"

"I thought that's what we were moving towards. That is, if you still want it."

"Of course that's what I want. Hell, it's what I've wanted since the moment I laid eyes on you. I'm sorry you've been feeling neglected, but I promise I'll make it up to you."

Melina shook her head and looped her arms around Mac's neck.

"I'm not talking about me. I'm talking about you."

"Me? I'm not feeling neglected."

"Well, you should be. You've been working non-stop, sneaking behind my back and paying my bills. Not to mention making sure I don't end up in a pine box. And during all of this, not once have you thought about yourself or your own needs. Tonight, I'm going to do something about that, provided we're done with business for now."

"Melina, a real man puts others' needs above his own. I learned that at a young age."

"I won't disagree with you there, but sometimes everyone needs someone to look after them and I want to do that for you."

Leaning forward, she kissed him softly before pulling back to smile at him.

"What did you have in mind?" His eyes danced with amusement.

"I could *try to* cook you a nice dinner, and we could enjoy a nice bottle of wine before moving on to dessert."

Mac raised an eyebrow as one of his hands traveled lower to caress her backside. "Dessert, huh? What kind of dessert?"

"A one-of-a-kind delicacy you've started to enjoy very, very much," she whispered.

"I'm sold. Your place or mine?"

"Mine. I've got the big bath tub, remember?"

"That you do, doll. How did I get so lucky to land a woman like you?"

Melina shrugged. "Maybe you did something good in a past life."

He laughed. "I'll go with that. Now let's get out of here."

Cupping her face in his hands, Mac kissed her

hungrily, silently promising that they had another long, hot night ahead of them. Melina's body heated in anticipation. When Mac pulled away and tapped her nose, she couldn't help smiling. She'd been doing a lot of that lately and it felt good.

Cars raced down the street behind Mac, except one. As it crept closer to where they stood on the sidewalk, the back window slowly lowered. Melina's body tensed as alarms rang in her head.

"Mac."

His head whipped in the direction she was looking and then gunfire exploded.

Mac pushed her behind a parked car and then to the ground. Melina barely had time to brace herself.

"Keep your head down."

Bullets continued flying and the sounds of glass shattering and screams filled the air. It was a drive by, and the only thing that was clear was that someone wanted blood. Hers or Mac's, she didn't know. What she did know, was that she'd had enough of this shit. Rolling away from Mac, she grabbed for his gun.

"Melina, don't!"

He reached for her, but she eluded his grasp as she scrambled to her knees behind the shot-up car that had shielded them. The gunfire had stopped. Melina peeked over the hood of the car and saw a silver Dodge Charger. Melina fired, putting a bullet in the back headlight. The car revved up, and Melina carefully aimed one more time.

The car rolled to a stop seconds after the bullet shattered the back window. Melina had managed to hit her target.

Mac grabbed her, jerking her to her feet.

"We have to get out of here. Now."

He snatched the gun from her and tucked it into his back pocket before nearly dragging her down the street to where they'd parked. Melina didn't know who was after them or why, but she could damn well guarantee that when word got out, they'd think twice about coming after her and Mac again.

CHAPTER TWENTY

"You have really got to stop grabbing people's guns and shooting with them," Mac muttered.

Melina shot a look over her shoulder, probably in the direction of the car. "Why? I get the job done, don't I?"

"Not the point."

"It's the only point that matters when someone is shooting at you."

"Fair enough."

"I thought so," she said.

"Your father?"

Melina nearly slipped in her heels, but Mac caught her around the waist and drew her to his side. It was becoming second nature for him to keep bringing Melina closer. She was better there, safer, and happier. She deserved to be there.

He just wasn't sure how to deal with it.

In his arms, Melina kept a steady pace, seemingly unbothered by the fact she had probably just killed a man. She never failed to shock Mac, but he liked it. He liked her.

A lot.

"What about my father?" Melina asked.

Mac made sure the gun was safely tucked into the waistband of his jeans. "Was he the one who taught you how to shoot like that?"

Melina laughed. "Yeah."

Mac nodded approvingly. "Damn. I would have liked to meet him. Shake his hand. Thank him, maybe."

She didn't respond. Mac didn't mind. He knew how touchy of a subject her father was.

Thankfully, Melina kept up with Mac's jogging pace down the sidewalk. The street had gone completely quiet of noise. When the first burst of gunshots had rung out, people dropped to the ground or scattered into the closest businesses they could find.

No doubt, the cops would be showing up soon.

Mac didn't need their brand of trouble. Neither did Melina. God knew the cops had been a big enough nuisance in their lives lately.

"Fucking surprising," Mac muttered.

"Hmm?"

Mac held Melina tighter. "I was thinking it was surprising that those dumbass detectives weren't following right behind us today. They usually are."

"Maybe we lost them earlier."

"Must have. Get in," Mac demanded the second they came up beside his black car.

Melina did as he wanted. No arguments.

It was a damn good thing she wasn't her usual combative and difficult self when shit was going down. Mac appreciated that about Melina, amongst many of her other interestingly wonderful qualities.

Mac went to shut the door, but Melina stopped him. Her brown gaze, wary and concerned, found his. Despite their situation, it calmed Mac just to take a moment, push aside his panic, and stare at Melina.

And that's how he knew.

That she was his?

His girl?

Yeah, that was how he knew.

"We don't have time to stand around and chat, doll. What do you need?" Mac asked.

"My father," Melina said.

"What about him?"

"He would have loved you, Mac."

Mac's hand tightened around the metal edge of the passenger door. A heaviness pooled in his stomach, grounding him. It didn't feel entirely bad, though.

"You think?" Mac asked.

"I know," Melina told him with her usual fierceness.

"I'm not the kind of man that fathers usually want their daughters running around with. There's not a whole lot about me that's good inside."

Melina never took her eyes off Mac for a second. "There's enough good where it counts."

Mac supposed she was right.

And as long as he was what Melina wanted, nobody else mattered to Mac.

"We have got to go," Mac told Melina.

Melina moved her hand from the door, letting Mac shut her inside the car. The pressure that had been steadily building in his chest deflated slightly. Melina wasn't entirely safe just yet, but being inside a vehicle was better than being way out in the fucking open.

Mac crossed around the front of the car quickly, sweeping both directions of the street with his sharp gaze. He didn't want to be caught up in another drive-by situation with whoever.

Mac's stare narrowed in on the silver car down the road. It was still resting where it had come to a stop after Melina shot the driver. It was still running, too. No one had even tried to approach the vehicle, yet.

Who, was the question.

Mac wanted to run down, take a quick peek at the driver, and get the hell out of Dodge. He couldn't afford to take the risk. He didn't want to stay in the area for any longer than was necessary.

As it were, they had already been there too long.

He wouldn't put Melina in more danger.

Mac would always take care of his girl.

No matter what.

Sliding into the driver's seat and shutting the car door, he slid the key into the ignition, shifted gears, and spun the tires on pavement when he pulled out of the parking spot. Melina cussed under her breath, her hands flying out to the dashboard to steady herself.

"Who did that?" she asked. "Luca? That enforcer—Vin—maybe?"

Mac tightened his grip on the steering wheel. "I don't know."

And that was a fucking problem.

Mac glanced over at Melina.

It was a problem he intended on fixing.

It had taken Mac the majority of the evening, but he finally convinced Melina to stop worrying and take a nap. Their plans of a nice dinner, a dessert, and a quiet night together had been ruined by her concerns and his lack of answers.

Mac felt bad.

He wanted to be able to tell her it was all right and mean it. He couldn't do that.

Leaning in the doorway of Melina's bedroom, Mac watched his lover toss and turn in the sheets. She was sleeping, but fitfully. More than anything, he wanted to crawl in the bed with her, bring her closer, and take away whatever nightmares were troubling her sleep.

Unfortunately, he couldn't do any of that.

Not tonight.

Mac had other business to attend to. No doubt, if Melina knew what Mac was planning, she would demand to go with him and be a part of his dealings. Mac couldn't bear the thought of putting Melina back into yet another position where she could be hurt or in some kind of danger.

As it were, she had enough attention; she had enough problems.

Too many were caused by his involvement in her life.

Mac fingered the cross hanging down from his neck. It hung off a leather cord, and he never took it off for anything. Not even when he fought. Usually, touching the cross would give him some sense of relief, or even hope.

He didn't find it.

Something else had taken its place for calming him when he needed it. That something else was Melina.

Tugging the leather cord up over his head, Mac watched the cross swing in front of his face for a second before he enclosed it into his fist. Crossing the bedroom as quietly as he could, he bent down over the side of the bed and pushed a few stray waves of hair from Melina's face. Her lips curved upward in her sleep, seemingly pleased at his touch.

She couldn't know.

But he still wondered if she did.

Mac carefully put the leather cord around Melina's neck, letting the cross fall by her hand on the pillow. If she woke up in the night before he got back, then she would find it. If he wasn't back to the apartment by morning, then she could have something to keep.

Because if morning came and Mac wasn't there with her, then he wouldn't be coming back at all.

Ever.

It had taken a few cautiously made, strategically chosen calls placed to the right people to find out where the Pivetti Don was for the evening. Melina had made a good point earlier in the day when she tossed out the only two names of people who might possibly be coming after them, wanting blood.

Melina had mentioned Vin, the enforcer who had caused issues for Mac in Guido's office. Mac honestly didn't believe the enforcer was the person who had come after them earlier for two simple reasons.

One, if Vin had come after them, they would be dead. Vin's job was first and foremost to protect the family. The man's specialty was killing. When he pulled the trigger, he wouldn't miss. Simple as that.

And for two, Vin was alive and well. Mac had made a phone call to a friend of a friend who stuck close to Vin's guys. If he were the one Melina shot earlier, he wouldn't be hanging out with his people.

That only left the other person Melina mentioned.

The Pivetti Don.

Luca.

He was the only person, who at the very moment, had threatened Melina's life, and by extension, Mac's life, too. After all, he was the man involved with her. Mac was the one who brought her into their world and told their secrets.

Luca wouldn't hesitate to kill Mac, too.

So, Mac wanted to find out why the man had chosen today, why the hit had failed, and why Luca didn't have the balls to just take the two out without problems. It was fucking stupid—foolish, even. Mac knew better than to go off half-cocked, demanding answers from a Cosa Nostra boss.

It didn't matter.

He had to know what he had done—what his girl had done—to deserve such a dishonorable hit. A hit that wasn't even fucking good enough to put at least one of them in a grave. And if he could help it, Mac wanted to put an end to it however he could. If that meant sacrificing his life so that Melina had a head start to maybe get away, then that's what it meant.

Stepping up to the entrance of the club, a beefy bouncer looked Mac over. Mac had bypassed the long line of people waiting to get in. It wasn't his first time at the joint. He'd come a time or two with Guido, so his face was known as someone who should be let in the door without question.

The bouncer nodded at Mac's jacket. Mac opened up the leather jacket wide and turned around to show the man he had no weapons on him. He'd left it at home with Melina. The bouncer grunted under his breath and moved aside to let him pass without a word.

Mac entered the dance club, feeling the heavy bass thrumming hard against the soles of his Italian leather shoes. Usually, he liked music and loved to dance. Tonight was not the right time. He swerved in and out of swaying, sweaty bodies, searching for a face in the crowd he might recognize.

It didn't take long at all for Mac to find Luca.

A small set of winding metal stairs led to an upstairs section that was securely monitored by two men in black suits. It was a VIP section that was only used by the most important people in the venue. Luca was definitely one of those people.

Mac crossed the last half of the dance floor, keeping his gaze locked up above on the Don sitting in a booth and sipping from a glass. Unconcerned, and with his arm around his wife, Luca seemed to be enjoying his evening.

He certainly didn't look like he was concerned about having put a hit out on two people earlier in the day. Then again, it was Luca's job to be cold and distant from his choices when it came to protecting the family by whatever means necessary.

At the bottom of the stairs, Mac was stopped by the men in black.

"I'm here to see the Don," Mac said.

"Boss is busy," said the one man on the right.

Mac didn't recognize either of the men. It wasn't such a surprise. Luca had a handful of guards that rotated duty, depending on what he was doing that day and who he was with. His wife had an entirely separate horde of guards.

"He's not too busy to see one of his soldiers, is he?" Mac asked.

Up above, Mac caught Luca's eye. The Don's brow furrowed as he looked down at Mac, and then snapped his fingers twice to gain the attention of the bodyguards.

"Let him pass, *cafone*," Luca barked. "He's one of Guido's best *soldatos*. Let him up, Johnny."

Luca's interest in seeing Mac only left him more confused. Surely, if Luca had put the hit out on him and Melina, the man would simply order the bodyguard to take Mac away. Unless, that was, Luca was being incredibly cocky and arrogant.

That was a possibility.

The guard allowed Mac to pass. Mac took the metal stairs two at a time, his hands thrown casually inside his pockets. As he rounded the last few stairs, his nervousness finally began to settle. He just wanted some answers. Luca could provide them.

"*Soldato*," Luca said, leaning across the table to grab a cigar from the top of a pile. The Don removed his arm from around his wife to pull out a gold zippo as he worked on lighting the cigar. "What brings you to the club tonight, Maccari?"

"I had something to take care of, Boss."

Neeya Pivetti smiled at Mac and waved at the seat across the booth for him to sit down. He took the offer, and sat in the booth. "Evening, Mac. I didn't think we would be seeing you again so soon. How's your girlfriend—Melina, was it?"

Mac took note of the fact that Luca didn't seem bothered or concerned over his wife questioning him about Melina.

"She's fine right now," Mac said. "At home sleeping without me. Earlier, however, she was nearly gunned down on the street corner as I was finishing up some business."

That caught Luca's attention. The boss's head snapped up, his gaze finding Mac instantly. Luca's eyes narrowed with a dangerous glint as he took Mac in for a second time, like he was reconsidering why Mac was there.

"Is that so?" Luca asked.

"*Sì*," Mac confirmed.

"And you felt the need to come here and what, confront me, Maccari?"

Mac leaned back in the booth. "Actually, I wanted to know why a Don couldn't manage to find a better hired gun to do the job, if that was the case and you had put out the hit. You didn't hide the fact you were uncomfortable with Melina, and you promised to fix the issue if need be."

Luca's lips thinned into a tight, angry line. "You're either terribly arrogant, or mighty stupid."

"Luca," Neeya said quietly.

"Hush, woman."

Neeya's mouth snapped shut.

"I was hoping to find out if you were the one who put the hit out," Mac continued without missing a beat. "And if that is the case, I'm more than willing to accept the punishment for Melina, if you leave her be and let her go."

"He's not going to kill Melina," Neeya said, quiet and sure.

Mac didn't know about that.

Luca still didn't look pleased. "Neeya, that's enough. Be quiet."

"No." Neeya flicked her wrist in her husband's direction, as if to dismiss him. "Luca won't hurt the girl—I like her. Tell him, Luca."

"Neeya, *mio Dio*. Stop it."

"*Luca.*"

Luca's gaze cut back to Mac in a blink. "I didn't put out the hit, not that I owe you a single fucking explanation for anything, Maccari. You're a good soldier, but you are seriously forgetting your fucking place in the food chain of this family right now."

"Disrespect is the first thing to get a man killed," Mac said.

"You're goddamn right," Luca replied smoothly.

"Then surely you can understand why I did come here looking for you tonight. I wanted to know if you had decided to fix the issue like you said you would. That was all."

"I didn't."

The two words had come out of Luca's mouth clipped and pissed. It was enough to tell Mac that the boss was telling the truth.

"But if I had, what would you have done?" Luca asked.

"Nothing."

Luca smiled coldly. "I doubt that."

"Coming here was all I needed to do," Mac said, shrugging.

"A distraction for me?"

Mac nodded. "If you want to see it that way."

"To give your girl a chance to run," Luca murmured.

Mac passed Neeya a look. "Wouldn't you do the same?"

Luca's expression remained passive. "I would. You have a problem, I see."

The darkness coating Luca's tone was enough to make Mac want to leave the man's space. "Do I?"

"Yes." Luca scoffed, adding, "Seems you have someone who wants to kill you, Maccari, and it's not me. Who is it?"

"I don't have the first clue," Mac admitted.

"That's not good," Neeya said, frowning at her husband.

"That's how it usually works, *bella*," Luca replied. "We never know who until it's too late."

Neeya didn't seem pleased with that answer, but she stayed quiet.

Luca patted his wife's knee, saying, "Worry not. I'm sure Maccari is more than capable of handling the problem. Aren't you, Mac?"

"Sure," Mac said.

Neeya glanced down at her lap. "I would like to invite your girlfriend to dinner again, Mac. Please make sure that she's alive to come."

Mac passed Luca a look, wondering how to take that statement.

Luca just shrugged. "You heard the woman. If you find out who is the person behind this nonsense, I give you full permission to take care of it, Maccari."

That seemingly flippant statement was anything but simple.

"Even if he's made?" Mac asked.

Luca smirked. "Especially, if he's made. If he is, then he likely wants to get rid of you for a reason. Maybe you know something. Maybe you're in his way. Who knows? Do you know something I don't,

Maccari?"

"No."

"Then I suggest you work on figuring it out," Luca said, turning away from Mac to give all of his attention to his wife. "Have a good evening, Maccari."

Dismissed.

Mac didn't mind. He left without saying goodbye.

Mac let the hot water beat down on his tense shoulders and back. Turning around, he tipped his head under the water. All of the sound around him was muted by the torrent of rain drumming on his head. He'd gotten back to Melina's apartment before dawn, and found that his girl was still sleeping in bed, unaware that he had left.

Well, he suspected she didn't know.

Sighing, Mac rolled his head back and forth, cracking his neck. It took away a little more tension still lingering in his muscles. After his meeting with Luca, Mac was left more unsettled than ever and with more questions than he had answers.

Who was coming after him?

Were they after Melina, too?

Was it both of them?

Mac didn't know. He hated not knowing things.

The slide of the glass shower door was the only warning Mac got that someone had entered his private space a second before small but strong arms wrapped around him from behind. He let out a contented sigh at the feeling of Melina's plump lips pressing to the spot between his shoulder blades.

"Morning, doll," Mac murmured.

"Morning," she whispered.

Melina hugged him tighter. Mac let her. Her perky

breasts pressed to his back, and her body molded perfectly against his.

"You wanted a shower too, huh?" he asked jokingly.

"I wanted to be with you."

Mac smiled. "I like that."

"Me, too."

Spinning slowly, Mac encircled Melina in his embrace. She tilted her head up, allowing him to bend his head just enough to capture her lips with his own. Her soul-brown eyes watched him with an intensity he hadn't seen from her before as her lips parted to let him deepen the kiss. The moment he did, Melina let out a little moan that was enough to make his cock harden. She moved closer, pressing her tight body harder against his.

Mac let his hand fall from her side and snake between Melina's thighs. He stroked her bare pussy, feeling her shudder under his palm. She was hot to the touch, and he loved that. Her body was always so responsive to him, no matter what he was doing. He was finding himself constantly needing her little sounds, and wanting to watch her face when he was buried deep in her pussy and fucking them both to a fast heaven.

He craved those things.

Badly.

Every day.

"Now this is a damn good morning," Melina breathed.

Mac stroked her sex again, spreading her open with two fingers before he let them sink inside. Her snug walls flexed around him, and Melina swallowed a cry. Her forehead fell against his, and she rubbed her cheek along the stubble dotting his jaw. Her hips rolled into his hand with every thrust as steam fogged up the glass surrounding them.

"No dirty words for me today?" Melina asked.

Mac chuckled. "You don't need it. I don't need it. Not this morning. This is enough, huh? Just feeling me, babe. Feeling you all over me. Loving all your little sounds and the way you move against me, wanting more. Loving kissing your mouth when you come, and filling you full all over again when you ask for more. What else do you want, doll?"

Melina's gaze found his, knowing and searching at the same time. "Love me."

The rhythm of Mac's fingers slowed for a second. Melina didn't stop watching him.

Love was a big word.

It was kind of scary, too.

The only love Mac had ever seen between a man and a woman growing up was one that had been unhealthy and untrue. He didn't think it was real—he wasn't sure he knew how to love someone.

But he did know how he had been seeing Melina for the last little while.

She was by his side every morning. He liked kissing her mouth, holding her hand, keeping her near, and needing her even closer. He made sure she was happy, pleased, and taken care of. He wanted her smiles, and fuck any other man that thought they deserved one, too.

Mac wanted her to be his. No one else's. Just his.

He wanted to breathe her air. He needed her like he needed the breath in his lungs.

It was still strange.

"Yeah," Mac said, kissing her cheek softly. "Love you, doll."

Melina's lashes fluttered closed as she trembled her way through a slow orgasm. "Oh, my God."

"Best thing to wake up and get, huh?"

"Keep giving me that when I wake up and I'll let you know."

There was his girl.

Without needing to be told, Melina turned around and faced the shower wall. Mac crowded her back, running his hands over her wet curves and the swell of her ass.

"Christ, you're so beautiful," he said.

Melina smiled coyly when Mac kissed the corner of her mouth. "Beautiful for you. Thank you for the gift, by the way."

"Hmm?"

"The cross."

Mac traced a line from Melina's shoulders to the small of her back. "It's safer with you."

"I'll make sure it stays that way."

"I've never taken it off, doll."

"I wondered about that. I think that's how I knew."

Mac found her watching him, and smiled. "Knew what?"

"That you love me, and that I love you."

That word in her mouth was enough to make Mac insane. He wanted her to say it again. Over and over. In however many different ways she could spin it, Mac wanted to hear it.

He fitted himself behind her, pushed her against the wall and up on her toes, and positioned his cock right at the entrance to her heaven. With no forewarning, Mac pushed in. Melina hadn't been expecting it, but she was wet enough to take his bare length with no trouble. In one hard thrust, he was seated deep in her pussy, and it felt like a drug seeping straight through his skin to his bones.

"Fuck," Mac mumbled against her shoulder.

Melina whined. "Yeah."

"Fucking *fuck*."

"You feel better like this," she said. "Bare. Just you. I can feel that."

Mac's teeth buried into the junction of Melina's

shoulder with a gentle bite. She sighed, and backed into him as he began to fuck her against the wet shower wall.

"Love me," he ground out.

Melina's hands fell from the wall and reached back to find his thighs. "Love you."

"Again, doll."

"Love you, Mac."

His stress finally floated away. He fucked her harder when she asked for more. His fingers raked over her skin, imprinting her to memory, taking from her body, and forgetting about the rest of the world still fucking them over.

She mattered.

They didn't.

CHAPTER
TWENTY-ONE

She, Melina Morgan, was in love.

Completely.

With every burning fiber of her being.

It scared the ever-loving hell out of her.

The silk sheets rustled against her bare skin, as she lay in bed naked. The past few days had passed in a haze for her.

A haze of fucking, lovemaking, and Mac.

Only Mac.

She bit her lip, trying to fight the smile that came across her face as she thought of him. It wasn't in her nature to be like this—giddy with happiness. For the first time since she could remember, hope for a real future bloomed hot and heavy inside her. If anyone would have told her that she would fall in love, Melina would've told them they'd lost their mind. It was amazing how everything had changed.

The sound of a key turning in a lock drew her attention. Slowly, she eased open the drawer of the nightstand beside her and pulled out a gun.

Her gun.

A Glock 19 Mac had reluctantly procured for her after they'd almost been gunned down. With a firm grip on her weapon, Melina calmly aimed it at the bedroom door. The handle turned and the door swung open. Mac stood in the doorway, bags in hand, staring at her.

"You can put the gun down, doll."

Melina smiled. "Maybe I will. Maybe I won't."

"And why wouldn't you?"

"Because maybe I'm thinking about ordering you to put those bags down, strip and please me in a thousand different ways while I hold you at gunpoint."

Mac moved closer to the bed, setting down the two bags he'd been holding onto the nightstand. There was a twinkle in his eye.

"Now, why does the thought of that get my cock so damn hard?"

"Because you have issues."

He raised an eyebrow as he reached for the sheet that was wrapped around Melina. "I have issues, huh?" he asked.

Melina's breath caught in her throat as he eased the sheet away from her body. Cool air and Mac's hot gaze met her body. Unhurriedly, his hand cupped her breast, toying with her nipple.

"Now, what man in his right mind wouldn't have issues, knowing he had perfection like this waiting for him when he got home?"

Melina's tongue touched her lips. "Home?"

Sitting down on the bed bedside her, Mac offered a smile and a shrug. "Yeah. Home. It's wherever you are, doll."

She turned away and fanned her face with one hand, while putting the gun away with the other. Tears were threatening to come, but she refused to give in to them.

"I hate you, Maccari. You're making me all mushy and weepy-eyed. I'm not that kind of girl."

She faced him and he placed a finger under her chin, forcing her to meet his gaze. "And that's one of the things I love about you the most."

Before she could answer, his lips were on hers. His kiss was hot, demanding, and all consuming. Melina leaned closer, easing her tongue into Mac's mouth. He groaned against her lips as he grabbed her waist. Why did he have the power to make her feel like this? Regretfully, she pushed him away.

"What's wrong? Can't handle the fire?" Mac teased.

"Hardly. I just don't need you having a heart attack from too much excitement."

Mac snorted. "A heart attack? I'm in the best condition of my life. You know that from much personal experience."

Melina shook her head and laughed before pointing at the bags Mac had set down. "Enough distractions. Give me my food. I'm starving."

"Bossy today, aren't we?"

Mac reached for the bags and began removing containers of food.

"Always, but what do you expect? You've been keeping me captive in this bed for days. I love sex much as the next person, but there is other sustenance you need to keep the engine running."

"You know, you constantly surprise me," Mac said.

He opened a container of shrimp lo mein and handed it to Melina.

She smiled. "That means you'll never get bored with me."

"I'm looking forward to a lifetime filled with surprises then."

Melina took a bite of the Chinese food and chewed thoughtfully. A lifetime. Was Mac hinting at something? Sometimes, she couldn't really tell with him. One minute, he was an open book with his full intentions right out there in the open. The next, he wore a mask that gave away nothing.

Putting down her chopsticks, she regarded him from beneath lowered lashes. "Did you mean something by that last remark?"

Popping open a Coke, he handed it to Melina before taking a long, healthy swallow of his Mountain Dew. "And if I did?"

Melina could feel her pulse beating in her neck like a steady drum.

"Don't you think it's a little soon to be thinking long-term?" she asked. "I mean, people are trying to kill us and the cops are on our asses. We're not exactly the Cleavers."

Mac laughed, but when he noticed she wasn't, he stopped and grabbed her hand.

"When it comes to something I want, I play for keeps. I never thought I'd find a woman who could hold my interest for more than a quick fuck, and then you came along and showed me differently. That's a big deal to me. When I told you I loved you, I didn't mean it just for right now. When I love someone, it's more than a passing moment." He leaned close and kissed her softly on the lips before pulling away. "Do you get where I'm coming from?"

She nodded. Looking in his eyes, she could see his sincerity. The depth of his real feelings for her and suddenly she was afraid.

"This is going to sound really stupid but the thought of forever with someone scares me to death. Dying in a barrage of bullets … not so much."

"That's because you are a rare woman," Mac said, smiling. "You were made for this kind of lifestyle."

"You think so?"

"Yeah. Someone shoots at you and you don't even bat an eyelash while you shoot back. I mention things getting even more serious with us, and you're ready to run out of here. That is definitely different from your average woman."

Melina took another few bites of her food before she spoke again. "That's because I've never been the girl who believed in a happily ever after … until you came along.

Realizing we could possibly have one, that a man would be crazy enough to want to have one with me? That takes some getting used to."

"Well, get used to it, because I'm not going anywhere. Every time you feel that cross around your neck, I want you to remember that."

Reflexively, Melina fingered Mac's cross. It was strange how it felt as if it had always been there, lying over her heart. A silent reminder of how he felt for her and according to him, would always feel.

A whole new world.

She cleared her throat. "And what about this mob stuff?"

"One thing we have in our favor is that it's not Pivetti. That means it's someone lower on the food chain and since I have his blessing to take out whoever it is, I'd say we're going to be okay."

"Don't forget, I was shot at, too. What makes you think I shouldn't be the one to take out whoever is coming after us?"

Mac closed his empty carton of beef and broccoli. "Because lately you've been the one doing all the shooting lately. Leave something for me."

Melina shook her head. "Selfish."

"Hardly, doll. A man protects his woman, and besides that, this kill is just what it might take to advance me up the ladder."

"Why am I not surprised you're working an angle?"

"Because you're starting to learn how I operate. Tomorrow, I'll start putting some feelers out."

"What's so special about tomorrow?" Melina asked.

"I'm going back to work. I figure I've more than overextended whatever good graces Guido might have towards me."

"So what time are we leaving?"

"We aren't."

Melina disposed of her empty carton and scowled at Mac. "And what the hell is that supposed to mean?"

"It means I want you to stay here. Out of sight. Out of mind."

"That's not going to fly with me. I am not the little woman who waits at home. I won't play the housewife, Mac."

"I'm not saying you are, but until we get things sorted out right now it will ease my mind to know that you're here. To know that when I am out there handling business, I can spend every second of my time working on who is out to get you and me. I can't do that if my only thoughts are of keeping you safe."

"I don't need you to keep my safe. I was protecting myself long before you sauntered your arrogant ass into my life."

Melina got out of the bed, unbothered by the fact that she was stark naked. She couldn't believe Mac. Did he really not know by now what kind of woman she was? Melina had never been and would never be a damsel in distress. If Mac didn't understand that quick, fast, and in a hurry, then their new relationship was headed towards its first major problem. Stomping towards the bathroom door, her hand had barely closed around the knob before Mac was spinning her around to face him.

"Doll, listen to me."

His eyes sought hers, silently begging him for a chance to further explain.

"You've got two minutes."

"You may not need me, but I need you and if that means I have to make decisions that you don't like in order to ensure that I always have you, then I'm going to do just that."

She swallowed hard. "I've already proven that I can help you and that I don't need protecting. I don't like this."

"I don't expect you to. I'm just asking you to give me some time. After the dust settles, you can come to work with me every damn day, if you want. Please, Melina."

She glared at him. The last thing she wanted to do was stay home, waiting and watching the door like some good little housewife, waiting for her man. The thought of it made her skin crawl in disgust. She was a go-getter, a doer. Sitting around had never been her style.

"And what am I supposed to do with myself all day while you're out having all the fun?"

Mac's hands slowly settled around her waist as his gaze lowered. He licked his lips as he stared at her bare body and Melina tried to ignore the rush of heat she felt beneath his gaze.

"Be here to remind me of everything good in this world and how lucky I am to have you to come home to."

With a smirk, he maneuvered them back over to the bed until the back of her legs were touching the edge. Slowly he pressed her down on the bed and got on his knees.

"This isn't over, Mac."

He grinned at her as he eased her thighs open. "It is now, doll."

His tongue touched her clit and Melina's retort died on her lips.

The bastard.

He licked her pussy from back to front and Melina knew it was truly over. She'd lost, but this was one battle she didn't mind not being the victor.

"Are you going to tell me where we're going?" Melina asked.

"No."

"I don't like surprises."

"Too bad. You're going to have to deal with this one, doll."

Melina pouted. It had been absolute hell staying at her place this morning as she'd waited for Mac to come back. She'd spent half the morning cleaning, and the rest of the afternoon surfing the Internet. Saying she was bored out of her mind was a true understatement. She'd decided to punish Mac for her suffering.

Too bad her brand of punishment had turned out to be a reward for both of them. Her knees still ached.

She touched his thigh. "Can't you at least give me a hint?"

"We're almost there."

Melina rolled her eyes. "Some hint."

Folding her arms, she sat in silence as Mac drove. Even her attempts at seduction hadn't made him reveal where he was taking her. All she'd managed to wheedle out of him was that they were going somewhere special.

Some place that mattered a great deal to him.

Some place he'd never taken a woman.

Melina still had no fucking idea where they were going. She watched the scenery around them searching for a clue as to where Mac was taking her. Finally, she saw a sign.

"Amityville?"

"Yep," he said.

They drove into town and after more twists and turns than Melina could keep track of, they entered a small neighborhood where Mac stopped the car at the end of the street. A small one-level house stood, looking welcoming and cozy from the outside. He put the car into park and killed the ignition.

"We're here," he said quietly.

He turned to her and softly grabbed her chin, before pressing a kiss to her temple. Melina unbuckled her seatbelt as Mac exited the car and came around to open the door for her. She allowed him to help her out before he closed and locked the door behind her. Melina tugged at the hem of her dress, a slow dread creeping into her heart.

"If we are where I think we are, you could've given me a warning to dress more appropriately."

"There's nothing wrong with what you have on. You look beautiful, like always."

Taking her hand in his, Mac led them to the front door of the small gray house and rang the doorbell. They waited for less than a minute before the front door opened.

"James."

James?

It took Melina far too long to realize that James was Mac.

She felt stupid.

"Hey, Ma," Mac said.

Standing in the doorway was a middle-aged woman with blonde hair lightly streaked with gray. Her eyes were the same as Mac's and right at that moment, those eyes were firmly focused on Melina.

"Good to see you, son. Who is this you've brought with you?"

The woman's gaze never wavered from Melina.

"Ma, this is my girlfriend, my Melina."

"*Your* Melina?" Mac's mother said as she raised an eyebrow.

"Yeah. Mine."

"I see."

Melina couldn't remember the last time that a person had made her feel so unnerved beneath their gaze, but Mac's mother was doing just that. She smiled as the woman appraised her from head to toe before extending her hand.

"Melina, welcome to my home. I'm Cynthia."

"It's an honor to meet you, ma'am," Melina said.

The two women shook hands, but there was no mistaking the tenseness that hung in the air between them. Though Cynthia Maccari wore an apron like she was Susie Homemaker, Melina wasn't fooled in the least. Mac's mom was an alpha female and she was sizing up the woman her son had brought home, looking for weaknesses.

"Thank you, Melina. Why don't you come in? Dinner's almost ready."

Cynthia motioned for them to follow her inside. Melina shot Mac a look as she entered the house behind his mother. She took in her surroundings. The home was small but nicely furnished in shades of black and gray. It was something Melina would've chosen herself. Well, at least she and Mac's mother had one thing in common. Cynthia took a seat on a black high-backed chair. Melina allowed Mac to lead her to the matching love seat.

"You know, James has never brought a girl home before," Cynthia said.

"Mac, Ma," Mac said.

"Not to me," his mother replied firmly. "As I said, never once."

"He mentioned that," Melina admitted.

"Did he? My son is usually a man of few words."

"Not all the time, Ma," Mac said.

"So it seems. Well, there's a first time for everything. If you two will excuse me a minute. I have a few things to finish up in the kitchen," Cynthia said.

"Do you need any help?" Melina asked.

"Do you cook?"

"Not particularly well, but I try."

Cynthia gave her a terse smile. "That's all right, then."

As the woman disappeared from the room, Melina buried her face against Mac's neck.

"Your mother hates me," she groaned.

"No, she doesn't, doll. She's just in shock."

"Yeah, she can't believe her son brought home a hooker."

Mac pulled her back to look at him. "What's going on with you? I've never seen you like this."

"Meeting your mother is a big deal. I want to make a good impression. It doesn't bode well for a relationship if your boyfriend's mother hates you."

"Melina, she doesn't hate you. She's just trying to figure you out. To bring you here means I obviously care about you, so she just wants to know what makes you so special to me."

"And you're sure it has nothing to do with the fact that I'm wearing a red bodycon dress, stilettos and I'm not some willowy, blonde, white girl?"

"Positive. Now stop stressing."

Mac pulled her closer and kissed her forehead. Her nerves were rattled, but Mac's quiet confidence in her and their relationship was easing some of her fears.

"Thanks."

"For what?" Mac asked.

"For believing in me."

"I'll always believe in you. That's what you do when you love someone and we both know how much I love you."

"Do I?" she asked.

"Yeah, you do, doll."

Holding her face, he kissed her softly on the lips. Once. Twice. Three times.

The sound of a woman's throat clearing made them break apart. "Dinner is ready."

Mac helped Melina to her feet. "It smells wonderful, *Mamma*."

"It should. I made all your favorites."

"You're in for a real treat, Melina. My mother is the best cook around."

Cynthia beamed at her son, basking in his praise. Anyone could see the love the two of them had for each other. Melina swallowed a lump in her throat as she thought of her own mother, gone from the world over ten years. Quickly blinking away tears, Melina followed Cynthia down the short hall to a small kitchen and dining area. A tall, raised mahogany table was covered with platters of food. It looked like Mac's mom was trying to feed an army.

"Wow. Ma, you outdid yourself," Mac praised.

"Thank you. Your sister's missing out."

"Where is Victoria, anyway?" Mac asked as he pulled out a chair for his mother.

"She was too busy to come for dinner. You know how your sister is. Speaking of siblings, do you have any, Melina?"

"No," Melina replied. "It's just me."

Melina sat down in a chair, staring at the food in front of them.

"Ah. Well, dig in you two. There's stuffed meatballs, lasagna, garlic bread sticks, and chicken parmesan. Oh, and tiramisu for dessert."

Mac rubbed his hands together with glee. "This was well worth waiting all day for."

"This is impressive, Mrs. Maccari. Have you always cooked like this?"

Cynthia smiled. "Yes. Cooking large meals is an Italian tradition. When we cook, we make enough to last for days."

Melina took a bite of the lasagna and moaned. "This is one tradition I could grow to love very much."

Cynthia smiled. "Thank you. Are there any traditions that your family celebrates?"

"It's just me. My mom died when I was eight from ovarian cancer and I just recently buried my father."

"I'm so sorry to hear that. Life couldn't have been easy for you."

"I had my dad. We made the best of things."

"Her father was a veteran," Mac said.

Cynthia's eyes widened. "How long did he serve?"

"Fifteen years," Melina answered.

"That's a lifetime," Cynthia murmured.

"Yeah, it was."

The doorbell rang.

"Are you expecting someone, Ma?" Mac asked.

Cynthia shook her head. "No. Just us."

She got up from her seat and left the table. Mac turned and faced towards the door.

"No one would follow us here, would they?" Melina asked.

"No. That would be the highest level of disrespect. My mother has always kept away from the business as much as she could. She doesn't approve, doll."

Still, Mac remained on edge as they waited for his mother to return.

"James, look who's here," his mother called.

Cynthia returned to the room, but she wasn't alone. Her face was set in a terse smile. Behind her stood a man with dark hair. A stripe of gray touched his temples and his eyes were black and cold. Beside Melina, Mac stiffened. There was no inexpressive mask this time. His face was lit with a quiet, seething rage.

"Son," the man greeted with a smile that looked anything but sincere. "It's been a long time."

CHAPTER TWENTY-TWO

Mac refused to stand from his seat as his mother stared at him with a silent plea in her gaze for him to move. He couldn't—wouldn't.

James Sr. watched his son with a knowing sneer curving the corners of his mouth upwards. Then, his stare flicked to the woman beside Mac.

Mac stiffened all over. His hand found Melina's thigh under the table and he squeezed gently. Just enough to say he was there, and that was it.

"No hello for your old man, Mac?" James asked.

Mac stifled his biting retort and settled for a terse, "*Ciao*, James."

Not "dad", or even "father".

James Maccari didn't deserve those titles.

He was useless.

Cynthia took a breath, clapped her hands, and then waved at the table. "Sit, Senior."

James nodded at his estranged wife, and kissed her on the cheek as he passed her by to make his way to a free seat at the table. "Where's my favorite girl?"

"Victoria couldn't make it," Cynthia said. "You could have called, if you wanted to come over."

"My house, too," James muttered under his breath as he reached for a breadstick.

"Actually—"

Mac's mouth snapped shut when his mother cut him

254

with a single look. He blew out a frustrated breath and felt Melina's hand cover his on her thigh. Above all else, Cynthia hated to see her son and her estranged husband fight. Mac knew it hurt his mother, but she understood why the two men weren't close.

James' entire lack of couth, care, and manhood being one.

It was a big one.

"Eat," Mac told Melina quietly.

Melina nodded, and took to eating once more. Mac followed suit, keeping one eye on his father and another on his mother. Conversation flowed, but it was awkward and stinted. It wasn't like he had a whole lot to say to his father.

Mac was starting to think his plan of introducing his mother to the woman he loved had been ruined by someone he didn't give a shit about.

Sad thing, that was.

"Who's this broad?" James asked, chewing with his mouth open as he waved at Melina.

Mac didn't want to dismiss Melina in front of her. But his bigger issue at the moment was making sure his father didn't have any ties to her, personal or otherwise.

"A friend," Mac said shortly.

Melina frowned, and her teeth cut into her lip. She passed Mac a look, hurt marring her features. He wished he could explain to her that the man sitting across from her didn't deserve to know who she was, or how important she was to Mac. James didn't get that right—Melina was too good for him.

The man shouldn't even be sharing her air.

James grinned, his stare traveling down over Melina's chest. Mac shuddered with fury, but he managed to somehow hide it.

"Pretty thing," James noted.

Melina didn't say a word.

"She is, isn't she?" Cynthia asked, smiling.

"A little dark, though," his father added.

Melina's fingers dug into the back of Mac's hand with enough force to leave a row of scratches behind. He took the pain, and her punishment. He wondered how many comments she had heard like that throughout her lifetime.

Like the color of her skin made her the lesser.

Like her heritage made her unworthy.

Like because she wasn't white, she wasn't good enough.

She was fucking perfect for Mac.

And he loved the way her skin looked pressed against his.

"What's Pivetti think of that?" James asked.

Mac glanced at his mother, taking in her puckered brow and hard eyes. Cynthia wasn't okay with Cosa Nostra business being discussed at her table. She knew the Pivetti name and what it meant.

"What do you mean, what's he think of it?" Mac asked.

"The girl—your girl." James tipped his chin at Melina. "Stop trying to play me for a *cafone*, son. I work around shit, just like you do."

"Language," Cynthia said quietly.

James ignored her. "I roll the block, Mac. I walk the streets and see people you know. Seems your little broad there's been kicking up a fuss. She's got some eyes on her, and that means eyes on you, son. So I asked, what does Pivetti think of it? I know he married one a little darker than her, but his came from good stock and she had Italian on her father's side. Plus, she brought the diamonds with her. You know you can't be running around making mixed-race *bambinos* with—"

"That's enough," Mac barked.

His rage boiled over.

There was no stopping it.

"Keep that filth inside your head, James," Mac added, a dark edge sharpening his tone.

No one—absolutely fucking no one—would disrespect Melina in that way. Not in front of him, and not behind his back, if he could help it. He'd cut their tongues out for even whispering something as awful and bigoted as his father had just said.

Melina's hand had progressively tightened around Mac's to the point his knuckles cracked. How she had stayed as quiet as she did, he didn't know.

God, he loved this woman.

"What I do in my personal life is none of your concern," Mac said quietly. "It's hasn't been your concern in, oh ... about twenty years, James. You know, around the time you left Ma to take care of her house and kids alone. About the time you ran the streets, fucking whoever you wanted and drowning yourself in a bottle along the way. When you snorted coke up your nose. Remember that? Yeah, that's when you lost the right to know or put your opinions in my business."

James' lips flattened into a thin line as he regarded his son.

Mac was surprised that the man was sober today. It was a first.

It was also a weekday.

"I—" James started to say.

"James is full-blooded Italian," Cynthia interrupted smoothly, her gaze jumping between Mac and Melina. "We can trace our family roots right back to Sicily, Senior. His children will still be half, and from his side."

Mac was stunned to hear his mother speak out like that, especially towards Melina. She had been a little cold earlier. Colder than he expected. He knew it was just her way of trying to handle a surprising situation.

His mother had never once met a woman he was seeing. Bringing someone home to her was a big deal.

Mac was her firstborn—her only boy. Italian mothers raised their sons a little differently than they did for their daughters. They taught their girls how to handle a house, manage a man, and raise her children right. They raised their daughters with the capability to take care of themselves, no matter what happened.

But an Italian mother—his mother—raised their boys with the ideal that she couldn't let him go until he found a woman who would handle his house, manage him, and raise his children right. An Italian mother needed to know that the woman their son chose would be able to take care of her family, no matter what happened.

She needed to be perfect.

That's what Cynthia would want. She expected it.

Mac knew Melina was, his mother just needed to see it, too.

His father, however, could take a flying fucking leap.

"You have a good point," James said, still surveying Melina like she was a piece of meat.

"Mac," Melina said quietly.

"Yeah, doll?"

He didn't take his eyes off his fuck-up of a father.

"I'd like to go," Melina told him.

Yeah, ruined.

Mac gave Melina a nod, and a sad smile. "Sure, babe."

"Don't go," Cynthia said softly.

Mac glanced between his saddened mother and his smirking father.

"Let them go, Cynthia," James said, reaching for more lasagna.

"Another time, Ma," Mac promised.

Cynthia twisted her hands together on the table. "But—"

"I promise, *Mamma*," he insisted.

He never broke a promise to his mother.

She raised him better than that.

Cynthia nodded, but she still seemed hurt. Mac would apologize for that later.

Mac helped Melina out of her chair. His girl politely said goodbye to Cynthia, and promised to visit again soon with a request to teach her how to cook.

He had to laugh at that.

Cynthia agreed.

Melina didn't say a single thing to Mac's father.

James didn't look like he minded.

As they were heading out of the kitchen, Mac heard his father call out his name.

"What?" Mac asked, not bothering to tamper his irritation.

"Proud of you," James said, cocking a brow high. "Got yourself noticed, Mac. Just like I knew you would. Don't let it be ruined, all right? Think smart, not stupid. No woman is worth the button—she ain't going to get you in after she's got you seen, son. Keep that in mind."

Melina was worth far more than his button for the Pivetti crime family, but his father didn't need to know that was how Mac felt.

Forever the opportunist, Mac thought.

He finally understood why his father had shown up today.

James had probably heard that his estranged son was gaining the attention and traction in Cosa Nostra that he had never been able to achieve because of his lifestyle and bad choices. Perhaps Mac could be James' ticket into the family.

It wouldn't happen.

Not on Mac's watch.

"Let's go," Mac said, tugging Melina into his side.

Melina smiled, but he could see right through it.

Mac didn't start the car. He held onto the steering wheel with one hand, and placed his other on the middle leather section with his palm facing upwards. Not a second later, he felt the warmth of Melina's hand slide into his.

"I'm sorry," he said softly. "That never should have happened."

"It's not the first time," she whispered.

His heart hurt just hearing that.

"I love you, Melina."

Mac tilted his head just enough to catch her frown out of the corner of his eye.

"I know you do," she said.

"You're beautiful."

She laughed quietly. "So you keep saying."

But it was more than that.

"You're worthy, doll."

Melina blinked, silent.

"You're so crazy; you're smart, quick, and sharp. You make me want to scream, love you, and fuck you all at the same time. You challenge me. You are perfect. You are everything I need and want, and the color of your skin has nothing to do with how important you are to me. It has never mattered."

She met his stare, smiling slightly. "Yeah, I know."

"But I'm going to keep telling you that."

"Will you?"

Mac nodded. "Every time someone tells you differently. I absolutely fucking will."

He shouldn't have to, but he would.

Because people like his father were everywhere.

They couldn't be escaped.

"*Ti amo*," Mac repeated.

Melina wove their fingers. "Always, Mac."

"*Tanto. Sempre*, Melina."

"I don't know what that means," she said.

"So much. Forever."

Melina stared out the windshield. She still felt a million miles away to Mac.

"Talk to me," he demanded.

"I thought, at first, that you didn't think I was good enough to tell your father who I was to you," she confessed, her tone barely above a breath.

"Never."

"I figured out really quickly that he just wasn't important enough for you to tell him."

"Exactly," Mac said.

"Your mom, though …"

Mac chuckled. "Doll, she's going to adore you. She just needs to know her son is in good hands. She's always going to be like that with me. With Victoria, she'll send her off with a smile. When it comes to me, she's insane."

"Can we just … go?" Melina asked.

Sighing, Mac ignored the heaviness settling over his heart. "Yeah, sure."

He started the car, but a familiar form leaning on the front steps of his mother's home stopped him from pulling away. James stood there in the shadows, watching and smoking a cigarette.

Mac had all he could do not to get out of the car and beat the man's head into the pavement.

He started the car instead.

Mac didn't say a thing when Melina lifted her middle finger to his father, either. The bastard deserved it.

"Maccari."

Mac straightened at the familiar voice, a drop of tension sliding down his spine. He spun on his heel to face the man who had called his name in the quiet warehouse.

"Anthony," Mac greeted the Capo.

Anthony strolled across the cracked cement floor with an easy, confident stride. He fiddled with his lapel on his suit jacket, ignoring the other *soldatos* in Guido's crew moving around the place. His focus was solely on Mac.

This didn't bode well.

Mac still owed the man for the truck fuck up.

"Guido said I would find you here," Anthony said.

Mac shrugged. "Work, you know."

"I hear you're good for that." Anthony smiled as he came to a stop just a couple of feet away from Mac. "Guido isn't the one who says it, however."

Mac's brow furrowed.

That wasn't the first time someone had mentioned how his Capo didn't openly give Mac credit when it was due.

"I don't think he realizes what he's got in you," Anthony said, looking around the warehouse. He watched the men work quietly and efficiently. The crew had heisted a truck full of electronics and was trying to get it sorted and ready for quick sales. "Here you are, making sure these young men walk the right line and get their business handled. Guido wouldn't have half the crew he currently has if it weren't for you. Isn't that right, Maccari?"

Mac knew better than to drum up his own deeds. Pride was a good thing to have, but too much of it got a man in trouble.

"I'm just doing what I'm told," Mac said.

"You're being a good *soldato*," Anthony replied. "I could use a man like you on my crew. You would have had your button by now, had you been my man."

Jesus.

Mac shoved his hands in his pockets, still wary and confused about Anthony's presence and the conversation they were having. "Would I?"

Anthony shrugged. "Sure. It's always a little dangerous when you've got a good solider getting attention from the higher ups in the family, you know. Because when attention is on someone else in *la famiglia*, that means it's not on you."

And every man wanted the boss's approval. Every man wanted to be noticed and for all the right reasons. It was a well-played game in Cosa Nostra.

Mac got it.

Unfortunately, he still didn't trust Anthony a great deal. He was a rival Capo, after all. The man was fighting for the boss's attention and approval against Mac's boss.

Considering there were only a handful of people who could want Mac dead, and he knew one of them wasn't the Pivetti boss, Anthony had taken a spot on the list. The truck accident had been a stupid mistake, sure, and one that Mac apologized for.

But stupid mistakes killed men.

Grudges killed men.

Fuck ups were how men like Mac died all the time in Cosa Nostra.

"Your boy in the far right corner has been watching us for the last five minutes instead of working," Anthony noted.

Mac didn't even need to look to know which man Anthony was talking about. "Stephano, quit standing around with your fingers in your ass or I'll make that a permanent look for you."

"Sorry, Mac," came the quiet reply from behind him.

"They like you," Anthony said. "Respect you."

"Aren't they supposed to?" Mac asked.

It's what made the crew manageable, for the

most part.

Anthony didn't reply, instead saying, "As much as I hate Guido, the asshole that he is, I do like you, Maccari."

"Thanks."

"I've decided how you can make the money, and get back in my good graces for the truck incident."

Wonderful.

Mac kept his face a blank mask. "And how is that?"

"I heard you have a thing for fighting in a cage. You're pretty quick on your feet. Practically unbeatable. Rumor is, you're known to step over into another family's stomping grounds to catch the best matches."

"I only fight when I need some extra cash," Mac said quickly.

He didn't want problems for messing with another family.

"Calm down," Anthony said, chuckling. "I'm not here to get you in trouble. Business is business, after all. How confident are you in your ability to win a fight?"

"Pretty confident, if I can size up my opponent beforehand," Mac admitted.

"I know a place—not like the one you go to for fights. It's an occasional thing, high stakes, and anyone can fight if they've got the right cash. Bets are instant and in the thousands. Fight for me for one night, give up all your winnings, and you'll never hear me say a bad word about you or our business again."

Mac held off his agreement for a moment. He wondered if Anthony was playing some kind of game with him. One that might get him killed.

"Can I bring someone?" Mac asked.

Anthony raised a brow. "Like who?"

"My girl."

Melina would have his back.

Mac trusted her above everyone in his life.

Anthony grinned. "Ah, I see. I don't have a problem with that, as long as she refrains from causing us any issues."

"She won't. And she likes seeing me fight," Mac added, smirking.

"Good." Anthony turned on his heel, heading back towards the warehouse entrance. "I'll give you a call, Mac. You won't see me around here again. Guido's home isn't a welcoming place for a man like me."

Guido wasn't all too fond of Anthony, either. Mac still refused to feed into Guido's nonsense about taking Anthony out. There wasn't any reason. Rivalry wasn't good enough to spill blood.

"Unlike Guido," Anthony said, still walking, "I know better than to toy around in another Capo's business or territory. Do me a favor, Mac."

"What's that?"

Anthony pulled open the old, rusted door of the warehouse. "Tell your Capo to stay behind his own damn lines, and leave my crew alone."

When had Guido gone into Anthony's territory? And why?

Anthony left the warehouse before Mac could ask.

Mac kicked off his shoes, hearing the womanly giggles echoing from the kitchen. Not one set of giggles, but two.

Both were familiar.

Confused, Mac quietly padded down the hallway and stayed in the shadows of the entrance of his apartment. He preferred Melina's place, but he needed a few things from his own apartment for the week. Melina agreed to stay at his place for a couple of days while he worked some things out with business.

Standing side by side, Mac watched as Melina copied her companion's actions as she kneaded a thick clump of dough.

Victoria—Mac's sister—smiled and nodded approvingly. "There you go. Just make sure you mash it good, and it'll rise great."

Something primal curled in Mac's gut, hot and twisted. He liked seeing Melina in the kitchen, working and cooking. She wasn't the homemaker type, as far as that went, but he liked the sight of it all the same.

It got him hot and crazy.

Mac tampered it down.

But only because his sister was there.

Why was his sister there again?

"I don't know," Melina said. "How is this going to help?"

"Listen …" Victoria grabbed a bit of flour and tossed it over Melina's pile of dough. "It's like this for my mother, she needs to make sure you're up to speed. Poor little Mac, he can't feed himself unless it's her cooking the food, or dress himself, or keep himself warm. I know, he's grown and can handle his shit, but not to my mom. This will help, trust me."

"I still think you're nuts."

Mac chuckled, unable to stop himself. Both women's heads snapped up, their gazes leveling on him. He stepped into the kitchen with a shake of his head.

"You think she's nuts because she is," Mac said, shooting his glaring sister a smile. "Vic, good to see you."

"And you. You've been everywhere but to see me these last couple of months. I was starting to think you must be dead," Victoria said, not hiding her bite in the least.

Melina laughed, but kept quiet.

"So you just showed up at my apartment looking for me?" Mac asked.

"Ma mentioned you brought a girl around. I wanted to come and see you, maybe find out why you didn't mention anything to me."

Mac scowled. "It's a new thing, Vic. I'm working on it."

"I saved you the trouble."

Melina jerked her thumb at Victoria. "I like her."

"Of course you do," Mac said. "She's just as difficult and hard on the head as you are, doll. Birds of a feather and all that."

Melina stuck out her tongue.

Victoria stuck her middle finger up.

"See," Mac muttered.

Now, he had two females in his place to bust his balls.

Perfect.

Melina seemed happy, though.

Maybe she had found a friend.

"What's for supper?" Mac asked.

Melina cocked a brow at him. "Whatever I cook."

Well, then ...

"Sounds delicious," he said.

Victoria laughed. "Ma raised him so well."

CHAPTER TWENTY-THREE

"You know, Melina, I have to tell you I'm really impressed."

Melina smiled. "Oh, are you now?"

"Yes. You went from barely being in the kitchen to whipping up some great dishes."

"What can I say? Your sister is a pretty good teacher."

Mac took another bite of his chicken parmesan before speaking again. "Nice to know Vic is good for something other than running her mouth."

Melina reached across the table and popped Mac on his hand.

"Don't talk about your sister like that."

"Since when did you two get to be best friends?" Mac asked.

Melina took a bite of her breadstick before answering. "Since she has so kindly been giving me cooking lessons in the hopes that it will make your mom comfortable relinquishing your care to Big, Bad Melina."

Mac touched her leg under the table. "Big, Bad Melina. Mmm, why does that sound as sexy as it does?"

Melina rolled her eyes. "Because you're sick."

"Sick over you." Mac winked at her.

Melina returned her attention to the dinner she'd prepared for them. Chicken parmesan, fresh baked garlic bread sticks, and New York Cheesecake. Forget Mac's mother being impressed with her. Melina was impressed by herself. Losing her mother at such a young age, some of the things she'd missed out on were time in the kitchen, learning how to cook, bake and sew.

A mother would have taught her all those things.

A mother would have explained to her what to expect when it came to life and love.

But fate had been a cruel mistress and so she'd been left to learn on her own and all things considered, right now she was doing pretty good.

"Hey. Where did you go? You have a far off look in your eye," Mac said.

Melina swallowed a lump in her throat. "I was thinking about my mom."

Mac put down his fork and reached for her hand across the table. "Tell me."

She shook her head. "It's silly really. The time Victoria and I have been spending together just reminded me that your sister was teaching me things my mother should have. It's weird in a way, how your sister and I have bonded. I don't usually deal well with women."

"There's nothing wrong with thinking about your mother and missing her," Mac said softly.

"You know I'm not one for sentimentalities most of the time, but a part of me sometimes can't help but wonder how my life would've been if my mom hadn't died so young. Would I be a different woman than I am now?"

"You are exactly who you are supposed to be, doll. Your mother would have been proud of you, no matter what. A mother's love is one of the few things money can't buy."

She nodded. "You're right. Just excuse me for being all sappy. Hanging out with your sister has just been reminding me of the lack of female companionship in my life. That's all."

"Things are different now. I know it's not easy for you to let people in, but Vic likes you. Trust me, my sister has a short attention span, and if she didn't enjoy hanging out with you, she wouldn't."

Mac leaned across the table and kissed her briefly on the lips before using his thumb to wipe away a smear of marinara sauce on her cheek.

"You could've told me I had sauce on my face."

Mac's eyes smoldered. "Not when I was deciding if I was going to lick it off or not."

"You are so bad."

"And that's why you love me," Mac said with confidence.

Melina's hand drifted towards Mac's crotch under the table. "Is that so? Are you certain it's not because of your amazing cock?"

She licked her lips as her hand found his hardness through his pants and rubbed.

"You're not playing fair," Mac said, eyes bright with lust.

"All's fair in love and war."

Rising from her seat, Melina came around to Mac's side of the table and slowly pulled back his chair. He watched her with an amused expression on his face.

"Doll?"

"Shh."

Melina straddled Mac's lap and took his face in her hands. She kissed him hard and hungrily, trying to convey to him the best way she could just how much his unwavering support and love meant to her. Mac's hands gripped her waist and lifted her up.

"What are you doing?"

"Bedroom. Now."

Melina laughed before Mac's lips were covering her own as he carried her towards the bedroom. Finishing their dinner would wait. Right now, dessert was calling.

"We're going to kill each other if we keep this up," Melina said hours later.

"Not a bad way to die is it?"

"Not in the least."

Melina lay on Mac's chest in the darkness of his bedroom. His arms were wrapped around her, holding her close to him. She snuggled closer as he played with a lock of her hair. As much as she loved the primal connection she had with Mac, she loved this part, too.

Afterglow.

The comforting silence of two hearts beating.

The feel of a hard body holding her like she was the most precious thing in the world.

It was a high she'd probably never get used to.

"You know, every time it just gets better and better," Mac said.

"Believe me, I've noticed."

Mac laughed in the darkness. "Glad to know all of my hard work is not going unappreciated. But on a serious note, there's something I want to talk to you about."

"Oh. What is it?"

"I had some business I was doing for Anthony that went south and so I owe him. He told me how he wanted me to pay up."

Melina's breath caught in her throat. "And what's that?"

"He wants me to fight for him. High stakes. Lots of money involved."

"How much of it does he get?"

"All of it."

Melina sat straight up in bed and frowned. "All of it? Is he out of his mind?"

"Doll, that's the way things work."

"That's bullshit, Mac. You're the one putting your life and health on the line every time you fight and he gets to sit back and enjoy all the rewards. I'm not okay with that."

Melina saw the outline of Mac's body as he shifted in bed. Seconds later, he'd turned on one of the lamps before he rested back against the headboard.

"I know it's not ideal, but I don't have a choice. If I don't do this, my reputation is dead and possibly me too, for not making things right."

Melina folded her arms. "There are too many stupid rules to follow if you ask me. Blink wrong and you're dead. A dollar short and you're dead. What's the point of dealing with all of this?"

Mac reached for her hand. "I was born into this life. I know these streets and I know what it takes to make it. I'm just paying my dues and giving respect where it's supposed to go."

"And once this is over with, are you good with him?"

"Yeah. He gave his word and in this life, your word is everything."

She couldn't believe how calm Mac was being. The fact that he was going to fight and hand over every red cent he made didn't appear to bother him in the slightest. Nor did the fact that he was fighting for Anthony, a man she wasn't fond of in the least. The man gave her the creeps.

"Then I'm going to be right there with you and I don't want to hear any arguments about it."

Mac smiled at her, showing his perfect white teeth. "There's no one else I would rather have in my corner."

"Like there's anyone else I would let be in your corner. You never know when you're going to need me to put another bullet in someone."

Mac pulled her down on top of him until they were

nose to nose. "So now we get to the real reason."

Melina smiled. "What can I say? I think I was born for this role."

Beneath the covers, Mac cupped her ass in his hands. "I think you were, too. In fact, I know you were."

The sound of Mac's phone ringing caught their attention. Melina shifted to Mac's left side so he could answer his phone. He answered on the third ring.

"Mac."

Melina sat up and listened, watching the expression on her lover's face. A muscle in his jaw moved.

"Guido."

Her body tensed when she heard the name. Why was Mac's Capo calling him so late?

"Yeah. We'll be there."

Mac ended the call and stared at her with a half smirk on his face.

"We'll be where?" Melina pressed.

"We've been invited to another get together at the Pivetti mansion tomorrow night."

Melina raised a brow. "Really? That's a surprise."

"Not really. The invitation came from Neeya and we have you to thank for that. You keep making an impression, doll."

"Excuse me for not jumping for joy at the thought of going into the lion's den again. Luca wasn't exactly very cordial to me the last time we went there and neither were his other guests."

"I know that, but this will give us a chance to size up the players."

"You mean find out who's trying to kill you or me, or possibly both of us?" Melina asked.

"Yeah, and you know the old saying, keep your friends close and your enemies even closer. Now we have a prime opportunity."

Melina twisted an errant stand of hair. What Mac said made perfect sense. Their lives were on the line and a dinner surrounded by all the key players in their corrupt world could put an end to the mystery once and for all. She'd rather walk on broken glass than attend another party, but Melina had never run away from anything and she wasn't about to start now.

"Fine. But I'm not going to be so nice this time."

Mac drew her back into the circle of his arms before turning out the light. "I'd expect nothing less."

Subterfuge and innuendos had become their way of life, but together they would figure things out. They had too much to lose otherwise.

"Doll, to say you look amazing would be an understatement."

Melina blushed beneath Mac's praise. She did look good after another morning spent being pampered, courtesy of her lover. A day at the spa had done wonders for her, although she couldn't help but wonder just how much the little retreat had cost him. When she'd asked, he refused to tell her. Part of her had wanted to argue, but she knew better than to keep pressing Mac about something when his mind was made up.

"I have you to thank for that."

She gave him a saucy wink before she faced him again.

"All I did was make sure that you got the treatment you deserve."

"Well, I want you to know that I appreciate it."

Mac cupped her chin in his hand. "You're welcome. Are you ready?"

Melina sighed. "As ready as I'll ever be. I still wish we

didn't have to go."

"Me too. There are better ways we could spend an evening than with sharks."

"You're right about that, but I never run from anything and I'm not about to start now. Let's go."

Melina took one last look at herself in the mirror, admiring the way the black fitted dress with strategic cutouts accentuated the curves of her body. The four-and-a-half-inch stilettos she wore did wonders for showcasing her calf muscles. Instead of her usual curly mass of hair that hung down her back, her hair was slicked into a low ponytail to show off the simple black cross earrings that she wore proudly to match Mac's necklace. A girl could get used to this kind of treatment.

She held tight to Mac's arm as he lead her outside and opened the car door for her. She didn't want to think that she was getting sappy and losing her edge, but her new relationship made her want to show more of her softer side. With Mac, she was realizing that she didn't always have to be a tigress. Sometimes, it was all right to let someone else take charge.

As Mac started the car, she couldn't help glancing at him. She was a lucky girl, indeed. The suit he wore fit like it was made for him, showing off his toned and fit physique. A physique that she hadn't been able to stop herself from enjoying every chance that she got.

"Doll, if you keep looking at me like that, we're going to be late for this party."

Melina licked her lips. "Why?"

"Because I'm going to pull this car over and fuck your brains out."

"As much as that thought appeals to me, we don't need to make a late entrance. I'm sure it wouldn't be looked on well."

"No, it wouldn't. You're learning fast how this life works."

Melina shrugged. "Only the strong survive."

"That's one way of looking at it."

Mac reached for her hand and brought it to his lips before he held it tight in his hand. They were silent as he drove. Melina couldn't help thinking about what the night ahead would bring for them. Obviously, Neeya Pivetti liked her, or else she wouldn't have been invited to return to the opulent mansion, but Luca still wasn't keen on her. Melina only hoped that at least he would be a little less rude than he'd been last time. Twenty minutes later, the Pivetti mansion loomed in front of them. The familiar sight of men patrolling the massive grounds greeted them.

"Time to walk into the snake pit," Melina said.

"Crush them with your heels, doll."

Melina smiled. If need be, she'd do just that. Mac helped her from the car and tucked her arm through his as they walked up to the large mansion. Before they could even ring the doorbell, the door was opened and they were ushered inside by the same woman that had cleaned their shoes the last time they'd visited.

"Welcome to the home of Luca and Neeya Pivetti. Our hosts await you in the ballroom."

The woman turned and snapped her fingers, and another member of the household stepped forward in the familiar black and white and beckoned for them to follow him to the ballroom. Opulence screamed at her from every corner.

Did it really take all of this to live?

No, it didn't, but one thing she'd learned in her short exposure to Cosa Nostra, was that appearance was everything.

When she and Mac entered the ballroom, all eyes focused on them. Melina felt like prey being sized up by a gang of predators. All conversation had stopped as she and Mac were stared at like a circus attraction.

"Ignore them. Keep walking," Mac whispered.

She nodded and plastered a haughty smile on her face. This was a game and she could play it with the best of them. Melina tossed her ponytail over her shoulder and walked confidently into the ballroom with Mac. Slowly, the conversations around them started to resume and she leaned closer to him.

"I don't like this," Mac said. "Something's not right."

"That's an understatement."

Melina took in the décor of the ballroom. Once again, no expense had been spared in the evening's decorations. Neeya Pivetti had impeccable taste.

"Mac, what a surprise."

Melina rolled her eyes as Guido approached them. A cigar stuck out of the jacket pocket of his designer suit, but it did nothing to hide his large form.

"Skip," Mac said.

Guido's gaze roved over Melina and she fought the urge to curl her lip in disgust.

"I see you've brought your girl with you. My, my, she looks good enough to eat every time I see her."

Mac's hand tightened around hers. She didn't need to look at his face to see that he didn't appreciate his Capo's comment. It was highly suggestive and downright disrespectful. If Guido were any other man, there was no question in her mind that Mac would've beaten him to a pulp for what he'd said. No doubt, Guido knew it, too, or he wouldn't be standing there with such a shit-eating grin on his face.

"A man is nothing without a good woman by his side," Mac finally said.

"Hmm. For some men that's true, I suppose. Me, I've always prided myself on paving my own way."

"That's one of the things I love most about Mac. He's a made man in all the ways that matter," Melina said.

Guido laughed and Melina's jaw tightened. The urge to kick him in the balls rose up strong, but she forced herself to remain calm. She and Mac were in enough shit, and despite her intense dislike of his Capo, she wouldn't allow herself to go off half-cocked and further complicate things.

Mac's eyes found hers. "You couldn't have given me a higher compliment, doll."

Guido rubbed a hand over his face. "Mac, I never thought I'd see you let a female take your balls like that. But then again, she is the only reason you're here tonight to begin with. Enjoy your evening."

Without another word, the pudgy Capo walked away, hands in his pockets.

"I got away with killing Tip and he was a made man. Think I could put a bullet in him too without consequences?" Melina asked.

Mac laughed before he kissed her on the cheek. There was a twinkle in his eyes as he looked at her. "Are you trying to make me embarrass myself in here?"

Melina raised a brow. "I have no idea what you're talking about."

"You holding a gun is enough to get my cock hard no matter the time, place or situation."

"Nice to know I have that effect on you but I'm serious. What the fuck was up with him? He was deliberately being an asshole."

Mac's eyes narrowed on a spot across the room where Guido stood, talking with Vin.

"Guido is an asshole on his worst days. There was something different about him tonight. It was almost like he was deliberately trying to goad me into something."

"I thought the same thing, but why? You're his best guy. It doesn't make sense."

"A simple little thing called jealousy, doll. It has been

known to destroy empires."

Melina looked around the ballroom, eyeing the rest of the partygoers. She recognized some of the botoxed, bone-thin women she'd seen the last time. A few of them tossed her mocking glances, baring their teeth.

"I thought men in Cosa Nostra were supposed to be above foolishness like that," Melina said.

"Maybe in times past. These days, honor and respect are not the staples they used to be for some men."

Melina rolled her eyes at some of the women staring at her before she turned her attention back to Mac. "Be careful. Please."

Mac smiled softly. "Always. Don't worry. I'm not going anywhere."

Melina cleared her throat. "Good. I've just gotten used to having you around. I'd hate to have to mess up my makeup by crying at your funeral."

Mac laughed. "Don't want to mess up your makeup, huh? That's a good reason."

"What can I say? I can't have you thinking I've gone completely soft."

"No danger there. I know firsthand your bark is as just as bad as your bite," Mac teased.

"Melina."

She turned at the sound of a woman's voice calling her name.

"Neeya," Melina said.

The regal-looking woman wore a deep burgundy gown that highlighted her slim waist and figure. The strapless dress showcased her toned arms. With easy grace, Neeya Pivetti made her way to Melina's side.

"You look wonderful, dear," Neeya greeted her.

"I can say the same. You look very queenly," Melina said.

"Ah, this old thing."

"You wear it well, Mrs. Pivetti," Mac said.

"I appreciate the compliment, Mac. Either your mother raised you right, or Melina has whipped you into shape quite nicely."

Melina laughed. "I can't take all the credit for this one. His mother is a formidable woman."

"Indeed, she must be. Now, Mac, if you don't mind, I'm going to steal your lovely date for a little while. I believe you'll find my husband in his study. He wants to see you."

"Yes, ma'am," Mac said to Neeya before turning to Melina. "Don't have too much fun without me, doll."

With a wink, he was off in search of Luca, leaving Melina alone with Neeya.

"My, I'd recognize that look anywhere," Neeya said.

"And what look would that be?"

"Of a woman in love."

Melina's eyes snapped to Neeya's. She wanted to deny it, but somehow she knew that it would be pointless to lie to a woman like the Pivetti Don's wife.

"Love makes you vulnerable. It's why I've always fought so hard against it."

Neeya offered her a smile. "I'm glad you didn't deny it."

"I'm sure a woman like you can spot liars a mile away. There was no point in lying."

"You'd be right about that. In this lifestyle, you have to be perceptive. It can be the difference between living to see another day or never opening your eyes again."

"So I'm learning. How do you deal with it? The backstabbing? The dishonesty?"

"I suppose I should tell you something about me, Melina. Though I grew up with wealth, it came with a price. My life now as Luca's wife is not so very different from mine in South Africa. There was death, dishonesty and greed around every corner. Everyone is and remains a suspect. How you survive is simply to trust no one and always, always have an escape path."

Melina sighed. "That sounds like a lonely way to live."

Neeya shrugged. "It can be, but life is all in what you make it. I'm used to living life at the top of the food chain and I will accept nothing less than the best. And if that means I have to be on my guard a little more than usual, then so be it."

"You're a stronger woman than I."

"You're stronger than you give yourself credit for. You came into this pit of vipers tonight, despite the fact that you were not greeted warmly on your last visit, and in spite of the whispers of unrest."

"It would've been rude to refuse such an invitation. I'm sure you or your husband would not have taken kindly to it."

Neeya folded her arms. "And you're avoiding what I just said. I know what's going on, Melina."

"Well, then you know that Mac and I have to watch our backs at every turn and we have no idea who is behind this."

"Don't you? Come now, dear, you're a bright girl. The answer is already in front of you. The question is when are you going to do something about it?"

A passing waiter stopped and offered them a flute of champagne. Melina quickly downed the contents of her glass before reaching for another one.

"I'm not like you. You're the wife of a Don. People respect you. Since I hooked up with Mac, I've been treated like the dirt on the bottom of a shoe because of the color of my skin. I've been called a whore of the worst kind. Sometimes, I wonder if Mac would be better off without me."

"Now you sound like the foolish women at this party. Your Mac is in love with you and a man like him doesn't fall in love indiscriminately. He saw something in you. That you could be not only a lover, but a partner as well. Don't let those who envy you destroy what you have."

"Easier said than done."

"I never pegged you for a quitter, Melina. Don't start now."

Melina took another sip of champagne. "I can't. Mac needs someone to watch his back and no one can do a better job of that than me."

"That's the spirit. Now excuse me for a moment. I have to check on the progress of dinner."

Melina nodded. When Neeya had gone, she drank the rest of her champagne. Her hostess was right. She had to grow a thicker skin. Mac needed her now more than ever. She didn't have time to let her petty insecurities get the best of her. Who gave a fuck if they didn't like her? She didn't need their approval, nor did she want it. She'd always been a rebel and there was no need now to do anything differently. As more snickering whispers reached her ears, Melina smiled.

Let's go, bitches.

There was nothing they could dish out she couldn't handle.

CHAPTER TWENTY-FOUR

Mac tossed his hands in his pockets as he strolled down the hallway leading to Luca's office. Just a few feet from the large, ornate doors, Mac noticed they were opened a few inches. It was enough that he knew no one inside would see his approach. From his spot, he could already hear quiet murmurs coming from inside the office.

Glancing back down the hallway, he took note that no one was behind him.

Knowing that both he and Melina had a target on their backs, it was tempting to listen in and see if he could find out something that might push him in the right direction. Still, Mac hesitated at eavesdropping on the Pivetti Don and his men. Luca had obviously ordered Mac to his office, and knew he would be coming upstairs right away. It was a demand from the boss—no man ignored one of those, or made a Don wait.

Simple as that.

It would not bode well for Mac to be caught spying, no matter his reasons.

Clearing his throat loud enough for it to be heard from within the office, Mac strolled up to the office doors and knocked. He waited to be permitted entrance, and it didn't take long.

"Come on in, Mac," Luca said, his voice slightly muffled.

Mac pushed open the doors, and took in the people sitting around the office. Luca sat behind his large desk, fingers drumming against the wood in what looked to be irritation as he glared at another man across the room. Enzo, Luca's underboss, seemed to be completely oblivious to his boss's glower. That, or he was terribly good at pretending. Matthew, Luca's consigliere, was shaking his head and sipping from a glass filled with amber-colored liquid.

"You're going to press that issue, then?" Luca asked Enzo.

Enzo shrugged. "Listen, Boss—"

"No. *Fermo!*" Luca barked, his palm smacking hard to his desk. "I am not the one who needs to listen between us, Enzo. You are clearly forgetting your place."

The underboss quickly tipped his chin lower, an action that Mac instantly recognized as a submissive pose.

"It's being seen as favoritism on your part," Enzo muttered quietly. "Consider that. It could do him more harm than good."

Mac wasn't entirely sure what he had just walked in on, but it didn't sound good. It also didn't sound like it was something he should be in the middle of.

"I can come back if this is a bad time, Boss," Mac said, directing his comment to Luca only.

Luca's cheek twitched, but he didn't give Mac a passing glance. He was still glaring at Enzo like he wanted the man to melt into the couch he was sitting on.

"Maybe the idea of favoritism is exactly what I am looking for people to think," Luca said. "Did you consider that?"

Enzo sighed. "And you will get the young man killed for it."

Mac stiffened, taking in Enzo's statement. Were they talking about him?

Who else, other than Mac, could be getting what would be seen as extra attention from the Pivetti Don?

Mac didn't believe that it was Luca who was making attempts on his life. But could the Don be purposely doing other things to push someone else into those attempts?

"I'm just going to step out—"

"You will stay where you are," Luca interrupted Mac, cutting him with a single look.

That was that.

Mac nodded. "All right, Boss."

Luca jerked his head towards the door. "Both of you, out. Mac, pour yourself a drink and take a seat."

"Luca," Enzo said, almost as if he was pleading with his boss for something.

"Do as I said, Enzo. You follow my orders, not the other way around."

Matthew pushed away from the window, drink still in hand. "Come on, Enzo. We're missing the party. Let's go find our wives, and see how drunk they've gotten since we last left them."

Enzo scowled as he stood from the couch. "You're playing with fire, Luca."

Luca didn't look like he cared. "Maybe so, but I only want the best, Enzo. I know he is, so let him prove it."

"To what sacrifice?" Enzo asked.

The boss didn't respond. He simply flicked a hand towards the door, silently demanding that his men leave again. Mac stepped to the side as Matthew and Enzo strolled past him to leave the office without another word of argument.

Enzo gave Mac a frown as he passed.

That, right there, was enough to tell Mac the conversation he'd walked in on was likely about him. That being the case, Luca was pushing the buttons of several men by giving Mac—an unmade man— private time and attention he wasn't giving to his made men.

"Close the door behind them," Luca demanded.

Mac complied, letting the heavy door click shut as quietly as he could manage. "I take it that was about me, huh?"

Luca smiled, slow and easy. "You're a smart man. You don't need me to say what you already know."

Well, then ...

Stuffing his hands in his pockets again, Mac tried to seem unbothered. It was nothing more than pretense. He didn't want to be someone's bait.

"Worry not," Luca said, glancing at Mac. "I can see that's what you're over there doing. Stewing, thinking, and worrying. Don't bother. It's pointless."

"From the sounds of that conversation, it's not exactly pointless."

"It is, Mac, because I expect you to come out on top in all of this, whatever it is."

Mac's brow furrowed. "You don't even know what's going on, but you're hoping that someone will react to your ..."

"Favoritism was the word Enzo used," the boss supplied.

"Fine, favoritism. You're hoping someone will react to it."

Luca shrugged. "Someone is messing with my people, Mac. Making moves and causing issues without consulting me. I do not want the trouble that may bring. So yes, I am hoping this will bring the fool out of the woodwork. Jealousy is strange in that way. It makes the best of men greedy idiots."

Mac still didn't like this at all.

The problem was, he didn't get a choice.

"You wanted to see me?" Mac asked.

The question was for show, and nothing more. He knew exactly why Luca had wanted to see him, now.

"Pour yourself a drink," Luca replied, waving at a table filled with spirits in bottles.

"Would you be offended if I refused?"

Luca cocked a brow. "Why would you?"

"Because I don't drink if I can help it. My father and all."

"Ah, I see. The last time you were in here, you had a drink."

"Refusing your offer would have been, rude seeing as it was my first invitation from you," Mac explained.

Luca grinned, pointing a finger at Mac. "See, smart man. Forget the drink. Have a seat."

Mac took one of the high back leather chairs closer to Luca's desk. "What now?"

"Now we give it a while, Mac," Luca said, resting back in his chair. "How's your girl?"

"Well."

"Neeya was happy to invite her tonight. I hear you and Anthony have worked out a solution to the little problem of you owing him money."

Mac kept his face a mask of calm. "Yes."

"Honorable men pay their debts. I'm pleased to see that you are one of them."

Always thank a boss when he gives you a compliment.

"*Grazie*, Don."

Luca picked up a glass on the side of his desk and took a drink of the dark liquor. "Be careful with Anthony. He's the kind of man who isn't as upfront with his motives as I would like him to be."

Mac nodded. "Thanks for the heads up."

"A good boss looks out for his *famiglia*—his men."

His men.

Mac remembered Luca's words to his underboss and consigliere from earlier.

He wanted the best men.

Did the boss think that was Mac?

Mac dropped to one knee and helped Melina slide her feet into sky-high stiletto heels. He fixed the straps around her ankles, and let his hands skim the soft skin of her bare legs as he rose up again.

"Keep that up and we'll be late," Melina said, smirking.

He dragged his hands a little higher under her bodycon dress, exposing her thighs and black lace panties. She looked damn good with her legs a mile long and her curves begging to be touched. "We can't be late for something when I don't even know where it's happening or how we're getting there, doll."

Melina wagged a finger at him. "We were told to be ready by seven."

Mac shot the clock a look. It was ten to seven already. Anthony had texted him those simple directions earlier that day. Nothing more.

"Ask me," Mac drawled, winking, "and I can make it quick."

She opened her pretty mouth to respond, but a knock on Mac's apartment door interrupted them both. Instantly, Mac was on guard. The building wasn't entirely safe—wait long enough and someone would come out and let someone in—or ring a bunch of buzzers and make it quicker.

Still, he wasn't expecting anyone.

Mac nodded towards the bathroom, not saying a thing. Melina followed his unspoken request, disappearing into the bathroom and closing the door behind her. Another knock echoed on the apartment door.

"Just a second," Mac called.

He grabbed his gun off the couch as he strolled towards the door. Resting the weapon down at his side, he looked through the peephole to find an unfamiliar man, wearing a tailored suit, behind it. In his arms, the man held a long box that was at least four feet in length.

"Who is it?" Mac asked, knowing he would be heard through the door.

"Anthony Corelli's second driver, sir," the man responded. "I was told to be outside at seven, and to make sure this gift was delivered to a Melina Morgan before leaving."

"You couldn't give it to us outside?"

"Those weren't my instructions."

Goddammit.

Mac's paranoia and wariness were way too high for this fucking nonsense. Why couldn't Anthony have just said he was sending a man to the building?

"I will leave the gift at your door, sir, and be waiting outside," the man said.

Through the peephole, Mac watched as the man did exactly what he said he would do. Five long minutes later, Mac pulled open the door and listened. The only sounds he could hear were the normal noises of the old building. He pulled the door open the rest of the way, found the hallway empty of the man, and grabbed the box.

Once the apartment door was closed, Mac called out, "All is safe, doll."

Melina came out of the bathroom looking less than impressed. "What was all that about?"

"Anthony's theatrics."

"Hmm."

Melina's gaze fell on the box in Mac's hands.

He shook it. "He sent something for you."

"What is it?"

"I don't know, but it's rude to refuse the gifts of made men. I assume whatever it is, he must want you to have it for the fighting event tonight. Come open it up."

Mac was less than impressed that another man was buying his girl gifts. Melina wasn't a quiet, easily-pleased woman. If she wanted something, she would let Mac know, and he would get it for her.

Other men didn't need to be buying her fuck-all.

She wasn't theirs to spoil.

She was *his*.

"Stop the scowling," Melina said as she walked up and took the box from his hands. "You're practically turning green, Mac. You know I think Anthony is a pig."

He did.

It still didn't help.

Mac followed Melina into the living room, still silent and scowling, despite her demand for him to stop. She put the box on the couch, and pulled at the red ribbon keeping it closed. Once she had that tugged away, she lifted the lid and tossed it aside.

"Oh, wow," Melina said, pulling the tissue away from the top of the long box.

Even Mac was a bit surprised at the item resting beneath the tissue paper.

"Is that …?"

"Touch it and see," Mac said. "It'll feel like air on your fingers."

Melina reached into the box and ran her hand over the gray-and-white-colored fur coat. It was long enough that it would fall to her knees, with an overly large hood and wide arms. It was a beautiful piece of clothing, to be sure, but Mac didn't even know if Melina was into furs. It was common for the women of made men to sport all different kinds of furs, despite how society liked to shame people who collected the rare coats, hats, and so forth.

The coat had to be in the thousands of dollars, at least.

Mac's gut burned a little hotter with his anger.

A gift of this magnitude, of this sort of flash, was not

acceptable. It was almost like a blatant offer from Anthony to Melina.

"So soft you can't even feel it," Melina said, running her hand down the coat again. "I'm not ... a fur kind of girl, Mac."

"Is there a note?" Mac asked.

Melina moved the coat around, and found a folded up piece of parchment paper beneath it. Opening it up, she read, "Melina, I hope you'll enjoy this gift and put it to good use tonight as you stand in the crowd. Chinchilla is the softest of the furs, and I thought it would look beautiful with your skin. Until tonight ... Anthony Corelli."

She tossed the note away like it had burned her hand.

Mac's jaw clenched. "He's a bastard."

"Am I the only one who feels like that was a proposition of some sort?"

"Without outright asking? Yeah, sort of."

Melina frowned as she turned on her heel to face him. "Don't do that, Mac."

"I'm not worried ... or whatever. But I don't trust Anthony a great deal right now."

"You don't trust anyone right now," she corrected.

"I wonder why, doll." Mac sighed heavily. "You're going to have to wear the coat, at least to keep his attitude at a bearable level for the evening."

"Is he going to expect something for it in return?" she asked.

"No. That would come after you had already accepted his proposition. This is basically him telling you to look at the kinds of beautiful things he could give you."

And it made Mac fucking sick.

And *angry*.

Fuck, he was mad.

"Don't do that," Melina repeated, quieter the second time.

His girl knew him too well.

Mac was damn good at hiding his emotions when he wanted to, but not where Melina was concerned. He was going to have to learn how to curb his instinct to react whenever she was involved, or he was going to find himself in a grave before it was his time.

"It's not you, doll," he said.

Melina nodded, her hand coming up to stroke his tight jaw. "Put that anger to use, yeah?"

Mac smiled, unable to stop himself. "Pardon?"

"Tonight, when you're fighting. Focus what you're feeling right now into something good. I do not want to spend my night in an ER after pulling you out of a cage, Mac."

There was a shining worry glimmering in Melina's eye. Mac couldn't miss it even if he tried.

"I'll be fine," he assured.

Melina didn't respond.

Mac hoped he was telling the truth, but he really didn't know.

***

"Three fights, total," Anthony said. "Spread out, so you'll have a bit of a break. I just confirmed your register."

Mac didn't show the nervousness that slipped through his bloodstream at Anthony's statement. One fight was nothing. Two was pushing it, but was doable. Mac would be exhausted and overworked after the second, and not up for a third round, but obviously, he wasn't being given a choice in the matter.

It didn't help that he had been far too busy lately to keep up with his usual workout regime. He hadn't even been able to have a good round of sparring to prep for this. He wasn't out of shape, as far as that went, but he might be a little rusty and out of practice.

It could still be bad.

Melina's hand tightened around Mac's arm like she knew what he was thinking. He patted her hand, wanting to reassure her. If he couldn't reassure himself, the least he could do was calm his girl.

"Your gear?" Anthony asked.

Mac held up a small black bag. "They checked it at the door."

There wasn't much in the bag but some long shorts, clean clothes, and protective tape for his fists. Anthony had already let him know the place didn't allow the usual protective gear, which meant Mac would essentially be fighting bare-knuckle with no way to protect his head or mouth, other than his own quickness.

"Thank you for checking in at the door as a fighter," Anthony said. "That made things a lot easier for me."

Mac shrugged. "I don't think they would have let me in otherwise."

Anthony held out a rack card, and Mac took it. Looking it over, he found the times of his fights, and his opponents. Thankfully, the stats of the men were right beside their names, just like his. His opponents were close to his own height and weight, which mostly made for a fair fight.

It didn't, however, tell Mac their specialties in the cage.

That could be dangerous.

Anthony glanced down at his watch. "You have an hour before your first fight."

So he did.

Melina grabbed Mac's arm a little tighter.

"Care to point out who I'm fighting so I can see

their faces?" Mac asked.

Anthony nodded once, and waved for Mac to follow as he spun on his heel. Mac took the chance to look over the large warehouse style venue that was being used for the makeshift fight club. From the outside, the building had almost looked decrepit. On the inside, it was a great deal nicer with velvet-lined walls, several bars, tables and leather chairs set up, and red carpeting covering the floor.

At the back of the place, Mac noticed a winding, metal staircase that led up to what looked to be a large space with mirrors for walls. Mirrored walls only meant one thing—one-way windows. He suspected it was probably an office of sorts. The money coming in and out of the place was likely kept there, highly protected and watched all night. Whoever ran the operation had a good view of the floor, people, and the fights where the office was positioned.

Large, brass chandeliers hung down from the high ceilings, lighting the place. Servers wearing black and gray ensembles moved in and around the throng of people without ever interrupting conversations or making themselves known unless asked. Melina was not the only woman in the joint wearing a fur coat, never mind the diamonds glittering on women's hands, wrists, and around their necks.

In the middle of the large venue, an octagon cage proudly rested.

Looming, almost.

Mac didn't wonder if he had made the right choice by agreeing to this night. He knew he had without a doubt. He owed Anthony a great deal of money—too much to pay back in a quick, normal manner.

At any point in time, Anthony could demand payment from Mac for the debt. And if Mac couldn't produce what he owed, then he would be officially fucked and marked for dead.

That's how it worked.

Before long, Mac had walked the entire building with Anthony before the man was able to point out each of Mac's three opponents for the night. He distinctly remembered Anthony telling him that he knew of a place. The Capo hadn't given the impression he frequented fights, but given his familiarity with the faces of fighters, this wasn't Anthony's first go round.

As far as his opponents went, Mac took note of each of them as they were pointed out. All three were with someone else, kind of like Mac was. It was probably their sponsor, or boss of sorts. Each, also like him, wore a tailored suit that didn't give off the impression that they were a fighter readying for a match.

Not one made Mac feel nervous.

They weren't all that intimidating.

Anthony directed Mac and Melina back towards the cage with a wave of one hand. At a row of black tables surrounded by leather chairs, he stopped.

"Let's have a seat for a moment," Anthony suggested.

Mac wasn't interested in sitting. His body didn't need to relax. It had been in that state for too long as it was.

Still, he pulled out a seat for Melina. She sat down, and Mac rested his hands to her shoulders over the fur coat she wore. He ignored the gazes of people as they strolled past, clearly taking him and Melina in, and probably wondering exactly who they were.

He suspected that new faces were a rare thing at these events.

Unless one was a fighter.

Considering the people barely passed Anthony a second look, Mac's assumptions about the Capo were only further confirmed.

Melina patted Mac's hand gently, and his attention was back on her in an instant.

"Well, what do you think?" Anthony asked as he took a seat across from Melina.

"Three is ... pushing it," Mac admitted.

Melina made a noise under her breath. "It's suicide, Mac."

Anthony chuckled. "I'm sure he can pull it off."

Mac wet his lips, his fingers tightening around Melina's shoulders. "I won't guarantee anything about the third, so I would suggest that be your lowest bet for the night."

The Capo rested back in his chair, tapping a finger to his mouth. "I'll take it into consideration. But frankly, I expect you to win."

Wonderful.

Then, Anthony's gaze cut back to Melina. He looked her new coat over, his smile growing into a more predatory look. "I hadn't asked earlier, but how did you like my gift, sweetheart?"

Mac could almost see Melina's fake smile when she said, "It was a surprise."

"Furs are the dresses of queens."

He couldn't stop himself. "Furs aren't my girl's thing, Anthony."

The Capo's gaze jumped to Mac instantly. "She's wearing one just fine right now, Mac."

"You know why that is," he replied coolly.

Anthony laughed, seemingly unbothered by Mac's tone. "You know, my first offer still stands."

Mac stiffened.

So did Melina under his hands.

"I can pull the plug on this whole night," Anthony said, waving a hand at the cage, "... for a single night with your woman, Mac."

Mac clenched his teeth so hard that his molars throbbed. He had to force himself not to grab Melina's shoulders so tightly that he might hurt her.

It wasn't her.

It was Anthony that pissed him off.

Somehow, Mac found his voice. "I'll let Melina speak for herself where that offer is concerned, Anthony."

Melina glanced up at Mac, one eyebrow lifted in silent question. Mac nodded to her, knowing she would handle the situation just fine. She turned back to Anthony, and rapped her manicured fingernails to the table.

"See," she said slowly, almost patronizing, "the neighbors already know Mac's name. I would hate to disappoint them by not being able to give them the same kind of performance, Anthony."

Mac squeezed her once, and hid his smirk by looking away.

That was quite a way to tell a man no and insult him at the same time.

Damn, he was proud.

Anthony didn't look all that impressed with Melina's response, but he shrugged it off and looked to Mac. "I guess you're fighting then, Mac."

Mac didn't even blink. "I guess so."

CHAPTER TWENTY-FIVE

Bruised.

Battered.

But somehow, Mac was still standing.

It spoke to his will and the deep inner strength that kept him going in times of adversity. Melina's throat was as dry as cotton as she watched Mac enter the cage for his last bout. He'd won his first match with no real issues, easily outpacing his opponent with his quickness and strong blows. Afterwards, he'd turned and looked out into the crowd, looking for her. When their eyes had locked, he winked at her. She hadn't been able to keep herself from smiling.

That was Mac.

Confident, no matter what he faced.

His second opponent had been a little more difficult, partially due to the fact that Mac had only received a one-hour break before his next match had started. He had to be tired. The other man had managed to land a few direct hits on Mac's face.

It was the first time that she'd ever witnessed that.

And it scared the hell out of her.

The cut above Mac's eye and the bruises on his cheek spoke to the battle he'd gone through. So did the dark purple bruise on his abdomen. She hated to see him hurt … in any way. The whole time she'd watched from the VIP section as his matches had gone on, she'd wanted to be there to shield him.

To deliver a few well-placed hits of her own.

There were easier ways to bring a man down than this fighting nonsense.

A kick to the balls would do nicely.

Speaking of a kick in the balls, she wanted to do that and more to Anthony.

The arrogant bastard.

She hadn't missed the smug looks and the wayward glances he'd thrown her way. Though he'd acted as if her refusal of his offer hadn't bothered him, Melina knew differently. Men—all men—no matter their position or how much power they wielded, hated to be refused by a woman. And not only had she refused him, but she'd praised Mac as the superior man … in all things.

"Well, my dear, do you think he can pull it off this time? He looks a little worse for wear," Anthony said from beside her.

"No thanks to you."

Anthony laughed. "I have to follow the rules like everyone else here, Melina."

"Is that the story you're telling now? Surely two matches would have served your purpose of getting your money back."

Her gaze narrowed at Anthony.

"Sounds like your faith is slipping in the indomitable Mac."

Melina folded her arms. "Never."

"Is that so?"

"Yes. All I am is a woman looking out for the best interests of her man. Don't screw him over, Anthony."

He put a hand over his heart. "Melina, you wound me. I'm the one with the most to lose here."

"You have nothing to lose. At the end of the day, you are still going to be a fat cat doing nothing but profiting off the hard work of a far better man." Melina couldn't keep the heat out of her tone.

Anthony scowled. "Some might say that you're crossing a line with that remark."

Melina shrugged. "You know what they say. If you can't take the heat, stay out of the kitchen."

With that delivered, Melina turned her attention back to the cage. She'd given Anthony more of her time than he deserved. After this evening, she hoped she never had to see the bastard again, other than in passing. This Cosa Nostra business was really starting to rile her the more she thought about it. Loyal men like Mac did all the hard work, took all the risks, and had little to show for it while they passed all the profits off.

It was bullshit.

When things settled down, she would mention her feelings to Mac, but now she had more important things to worry about. Mac's last opponent entered the cage and Melina held her breath. The dark haired man was about the same height as Mac but his build was stockier. He was large muscled, like a wrestler or UFC fighter. She watched him bounce around the cage, smirking. Clearly, he thought he had this fight in the bag.

Melina's eyes softened as she watched Mac in his corner. He leaned against the wall of the cage and though his face betrayed no expression, his body language told a different story. He leaned all of his weight against the wall as he waited.

And then she saw it.

When he took a deep breath, he winced briefly before quickly schooling his features.

He was hurt.

How badly, she had no idea.

She tried to catch his gaze, silently pleading with him to look at her but he didn't. His sole attention was now on the man standing between him and freedom from his debt to Anthony. Mac had to prevail and she knew he would, even if it nearly killed him.

The bell rang, signaling that the match was about to begin. Mac moved from his corner and to the middle of the ring. The referee nodded for Mac and his opponent to touch gloves. Mac offered his glove, but his opponent only smirked, refusing to offer his own glove.

Prick.

The ref stepped away from the two men and Mac's opponent struck first, nailing him in the jaw. Melina bit her lip hard. Mac backed away a few steps but quickly recovered. She watched a cut on his lip begin to bleed. Her fingernails dug into her palms as the man lumbered towards Mac. Her eyes barely followed as her lover landed a series of hard body blows. Surprise doted the other man's face, before he tried to hit back. Mac sidestepped him, but not before he took a shot to the gut. Spit flew from his mouth at the force of the hit.

"That was a nasty hit."

Melina ignored Anthony's comment. He was inconsequential now. All that mattered was Mac. She continued to watch as the match went on. Mac gave as good as he got, but the two previous fights had taken a real toll on him. He wasn't shielding himself like he normally did, and he wasn't able to dodge his opponents strikes as quickly as he needed to. Her man was wearing down, but there was a fire in his eyes.

She recognized that look.

Mac was going to go for broke.

In a flurry so fast she could barely follow him, Mac struck, delivering blow after blow. Melina rose to her feet. Mac's fists rained down on the other man, and his opponent staggered to the ground. The ref quickly got between Mac and the man as he started to count. She barely breathed. An eight count and the man made it to his feet.

Melina cursed under her breath as her eyes shifted to Mac. His chest heaved but his fists were up. Sweat poured from his forehead. He'd just unleashed what was no doubt his last barrage. She didn't know if he had anything left to give. His opponent came towards him, attacking with body blows. Mac tried to shield himself, but he couldn't escape some of the hardest hits. He staggered back and then just when she thought Mac would fall, he came back, landing a direct hit in the face.

Melina heard the man's nose crunch from the force of the blow.

Blood poured from the man's nose as he stumbled and hit the mat. Mac backed away as the ref started to count. Melina had never much believed in praying, but there was a first time for everything. Silently, she moved her lips, praying for the man to stay down. Finally, the ten count came and Mac's hand was raised in victory.

He was bloody and beaten, but he was the winner.

"Well, well. Mac is a man of his word," Anthony said.

"He always is."

"So I see. You know, it's too bad, Melina. You and I could have had a real good time."

Mac had won and she'd had enough of Anthony's arrogance. She turned to the man and glared down at him.

"In case you didn't get me the first time I said it, Mac is all the man I will ever need. To him, I'm not some trophy or a piece of ass to toss aside once he's gotten his rocks off. He values me, and he shows me that in ways that men like you will never understand. Money doesn't make the man, Anthony, and it will never be enough to impress a woman like me. Now, if you'll please excuse me."

With a smile on her face, Melina turned and made her way to the cage. She waited as Mac climbed over the wall and came to where she stood. He gave her a lopsided grin.

"Doll," he said, still smiling.

"If you ever scare me like that again, I'll have your balls. Do you understand me?"

"You already own them and my heart, too."

"Good answer, Maccari."

Wiping the blood from the corner of his mouth with her thumb, Melina kissed him hard. He'd won the battle today, and whoever was making war against them, she was certain he would win that battle, too.

"You know, if I hadn't seen and experienced this for myself, I would never believe it."

"What are you talking about now?" Melina asked.

She leaned on her elbow, drawing lazy circles on Mac's chest.

"That you could be such a sweet little nursemaid. I don't think I've ever been taken care of so well."

"Don't get used to it. All of this sweet girlfriend nonsense can get a little sickening."

Mac laughed. "Only you would say something like that. There's nothing wrong with being sweet sometimes."

"I didn't say there was. If you recall, my sweetness had you begging and pleading a few hours ago."

"Touché."

Melina smiled. Nearly four days after Mac's wins in the cage, he'd walked away with bruised ribs, a tender kidney, and thankfully nothing worse. She'd had to beg and plead with him to go to a doctor to begin with. But after threatening to add to his injuries, he'd reluctantly agreed to be checked out.

Since then, Melina had done her part to nurse him back to health. He still had bruises, but they were fading and his soreness seemed to be all but gone. But even though Mac teased her about playing nursemaid, she hadn't minded it. Cooking for her man and tending his wounds had made her feel empowered. Mac made her feel like she was vital to his existence. Sometimes, she caught him looking at her as if he couldn't breathe without her.

A year ago, she hadn't even known this man existed and now they were so intertwined and in sync together that Melina couldn't imagine what her life would be like without him. Especially now.

"Hey, I call it like I see it," she said.

"I know you do, doll. You're a straight shooter, in more ways than one."

Melina laughed. "Ha. Speaking of which, when am I going to get a chance to do that again? I'd say Anthony could use a bullet after the highway robbery he committed by taking all of your winnings."

Mac pulled her into his arms. "Are you still sore about that, Melina?"

"Hell, yes. You could've been seriously hurt, and he makes off with all the damn money. A reasonable man would've at least given you a cut of it after the shit you went through to earn it."

"That's not the way things work. I made more in the fights than the truck was worth, but taking all of it was supposed to teach me a lesson about respect and not fucking up again."

"Bullshit."

"That's the way things are," Mac said simply, offering little else.

"You know, if women ran the mob, things would be completely different."

"Really? How so?"

"For starters, there would be none of these antiquated rules you guys have."

"I like some of our rules," Mac said.

"Like what?"

Mac kissed her forehead. "Respect and loyalty. It is what Cosa Nostra was built on."

"That may be the case but the men you work under now know nothing about such things. You have more respect and loyalty in your pinky finger than them."

"Now I definitely could get used to compliments like that."

His lips found hers and Melina moaned as Mac's tongue invaded her mouth. She nearly lost her breath. His kiss was possessive and demanding. When his hand found its way between her legs, rubbing her clit hard she moaned pressing herself closer to his hand. Mac responded by slipping a finger inside of her and curling the digit hard in just the right spot to make her shake so *hard.*

His mouth lifted from hers. "You're so soft and wet and sweet for me, doll. I love it when you're like this." His tongue licked the seam of her lips.

And then his phone rang.

"You've got to be kidding me," Melina said.

"Just give me a minute." Mac reached for his cell phone next to the lamp and answered it. "Mac."

Melina noted the frown on Mac's face as he listened.

"Yeah, Skip. I'm on my way."

Mac ended the call.

"What is it now?" Melina asked.

"Guido wants to see me, and from his tone, he doesn't sound happy."

"When is that fat bastard ever happy?" Melina asked.

Mac laughed as he got out of bed slowly. "I'm still sore right now. I can't take too much of your humor."

Melina admired the firm curves of Mac's ass while he dressed. "With the folks you're dealing with, you need my humor and everything else."

"No arguments with you there, doll."

"Good. You're learning. Now, where does your illustrious Capo want us to meet him?"

Mac turned to face her, a frown on his face. "Not us. Just me."

Melina threw back the covers and moved to the end of the bed, folding her arms.

"What would make you think I'm just going to wait around here, if he's pissed off with you?"

Mac put on his shirt. "I can handle Guido."

"I didn't say you couldn't, but I don't like you meeting him alone. We still have targets on our backs."

"I know that. Finding out who's after us and ending this is all I've been able to think about, but I can't risk anything happening to you. I need to meet Guido with a clear head."

"What the hell are you saying, Mac? I'm a distraction?"

"Yes."

There it was.

One word.

Why did it stab her through the gut like a knife ripping her insides out?

"I didn't mean it like that, Melina."

When he moved towards her, Melina held up her hand to ward him off. "Don't. Just don't."

"There is no one in this world that I trust more than you. I love you in a way I never thought I could love, but the thought of losing you … I couldn't take it, doll. If Guido is on the warpath, then I need to be able to deal with him. If I know that you're here out of harm's way, then at least I know that no matter what happens, you'll be all right."

Melina sighed as she looked at Mac. She could see the

love he had for her shinning in his eyes. He wasn't asking this of her because he didn't think she wasn't capable of watching his back.

He was asking this because he loved her.

Because he wanted to protect her at all costs … even if it meant leaving himself exposed.

"Sometimes you have to think of yourself, Mac."

He sat down on the bed and took her hand in his. "When you love someone, you put their needs ahead of your own. What kind of man would I be to risk you?"

"You're not risking me, Mac."

"Yes, I would be. Please, Melina. I don't ask for a lot of things, but I'm asking you to give me this. If things go sour, you'll be the first person I call. I promise."

He kissed her softly on the lips. Her heart was tight in her chest. Staying behind was the hardest thing he'd ever asked of her.

"This goes against everything screaming inside me," she said.

"I know, but I'll be fine. Remember I was doing all right before we met."

Melina laughed. "Yeah. *Just* all right, but if it will put your misguided conscience at ease, then I'll stay here."

"Thank you. I know how hard this is for you."

"No, you don't. Now go and see what that pompous ass wants and don't keep me waiting too long."

She kissed him hard, deepening the kiss the very moment he parted his lips to let her into the heat of his mouth. He groaned against her lips before she pushed him away.

"You're not playing fair, doll."

"All's fair in love and war. Now go."

Mac stood up and grabbed his keys from the

bedside table. "I love you, Melina."

"I love you, too. Come back to me."

"Always."

And then he left the bedroom. Melina sat on the side of the bed and listened as the front door slammed shut. The longer she sat there, knowing he was alone and she was stuck there waiting for him to come back, the worse she felt.

Deep in her heart.

Burrowing into her soul.

Needling into her bones.

Something wasn't right.

She felt it in her gut and her gut had never been wrong.

Could Mac be walking into a trap?

Melina rapped her fingers to her knees, and shot a look at the clock. A fleeting thought passed through her mind—a conversation, actually. One she had with a much smarter woman when it came to the mafia and the lifestyle Melina was now surrounded by.

She had told Neeya Pivetti that she didn't know who was coming after her and Mac.

Neeya disagreed. *Don't you? Come now dear, you're a bright girl. The answer is already in front of you.*

Had it been in front of them for a long time? Longer than maybe Mac wanted to admit? Was it Guido showing his jealousy over a solider he wanted to keep to himself and out of the limelight of the family?

Mac trusted Guido. He didn't always like him, but he trusted the man because he was his Capo, Melina knew. He wouldn't look to Guido as the person who might want to harm them. But to her, the Capo was no better than other men of his position—men like Anthony.

The difference between those two men? Anthony had gotten what he wanted from Mac, and he didn't hide the asshole he could be while he got it, either. And then he walked away.

But Guido?

He hid everything, including Mac.

Melina didn't like this at all.

Getting up, she quickly dressed in a black tank top, jeans and spike heeled boots before she threw on a leather jacket. Opening her nightstand, Melina pulled out the gun Mac had given her and tucked it in her waistband.

No way was she walking into a lion's lair without a means to take it down.

Cosa Nostra be damned.

The man she loved was not about to pay the price for another man's greed.

CHAPTER TWENTY-SIX

Mac pulled his car into the parking lot of Guido's club. He cut the engine and pulled his keys from the ignition. Shifting in the seat, he took some of the pressure off his injured side. Despite how much he had done over the last few days to hide it from Melina, his ribs and sore kidney were still giving him hell.

His girl worried enough.

She didn't need him adding to it.

Still, he had a feeling that whatever this meeting was with Guido, it wouldn't be fun. The Capo sounded like he was in a right and proper fit when he'd demanded Mac get his dumb ass out of bed and make his way over.

The "dumb ass" thing being Guido's words, not Mac's.

Mac couldn't figure out what in the hell he had done to not only warrant his Capo's anger, but also the man's verbal abuse. Sure, he had seen Guido turn his nasty self on other people in that way over the years, but never Mac.

Long ago, he had earned the respect—and he thought the admiration—of Guido for his loyalty, respect to the life, and his hard work. It was the only thing Mac strived for in his life—to be a made man was the most important thing.

Guido knew that.

So yeah, Mac didn't understand.

Brushing off his lingering irritation, Mac grabbed the

small white grocery bag and opened it up. He'd stopped at a corner store quickly to pick up an item he needed, but Melina had refused him over the week, due to the doctor's orders. Popping open the plastic package, he quickly unrolled the long, flesh-toned support bandage. Lifting his shirt up, he made quick work of wrapping his injured ribs as tightly as he could. The pressure of the bandage allowed him to breathe better, and he figured he would at least be able to move without showing he was in pain.

Mac didn't need anyone thinking he was down and out, never mind weak. It would only lead to some fool thinking he wouldn't be able to hold his own.

No one needed that.

Knowing he had already made Guido wait too long as it was, Mac grabbed his Beretta, which was resting in the passenger seat. He slid it into the back of his pants, but he didn't think he would need it.

The quicker he got this over with, the faster he could be back with Melina.

That's all he wanted.

Mac was surprised to find Guido's club entirely empty of people. While it wasn't business hours for the club, the Capo almost always had a few men wandering around. There hadn't even been any enforcers outside, watching Guido's car like normal.

It irked Mac.

Something didn't feel right about this at all.

Mac expected Guido to be in his upstairs office, but found him sitting at the bar. The man's large form rested on a barstool. Guido didn't make a sound as Mac approached loud enough that he knew he was heard.

Silently, Mac slid onto the barstool next to Guido. He found a bottle of whiskey and two shot glasses resting in front of the Capo. One shot glass was filled with amber-colored alcohol, while the other was overturned and unused. Down a couple of feet from Guido on the bar, Mac noticed a gray tub the servers used to transport dirty dishes from the floor to the kitchen. By the looks of it, it was filled with soapy water.

Yet, no one was around.

"Slow day around here?" Mac asked.

Guido snorted under his breath, making his large form shake. "Something like that, kid."

Mac bristled at the term, since it didn't sound entirely praising, but rather, mocking.

"What took you so fucking long?" Guido asked.

"Traffic," Mac lied smoothly.

"Sure it wasn't that woman of yours?"

"She was sleeping when I left."

Another lie.

Mac figured it was better to keep the man in the dark, regarding details about his personal relationship with Melina, never mind her opinions of Guido. It wasn't like they would impress the man or anything. Mac didn't see the point in filling him in.

Guido cleared his throat. "She doesn't know you're here, then?"

"No. I'll bring her home some chow and say I went out to grab breakfast. She doesn't ask much about any of this."

"Sure."

He didn't sound like he believed that.

Mac chose not to push it.

He took note of the crumpled appearance of Guido's black suit, his wrinkled dress shirt, and the loosened tie around his neck. His eyes were bloodshot, and his usually kept hair was a mess sticking up in every direction. It wasn't like the Capo to look so … slobby. Guido was all about appearances, and his current state spoke of liquor, stress, and a couple of sleepless nights.

Again, that uneasy feeling settled in Mac's gut.

He tried to never ignore it. It was there for a reason, after all. His hadn't once let him down before. It had saved his life a time or two, out on the streets.

What was it trying to tell him this time?

"You're looking a little rough," Guido noted.

Mac chuckled, and ghosted the pads of his fingers over the cut above his brow. He still sported a slice on his lip and a couple of bruises on his cheek, too.

The marks and pain were worth it.

He was free of his debt.

Free to be made.

"It's nothing," Mac assured.

Guido pursed his lips, giving Mac another one-over. Then, he grabbed the overturned shot glass and set it back upright in front of Mac. "Have a drink."

Mac flashed what he hoped was a confident smile. "You know I don't drink, Skip."

"You do today."

What?

"Skip—"

Guido cocked a brow, shutting up Mac's second attempt at a polite refusal. "Drink, I fucking said."

Damn.

He did not sound pleased.

Apparently, they were back to pissed off Guido, just like that.

Mac grabbed the bottle of whiskey and poured a shot. Quickly, he downed the drink, barely holding back his grimace as it burned his throat all the way down.

Guido nodded at the shot glass. "Another."

"Are you trying to get me drunk or what?"

"My father used to tell me you couldn't trust a man who wouldn't drink. So put some liquor in that glass, and drop it back, Mac."

Mac steeled his features, wondering what game his Capo was playing now. He poured another shot, and drank it down. The second was a lot smoother than the first. He let the shot glass hit the counter with a clink.

"I take it your father never met mine, then," Mac said quietly.

Guido barked out a laugh. "Probably not."

"I'm not drinking any more of that shit," Mac said.

"I don't expect you to." Guido waved a hand and added, "There's a glass of water on the other side of you. Grab it and wash it down. I know you're not a man with a taste for good liquor like the rest of us."

Mac ignored how that sounded like a digging jibe meant to hurt his pride, and turned on the stool to grab the glass of water that had been placed on the bar just a foot down the way. Leaning over to grab it, Mac had just grasped the glass when he felt Guido move behind him.

He didn't get the chance to turn back around.

A shout died in Mac's throat as something wrapped around his neck, and he was pulled up off the stool. The glass of water he had went flying at the same time, shattering and spilling across the club's floor. Guido heaved behind him, grunting as he threw his weight backwards, taking Mac with him.

Instinct kicked in for Mac and nothing more.

He couldn't breathe.

And that was the only thing that mattered.

Not fighting. Not getting away.

Catching a *breath*.

Guido was pulling whatever was around his throat even tighter. Mac's back hit the bar top as his legs kicked out and he clawed at his throat. Pain bloomed in his ribs, taking with it most of his fight and strength. His body was already weak from the fights a few days before. He wasn't up for this shit. Unable to even shout, as he had already lost all of his breath, Mac tried to weave his fingers in under the long length of material around his neck.

His vision tunneled suddenly, blackening at the edges.

Jesus Christ.

Using one hand, he made a fist and struck out at Guido. The man barely dodged it. Mac tried again, but quickly decided trying to get whatever was around his neck off was more important. He couldn't fight back if he couldn't fucking breathe. Then, Guido started dragging Mac along the bar. He felt his gun fall from his pants, but he didn't hear it hit the floor. Mac tossed his weight back and forth, but his weakened strength had nothing on Guido's extra hundred or so pounds forcing him along.

He still couldn't even catch a breath.

"What'd I fucking tell you, huh?" he heard Guido ask.

Mac's mouth opened, and he found his Capo watching him from up above. The cold blackness in the man's eyes was new. Who was this man?

"Fucking me over, that's what you were doing," Guido continued, ranting away.

Mac felt his head hit something firm, and Guido finally stopped dragging him along the bar. His body felt weaker than ever with no oxygen running through his blood. His lungs fucking burned like hell, and each time he tried to fight to get his body off the damn bar, his ribs ached.

"Working with Anthony behind my goddamn back; cozying up to Luca like I wouldn't see it," Guido snarled. "I see that shit, Mac. And I made you, kid. You're not going anywhere that I don't let you go. Do you fucking understand me?"

God.

Mac swallowed convulsively, nodding. If it would help to let him catch a breath, he would do it.

Guido barked a laugh. "Liar. You're just like your old man, Mac. A dirty liar. And a sneak. You're not going anywhere in this *famiglia,* unless I put you there. I fucking made you—you are my *soldato,* not Anthony's, and you're certainly not Luca's little bitch boy to do with what he fucking pleases. I thought the first little message of mine would be enough for you to get the hint. I thought scaring you and your girl would be enough for you to realize you needed to lie low, and get the fuck out of the spotlight. But no, you had to put yourself right back in it."

"I—"

It was the only word Mac managed to get out—raspy and aching.

Guido grabbed the tub of soapy water and tipped it up. Mac instantly arched off the bar as steaming hot, soapy water poured over his eyes, down his face, and flooded his open mouth. Being choked like he was, he couldn't even force the water out of his throat. Instinct caused him to cough, which made him swallow and choke on even more soapy, hot water.

Over and over, Guido repeated the process.

Mac was still trying to get the damn tie off from around his neck. Yeah, he figured out what Guido was choking him with, when he realized the fat fucker wasn't wearing his loosened tie anymore.

Kicking against the bar did him no good. Fighting against Guido's hold got him nowhere. Instead, the Capo just slammed Mac into the hard bar top, causing his head to snap against the surface.

More water poured over his face, but Mac had finally closed his mouth and it didn't choke him this time.

Not that it mattered.

He was running out of time to figure something out.

Muddy in his mind, out of air, and blurred in his vision.

"I fucking made you," Guido repeated darkly. "And this is how you repay me?"

But I didn't, Mac thought.

He hadn't done any of that to Guido.

What difference did it make now?

His vision blinked in and out. He no longer had the strength to fight at all as his legs began to go slack against the bar top. No matter what, he refused to give up.

Mac kept trying to pull the tie away from his throat, knowing it was pointless. Guido was holding it firm, determined to see his plan through.

But he wouldn't give up.

It wasn't Mac's style.

He'd die trying—honorable men always did.

A rushing sound filled his ears. His blood, likely.

Just as his eyes began to close, the tie loosened and Guido flew backwards with a roar. It took Mac several gasps of air before he realized he could breathe. Each breath hurt him a little bit more than the last to take.

"Move." He heard the word screamed.

Mac shook his head.

"Fucking bitch!"

He clenched his fingers, moved his legs, and tried to see straight.

"Mac, please!"

A loud pop cut through the club, but it was still dulled to Mac's senses. It was almost like he was underwater listening to it all.

Turning his head to the side, Mac blinked and focused.

It was just a second.

One split second for him to see her.

Melina.

Gun drawn and pointed, tears streaking down her face, and she was shouting at him again. Mac's mind just wouldn't work like it needed to. He took another deep breath, willing the air and oxygen to do what it needed to do.

Suddenly, Melina dropped to the floor, and Mac heard another round of pops fire off. It wasn't from her gun that time.

"I'll kill you, cunt," he heard Guido growl.

Finally, Mac moved. And he moved a hell of a lot faster than he thought he could, as his knees met the bar top and he scrambled fast towards where he had started out before Guido dragged him along.

The item he wanted was just inches from his fingers.

His gun.

Melina rose to stand again, but her gun was down at her side.

Mac turned at the same time with a gun in his own hand as he flicked the safety off and cocked back the hammer.

She shouldn't have stood up, he realized.

Guido was already aiming and his finger was twitching on the trigger.

Mac didn't think.

Not about the consequences, Cosa Nostra, or anything else.

He just pulled the trigger.

Guido didn't even notice Mac had moved, that he was alive, and he certainly didn't see the bullet coming until it entered the side of his head. Blood and brain matter sprayed from the exit wound on the other side of the Capo's head a second before his large body dropped to the floor with a loud thud. His gun clanked out of his slack hand.

Mac swayed for a second, still not right in the head or all that steady on his feet. He heard Melina scream for him as the gun fell from his hand and he dropped sideways, tumbling off the bar with a groan as pain shot through his throat and chest at the same time.

He barely even felt the floor when he hit it.

At least Melina had finally let him shoot the fucking gun for once.

"Mac!" Melina was at his side in a flash, her soft hands roaming over his face and neck. She was still crying, and while Mac wanted to reassure her that he was fine, his throat was raw and dry. The words didn't come. Or maybe they didn't want to. "Oh, my God."

Mac swallowed, grabbed her wrists, and stopped her movements. Melina caught his gaze, quieting. "I told you … to stay home."

Melina gave him a look. "You knew I wasn't going to do that."

"You could have been hurt, doll."

"I figured it might not be me they were coming for," she whispered.

Yeah, shit.

Mac rested his head to the floor of the club. From his position, he could see that the bar was a fucking mess.

Melina was already moving onto another topic. "We have to get rid of it."

"Get rid of what?"

"The body, Mac."

Mac wished his throat didn't feel like scorched flesh. "It'll be fine."

"I'm sure," Melina muttered above him.

It would be.

Luca gave his word—Mac had to trust that.

Mac perched on the edge of the bar, waiting for their guests. Melina slid in between his legs without saying a word. He knew she was scared, but the woman was too headstrong to admit it. She was also fretting over him, and pissed off because he told her to chill out for a while.

Sliding an arm around Melina's waist, Mac pulled her closer and rested his cheek to the top of her head.

"Almost over," he said quietly.

Melina nodded, but stayed silent.

Mac expected her shock to wear off at least by the time they were home.

He heard the front door of the club open, and Melina stiffened in his arms. "Don't worry, doll."

"Easier said than done," she replied.

Mac knew she was right.

Before long, Luca Pivetti and his two closest men were standing in the middle of the club. Not one said as word, but all scanned the place, taking in the mess at the bar, the body of Guido still unmoving on the floor, and the puddle of blood that had finally stopped spreading.

Finally, Enzo spoke up.

"Your suspicions were right," he said to Luca.

Luca gave a single nod. The boss flicked Mac with a look, saying a million and one things without even opening his mouth.

Mac saw what was most important.

Gratitude.

"Get rid of it," Luca said to his underboss, waving at Guido's corpse. Then, he jerked a thumb at his other man. "Matthew, clear the security footage in his office. Call someone if you need help."

Luca spun on his heel, leaving.

Mac cleared his throat, wincing at the ache it left behind. "And me?"

Slowly, Luca turned back around with a smile. Usually, when the man smiled it came off as cold. This didn't feel like that at all.

"Go home," Luca said. "I will call you when, or if, I

need you."

Mac's arm tightened around Melina again. "Okay, Boss."

"Well done, Mac."

Mac sipped hot coffee and stared out the window. He'd made a place on the corner chair, and decided he really didn't want to move for a while.

That happened to a man when he was almost killed.

Melina asked him several times to go to the hospital and get checked out. She wanted to make sure his windpipe wasn't injured in some way. Thankfully, she didn't put up too much of a fight when he refused.

But she did go into the bedroom and closed the door behind her.

It was like radio silence.

Mac wasn't sure what to do. He wanted to go to her and make whatever was wrong go away, but he also needed to process everything that had happened.

Melina would understand.

She always did.

Mac finally shed his clothes and crawled into bed, well after midnight. He found Melina on his side of the bed, hiding under sheets and blankets, so he settled into her side with his back to the bed and an arm behind his head acting as a pillow.

In the darkness of the bedroom, he watched the outline of Melina's bare shoulder rise and fall with her breaths. It was almost soothing. He wasn't sure how long he stayed like that, watching her sleep, but eventually he moved closer and closer to his girl until they were both under the sheets and she was firmly tucked into his body.

Mac only realized it once he had Melina as close to him as he could have her, but he finally felt like he could really breathe and think again.

He'd needed that so badly.

"You finally came to bed, huh?"

Mac wasn't surprised that he had woke Melina. "Sorry. I was just ..."

"It's fine, Mac."

"It's not, but I am now." He pressed a kiss to the back of her neck, feeling her back push into his chest.

"I still think you should go to the hospital. You sound terrible. It hurts just hearing your voice."

Mac sounded raspy, mostly, but the ache had left. It still hurt when he swallowed most of the time. "I will. First thing tomorrow. I promise."

Melina turned in the bed, tucking her head under his chin, and wrapping her arms around his sides. Mac held her tighter, too, because damn ... closer was better.

With her, closer was always better.

"Thanks for having my back again," he murmured.

Mac should have told her that hours ago, but he had been stuck in his own thoughts, trying to figure out all the shit he had missed that led up to those final moments.

Melina smiled against his skin. "Isn't that my job?"

"Seems so."

"You're not mad at me?"

Mac stilled. "Why would I be mad at you, Melina?"

"You told me to stay here, and I didn't."

Oh.

Maybe that's what Mac was missing. It wasn't that she

needed space from him to process what happened; she wrongly thought he was angry with her for disobeying his request for her to stay where it was safe.

"I'm not mad," he said softly. "You did the right thing."

"By default, right?"

"You've got a good gut instinct. I'm not going to fault you for following it."

Melina nodded. "Okay."

"I'm not mad," he repeated again, just in case she needed to hear it a second time.

She quieted in his arms for a long while. Long enough that he wondered if she might have fallen asleep. He quickly figured out she hadn't when her head tipped up just enough to allow her sweet mouth to find his in the darkness.

Mac took her kiss, he let her deepen it until their tongues danced together, and her hands were traveling all over his body. The sweetness of the kiss quickly burned hot when he pushed against her lower back, driving her lower half into his growing erection.

Softness was gone in a blink.

Their movements, their intent, became a lot faster and more frantic in the dark.

Nails scoring over his chest. His teeth buried into her shoulder. She shoved his boxer-briefs down as he pulled her silky chemise up.

Melina's sighs echoed in Mac's ear when he rolled her onto her back and spread her thighs wide with the same roughness she had shown him. Sometimes, he just needed to connect with his girl on a level beyond words and passing glances.

Sometimes he needed to feel more.

Touch more.

Taste more.

…have more of her all over him.

Mac grabbed Melina's jaw in his hands, forcing her head up so that he could see her brown eyes watching only him and nothing else for the moment. His palms slid down the slender column of her throat, the pads of his thumbs dragging along her pulse points and feeling her swallow beneath his hold.

She was so beautiful like this under him.

Waiting.

Watching.

Silent and still.

Perfect, really.

Melina shifted under him, flashing him one of her sexy, knowing smiles. He groaned at the sensation of her fingertips dancing across the underside of his cock just before her fingers wrapped the base in a firm grip. She stroked him slowly, but tight enough to make his breath catch in his chest.

"Jesus," he mumbled.

Melina's legs hooked around his hips, and then her heels pressed into his lower back, demanding without even saying a word. Mac knew what she wanted, and so he gave it to her. Taking one hand off her throat, he wrapped his arm around her lower back and pulled her up a little higher so her ass was almost in his lap. Stroking his cock once more, Melina shifted her hips just enough to let the head of his dick slide along the soft, wet lips of her slit.

She was always wet for him, no matter what.

Her body was made for his. He was sure of it.

"Come on," she urged low. "Take it, Mac."

How was he supposed to deny her when she talked like that, all breathless and dazed eyes?

Mac flexed his hips, and just like that …

Just like that, he found heaven wrapping him in a tight, hot grasp.

All over.

Melina shuddered from the force of the thrust, but she still met him there. Mac didn't give her much time to adjust, because he couldn't. Already, the need, his lust, and their love was surrounding his senses and coloring his vision red. He started a rhythm between them that was as punishing as it was good. Pushing up on her elbows, Melina's body was suspended above the bed, and she was backing into him again.

And she watched him like that.

Saw his body tremble.

His cock taking her.

She looked so enraptured with them.

He was already lost in her.

"Yeah, *ciao?*" Mac blinked awake at the same time he put the phone to his ear. "Mac, speaking."

At first, no one responded on the other end of the call. It made him wonder if he had actually heard the phone ringing in his dead sleep, or if his head was just making things up. It wasn't like he had gotten a hell of a lot of sleep the night before, and frankly, neither had Melina.

Finally, someone spoke on the other end.

Mac felt a little less crazy.

"Mac, my home, two hours," Luca ordered. "I know with girls like yours, she won't let you go too far from her. My wife will have a breakfast spread waiting for Melina to choose from. You, however, will find me in my library today. Do not make me wait."

"Okay, Boss. Do you want me to—"

Luca hung up the phone before Mac could finish his question. Confused and a little frustrated, Mac dropped the cell phone to the bedside table, and fell back into the bed. Melina met him there, her soft hands roving over his chest as her lips pressed to his bicep.

"What's going on?" she asked.

"Luca," Mac said.

Melina groaned, her forehead hitting Mac's arm with a quiet smack.

Mac laughed. "I don't think it's bad, doll."

"It never seems like it is until guns get pulled out."

"Neeya invited you to breakfast," Mac said, hoping that would soothe Melina's worries.

She scrunched her nose. "Yeah?"

"I think you made another friend."

"How long do we have?" she asked.

"Two hours."

It was a half-hour drive, at least.

"And there's already breakfast waiting, so we don't need to bother with that, right?" Melina asked, dragging a single fingernail down over his happy trail.

Mac's throat tightened, and his cock hardened. "No. I can't be late, according to him. I don't even know what he wants."

He figured it couldn't be bad, given Luca could have killed him the day before if he wanted to after what happened.

Melina was on top of him before he could think. "We'll make it fast, I promise. You won't be late, Mac."

"Make it worth it," he argued, grabbing her hips roughly.

She laughed. "That, too."

Mac walked into Luca's library with his hands tossed in his pockets. The library was done in similar design to Luca's office, but it was larger, with a second level. Books lined every wall in custom-made book shelves to fit the circular shape of the room. Brass ladders on wheels rested against the shelves attached to tracks.

Luca stood by one of the only windows, smoking a cigar. He didn't turn at Mac's entrance.

"Boss," Mac greeted.

Luca waved a hand, as if to tell him to continue on in. Mac did, only stopping when he was in the middle of the large library.

"Everything has been handled," Luca said, tossing Mac a look.

Mac understood the words that weren't said: Guido had been taken care of and dispatched without issue.

"Thank you," Mac said. "I didn't intend to cause a mess."

"Yet, it always does." Luca waved at a couch in a sitting area just a few feet to the left of them and said, "Sit."

Mac's eye caught the items on the couch, and he froze.

A silver knife.

The picture of a saint.

A gold zippo.

A gun.

One bullet.

"Don't let it bother you," Luca said, hitting Mac on the back as he passed with a smile. "It looks more intimidating than the process of initiation actually is."

Initiation.

He was going to make Mac a made man.

Today.

Mac finally snapped out of his daze. "Shouldn't there be other people here for this?"

Luca chuckled. "Should there be? I'm the boss—while unprecedented to do the Omertà like this, it's not entirely unheard of. My word, my choices, are law."

Well, then.

Luca picked up the gun, slid the cartridge out, and inserted the one bullet before replacing the cartridge. Turning off the safety, he cocked the hammer back, and set the gun back on the couch with a great deal more care than he had picked it up with.

"Are you just going to stand there, or are you going to sit like I told you to?" Luca asked.

Mac was still pretty sure other men in *la famiglia* were supposed to be there. Luca seemed to pick up on Mac's dilemma.

"I don't need the permission or approval of others for what I already know," the boss informed him quietly. "I can make who I want, if I feel they are deserving of it. And I would prefer to do it without the issues and jealousies of other men who might want someone else in your place."

"Okay," Mac said, understanding his boss a bit better.

"You will not waste time after today, Mac," Luca continued, "not in this family. You have a ready-made position waiting for you where Guido's old spot is concerned. You have proved yourself more than capable of handling it all. I know you do a great deal of the work as it is. There will be no apprenticing under another Capo to learn the position—you don't need to."

Mac nodded, surprised. "People might not like that."

"That is something *you* will have to learn to manage and handle appropriately, as a made man."

He could do that.

Probably.

"You're never to speak of what happens in this library after you leave it," Luca said firmly. "Not to your friends, other made men, or even your girl. It is sacred—so protected by us all. Do you understand?"

"Absolutely."

Luca picked the knife up. "Sit, I said."

Mac did as he was told.

"Are you ready?" Luca asked.

Was he?

Mac had waited a long time for this.

Did he deserve it?

"Yes," Mac said.

Luca smiled. "You don't sound sure."

"I wasn't expecting this. I didn't think it would be like this at all."

"We never do. Palm out, and repeat after me."

Mac put his palm up for the boss, and he didn't even flinch when his blood fell in droplets to the hardwood floor.

But he repeated every word.

CHAPTER TWENTY-SEVEN

"Melina, dear, is everything all right?"

Neeya's voice startled Melina who nearly dropped her fork.

She met her hostess' gaze and nodded. "Everything is fine."

Neeya tapped her manicured hand against the table. "Now why would you want to insult my intelligence and mock my hospitality by lying to me?"

Melina swallowed hard, noting the edge in Neeya's voice, despite the smile on her face.

"I meant no disrespect. This is all new to me. I'm not used to being the type of woman who worries about a man. It's unsettling."

Neeya waved a hand. "Is that what this is all about? Dear, the worst is over now. Relax. Take a breath. Good times are ahead."

"I'm sure you're right, but after being on edge for so long, it's hard to let down your guard."

"I never said to let down your guard, but it is okay to realize you can start to enjoy life again. Never let anyone take that from you."

Melina speared a strawberry and took a slow bite before she spoke again. "But what is my life now? Everything is different."

"Melina, I never pegged you for an indecisive woman."

"Neeya, can I be frank with you?"

"Of course."

"I'm not sure how to handle being a part of this lifestyle. I'm not talking about the danger or anything like that. I'm talking about all these traditions and unwritten rules I don't understand. The last thing I want to do is step on any toes or cause any problems for Mac. He's had to deal with enough."

Neeya offered her a wide smile. "Spoken like a true woman in love. It's amazing how you've changed in the short time I've known you."

Melina laughed with a touch of nervousness in her voice. "You mean from being an independent, take-no-shit woman to some sap who constantly worries? I have to say, I'm not much of a fan of the new me."

"You still are an independent, take-no-shit kind of woman. That's why we get along so well. Not to mention, you know your way around a gun. But listen to me well, Melina. Just because you love, does not diminish who you are as a woman in any way."

Melina nodded. "I guess I didn't think of it like that. I was so worried about losing my edge."

Neeya sipped her mimosa before she responded. "I seriously doubt that will be happening anytime soon, and in regards to your other concern, there's an extremely simple way to avoid the headache of any of it."

"And how's that?"

"Take your cues from Mac. If he wishes to discuss things with you, then fine. If he doesn't, then respect his silence. Undoubtedly, he has a good reason for keeping some things to himself."

"Is that how things work with you and your husband?" Melina dared to ask.

"Yes."

"And you're all right with not knowing things? It

doesn't bother you?"

Neeya laughed. "Of course not, because at the end of the day, I know that Luca is good at what he does. He would not be the boss if he did not earn the spot. And in the event there ever was a real reason for concern, he would have balls enough to tell me."

Melina nodded as she popped another fresh strawberry in her mouth. Maybe Neeya was right. Maybe she really was worrying and obsessing over nothing. Guido was dead, and Mac was very much alive. Surely they'd come through the worst of whatever Fate had to throw at them. Maybe it was time to really live a little.

"You two need to hurry up."

The sound of a girl's voice drifted into the room where Neeya and Melina were eating breakfast. A few minutes later, three young women entered the room. Melina recognized them as Neeya and Luca's daughters from the painting immediately.

"If I didn't know any better, I'd have thought that I taught you girls better manners than yelling through the house," Neeya said.

The tallest of the girls gave her mother a small smile. "I'm sorry, Ma. We're going shopping and as usual Hope and Lora are bringing up the rear."

"Rose acts like we're actually going to have to wait or something. They shut down every store we shop in and give us exclusive access. It's not a big deal," the shortest of the girls said.

"Lora, just because you have a privilege doesn't mean you have to abuse it."

"Wrong. If you have a privilege, I expect you to abuse the hell out of it," came a new voice.

Melina's attention shifted to the staircase. Luca and Mac were descending and for the first time since she'd met the Pivetti Don, he seemed to be in a good mood. A real smile tugged at the corners of his face as he approached his daughters.

"After all," Luca continued saying, "I didn't provide all of this to you girls for nothing."

Melina's gaze shifted to Mac. There was a look in his eyes she hadn't seen before.

A look of wonder.

His steps seemed lighter as he stood near his boss. A white bandage had been wrapped around his left hand.

Something was going on, and she meant to find out what it was.

"Luca, I thought we talked about this."

"Nonsense. Nothing is too good for my *principessas*. Let your enforcers know you're leaving and have a good time."

"Thank you, Daddy," Lora said.

She leaned close to her father and kissed his cheek. Rose and Hope rolled their eyes before they quickly bid their parents goodbye, and dragged Lora from the room.

"When our girls become incorrigible, spoiled brats that no man wants, you shoulder all the blame for it, Luca," Neeya said.

"I will happily take that blame, wife. That simply means I don't have to give them away. Now … a friend of mine and I are going to take a walk around the grounds, if you need us."

Luca kissed his wife on the cheek before he turned to leave the room. Mac gave Melina a thin smile before his face became an impassive mask. When she and Neeya were alone, Melina cleared her throat.

"What was that all about?" Melina asked.

"You really don't know?"

Melina shook her head. "No."

"Whenever a man has been made, he is introduced as 'a friend of mine' by another made man. The man in question is never to speak of his initiation or his new status."

Mac had been made.

She was quiet as she let Neeya's words sink in. He'd done it. Mac's hard work and loyalty had finally been rewarded. Wow.

"Speechless?" Neeya asked.

"Something like that."

Yeah.

Something like that.

"Doll, are you sure you're not Italian? Every meal you make gets better and better."

Melina smiled at Mac's praise. In the two weeks since Mac's "promotion", they'd settled into an easy routine. He usually left around nine in the morning, before returning home for lunch and a quick round with Melina in bed. Afterwards, he'd leave for a few more hours before he was home around five in the evening. Some days he came home even earlier. Melina had no complaints about his new duties. They spent more time together and much of the stress he'd been under as just simply a soldier was gone.

Not to mention that every night he did come home, she made sure he had a hot meal. The cooking lessons Victoria had given her were really paying off. She found she enjoyed cooking, so she didn't mind. Mac had confessed how much he looked forward to seeing what she was whipping up next.

"Not that I know of," Melina finally replied.

"Well, this is another amazing meal. You've really outdone yourself."

"Thank you. A full stomach is the way to a man's heart, I've always heard."

Mac reached across the table and grabbed her hand. "You had mine before you learned your way around the kitchen, doll."

"You know, you're right. I guess being a domestic is really not that important in the grand scheme of things."

"No, but it is a bonus that I appreciate."

Mac rose from the table and came around to Melina's side. She watched him warily as he reached for her.

"What are you up to, Maccari?"

"Just wait and see."

In one swoop, he lifted her from her chair and into his arms before he kissed her on the mouth. Melina moaned as his tongue teased her lips. Instantly, she was aching for him.

"You're not playing fair," she whispered against his lips.

"Weren't you the one who told me all is fair in love and war?"

Melina could only smile as Mac took them into the bedroom.

***

Seeing the kids at the center again had been so nice. The moment she'd walked through the door, they'd been all over her, asking where she'd been and complaining that she'd forgotten about them. Melina had spent the next two hours catching up with everyone at the center. Before leaving and promising to return soon, she'd left a little gift for the center. Mac's generosity was at an all-time high since he'd taken over Guido's territory. Even now, she still had a wad of money in her pocket.

It was strange in a way though. Her financial worries were over. If she wanted something, she could have it and there would be no questions asked. Her life had changed and in the best of ways. She wondered for the first time what her parents would think of her now. Would they be proud of her? Or would they be disappointed that she hadn't accomplished more?

If you're happy, they'd be happy.

Melina smiled. Yes, they would be and she knew someone else who would be happy to hear about her recent turn of good fortune. Before she could talk herself out of it, she found herself heading towards the old neighborhood. Since hooking up with Mac, she'd become so removed from her old life. It would be nice to see a familiar face again. Melina looked around before she entered the building.

She heard laughter as she headed towards the stairs. And then she saw Dulcea and some of the girls sitting and drinking wine. A few of the doors to the bedrooms were closed.

"Melina? What are you doing here?" Dulcea rose from her seat and came over to where Melina stood.

"I was just in the neighborhood and thought I'd drop by."

"You mean you still have time for us little people? Word on the streets is, you're living the life now."

Melina laughed. "Is that so?"

"Yeah. You've done well for yourself. I always knew that someday there would be a man out there to catch your eye and make you settle down."

"Settle down? You act like I've gotten married or something."

"Maybe not yet, but I'm sure that's coming. The way I hear it, your new man is smitten with you. I'm glad to hear that. You deserve someone who appreciates you."

"Thank you, Dulcea. That means a lot. It's actually one of the reasons I came by. When I needed a way to support myself, you gave it to me. You treated me with respect and you didn't cheat me. If it weren't for you, things probably wouldn't be as great for me as they are now."

"Hear that, girls? Stick with me and you'll go places just like Melina. Feels good to be thanked every now and then."

A few of the girls gave Melina some less than friendly looks, but she ignored them. She'd never cared much for the opinions of others and she wasn't about to start now.

"You're welcome. Now, I guess I'll be going."

"It was good to see you, but it's probably a good idea if you do get going. We're entertaining a few VIPs and your presence here might be a conflict of interest for all parties involved."

Melina nodded. "I get your drift. Well, it was good seeing you, Dulcea."

"You too, Melina."

Before she could talk herself out of it, Melina hugged her former boss before she turned and headed back towards the stairs.

Her feet never touched the first step.

"Everybody down. Hands on your heads right now."

Armed men wearing black vests stormed the room.

Badges flashed in her face as they passed.
Police.
Holy fuck.

❧

Melina turned, trying to get comfortable.

It didn't work.

The concrete slab was murder on her back. Day after day, week after week, this eight-by-eight cell had been her new home.

Solicitation.

Prostitution.

Resisting arrest with violence.

Illegal possession of a firearm.

The pigs were trying to railroad her and right now, they were succeeding. Her bail had been firmly denied and every day the pigs had another go at her. They wanted information about Luca Pivetti and Mac.

She told them nothing.

Her silence infuriated them.

The money she had on her during her arrest—and mostly the basis for the official's case—was thoroughly tied up in Mac, and his work in Cosa Nostra. The pigs believed the money came from whoring. Melina couldn't out the truth without talking about Mac in some way.

Her hands were tied.

Literally.

They threatened her and when that didn't work, they tried to make deals with her. She would be released with all charges dismissed, if she told them what they wanted to know. Not once was she tempted.

Freedom meant betraying the man she loved.

Freedom meant putting his life in danger.

Freedom meant taking away everything he'd ever worked for.

She wouldn't do that to Mac. Not now.

Not ever.

She missed his kiss and his touch.

She missed waking up next to him and going to sleep in his arms.

They had started to build a life together and in one fell swoop, it had gone straight to hell again. She'd been a fool to think things would stay the way they were. Fate always had a way of stepping in and delivering a well-placed kick in the gut when you least expected it.

CHAPTER TWENTY-EIGHT

"**W**ell, what of it?" Mac asked.

Randy set his briefcase to the courthouse steps, and pulled out a pack of cigarettes. Despite it being illegal to smoke on the steps, the lawyer lit one up and took a heavy drag. "No dice, Mac. Bail denied again."

Cursing low, Mac smacked a cement pillar with his palm, wishing that would help with his irritation. It didn't help at all.

"Calm down," the lawyer mumbled around his cigarette. "We've got eyes all around this place watching us right now."

Mac's gaze swept the courthouse, looking for the people Randy mentioned. While he didn't immediately see anyone, he knew the lawyer was probably right. Mac, being who he was, being affiliated to the mafia, was the only goddamn reason Melina was behind bars right now and he couldn't get her out.

"She's going to have to talk or do a bit of time," Randy added after a long moment. "They've got all their strings tied up in nice little bows, and in the process, they've tied her up. She can't admit to the money not coming from Dulcea's place without explaining where it did come from, and that'll lead back to you. Then, they're opening her up right there for questioning about you, your money, and where it comes from. Melina's not going to do that."

"And therefore, not going to talk about the money at all," Mac muttered.

"Guilty by her silence," the lawyer confirmed. "It's a shitty situation, but we're not looking at a lot of time right now. A great deal of those charges will be dismissed in the end."

"Except the possession of an illegal firearm, resisting arrest, and assault on an officer."

Randy shrugged, taking another drag from his cigarette. "What can I say? She got angry."

Mac scowled, knowing damn well Melina didn't do well with cops. It wasn't like he had thought to tell his lover that if something came up in that kind of situation, her best bet was to comply and shout for a lawyer as often as she could.

Things had changed since a few months ago.

Now that Mac was made, the changes were all the more apparent.

Like the fact that Melina wasn't his wife and that put him in a bad position with the family. When a man's woman got locked up, he had to concern himself with keeping his own image clean. If the woman was his wife, it was easier to get by with visiting her or working to her benefit to get her out.

Mac had to do all of that on the low for Melina.

"Four months in lockup, and it won't be a prison out of state," Randy said. "Seven months, max."

Mac clenched his teeth, holding back his groan.

Seven months was too long.

"It'll be quicker and easier, if she pleads it out," the lawyer added.

"She won't do that," Mac replied, already distracted and wishing there was something he could do.

More.

He wanted to do more for his girl.

Mac knew Melina, and there was no way in hell that girl was going to plead guilty to those charges.

"No contest, then?" the lawyer asked. "She's not admitting guilt, just saying she's not willing to contest the charges or go to trial."

The longer Mac stood there, talking about his girl's freedom like it should even be in question, the more agitated he became. None of this would have even happened, if he hadn't come into Melina's life and put her in the spotlight.

It wasn't fair.

Mac would much rather take the seven months off Melina's hands then make her do it. God knew he had done more than enough in his life to deserve time behind bars.

"I need an answer on that," Randy said, tossing his cigarette away.

Mac sighed, eyeing the courthouse.

He wanted to talk to Melina.

Luca ordered him to stay away.

What the boss wanted, he got.

Finally, Mac nodded. "Convince her to plead no contest."

"Will do. Anything you want her to know?"

"Just tell her I'm around—I'm here."

That would be enough for Melina to know Mac was keeping an eye on her, trying to take care of this bullshit, and that he still loved her.

Of course, he did.

She was his gun moll.

No man was worth shit without his girl.

Mac couldn't do much else for Melina, without disobeying his boss.

And that right there was his new life in a nutshell. All he worked for, he finally had. But the thing he wanted the most, the person who had helped to get him there, was now out of reach.

GUN MOLL

Mac hit the lock button on the fob in his hand, making sure his Dodge Challenger was closed up tight. Sticking his keys back into his pants pocket, he fixed his suit jacket and scanned the street up one side and down the other. People milled about, going in and out of the busy hub that was the very center of Hell's Kitchen.

They barely seemed to notice the Capo with a black bag in his hand as he strolled across the street and entered a small pizzeria known for its sauce on pizzas, not to mention the man who owned it.

Mac passed the tables without picking one, nodding to an older gentleman he recognized that was playing a game of checkers with a friend. The old man tipped his black, wide-brimmed hat in Mac's direction, and nothing more.

Respect was everything—more importantly, it was everything to the men whose time had already passed in the business of *la famiglia*. Despite their time having come to an end when they passed on their reigns to other, younger men, the old timers still hung around their familiar haunts.

And when they were there, they deserved a proper acknowledgment.

Mac walked right on past the cash where a woman was working at the register. She offered him a look and a smile, but didn't stop him as he went back into the kitchen of the restaurant. The closer he came to the private offices at the rear of the restaurant, the louder the voices became. Laughter and murmurs echoed above the clanging noise of the chef in the kitchen.

The door to the office was open, so Mac didn't bother to knock.

It wasn't the time for knocking, anyway.

The moment he stepped into the room, the voices quieted instantly.

At the head of the office, sitting on the corner of a mahogany desk with a smoking cigar dangling between the tips of his fingers, was Luca. The man waved a hand high at Mac's appearance.

"There you are," the boss muttered.

A good eight pairs of eyes focused on Mac. Six other family Capos, and Luca's two men, Matthew and Enzo.

Mac checked his watch. "Three minutes early, Boss."

"Cutting it too close, Mac."

He didn't argue with the man. It wasn't his place to do so, and here in this spot, he was not to act familiar with Luca in any way. Luca was his boss, and nothing more.

Mac didn't bother to excuse his almost lateness to Luca, because the man wouldn't be pleased to know it was caused by Melina's second bail hearing. Luca had warned Mac repeatedly to let the lawyer handle it, and to keep a distance for the sake of his new status in the Pivetti family.

Luca slid off the desk, snuffing his cigar out in an ashtray. "One rule about today. What is it, Mac?"

"Never be late," Mac said.

"Exactly. You do not want to find out what happens if you are late."

Enzo chuckled from his seat on the couch. "Go easy on him, Luca."

Luca cut his man with a single look that shut him up instantly.

No favoritism.

Nothing else mattered.

"It won't happen," Mac promised, lifting his black bag higher for the boss to see. "And we've all got better business to be getting to, yeah?"

Luca smiled. "We do."

GUN MOLL

Every second Wednesday of the month was dedicated to nothing more than a Capo paying dues to his boss. Mac had learned quickly in the last few weeks, since his rise in the family that every second Wednesday was held with a sort of higher respect than most other days. Money had to be down to the very last penny. Each and every bill and coin was accounted for.

Mac quickly learned how to keep books to prove where his money was coming in and out of, in case he got questioned about certain cash flows like he had that first Wednesday. Being a soldier for Guido all those years had been helpful, especially when it came to taking control of a crew that Mac basically managed alone for years, but it was nothing compared to having the actual title.

Being a Capo was fucking tedious.

Penny-counting, money-watching, time-crawling fucking tedious.

But Mac enjoyed every second of it.

Over the next two hours, Mac and the other Pivetti Capos paid the money due to their boss for tribute. It seemed like issues rarely happened on tribute, because Luca was known for his penchant to turn violent to make a simple point very clear to his men.

Mac was not interested in being one of them, but he was learning that he was expected to be no different with his crew. In a matter of weeks, Mac had gone from being one of the soldiers in the crew to essentially being their boss.

It was difficult for some of them to separate the man they knew him to be for years, to the Capo that didn't have the time or patience for their bullshit.

But he made it work.

His crew was easy.

It was the other Capos that were making the

transition of welcoming Mac into the folds more difficult than it needed to be. He had heard enough whispers to know that not all of the Capos felt he had earned his way into their Cosa Nostra, while others felt that his initiation was invalid, as it hadn't involved all of the made men in the family.

If and when Mac needed to deal with those issues, he would.

Luca had given him fair warning about it, after all.

Once the men began to trickle out of the back office, finished with tribute and dismissed by their boss, Mac turned to leave as well.

Luca's call stopped him. "Wait a moment, Mac. Take a seat."

Mac dropped into the closest chair by the door, waiting as the last few men left the office, some eyeing him from the side as they went. Once it was only Luca, Matthew, Enzo, and Mac left behind, Luca nodded at the door.

Reaching over, Mac closed it without a word.

"What can I do for you, Boss?" Mac asked.

Luca thumbed through a stack of bills on the table, handing over a pile to Matthew without a word, and then another to Enzo. "How is the court thing going?"

Mac drummed his fingers to his thigh. "Not well."

"You're keeping a distance like I told you to, right?"

"As much as I can."

Which wasn't a complete lie.

Luca didn't seem to be satisfied with that answer. "Let the lawyer handle it. You do not need attention on you right now being newly made, Mac. Cops have a way with fresh meat, like you're an easy way in for them. Do not give them that opening."

"I wouldn't."

"Still, I'm watching," the boss warned.

"She's not going to talk, Luca."

Luca's gaze lifted, and his lips drew thin. "For both

your sakes, I certainly hope not."

"The lawyer is going to have her plead no contest to the charges, and that'll force the cops to drop the questioning and demands on our side of things," Mac explained. "They'll get something, but nothing from us."

"And your woman will be ... where?"

Mac's jaw ticked. "Randy said seven months, maximum time."

"That's a bit of a wait for a woman, isn't it?"

Not when a man loved that woman.

Mac chose not to say anything about that. "I have a request."

Luca sighed, sitting down on the edge of the desk. "Go ahead."

"Melina's sentencing. I want to go. I'll be in the back, out of sight. I haven't even gone to visit her. I've kept my head down like you wanted. I want to be there for that, Luca."

"I'm not sure that's a good idea."

Mac shook his head. "If she were my wife, this wouldn't even be a question of asking, Boss, and you know it. You would already have her out of jail."

"And whose problem is that?" Luca asked.

"I was working on the wife thing before the arrest happened."

"But she still isn't your wife, Mac. And I can't allow a man of mine to handle just any woman with the same treatment a wife would receive."

Mac blew out a frustrated breath. "She's—"

"I know the woman is important to you," Luca interrupted. "You will stay in the back?"

"Head down," Mac promised.

"Do your best to keep from being pictured."

"Absolutely, Boss."

Luca waved a hand in Mac's direction, saying nothing. He didn't need to. His actions were clear.

Dismissed.

Mac heard the click-clack of heels approaching the door, and his smile was already growing. It felt like he hadn't smiled in weeks. Well, since Melina was taken from him.

As the door swung open, revealing his mother, Mac's grin widened even more at her lit-up eyes. She wore a navy blue dress that fell just below her knees. Her hair was pulled up into a neat up-do, her makeup done modestly.

Cynthia looked more than ready for Sunday services.

"I thought you weren't coming," she said, reaching for him.

Mac let his mother pull him into a tight hug. "Of course, Ma. You invited me to church."

And now that he was finally free with his schedule, for the most part, and wasn't running around for Guido all the damn time, he could spend Sunday mornings with his mother in a church pew. Mac knew it made her happy when he attended, so he agreed.

Cynthia peered over Mac's shoulder, her brow furrowing when she couldn't find what or whom she was looking for. "Where is your girlfriend? Melina, right?"

Mac cringed, but hid it quickly enough with a smile. He knew that his sister had been singing Melina's praises as much as she could to their mother. Victoria loved the time she had spent with Melina, and she wanted their mother to like her, too. No doubt, Cynthia had assumed her son would bring his girlfriend along.

She couldn't think any differently.

Mac hadn't told her about Melina's recent troubles.

He also didn't want his mother to worry.

"Melina had a last minute trip she had to take," Mac

said.

It wasn't a complete lie.

Cynthia frowned, stepping back from her son. "Oh. Why?"

"Emergency stuff. We weren't expecting it. She might be gone for a little while."

Again, not a total lie.

Mac would lie his ass off to just about anyone, if he thought he could get away with it, but he didn't like lying to his mother. It wasn't right—she raised him better than that. But he didn't think his mother would appreciate knowing about Melina's legal problems, given she barely knew her, and already had an opinion as it was about the type of business Mac was involved in.

Some things were better left unsaid, or in his mother's case, unknown.

"Family things?" Cynthia asked.

Mac shrugged, not giving a verbal answer. "Are you almost ready? Victoria said she would meet us at the church. You don't want to be late, huh?"

Cynthia nodded at the reminder. "Just let me grab my purse, James."

He chuckled as she disappeared back into the house. No matter how many times he told her to call him Mac, as he preferred, he would always be James to his mother.

Once Cynthia was back outside, Mac tucked her hand around his elbow and led her down the walkway towards his car.

"How have things been?" she asked.

Mac patted her hand. "Great, Ma."

Okay.

That one was a total lie.

Things were awful. He was lonely as shit. And nervous as hell for Melina.

Thankfully, his mother didn't notice his fib.

Cynthia tightened her hold on his arm.

Mac noticed her slight frown, and wondered what was going on in that head of hers. "Something wrong, Ma?"

She shook her head. "Not exactly."

"That doesn't sound like everything is right."

"Well, your father has been coming around more often. And you know I don't like to tell him to go away …"

Mac scowled nine ways to Sunday. No doubt, his deadbeat father had heard the rumors of Mac's recent initiation into the Pivetti Cosa Nostra and wanted his little slice of the pie, if he could manage to get his useless hands on a piece.

No way.

Mac worked too fucking hard for that nonsense.

"Has he mentioned why?" Mac asked.

Cynthia shrugged. "No, but he's been mostly sober."

Mostly.

Mac's irritation climbed a notch. "If he bothers you, let me know."

Cynthia patted his arm gently. "He's still your father, James."

Right.

Because that made all the difference.

Not to Mac.

Head down, Mac rapped his knuckles against his knee. Knowing he was being far too jittery, and that might draw attention, he forced his nerves back and sat a little straighter in the hard courthouse chair. He rested his ankle over his knee and sat still, surveying the throng of people in the courtroom.

Straight ahead, about ten rows up, Melina sat with her lawyer. When the judge demanded she stand for final sentencing, she did as she was asked with no question.

Mac had to bite his inner cheek just to keep himself from calling out her name. He didn't know if the lawyer had filled her in on his presence in the courtroom or not. He'd let Randy know earlier in the day that he would be there, but that he needed to stay out of sight—Luca's orders.

It fucking killed Mac.

Seeing Melina in a drab gray suit, hands cuffed and simple white, slip-on shoes with no laces killed Mac. Her hair was pulled back into a tight ponytail at the nape of her neck, and her face was clean of any makeup.

The girl was still goddamn beautiful.

But it was *killing* him.

All over again, Mac started rapping his knuckles to keep his attention diverted on something other than the swirling mass of emotions beginning to compound inside his chest. Maybe Luca had been right. Maybe Mac shouldn't have come here today, seeing as how he could barely fucking keep control of his anger and sadness.

Mac heard the sentence come down in the background of his thoughts.

"Two hundred and ten days to be served consecutively in the jail, time already served reducing the sentence to one hundred seventy-five days."

Mac did the math in his head.

A little over five and a half months.

His chest constricted as the gravel banged down, serving the judge's words as final.

Mac caught sight of Melina's profile as the bailiff approached, and she turned to speak with her lawyer. He stood, because other people were beginning to move for the next case to be heard, and he couldn't see Melina anymore.

Standing was the wrong thing to do.

Seeing her made him feel bad all over.

She was frowning, her lips moving as she spoke quickly to Randy.

Pain. Sadness. Desperation.

Mac couldn't stop himself, he was already moving forward into the side aisle, approaching Melina from behind the railing separating the floor from the viewing area.

"Doll," Mac called out.

Melina didn't hear him. She held her hand up to the bailiff, asking for just a moment as Randy shrugged in response.

"Melina," Mac said, louder the second time.

Finally, she turned. All that pressure and pain in his chest suddenly deflated in an instant. The very moment her eyes met his.

He could see relief there.

And confusion.

Mac's hand met the wooden rail, and he was reaching over it towards Melina with his other. Despite the bailiff telling him to step back, and moving towards Melina, she reached out to Mac with her shaking, shackled hands.

The second her skin touched his, he was okay.

And he hoped she was, too.

"I love you, doll," he murmured.

Melina nodded. "I love you."

"Take a step back," the bailiff ordered again.

Mac ignored the man, tugging on Melina so that she was just close enough for him to lean forward and catch her lips with his own. The kiss didn't last long, but it was enough for him to hear murmurs around them, and see the flash of a camera going off.

He cursed silently.

Already, he could see the headlines.

GUN MOLL

Suspected Mobster Kisses Hooker Girlfriend Goodbye.

Fuck them.

Mac would take Luca's anger when it came.

Melina was far more important.

She would always be.

"I love you," he told her again, holding her gaze strong. "I'm sorry, doll."

Mac didn't have to explain what he was apologizing for; Melina had to know. His distance, not being able to come and see her, and the next few months she would be alone without him.

All of it.

He was so goddamn sorry for those things.

"I will be waiting to pick you up wherever you are, the day you get out," Mac promised.

Melina swallowed hard. "Promise?"

"With everything I am."

And he was nothing, if not a man of his word.

Mac squeezed her hand tight.

"You have to let me go," Melina whispered.

Mac did, but his whole body ached the second she was gone from his reach.

"Wherever you are," he repeated, "I will be there."

Melina smirked.

Cocky to the very bitter end, he knew.

Mac didn't want this woman any other way.

"You better be, Mac."

ABOUT THE AUTHORS

Bethany-Kris is a Canadian author, lover of much, and mother to three very young sons, one cat, and two dogs. A small town in Eastern Canada where she was born and raised is where she has always called home. With her boys under her feet, a snuggling cat, barking dogs, and a spouse calling over his shoulder, she is nearly always writing something ... when she can find the time.

Find Bethany-Kris at:
Her website www.bethanykris.com,
or on Facebook at www.facebook.com/bethanykriswrites,
on her blog at www.bethanykris.blogspot.ca,
or on Twitter - @BethanyKris.

Sign up to Bethany-Kris's New Release Newsletter here:
http://eepurl.com/bf9lzD

A proud Alumna of the University of Central Florida and Florida State University, Erin Ashley Tanner writes stories featuring fierce females and the men who love them.

Prior to journeying into the world of contemporary

romance, Erin wrote paranormal romance for Evernight Publishing. Her debut novel, Goddess of Legend released in October 2013, was the first in her Demi-God Daughters paranormal romance series. The follow up, Goddess by Chance was released in November 2014.

Dirty Little Secrets, a sexy contemporary romance was published by Samhain Publishing in July 2015. Her next release with Samhain, Devious Little Lies is scheduled for release in June 2016.

Find Erin at:
Her website: erinashleytanner.wix.com/erinashleytanner, on Facebook: www.facebook.com/ErinAshleyTanner, or her Twitter: https://twitter.com/ErinTheAuthor.

Made in the USA
Charleston, SC
01 June 2016